A Sort of Virtue

Stopper looked at the body on the bed, the unharmed white thighs and the elegant legs, and pronounced an epitaph: 'Poor cow.'

When prostitute Lily Devon is found viciously slashed to death in south London, government phones begin to ring . . . A few days later the police are handed their prime suspect on a plate and, with the evidence mounting up against him, Derek Allgood confesses. Case closed.

Only Detective Chief Superintendent Hilary Catchpole knows for certain that Allgood is not their man. Have the police – and Allgood – been deliberately set up?

Catchpole begins to dig deep, and uncovers a trail of deception, personal ambition and corruption that leads right to the heart of government. What was the role played by the Home Secretary Rex Calendar, currently waging a shrewd battle to dislodge Prime Minister Bladon from office and discredit National Liberal leader Allen Pitcombe? Or the role of his brother Donald, ex-porn publisher and now the proprietor of one of Britain's biggest selling tabloids?

And what exactly did Bernard Bannock MP uncover about the Calendars' past just before his sudden – and untimely – death . . .?

Julian Symons

A Sort of Virtue

A POLITICAL CRIME NOVEL

MACMILLAN

First published 1996 by Macmillan

an imprint of Macmillan General Books
25 Eccleston Place, London SW1W 9NF
and Basingstoke

Associated companies throughout the world

ISBN 0 333 65216 9

1 3 5 7 9 8 6 4 2

A CIP catalogue record for this book is available from
the British Library

Phototypeset by Intype London Ltd
Printed by Mackays of Chatham, Chatham, Kent

Contents

1	Poor Cow	1
2	Telephone Conversations	5
3	Jacko Investigates	13
4	Cabinet Affairs	30
5	Jacko Wraps It Up	50
6	The Unwrapping	68
7	What's Right is What's Necessary	79
8	Difficulties of a Prime Minister	107
9	Garry and Faz	124
10	Pitcombe's Dog	140
11	Roselands	154
12	The End of a Story	203
13	Reactions: People	245
14	What the Media Said	257
15	Logical Solutions	265
16	Wrapping It All Up Tidily	292

DUKE FERDINAND: There's gold.
BOSOLA: So:
                    What follows? Never rained such
                    showers as these
                    Without thunderbolts i' the tail of
                    them: whose throat must I cut?

                                    (John Webster,
                                    The Duchess of Malfi)

The General Public has no notion
    Of what's behind the scenes.
They vote at times with some
emotion
    But don't know what it means.
    Doctored information
    Is all they have to judge things
by;
The hidden situation
    Develops secretly.

                        (W. H. Auden and Christopher
                            Isherwood, *The Dog
                            Beneath the Skin*)

ONE

Poor Cow

JACKO ROSE stood in the doorway, looked round the room and thought, a mess, then, a bloody mess. And on a Saturday.

A block of flats in Kennington, six storeys, red brick, put up in the fifties. An apartment on the ground floor, distinguished from the rest only by the number on the door. Bed-sitting-room, another bedroom, galley kitchen, bathroom with basin and lavatory.

Gum shifting from one place to another in his mouth, jaw rotating slowly, Jacko amplified the unspoken words to: the sort of bloody mess I've seen too bloody often. But did he mind, was he fazed by it like young Sergeant Stopper, who still looked milk-faced at the way someone had slashed away at the girl, and especially at her face as if in an attempt to obliterate the features, so that you couldn't tell what she might have been like? He was not.

He had seen it all before, Jacko would have said, and yet, rolling the gum around, he would have acknowledged that there was something unusual about this tart's boudoir. That it *was* a tart's boudoir the big circular bed testified, along with the mirror that covered half the ceiling. But the rest of the room wasn't done in the shocking pink Jacko thought of as Tart's Own Colour. Instead it was dove grey, the carpet, striped wallpaper and the covers of the sliding wardrobe. Some prints on the walls looked as if a kid had done them, which Jacko knew was the thing nowadays, and they were in grey and silver frames. The lighting was indirect, seemed to come from around the walls. Even the mock coal fire, switched on so that on this day in early June the room smelt sweetly and sickeningly warm, even that had a grey surround. Tarts often liked fluffy animals, cuddly dogs and even teddy bears, but there wasn't one in sight.

Mind you, the room was still a bloody mess. The chaos looked greater than it was because a triple mirror on the grey-skirted dressing-table had been knocked to the floor, so that glittering shards of glass lay about everywhere. Several pots and bottles from the dressing-table had also been knocked to the floor. One or two were broken, and their scents mingled with the sweet smell of blood. And of course there was the figure on the bed, reflected in the ceiling mirror. She lay on her back, one arm by her side, the other stretched above her head as if making a semaphore signal. Head and trunk were covered with blood, and the black sheet on which she lay was stained, although the colour of the stain could not be told. Above the bedhead drops of blood spattered the wallpaper.

Jacko approached the bed. He trod delicately, but there was still a crunch of glass beneath him. He bent over the body, moved gum from left to right within his mouth. There was a wound in the throat, and a dozen or more cuts around her breasts and stomach.

'Punter gets cross, tries to cut her head off maybe, way it looks. Weapon?' Stopper shook his head. 'So it's a bring your own knife party, then take it away afterwards.'

'Maybe he washed it, washed himself. There are bloodstains in the basin and on a towel.'

'Something for forensic. Plenty for forensic it looks like. What else do we know? Who's the lady?'

'Called herself Luisa Devane. Lets a room here to a singer with a rock group, Bobo Miranda – '

'As in Carmen?'

'Sir?'

'Joke. Skip it.'

'This Bobo was with the band at something called the Hallo Club in Camberwell, went to a party around there in Denmark Hill, got back here just before seven a.m., went in the bathroom, saw the stains, knocked on Luisa's door thinking she'd had a nose bleed or period trouble, saw the body, called us. I've talked to her, though she's pretty much in shock. Doesn't know a lot about Luisa, met her at a gig a few weeks back, they got on, she moved in, pays rent. Says she didn't know Luisa was on the game, not her business.'

'A likely story.' Jacko chewed reflectively. 'This Bobo, did she see anyone around? Anyone who might have been running Luisa?'

'Nobody. She asked Luisa one day did she have boyfriends, answer was no she didn't. Then she loosened up a bit, told Bobo she did have friends, they came back here sometimes, some of 'em important people.'

'Important people? And she lived here in Kennington?'

'Nothing wrong with Kennington. Or this block. Entryphones, caretaker, no graffiti.'

'But Mayfair it ain't. Wrong side of the river. She keep a diary, phone-pad, notebook, anything that might have names and addresses or phone numbers of these important people?'

'Bobo says she kept a diary by the phone, one of those with a page for every week. We haven't found it. Or anything else useful.' Stopper anticipated the next question. 'I've talked to the caretaker, name's Fraser, flat in the basement. He was cagey – far as he was concerned Luisa was a good tenant, quiet, paid the rent. Seems she'd taken a year's tenancy, then had the place done up to her own taste. Says he knew Luisa had a friend staying, understood it was just a few days, subletting not allowed.'

'She paid a backhander to friend Fraser if I know my caretakers.' Jacko chewed slowly and thoughtfully, a red-faced man in a shiny blue suit. He delivered himself of a profound truth. 'There's problems for a brass in having a ponce, and a lot of 'em are bastards, but she does get some protection. Going it alone, if that's what she was doing, is asking for trouble. And trouble's what she got.'

'So what next, sir?'

'We go through the motions, hope forensic turns up something useful, hope we get lucky.'

Stopper looked at the body on the bed, the unharmed white thighs and the elegant legs, and pronounced an epitaph: 'Poor cow.'

TWO

Telephone Conversations

HALF AN HOUR earlier on that same Saturday morning the telephone rang in Jonathan Reed's apartment. The instrument was on Belinda's side of the bed, so she picked it up. Johnno, two-thirds asleep, gave a grunt of dissent. She said, 'Hallo,' then whispered to Johnno: 'Him.'

'Christ.'

'Jonathan. Good morning to you. Have I disturbed you at breakfast?'

'No, sir.' Sarcastic devil. Or did he mean it? You could never be sure. 'Not at all.'

'You have a link with the Yard, I believe.' What was he talking about? 'A relative. You've mentioned him.'

'Oh, yes, right. My mother's cousin. People call him the Big Man. We see him three times a year. He comes down at Christmas, brings enormous presents.'

'How interesting.' Sarcastic, sarcastic. 'I want you to call him, have him deal with a particular matter personally, keep you in touch with developments. I'll give you an address to pass on to him. 11 Blewbury House, somewhere in Kennington. Near the Oval, where they play cricket.'

Johnno made frantic writing gestures to Belinda, who had got out of bed and was looking at her tongue in a glass. She brought him a writing-pad and a pen.

'What else should I know, sir? To tell the Big Man, I mean.'

An unexpected laugh. 'That's all you'll need.'

'He'll know what I'm talking about?'

'If not he'll find out. I think he may deduce your interest is not wholly personal. But you understand *you* are making the inquiry, and it is to you he'll report any news. If you need me I shall be at Blundells this weekend.'

'I understand.' The connection broken, Johnno stared at the bit of paper with the address on it.

'What's all that about?'

'I can't tell you. It's hush-hush.'

'Johnno, don't be stupid.'

'I'm not, it's confidential. That call was never made, you didn't take it.'

'Johnno, you know what you are, you're a creep.' Belinda turned round on the dressing-table stool. 'What I mean is you're OK most of the time and nice to be with, but when you hear his voice you crawl.'

'He is my boss.'

'And don't you know it?'

'And he's important, he's the Home Secretary.'

'That's just it, you thinking he's important. He's just a man, for Christ's sake. I think we've had it.' She got clothes from a cupboard. 'It's bloody George. You try to copy him, then when you hear the boss's voice you say, "Yes sir, please sir, thank you sir," and pretend to yourself it's something secret and important.'

'That's not fair.'

'Oh, grow up.' She had been living with Johnno for a month. He shared the apartment in Fulham with George Kaiser, who always seemed to have plenty of money, was often away for days at a time, and dropped occasional hints that the absences were connected with secret government work. Johnno envied him.

'You can't go now, Belinda, you've not had breakfast.'

They ate breakfast in silence, then she repeated that they'd had it, and left. Later in the day George Kaiser came in, on what he said was a flying visit, and Jonathan told him Belinda had left. George clapped him on the shoulder, closed an eye. 'She'll be back.'

'A little twerp who works for Rex Calendar,' the Big Man said. 'Some sort of secretary, distant relative of mine. Perhaps I should say twat, not twerp.' He got a laugh of acknowledgement rather than amusement. 'Didn't seem to know what he was talking about, something to do with trouble at a flat in Kennington, near the Oval.'

'Dear me, the Oval. That brings back memories. Seeing Ted Dexter, beautiful bat.'

First I talk to a twerp, then to an old woman, the Big Man thought. Sure enough, the voice of the Assistant Commissioner suddenly pitched up a note or two in a complaining whine. 'Why are you calling me? What's it all about?'

'All I've learned so far is a brass has been killed in a block of flats. The body was found early this morning. Point is, anything that comes via the twerp is something Calendar wants to know. I thought you'd like to be kept in the picture.'

'Yes, of course.' A pause. 'I've got a new motor-mower, one of those you sit on. Want to try it out. Lot of grass here, you know, lot of grass. What's his name?'

'The twerp? Jonathan Reed. He's called Johnno.'

'Ah yes, cousin of yours I think you've told me.' The AC might be an old woman, but he wasn't forgetful. 'Keep me in touch by all means, but you're the point of contact.'

Later that same morning Garry Johnson sat down to work on his speech. He had four racial harmony speeches, adjustable for different audiences. This one was for a Rotary Club, who would expect a pat on the back for inviting a black to talk to them. He was putting in a couple of jokes when Debbie shouted from below: 'Telephone.'

'Too busy to talk. You know that.'

'It's Faz. Wants you.'

'Say I'm on the throne, call him back.'

Her feet clattered on the stairs, then she appeared at the door of the tiny study. 'You better speak. Says it's important.'

He held up the sheet of notes. 'This important too, woman. Don't want interruption, you know that.'

'Suit yourself. You say you never want to get

across Faz, I hear you a dozen times. Up to you.'
Garry picked up the telephone.

Ryton Fazackerley, known to everybody as Faz,
was the senior partner in Fazackerley, Milton and
Close, a firm of solicitors famous less for what they
did in court than for keeping their clients out of
court. Faz did not deny that he knew half the people
in London who'd been inside – and, he'd add with
a slow smile, the much more important ones who
might be inside but aren't. Faz was short and square,
went two hundred and fifty on the scales. He said
now, in a voice that seemed to roll on castors, 'Garry,
my friend, how are you keeping? Busy, I gather.'

'Since you ask, Faz, I'm in the middle of a speech
telling those Rotary Club fellers what a privilege
it is to be addressin' the finest bunch of British
businessmen still managing to stay out of the slam-
mer. Any time they're in trouble, I'll tell them, they
want to pick up the phone, call Mr Fazackerley.'

'You like your joke.' Faz's laugh rolled along
comfortably. 'I like it too. Someone asked me this
week, what's with Slim?'

'Slim? You mean my brother Slim?'

'No one else, Garry, I can't remember mentioning any other Slim to you, not ever. Not sure I even
know any other Slim, though I recall a film actor
called himself Slim Pickens. You ever see him?
Comic actor, I think.'

'What you want with Slim? He's been in Jamaica,
been there eighteen months, more.'

'I'm glad to hear it. That little problem he had,
remember, over the cars he sold as demos done
only a few hundred miles, turned out they were
cannibalized, when one crashed – '

'It was that partner he had, that Derrick. He went down for it. Slim, he was just the salesman.'

'That was how we played it. You remember my advice, Slim should take a long holiday. And we kept your name out of it.'

'I don't know what you mean, Faz. I was never involved.'

'I said, that was the way it played. Derrick is out now, I hear he's looking for Slim. So you tell him, stay in Jamaica, right?'

'Right.'

'And so far I don't hear your name mentioned, about the business you put Slim's way. It should stay that way, you understand me?' A touch of grit was mixed with the oil. 'I hope it always stays that way, no reason why Derrick should hear your name. Hope you'll never be too busy to talk to me.'

'Never, Faz. Did I say that, did that stupid Debbie say that?' With an effort he added: 'Glad to have the word. Thanks.'

'No need. Now, something else. A little problem, you might be able to help.'

'If I can I will.'

'A woman attacked and killed in her flat, a block called Blewbury House in south London, Kennington. On the game I'm sorry to say, and it seems this was a frenzied attack, really unpleasant. Not the kind of thing happened when I was young or you either, though I can give you a few years. This girl, woman, supposed to be respectable. The name was Luisa Devane, ring any bell?'

'She black?'

'What's that?' For a moment Faz sounded discon-

certed. 'I don't think so. I understand the man handling it is named Rose, an Inspector.'

'When did it happen?'

'Some time last night, Friday night.' You're quick
off the mark, Garry thought but did not say. 'A
frenzied attack, as I say. Only too common nowadays,
blot on our civilization. The sort of thing should be
cleared up quickly.'

'Sure.'

'And it's your bailiwick, you know everybody.'

'Not everybody, only a sprinkling.'

'Lots of contacts, Garry. You're a politician, know
the ropes.'

'Not a politician, just a local councillor. Strictly
a local man.'

'And my reading is this was a local matter, this
Luisa picked up a man, took him home, made a bad
choice. You know the area, Garry, you know the
people, I'd like you to put out the word. This policeman, Rose, he'll need a name. I'd like to have it
soon.'

'You know some of these people too. Acted for
them.'

'Not the way you do. I'm not local. And there
are reasons I shouldn't be involved.'

'OK, I'll do some asking around, see what comes
up.'

'It's not just asking around that's needed, Garry,
here we need a name. And we need a result. Whatever the name is the label's got to stick, you understand me?'

'I hear you.'

Faz was running on pure oil again, no grit. 'Many
thanks, Garry. It's something should be cleared up,

you understand me. And we forget this conversation.'

'I forgot it already.'

When he put down the telephone Debbie asked, 'What was it then, what did that load of blubber want?'

'Just screwing me. Threatening give me trouble I don't do what he wants.'

'And what is it he wants?'

Garry smiled, showing beautiful teeth. 'Baby, he wants you to kiss my arse.'

THREE

Jacko Investigates

FOR A BRASS to be attacked in the course of her profession is a common hazard; for the attack to be violent is uncommon but far from unknown. Jacko Rose saw no need to do more than go through the customary motions. From forensic he learned that sexual intercourse had not taken place, but there was semen on the woman's stomach. Marks on her wrists and ankles indicated that she had been tied to the bed, something confirmed by the presence of ropes and handcuffs in a drawer. This suggested to Rose a course of events that began with bondage, continued with the client perhaps unable to perform sexually, the girl asking to be released or more likely able to release herself if the spring-operated cuffs were in use. The punter became angry at his own frustration, attacked her, and came to orgasm only after killing her.

Nothing very unusual in that, and going through the motions in such a case meant getting Stopper to check through the computer the list of sexual deviants interested in bondage and liable to turn nasty if unable to obtain satisfaction, with preference given to any living locally. The computer had turned up several names, and Stopper was engaged in checking their activities on Friday night. So far he had cleared more than half of them. Rose himself had talked to Bobo Miranda, aka Jenny Gresham, and persuaded her to admit a little more knowledge of Luisa's activities, including her belief that Luisa put advertisements into sex magazines. It seemed she had managed to avoid attracting the attentions of a ponce. It was possible one had come along in the guise of a punter, and attacked her more savagely than he intended when she refused to join his team, but the nature of the injuries made that unlikely. Ponces were generally too calculating to make mistakes that ended in death rather than injury.

There was another possibility suggested by forensic, although they could not confirm it. Bloodstains on an armchair and marks on the towel used for cleaning up afterwards suggested that two people might have been involved, one simply watching, a voyeur. Otherwise forensic had been what Jacko considered characteristically unhelpful. Death, the pathologist said, had occurred between nine and eleven o'clock on Friday, and he refused to be more specific. 'You tell me when the room began to be warmed up like an oven. You can't? OK then, I don't stick my neck out about the time.' That was the way with pathologists, they were either similarly uncooperative or else dogmatically certain about their conclusions. Either way, you couldn't rely on them. And he disregarded the vague idea about two people being present, on the ground that it would have been very unusual. Besides, it was much easier to look for a single villain. If a second candidate turned up, so much the better.

The diary or notepad Bobo thought she remembered seeing by the telephone had presumably been taken away, confirming Jacko's view that the killer was a punter, not a ponce. Luisa had told Bobo she knew some important people, but had not mentioned names, and since Bobo was interested only in rock music, never read newspapers, and did not listen to the news on TV or radio, it was unlikely that any name other than that of a rock musician would have stayed in her memory. Did she even know the Prime Minister's name? Jacko didn't ask, but wouldn't have been surprised by a negative answer.

A photograph of Luisa appeared in the papers, from a snap taken by Bobo when the two had had a day out together at Eastbourne. It brought the unsurprising news that Luisa Devane was no more genuine a name than Bobo Miranda. The dead girl's name was Lily Devon, she was twenty-one years old, and she came from somewhere Jacko had never heard of in Worcestershire. She had done well at school, briefly worked in a local solicitors' office, but left home at eighteen for what she told her parents was a job with a music publisher. Her parents came to London, and Jacko talked to them. Or rather, listened to what seemed to him a typical retired stuck-in-the-provincial-mud couple as they expressed astonishment, almost disbelief, about their daughter's occupation. Lily had come home at weekends once a month fairly regularly, and always seemed cheerful.

'She was doing so well,' Mrs Devon chirped. 'Had lots of new clothes, been promoted to assistant manager at the music publisher. We asked about boyfriends, and she said there was nobody at the moment though she went out with boys . . .'

She looked at Jacko in the hope that he might make her fiction reality. He nodded sympathetically, she sobbed.

John Devon said: 'No use taking on, Mother, she told us a pack of lies. No truth in them, was there?'

'She wasn't working for a music publisher. Never had done, so far as we've discovered.'

'She stayed in London at first with another girl — what was her name, Mother?'

'Myra Gray, she was older, had an apartment, Lily stayed with her for a while. We never met her, thought as she was older she'd look after Lily.'

Jacko said they'd talked to Miss Gray, but Lily had stayed with her only briefly, then moved into Blewbury House. He did not say Lily had told Myra Gray she was sick to death at being expected to live at home, work for pocket money and be treated as if she were a kid, or that Myra had said Lily had a habit, hash, pills, maybe something stronger, she didn't do drugs herself. Myra had suggested she should move out, and she did.

Mrs Devon said something about Lily picking the wrong boyfriend, they had always worried about the interest she took in some of the village boys. Jacko became impatient, saw no reason why Mrs Devon shouldn't be acquainted with the facts of life.

'It wasn't a quarrel with a boyfriend, Mrs Devon, perhaps I didn't make it clear. Lily was using drugs — some cocaine was found in the apartment, and that costs money. She was paying for it by bringing back men.'

Mrs Devon wept. Her husband said there was no

need to put things so bluntly; Jacko apologized but said facts had to be faced. If he had been candid he would have told them that killings like this happened not every day but most weeks, and that there were hundreds of bloody raving psychos roaming around loose in what everyone now called the community, and in his view they should all be locked up. But who would listen to common sense like that rather than theories of do-gooders who'd never seen a skull cracked open or a body razor-slashed, Jacko would ask after his third large Scotch.

The killing of Lily Devon wasn't the most important item on Jacko's plate. It took second or third place to a battle he was conducting with accounts about expenses, which seemed to involve answering dozens of questions on different-coloured forms every day. Quite frankly, he wouldn't have thought Lily Devon's death was of deep concern to anybody except her parents, and perhaps to Stopper working through that list of possibles, and so he was surprised to get a call from the Big Man one morning. Jacko was at once scornful of the Big Man's superior airs and a little afraid of him, so that he tended to exaggerate his natural tendency to voice Plain Man opinions in appropriately robust terms. Concealing his surprise at the Big Man's interest, he said they had a number of possibles lined up, and were slowly reducing them.

'That's routine. You're doing more than that, I hope.'

'Of course, sir. Though it's often routine investigations that turn up someone in cases like this.'

'I don't want to hear about *cases like this*. Every

case is individual. What lines are you pursuing, other than going through the computer?'

'I've talked to the dead girl's parents. She'd conned them into thinking she worked for a music publisher. And to her flatmate, talked to her. Flatmate said some of her punters were important people – '

'No names?'

'No names at all. Flatmate thinks she had a diary or something with notes for appointments, but if she had one it's been taken. This kind of case, dates for sex fixed on the blower and maybe fifty possibles, I'll be frank – '

'No, let *me* be frank, Jacko.' Rose flinched at the informality, which had something ominous about it. 'The clear-up rate on cases like this in the Met's area over the last two years is highly unsatisfactory. I want to see a result with this one. And I'd like to be sure effort has gone into it, which is not the impression I've got at the moment. Am I making myself clear? I'm sure I am. I should like to have a note of progress this day week.'

Blah blah blah, Jacko thought. A note of progress, more bloody paperwork. Or worse still, another chat with the Big Man. He gave a raspberry to Stopper, who was more than half-way through the sexual misfits. Seven had reoffended and were banged up again, five were living with their families and doing jobs of a sort, four had disappeared from their last known address and were probably living rough or in squats, and Stopper was trying to trace them. What more did the Big Man want? And what else could you do? Jacko was not sufficiently curious to wonder why the Big Man wanted to keep tabs on the case.

But still he put the word out more urgently than he had done before, and a couple of days later was told Pisser Jones could have something for him. Pisser was one of Jacko's snouts. He had been given the name because of the frequency with which he said, 'Got to do a piss,' or, in mixed company, ''Scuse me, I need the toilet.' Sometimes he used this as a means of retiring briefly from awkward situations, but the consensus of those who knew him was that Pisser really did have a weak bladder. He was a very petty crook, a thief unable to resist temptation, whether it came in the form of a jacket carelessly thrown down with a wallet waiting to be taken from an inside pocket, or the chance of half-inching a delicacy at a supermarket.

Some detectives have nothing but contempt for their snouts, others tolerate and even feel something like affection for them. Jacko belonged to the latter group. Most snouts are of limited intelligence, and Jacko enjoyed a sense of superiority in dealing with them. He also liked the way one or two of them relied on him for good advice, and for help when they dropped themselves into trouble. He had kept Pisser from being charged half a dozen times, saying almost with a sense of wonder: 'It was stupid, Pisser. You'll never learn, will you?' Pisser would respond with: 'Dunno what made me do it, Mr Rose, just came over me, can't help it.' Contempt and affection were inextricably mixed in their relationship, and although life had taught Jacko not to trust anybody, he thought Pisser would be less likely than most to do him down.

Pints of bitter in front of them, settled in one of the darker corners of a dismal pub near Waterloo

station, he went through a ritual of inquiry about
Pisser's wife and mother. The mother, who lived
with them, had all kinds of things wrong with her
and complained continually about them; the wife
was a termagant who in Rose's opinion needed
several belts round the ear. Pisser loved them both.

'The old lady, she's not herself. These pains she
gets, Mr Rose, you wouldn't believe, just *here*.' A
slightly wavering finger indicated an area below the
chest.

'Tell her to lay off the fish and chips, Pisser.
Doctor said less fats, you told me yourself.'

'Yeah. Right. I know it. Can't make her though,
can I?'

Jacko dismissed this unprofitable subject. 'So
what's it about, Pisser? What's new?'

Pisser downed half his pint. His eyes, always red-
rimmed, always glancing away from the person he
spoke to, fixed momentarily on a corner window.
'That Kennington job, the girl that got done, I don't
reckon that sorta thing. I mean you and me, Mr
Rose, we know there'll always be toms, brasses, pros-
sies, whatever you call them, stands to reason, but
that sorta thing is right out of line.'

'You've got a name for me, is that what you're
saying? If so, cough.'

'Not exactly. I mean, I gotta name but it ain't
the one you want. You better let me explain.' Jacko
did not say, what's stopping you? He knew Pisser's
approach was often circuitous. 'The wife plays bingo
Tuesdays and Thursdays, and last week or so she's
been going with this Maureen, dunno her other
name, tell you if I did.' Again Jacko nodded, refrained
from saying get on with it. 'This Maureen, useta be

Jimmy Silver's girl, you know Jimmy Silver.' Jacko nodded once more. Jimmy Silver was a leading member, perhaps even the leader, of a gang of drug dealers who called themselves the Tooting Boys from the south London area where they lived. 'But now she's moved in with Speedy Walters and Jimmy don't like it, not at all.' Pisser stood up. 'This beer, it runs through you. I gotta go.'

He was away five minutes, minutes in which Jacko's temper did not improve. 'If you're sodding me about, Pisser, you'll be sorry.'

'Mr Rose, would I do that?'

'I hope not for your sake. Let's have it, whatever it is.'

Pisser lowered his voice. 'Maureen told the wife, Jimmy knows who it is done the Kennington job.'

'You got a name?'

The lowered voice became almost a whisper. 'Somefin to do with some sorta relative of Jimmy's is all I know. Likes little girls, this relative, Maureen told the wife. Be on your records, bound to be.'

'But you don't have a name?' Shake of the head. 'So what you want me to do, bring in Maureen?'

'Don't you do that, Mr Rose.' Pisser was alarmed enough to look directly at Jacko. 'You do that, Jimmy finds out Maureen talked to the wife, links it to me – you got to find another way. I'm your snout, you know that, always give you stuff straight. You do what you say, you'd drop me right in it.'

'I see that. But what you tell me, it gets nowhere, not without a name. If we've met this lad who likes little girls he'll be on our books, but – you a betting man?'

Pisser spread his hands. 'You know me, I got no

vices, just weaknesses is all. Something comes over me, otherwise I'd never be in trouble.'

'If you were a betting man, I'd say it's fifty to one against our having any link between this lad who may have done the job and Jimmy Silver. I need a name, Pisser. You talk to your wife, tell her to get a name from Maureen.'

'Couldn't do that.' Pisser began to shake, hands body, even his nose quivered.

'Sorry to hear it.'

'It's a help, what I told you, must be. Must be worth something.'

'Not without a name.'

He left Pisser shaking, looking forlornly at his empty glass. Back at the Yard the computer spat out a lot of names and details of men interested in girls and bondage, but none of the details showed a link with Jimmy Silver. So this bit of information looked as if it was the first step on a road to nowhere. Jacko forgot about it. He talked again to Bobo, who convinced him she had deliberately kept clear of her flatmate's money-making activities. Then he set Stopper to making more inquiries in the area about people Luisa/Lily knew, visitors to the flat who'd been seen going in. None of this brought any joy. Luisa was not known in the pubs round about, did her shopping in the anonymity of a supermarket, seemed to have no friends. Her bank and building society accounts showed a balance of more than fifteen thousand pounds, so she had evidently occupied her time profitably since leaving home. Nor was there any luck in getting a line on her drug supplier, although this might have been Bobo, who under a little pressure admitted popping pills and smoking a reefer from time to time.

It would have been wrong to say Jacko was at his wits' end. He wouldn't have let Luisa bother him, but for the intervention of the Big Man. When Pisser rang again, Jacko agreed to another meeting without asking questions. It was a different pub – Pisser had a touching faith in his snouting activities remaining unknown to anybody – but the same old Pisser, going off to the Gents after taking a quick gulp at his beer. He returned smelling faintly of urine, and complaining that he had not been treated well last time.

'Walking away like that wasn't right. I always give you genuine info, I do somefin for you, you do somefin for me, ain't that right?'

'I told you, what I need is a name. You got one?'

'I got somefin. It's what Maureen – '

'What Maureen told your wife, I know that. And I know you got to make a living. But what goes out I have to account for, Pisser, I start giving hand-outs to everyone says they've heard second or third hand someone's been a naughty boy and needs his wrist slapped, it'll be me gets a one-two from my bosses, I make myself clear? So you tell me what you got, if it sounds like there's anything in it you collect, understand?'

It was just after midday, no more than a dozen people in the pub. The barman, a Chink or Jap (how many of those would you have found behind a London bar twenty years ago, Jacko wondered), seemed to be looking at them more closely than he should have done. Across the table Pisser glanced at Jacko, then quickly away and round the bar as if searching for someone. He said in a voice not much above a whisper: 'Jimmy's sister.'

'What?'

'Jimmy Silver's sister. She lives with this bloke Derek, Derek Allgood.'

'So?'

'Maureen, she says Mary knows it's him, Mary Silver that is, but she won't do anything about it. He has these fits, Derek, don't know what he's doing. He's the one.'

It was thin, but it was something. And it was no skin off Pisser's nose, so why did he look unusually nervous? Jacko made it clear he had hoped for, even expected, something much more detailed, but money changed hands and he promised if there was anything in it he'd make sure the tip-off remained anonymous. Watching Pisser slouch away, looking left and right as he moved out into the summer sunlight, he wondered if the cash had been wasted.

Derek Allgood was on the computer. He was thirty-five and in the past seven years had been charged three times with indecent assaults on girls, all of them under twelve. On each occasion he had pleaded guilty. The first time he had been bound over, the second he had been given a suspended sentence, the third, eighteen months back, he had been put into a psychiatric unit and given a course of therapy. The psychiatrist's report was in the file and, so far as Jacko could understand the language, said Allgood suffered from a kind of delusory schizophrenia in which he imagined his blood to be diseased, the disease curable only by the mingling of his infected blood with the pure blood of a young girl. (The psychiatrist provided a lengthy analogy with the Victorian belief that venereal disease could be cured by sexual congress with a virgin, which Jacko skipped.) Allgood became sexually excited by the act of purification, which involved cutting himself and the girl, and rubbing her blood into his wound. He made no attempt at penetration, but the girls were frightened. Allgood said, and the woman psychiatrist believed him, that he had no recollection of the attacks although he accepted that he made them. She concluded that Allgood was probably impotent, now understood his condition, and was capable of living successfully in the community, although he should be monitored every quarter. Since his release nine months ago he had been working as a clerk in an employment office, and reporting punctually for his check-ups.

Jacko and Stopper were both disgusted by the report. ' "Reporting punctually for his check-ups," ' Jacko repeated. 'Then going off cutting up young girls. *And* he gets a job just like that when millions are out of work. I just don't know.'

Stopper agreed. But Allgood had not been on his list of possibles, because his activities did not fit the crime. He had not attacked any of his victims. They had been lured by gifts of sweets into going home with him, and had then thought they were playing a game until the moment when the game turned real with the cutting. And both men recognized that taking blood from a young girl's arm (Allgood's favourite place of incision) was a long way from bondage and what had happened to Lily Devon. But still, it seemed worth going to look at Allgood. The address on the file was a small house in a street off the Brixton Road, less than half a mile

from Blewbury House. The road was temporarily a
cul-de-sac. Several houses just beyond Allgood's
place were roofless and windowless, one or two a
mass of rubble. A barrier said, unnecessarily: 'Road
Up'.

The man who answered the doorbell was short
and sandy, his expression mild. 'Mary's out,' he said.

'Mr Allgood? It's you we came to see. May we
come in?' Jacko showed his warrant card and was
inside a moment later.

Allgood led them into a small back room with
three cats in it. He sat down, and a ginger and white
cat immediately jumped on his lap. The other two
moved round the detectives' legs purring. Allgood
stroked the one on his knee.

'She's Marilyn. After Monroe, you know. Keeps
herself beautifully clean. Please sit down. Do you
like cats? They have to stay in here, if they get in
the kitchen they're at the food in a minute. Hump's
so clever he can open the refrigerator.'

Jacko sat down, and Stopper followed suit. A
tabby cat jumped on Jacko's knee, moved up to his
chest, dug in claws affectionately. Jacko put him
down, pushed him away with one foot.

'That's Robert. He's very friendly too. I'm afraid
Hump's rather wild, he can be really naughty.'

Stopper gave a laugh, quickly choked off by his
superior's glare. Jacko said: 'You don't seem surprised
to see us.'

'No, we've had two officers here already. But we
couldn't tell them anything, we were out at the time.
It is about the bomb, isn't it?'

The penny dropped. Less than a week earlier an
IRA bomb intended to cause havoc in a shopping

centre along the main road had barely touched its
target but had damaged and destroyed several houses
near by.

'The cats were so frightened. Except Hump, he
couldn't care less.'

'Robert and Hump,' Stopper said. 'Mitchum and
Bogart?'

'That's very clever.' Allgood smiled shyly. 'I love
those old movies, don't you?'

Jacko said: 'We're nothing to do with the bomb,
Mr Allgood. We're investigating the murder of a
woman known as Luisa Devane a few days ago. It
took place at Blewbury House in Kennington Road,
not far from here, and our information is you may
be able to help us with our inquiries.'

'Me? I've never heard of her.' Allgood's clutching
hand grasped Marilyn, who gave a penetrating
miaow. A door opened, closed. 'That's Mary. She'll
tell you I had nothing to do with it.'

The woman who appeared in the doorway was
an inch or so over five feet tall, with black hair worn
long, thick dark brows that met in the middle, and
a square tense body. Flat-heeled shoes accentuated
her shortness and squareness. She looked like a
female boxer. Her voice was a rasping growl. 'The
filth. You don't wanta talk to them.'

Allgood nodded emphatically. 'That's right. I
don't want to talk to you.' The cat named Hump
squeezed past the figure in the doorway and disappeared, followed a few moments later by Robert and
Marilyn.

Jacko said: 'You're Mary.'

'Mary Silver.'

'Jimmy's sister. How's Jimmy keeping?'

'OK, far as I know. We neither of us got anything to say to you, so you can get out.' Her expression did not change when Jacko told her about the inquiry. 'I heard about it, that's all. She was a slag.' The last words were to Allgood, who looked away. 'You trying to plant it on Derek, that it? He never hurt anybody, hasn't got it in him. Or are you tryin' to lay something on Jimmy, that it?'

'I'm not trying to lay anything on anybody.' Jacko felt he had been patient long enough, and his voice was louder than usual. 'All we're asking for at present is answers to a few questions. If Derek here can tell us where he was the night this girl was topped, and we satisfy ourselves what he says is kosher, you can kiss us goodbye. We're trying to find who killed her, not lay one on Jimmy or anyone else.' He paused, waiting for comment. None came. 'Evening of the third. A Friday.'

The words were hardly out of his mouth when the woman said: 'He was with me. All evening we were together.'

Jacko popped a piece of gum. 'The whole evening sitting round the fireside except there was no fire, it's too warm, just home bodies together. I call that sweet, Stopper, don't you think so?' Stopper confirmed its sweetness. 'Any reason you happen to have that instant recollection?'

'There's a TV programme on every Friday, *Coronation Street*, on at seven thirty, we always watch it. Right, Derry?' Allgood agreed. 'But I never said we was sitting here all evening. We saw *Coro*, then had our supper, then went down to the Four Feathers, just down the road before you get to Bon Marché. We was there till just before eleven, then back here, had a cuppa, went to bed. That's it.' She glared at Jacko. 'So you can get stuffed, try planting it on someone else. I dunno where you got Derry's name from – ' She looked from one to the other, and the detectives looked blankly back. 'But it's someone trying to lay one on Jimmy, I know that.'

Afterwards Stopper said: 'If that mouse ever killed anyone my dad was Jack the Ripper.'

'Say you don't know.' Jacko shifted his gum, but was inclined to agree Allgood didn't fit the bill. 'The whole story comes from this Maureen, and she was Jimmy's girl. Could be she wants to lay one on Jimmy the way that cow said, or maybe Speedy Walters wants to cause him a little grief. Though if that's so it's a funny way of doing it, doesn't land Jimmy in trouble, just his sister's boyfriend. But it all doesn't smell right. You been around as long as I have you get a nose for these things, and my nose says someone's trying to play games with us.'

'Your snout?'

'He wouldn't do that. I dunno who or what it is. So what's next, Stopper? I'll tell you. We go on looking at Allgood, check out what the cow told us, and you go back to that list of yours, find out where they've all gone.'

He didn't report in quite those words to the Big Man, but said they were following up a particularly promising lead. He was braced for a rocket, but the response was comparatively mild, even understanding. It made Jacko feel the Big Man knew when to use the big stick and when a little soft soap might be helpful. Their chat had the effect of making him feel he should go out and get a result. Which, he recognized, might be the usefulness of soft soap.

FOUR

Cabinet Affairs

THE GENERAL ELECTION had seen Patrick Bladon
and his party losing seats, so that if they were to
form a government they had to come to an accommodation – he rejected the word coalition – with
the National Liberals, whose campaigning on Green
issues had been surprisingly successful, or at least had
surprised the two main parties. The accommodation
had seemed logical, even inevitable, but now that he
was more than two years into his second term as
PM there were times when Bladon wished he had
rejected the idea.

It was true that like all politicians he preferred to
be in office rather than out of it, but having the
NatLib leader, Allen Pitcombe, in the Cabinet was
a heavy price to pay. When Pitcombe had accepted
the post of Environment Minister rather than one
of the plums he might have asked for like Minister
for Europe, it had seemed an agreeable recognition
on his part of the political reality that the NatLibs
were very much the minority party in the government. In the event, he and his do-gooding party had
caused so much trouble about the building of factor-
ies and roads on green-field sites, a process the press
had called the brutalizing of Britain, that Bladon

now regretted offering Pitcombe the Environment job. If he had been Minister for Europe he would at least have been out of the country part of the time. Instead every Cabinet meeting was a squabble, with one or two of the weaker brethren supporting Pitcombe and his single fellow-NatLib in the Cabinet in their interminable droning on about damage to the quality of life involved in what to most of their colleagues was the obvious need for better communications leading to a more efficient use of resources.

This morning it was squabble as usual, the chief subject the proposals of the Home Secretary, Rex Calendar, for checking the ever-increasing amount of violent crime. Some of Calendar's suggestions, stiffer sentencing and more money for the police, had been accepted even by the NatLibs, but they indignantly rejected Calendar's ideas about dealing with hardened violent criminals, and arming the police with the recently developed Baybee automatic pistol. When that discussion was cut comparatively short, Pitcombe reiterated his opposition on Green grounds to the new toll-road developments suggested for the South-west and the Midlands, developments quite obviously needed now that the companies running the privatized railways were pricing themselves out of passengers. And the Channel Tunnel – of course there were still arguments about the Tunnel, and the government's refusal to subsidize it. Bladon knew people said he should exercise more control – the tabloids said it every week – but that ignored the facts. He had exercised control over his first government without difficulty, but after this damned accommodation it was another matter. It

was a fact that a group in the party and a large
section of the public admired Rex Calendar's zest
for privatizing everything in sight and his steamroller
approach to everything and everybody in his way. It
was a fact also that Pitcombe had supporters for his
insistent whining about the quality of life and the
need to preserve it. There was a Calendar faction
and a much smaller Pitcombe faction, but there was
no PM's faction.

The art of keeping together a minority government, Bladon had recently told a TV interviewer,
was to bear in mind that it was a bird with two wings,
left and right, and they must move in harmony if
the bird was to fly.

'What if they don't?' the interviewer asked.

Bladon gestured with his hand, a downward
sweep. 'The bird falls. But it's my job to see that
doesn't happen.'

The interviewer smiled. Bladon noticed for the
first time that she was attractive, and doing her best
to make him aware of it. 'That sounds like the art
of staying on top of a greasy pole.'

'You could say that. But I like the idea of guiding
those wings so that they fly in harmony better.'

She smiled again. He could have pursued it, perhaps come to a discreet arrangement, but it would
have been less than wise and he really couldn't
bother. He was in his sixties now, and sometimes
felt everything was too much bother. He'd like to
retire to Deemings and play at being a farmer. Clarissa might be pleased, she'd never cared for the hustle
and bustle of politics, the counting of heads and
promising of favours. For a decade now she had been
occupied with her history of costume. She had made

herself an authority on costume and fashion, something he admired. And what was he an authority on? Perhaps the art of going near the edge but making sure you didn't overstep the mark and go tumbling down the cliff. All that balancing of one power group against another, cutting corners, making deals, had fascinated him and had been his life for years, but now seemed rather a bore. Looking across and down the Cabinet table at the white intense face of thin-nosed Pitcombe and at Calendar's square jaw and hair sticking up like a hedgehog's prickles, he felt nothing but irritation.

Pitcombe was on about SuperPlus, one of the companies formed to run power supplies when British Gas had been broken up. SuperPlus, he said, was inefficient, wasteful, and had a unit cost thirty per cent higher to users than any of its rivals. There was a hubbub of assertion and refutation, from which the rasp of Calendar's voice emerged saying the figures Pitcombe used were inaccurate, out of date, and took no account of the enormous capital expenditure SuperPlus had been involved in last year because the local NatLib administration that controlled its area had run down the equipment. In any case, why was it the concern of the Environment Minister?

Pitcombe's manner as always was one of complaint. 'My concern is that the proposed new equipment would be one further encroachment on rural England, one further step in the brutalization of Britain.' And the fact that Rex's brother Donald has been recently dabbling in SuperPlus shares has something to do with it, Bladon thought. He intervened, and shifted discussion to the comparatively harmless subject of the Channel Tunnel, harmless since the Tunnel itself was a *fait accompli*, but no politician or party was prepared to accept responsibility for the expense of doing what was necessary to make it potentially profitable. Today, however, Pitcombites and Calendars, as Bladon mentally characterized them, argued even about the Tunnel, and then were off again about whether Britain was being brutalized or just made efficient.

Afterwards Bladon asked Calendar to stay on, and suggested he should call off the hounds. The Home Secretary asked what he meant. Bladon said a Cabinet so divided about every issue made effective government impossible.

'Say that to Allen Pitcombe. We're the majority party in the government, very much so. We have a programme.'

Bladon sighed. 'When the NatLibs entered the government there was tentative agreement that a number of measures would be delayed – '

The bristles on Calendar's head seemed to stand up straighter. 'Delay is one thing. What they're doing is saying no to every measure of any importance that's put forward, even though it was part of our platform. Another thing. Pitcombe's conducting a deliberate personal campaign against me. You heard him trying to sabotage the work Donald's doing to get SuperPlus out of the mess the NatLibs left it in. I was the target.'

'Surely not.'

'Is that the famous Bladon sense of humour? Anyway, it's obvious. Face it, Patrick, this coalition or whatever you call it isn't working. The sooner we go to the country the better. We should be thinking about the spring.'

'What makes you believe we should win an election then? The polls mostly say we'd lose.'

'Who cares what the polls say?'

They were in the upstairs study that had once been the PM's bedroom. He had ordered a number of things shifted – the Zoffany of the Rosoman family had gone back to the drawing room, where he felt it belonged. The portrait of Nelson so much admired by Thatcher had also gone elsewhere, replaced by some seventeenth- and eighteenth-century costume drawings reflecting Clarissa's interests. The Staffordshire figures of Victorian politicians had been brought in from the white drawing room. Their presence gave Bladon a comfortable feeling, just as Calendar's made him uneasy.

Calendar took out a cigarette, lit it. His fingers were nicotine-stained. Bladon realized how much he disliked everything about the Home Secretary, his lower-middle-class background and deliberately uncouth manner, the square head and the bristles on top of it, the busyness people called zest and buzz and other bee-sounding characteristics. Brother Donald was a less prickly article but really they were a pair; one had married money and the other had made it in the most disgusting way, and both had that unpleasant desire to rise to the top. 'What rises to the top?' had been a question his father had often asked, and he had provided the answer with the assurance of a landowner who could trace his family origins back in the same area for three centuries. What rises to the top, he had said, is scum. Those who own the land and care for the land should rule the land, George Bladon had believed, and really his son thought so too, although it was not possible to voice such a belief nowadays. Instead he said, 'I envy your confidence. I think whisky is your tipple?'

'Whisky and a little water. No ice, can't stick it.'

The drinks poured, Bladon moved to the reason he had asked Calendar to stay behind. 'This story in today's papers leaking memorandums about the Baybee and the Outcast Islands – do you have any idea how the leak happened?'

Calendar's denial was accompanied by his smile. The smile was roguish, transforming him from a powerful aggressive boss into a boyish charmer aware that he could get away with almost anything. Bladon was proof against the smile, although he admired the way it was used. He had no doubt Calendar had prompted or authorized the leak, but it would be pointless to say so.

The three Outcast Islands were dots in the Atlantic, the nearest point of land St Helena. The Baybee had been developed by British gunsmiths, engineers and scientists working in collaboration. It looked like a child's cap pistol, and fired twenty five-millimetre bullets without the need to reload. Calendar's programme for crime prevention or reduction called for persistent violent criminals to be sent to the Outcast Islands rather than to British prisons, and for all the police to carry Baybees at the discretion of the Chief Constables in their area. The ideas had got no further than memorandums and animated Cabinet discussion. The Outcast Islands plan, which would have been confined to gang-leaders and big-time drug-smugglers, had been thought impracticable, but there was a lot of support for the Baybees, not least because it was thought they would be immediately popular with the public.

Now Bladon, speaking in a measured unim-
passioned way that he knew would annoy the Home
Secretary, said he would take very seriously any
attempt to pre-empt a Cabinet decision by taking
argument about these matters into the public
domain. The government, not the public or even
the Home Secretary, would make a final decision
about them.

Calendar said of course he agreed, and returned
to the attack on Pitcombe. 'He was damned insulting
about Donald. You can't expect me to sit still and
listen to such stuff.'

'He meant to needle you.'

'And he bloody well succeeded. You say I should
call off the hounds. What I'm telling you, Patrick,
is it's Pitcombe who should be brought into line.
Tell him to stop this nonsense about us planning the
brutalization of Britain. Pick an issue, challenge him
on it, see how many NatLibs he can lead into the
"No" lobby. They'd all be shaking like jellies, and
so would he.' He paused, then added: 'It may be
that the best way to persuade Allen is through
Gwenda, that's a possibility. And I don't have any
feeling against him, you know, there's nothing personal. I'd just like someone to tell him not to keep
throwing sand into the machinery. As for the leak,
Patrick, all I can say is I'm sorry and I'll try to find
out how it happened, though I can't see any harm's
done by giving the subject a public airing. But
whatever you do, you know you always have my
support.'

Bladon thanked him. A lunch was being given
for a visiting ambassador, and with Calendar gone
he sat down to read the notes prepared for him about

improving the relationship between their countries. After a couple of minutes boredom overcame him.

At Eton and at Magdalen, and even now that he was private secretary to one of the most important members of the government, it seemed to Johnno that he was waiting for life to begin. His father, an only moderately distinguished Major-General in the Catering Corps, had said: 'You're a dreamer, boy, that's your trouble,' but it seemed to Jonathan that dreaming was full of pleasures and possibilities, and that life was the unsatisfactory thing. His dreams he knew to be fairly conventional, involving as they did being asked to undertake secret missions, bedding dazzlingly beautiful women, becoming involved in dangerous affairs like those which he was sure George Kaiser encountered in the course of any month. Surely such things must happen to him one day?

In the meantime there was Belinda, with whom he had had an on-and-off relationship for some months, and there were the steps up the Civil Service ladder that had led to the secondment in Rex Calendar's office. Wasn't that enough, wasn't it success? The Major-General thought so. He had been pleased and almost respectful, regarding Johnno as the repository of state secrets. Johnno, although he did not discourage this idea, felt he was doing an office job, marking time. He really wanted to be like George Kaiser. George was tall, thin and untidy, occasionally remarking on Johnno's neatness of dress and appearance as if his attitude to life was the height of absurdity. At Oxford George had sometimes disappeared for a day or two at a time, never mentioned his parents, who remained invisible during his time there, and seemed unconcerned about his poor degree. He had casually agreed to Johnno's timid suggestion that they might share the expensive Chelsea apartment, and always paid his share of the rent.

George never spoke of his background, or the means by which he maintained himself. Belinda said Johnno should ask him straight out, and one night he did.

'Where do I come from? I thought you might have guessed. The name's a bit of a giveaway, I've sometimes thought of changing it. But I was given it as a kind of relic.'

'I don't know what you mean.'

'I mean Kaiser Wilhelm, the last Imperial ruler of Germany, had relatives. The name was a sentimental gesture.'

'Your father was one of the Hohenzollern family?'

'Did I say that? What does it matter, we live in a democracy.'

'Is he alive?'

'I've no idea, I never met him. But the background's been useful in my work, I can tell you that.' When Johnno asked what the work was, George gave his lopsided smile. 'Helping to make the world safe for the innocent. Like you.' He was never more explicit, although he sometimes referred casually to events in Ireland and Eastern Europe in a way that suggested personal knowledge of what was going on there, and to arms shipments in a way leaving it to be conjectured that he often met arms-dealers. He said once that if Johnno was in any sort of trouble where a strong arm might be useful, he would be able to help. Belinda was present, and asked what he meant. She got the lopsided smile.

'My dear Belinda, some things are better not spelt out.'

'Don't condescend to me. Do you mean if someone was giving Johnno trouble you'd *eliminate* him? Make sure he was *terminated with extreme prejudice*?'

'I don't answer questions like that. Forget it.'

Belinda said to Johnno afterwards, 'I don't know how you can be friends with him, he's such a phoney.' Johnno tried to make her understand that George had always been like that, he really was a mystery. Her response was that he would find out it was not one worth solving.

Johnno's feelings about his boss blended fear, dislike and worship. He admired Rex Calendar's decisiveness and refusal to admit defeat about anything whether important or trivial, but disliked it especially when his insatiable curiosity about everything was extended to Johnno's private life and background. Had there been much homosexuality at Eton, did the Major-General take such things for granted as part of his son's schooling, what allowance had he been given at Magdalen, what had it been like to make the adjustment from school and Oxford to real life? It was mostly teasing, he knew that, but the knowledge didn't make it any better. Today he rebelled. When Calendar asked: 'How's your sex life, Jonathan?' he replied: 'Minding its own business.'

The square head nodded approvingly. 'Always give as good as you get, never knuckle down till you have to. That's one lesson of the Calendar Training

School. Another is, if you know you'll have to give way do it gracefully as if it's voluntary, not forced on you. I wouldn't say you've mastered that yet.'

No comment seemed needed. He asked how Cabinet had gone. Calendar took a cigarette from the box on his desk and lit up. 'As usual, nothing decided. Bladon wanted to know if I had any idea who'd leaked my law and order ideas. I said I hadn't. It wasn't you, I hope.' Johnno got the smile. 'Bladon's a fusspot, thinks if you do nothing about problems they'll go away. Indolence be my friend is the PM's motto, and he's wrong. At present indolence is nobody's friend, what's needed is action.'

'So there's been no decision about the Baybee?'

Calendar shook his head, opened his desk drawer, took out the little toy, aimed it at Johnno. He heard click-click-click, flinched, then said: 'Would it kill anybody?'

'It could if it was aimed in the right, or maybe I mean the wrong place. But it's a stopper, not a killer – spray a dozen of these little bullets at a group of thugs and they'd damage them where it did most good.'

'I don't see why there's so much fuss. From what you've told me, and the papers I've seen, the suggestion is only that they should be distributed if the Chief Constable thought it necessary.'

'That's a sop to the lily-livered. What Chief Constable wouldn't welcome the chance to arm his whole force with these little beautiful babies if he could? If it happens – *when* it happens – I'll guarantee violent crime, not your everyday household husband-and-wife killings, I mean organized crime, would be cut by thirty per cent in a year. Any word from your cousin about Blewbury House?'

'Only that inquiries are proceeding. They've got several leads.' His boss did not comment, merely raised his eyebrows. He was emboldened to continue. 'I've mentioned this before, sir, I don't know the details but my guess would be that it's concerned with state security?' He ended on a note of interrogation, but Calendar still said nothing. 'If I'm right, isn't it maybe something for Special Branch or MI5 rather than Scotland Yard?'

'Another lesson. Avoid stating the obvious. If it was a matter for them, should I have asked you to speak to your cousin? Nor should you ask, as I can see you're on the verge of doing, if you should call him again. If I want you to gee him up I'll tell you, till then forget it. But remember it too. Now, what else have you got for me?'

Much of Calendar's morning was spent doing an interview for a radio programme. The interviewer homed in on the Outcast Islands plan and especially the Baybee, and was also curious about the source of the leak. Calendar stonewalled dutifully, but left the impression that if it was left to him the necessary measures would be put through Parliament very quickly. In the afternoon he found time for a meeting with Rosie Raymond, whose agency, Hamilton Raymond Associates, was planning a campaign designed to convince the public that the police force was friendly, efficient and trustworthy. These, as he stressed to her, were just two more ideas suggested by a department concerned solely with the preservation of law and order.

At the preliminary discussions Rex had made

clear his preference for dealing with Rosie. She brought layouts and slogans to his London flat behind Harrods ('He's On Your Side' and 'The Man You Can Trust' had been quickly rejected), but on her second visit and thereafter much of the time was spent in bed. Rosie was divorced so there was no potential husband problem, and she was some kind of distant relative of Pitcombe's animal-loving wife Gwenda. Shafting Rosie made Rex Calendar feel he was doing Pitcombe a bad turn, even though he knew this to be an illusion.

'Wow,' Rosie said on this occasion. 'You're certainly energetic.' She was about to add *'for your age'* but checked herself in time. Calendar was approaching fifty, she more than ten years younger, a lean brunette who preferred going to bed with Asian and African rather than Western men. Her performance with Calendar had been in the line of duty, although it was enjoyable enough. Afterwards he asked how often she saw Gwenda.

'Now and again. We do the publicity for APL, the Animal Protection League she's so keen on. I don't get invited home for chats, we're not bosom pals. I don't talk secrets with her if that's on your mind.'

'Of course not. There's something I'd like her to know, that's all.'

'What stops you picking up the phone?' She stopped when she saw the look on his face. 'Look, I'm a publicity girl. I'm not interested in politics, don't want to get mixed up in them.'

'Nothing to do with politics. You can say you've heard this on the grapevine or through a client. I'm a client.' The Calendar look was succeeded by the

Calendar smile, and what she was asked to say seemed harmless enough.

Bernard Bannock held a seat in Surrey, one of those captured by NatLibs in what had been thought a Tory fief. He was Allen Pitcombe's indispensable man in relation to the public and private lives of supporters and enemies. He knew which NatLib MPs were losing enthusiasm for their leader, which were in financial trouble, neglecting their constituencies, having affairs. And the magnetic filings of gossip Bannock drew to him extended well beyond his own party. Every bit of scandal, financial, sexual, and possibly criminal or actionable, involving those engaged with the Westminster talking shop came to him, was chewed on as one might say for flavour, and when chewed thoroughly regurgitated as a story and sent on the rounds. Sometimes the story proved incorrect, but that did not shake Bannock's faith in the authenticity of the next one. Even art experts have been deceived at times in their identification of a Vermeer or a Picasso.

There were drawbacks to Bannock. One was his inability to distinguish between the insignificant and the important, another the fact that although strong about moral values and the importance of the family, he was unmarried and was said by his numerous enemies to be a closet queer, although nobody had ever provided hard evidence of this. Pitcombe did not particularly like him – there was something displeasing about the fervour with which he nosed out moral and financial corruption in others – but had found him immensely useful. He talked in an interjectory way, with vital phrases often elided. In the House his speeches were sometimes disasters.

There was also something disturbing about his appearance. He looked like a horse, eyes bulging out of his head, nostrils wide and snorting, large feet occasionally stamping in irritation. He stood snorting beside Pitcombe now in the House urinal, muttering something made inaudible by the flushing water. He muttered again, and Pitcombe heard Calendar's name.

They went along to Pitcombe's room. He sat at his desk. Bannock momentarily lodged himself in a chair opposite, then began to walk about talking, large head bending forward occasionally, eyes bulging, phrases spurting.

'Weekly surgery very important – satisfies people – direct contact with MP, listen to what they say – half the battle – votes – someone to complain to, don't expect miracles – do what you can – minority partners – ' Another of Bannock's limitations was longwindedness. Pitcombe ceased to listen until he heard the name of Calendar.

'Say that again, Bernard.'

'Trevelyan, I said, Mary Trevelyan.'

'What has she to do with Calendar?'

'Came to me – lives with her mother – fine old woman, being turned out of her cottage – disgrace, council building new estate – no care for the individual – doesn't want to move, taking a stand – '

'Bernard, what has this to do with Calendar?'

The horse snorted, glared. 'I told you. Mrs Dawson – mother – worked for the Calendar family.'

'What then?'

'One of the boys was tortured – father a sadist,

mother did nothing – boys took part – couldn't bear it – left, thought of reporting case, never did.'

'I'm not clear about this. Which of the boys are we talking about, Donald or Rex? Are you telling me Donald tortured Rex?'

'No, no – Eugene – lovable, Lucy said, Lucy Dawson, only backward, nothing serious – there three years – couldn't bear it, left.'

Pitcombe traced it out. 'There was a third child, the youngest? And the father and the other boys ill-treated him. Lucy Dawson was the household help or whatever. Have you talked to her?' Bannock nodded triumphantly, and expanded on this. Lucy Dawson was old and arthritic, but still in full command of her wits. The senior Calendars were both long dead, but Lucy would be prepared to repeat her statements.

'Would they have any other authentication? No? So they'd just be unconfirmed gossip.' Bannock snorted. 'What happened to Eugene?'

Bannock plumped himself in the chair, became splendidly coherent. 'He disappeared. Mrs Dawson thinks he was murdered.'

Pitcombe stared. 'What basis does she have for that?'

The story, which Mary Trevelyan had often heard from her mother, was that having worked as house-hold help to the Calendar family and seen little Gene beaten and bullied until she could bear it no more, Lucy left. In her time Gene had been shut into cupboards, pushed down a flight of stairs, tied to a tree for several hours, and made to take part in an initiation ceremony involving his head being held under water. The father beat the little boy for being stupid, but it was his brothers who tortured him. He was seven years old when Lucy left; Donald was thirteen and Rex ten. Gene was rather simple, the other two very bright. Apart from what she called the torture, the initiation ceremony and the tree-tieing, the older boys lured Gene into doing things that got him into trouble. Their father then beat him with a slipper, and Mrs Calendar agreed that Gene was a naughty boy who must be punished. Sometimes, Lucy admitted, he *was* naughty. He had fits of rage in which he smashed things and was uncontrollable, something she put down to the persecution by his brothers.

Shortly after leaving the Calendars' employment, Lucy Dawson got a job in London and married a man who did all sorts of occasional odd jobs. He wasn't approved by her family, and Lucy didn't go back home to the Kentish village where she worked for the Calendars until he left her for a barmaid. On her return to New Valley she learned that the older boys had done well, one was now an MP. And Gene? He had dropped out of school at ten or eleven, and nobody seemed to know what had happened to him. The village shop run by the Calendars had changed hands after Mr Calendar dropped dead from a heart attack, and Mrs Calendar was in a home suffering from what was then called senile dementia. Gene seemed to have vanished, and when she asked around nobody wanted to talk about him. Her conclusion was that the brothers had persecuted him once too often, he had resisted and perhaps been killed in a fight. If he was still alive, what had happened to him? Bannock was still trying to find out.

Pitcombe said it was an interesting story. He would think about what might be done with it, and was grateful to Bernard for the trouble he had taken. The horse nodded, moderately pleased with this lump of sugar, then suggested they should give the story to one of the tabloids and let them follow it up. Not, of course, the *Bulletin*, which was owned by Donald Calendar.

That evening Pitcombe told Gwenda. They looked so much alike they might have been brother and sister, both tall, thin, long-nosed, with clothes rather hung on them than worn. About most matters they thought alike, but Gwenda had not been contaminated by practical participation in politics. At the mention of Bannock her long nose lifted in distaste.

'Mucky,' she said when he had finished. 'It's mucky, Allen.'

Pitcombe was proud of his wife's sensibility, which he knew was finer than his own, but now he protested. 'It tells us something about the Calendars. Even as little boys they were ruthless. Tearing the wings off flies, torturing their little brother.' She did not comment. 'Bannock wants us to leak the story to a tabloid, who'd follow it up more easily than we could.'

'I hope you won't do that.' She turned a gentle gaze on him. 'It would be lowering yourself, dabbling in dirt.'

'If I let Bernard dabble for us is that any better?' She did not reply. 'Donald Calendar's a nobody who has made a fortune partly by luck. But Rex is another matter.' He shook his head. 'He really does stand for the brutalization of Britain, you know that as well as me. These law and order ideas of his that have just been leaked, they'd lead to a police state. And if he has his way we shall be a nation of scientists who know nothing except their figures, producing nothing but high-tech video games, and cars built by automation for the profit of firms owned by Japanese and Germans. Most of the population will be morons who spend all their spare time watching television. All the things decent people love and enjoy will be destroyed by something Calendar calls progress.' It occurred to him that with a little polishing the phrase might be an effective climax to a speech. The next words seemed to him, even as he spoke them, rather a let-down. 'He has to be stopped. If this story might damage him we should use it, not through a tabloid but in some other way.' She turned her head away. 'You know how much I value your judgement. So often you see things I don't.'

'I think you've made up your mind.' She kissed him on the cheek. 'You know I never criticize except when we're alone. But don't get mixed up with anything dirty. Please, Allen, don't do that.'

He said he would sleep on it. By the morning he had decided there could be no possible harm in encouraging Bannock to dig a little deeper.

FIVE

Jacko Wraps It Up

WHEN JACKO had decided there wasn't enough on Derek Allgood to charge him, and that anyway his face didn't really fit, he put out the word again more urgently, and gave a rocket to Pisser for bringing him stuff not good enough to wipe a donkey's arse. In the following week he heard rumours about a ferment in south London's criminal gangs, with Jimmy Silver swearing he would get level with those who were trying to do him, Mad Monty Morris and Yellow Face Arbejay disappearing from their usual haunts, and other smallish fish scurrying around the pond as if their lives depended on perpetual motion, as perhaps they did. He expected Pisser also to run for cover, and was surprised when he rang one day and asked for a meet. It took place in the Waterloo pub and Pisser was less jittery than usual, indeed reproachful when Jacko asked if this was something else he'd dreamed up.

'That it is not, Mr Rose, that I would never do.' He buried his nose in the beer, drank half of it, wiped his mouth, sighed with pleasure. 'Warm weather, first of the day, nothing like it. I got something for you, a name and some details.'

'About Jimmy Silver, is it? I hear he's not pleased

by what's going on, whatever that may be. I don't want to hear about him, not unless it's to do with Blewbury House.'

'Not to do with Jimmy, no. This Blewbury House job, there was some stones taken, is that right?' Jacko said it could be. 'Now, I got a name for the handler. I give you that it's worth something, right?'

'It's not worth the pint you're drinking till I've checked it out.' Pisser stood up. 'Where do you think you're going?'

'Gotta take a leak.' When Pisser came back he gave Jacko the name of Moshe Davis, well known as an occasional fence for anything other than really big stuff. Moshe mostly handled jewellery, and had a shop off Ludgate Circus he ran as a cover, but he was prepared to deal in krugerrands, slush, pretty well anything except drugs. Moshe disapproved of violence, and there were times when he had volunteered useful information. According to Pisser, two or three days after the murder at Blewbury House Moshe was handling some items that could have been taken from Lily's flat. Where had his information come from? About that Pisser was evasive. He said he kept his ears open, heard more than he remembered, could have been something Maureen mentioned to his wife, but wherever it came from he was sure Moshe was handling some stuff that might be from Blewbury House.

The shop off Ludgate Circus had an unostentatious display of rings, bracelets, watches and earrings in the window. Moshe, a dignified moustached figure in his sixties, greeted Jacko and Stopper courteously, though without warmth. He stroked his moustache when he heard what they wanted, then said it was possible he had been offered some of the things they described.

'And bought them?' Moshe inclined his head. 'They were on the lists. Sight going, is it?'

'I read the lists. But there are so many items and often the designations are, what shall I say, meagre. "A ruby and diamond brooch", now, is it modern, fifty or a hundred years old, how are the stones set, what shape is it? I have perhaps a dozen brooches like that through my hands in a year. Would you say thank you if I was on the line every month saying this or that item might just possibly be what you're looking for?'

Jacko nodded. It was true Bobo had been unable to give any really useful description of the missing pieces – had only been shown them once for a couple of minutes, she said – so that the listing of them was vaguer than he'd have liked. At the same time he had a feeling Moshe had expected their visit, or at least was not surprised by it, although his manner was unusually nervous. The jeweller now produced three pieces roughly corresponding to those mentioned by Bobo. All of them looked modern. He showed them a book entry saying he had bought them for two hundred and ten pounds, with a scrawled signature from the seller that could have been anything. Asked how much he would expect to sell them for, he said only the emerald necklace with a diamond cut into its centre was worth much. How much? Five hundred, a thousand, five thousand? Moshe wouldn't be drawn.

'You understand, Mr Rose, I'm in business to make a living. And as for selling this stuff, maybe I have it on my hands for months, years. When I sell it, *if* I sell it, maybe I ask twelve hundred, take a thousand. It's a nice diamond, no flaws, the emeralds are well cut.'

'A nice diamond, a nice profit. We'll be taking these away for further examination; you won't object, I'm sure. Stopper, make out a receipt for Mr Davis. And now, Moshe, the thousand-pound question. Who did you buy these from, where did he say they came from, is the date in your book the right one? Because as Stopper here would point out if I hadn't done so already, this loose-leaf book you use could be very handy for putting in an extra item or taking several out for that matter. If the date is right it's the Monday after the presumed owner of these items was beaten up and killed in her apartment, so I'm sure you'd like to be helpful.'

It was very warm in Moshe's back room, and now a sudden surge of colour came into the jeweller's cheeks. His eyes closed for a moment. Either the appearance of shock was genuine or it was good acting, yet he must have known he might be questioned about the jewellery. Did he know the pieces were hot, but not that violence had been involved in getting them? In any case, now the fence fenced with them, at first saying he remembered nothing, then that it was a medium-sized man in a brown jacket who said they belonged to his mother, who had died recently. When Stopper showed him a photograph of Derek Allgood, taken just outside his house in Brixton, he said it was possible that was the man, but he spoke hesitantly.

'This is black and white,' Stopper said. 'Remem-

ber anything about him, do you? Colour of his hair
maybe?'

Moshe gave a great gulp. 'Yes. His hair was red-
dish, an unusual colour, I remember that.'

Stopper persisted. 'Someone brings in stuff like
this, stones worth a thousand or so, you're bound to
take a good look at 'em.'

'Let me see the photograph again.' This time he
nodded. 'I believe this to be the man, yes, although
I could not swear it. You say the girl was killed,
Inspector?'

Jacko had put in some gum, and felt more
comfortable with it in his mouth. Moshe's reaction
still puzzled him, but there seemed no point in
understating things. 'She was badly beaten up, sex
games of some sort that went wrong, then slashed.'
Moshe shuddered. 'Then this laddie in the picture,
if it was him, snitched these pieces and walked out.
That was Friday night, Monday he brings the stuff
to you. And you, you just buy it for a lot less than
it's worth, never asking a question. That putting it
fairly? I think so. So the wisest thing you can do is
to be really cooperative from now on, wouldn't you
say? We may ask you to pick him out in a line-up.'

Moshe Davis nodded. He did not look happy.
Which was reasonable enough in a way, since no
fence likes having anything to do with court cases
or line-ups. But would he stick to his story if he was
got at, had he perhaps been got at already? And did
they have enough now to make it worth bringing
Allgood in, questioning him and then putting him
in a line-up? On the whole he thought not, but he
was still brooding on it when there were two bits of
good news. They got a result from the patient trawl-

ing going on in the Kennington area, and a piece of physical evidence turned up.

The trawling had involved house-to-house and flat-to-flat calls, in the hope that someone had seen Lily and a companion near to or entering Blewbury House that Friday evening. It had produced little, except for a man who had been calling on his parents, who lived on the third floor, and had seen two men in the hallway near Lily's apartment just before nine o'clock. The man had no idea what they looked like, or whether they had in fact rung Lily's bell or called at another flat on that floor, and Jacko pigeonholed the information in case it was confirmed at some time. Now, however, a man came forward to say he had passed two people, a man and a woman, standing outside Blewbury House at nine o'clock or just after, talking or arguing. He stood and watched for a minute or so in case they came to blows, but instead they went into the block. The two were almost directly under a street light, and from the description the witness gave the woman could have been Lily Devon and the man Derek Allgood. The witness, Billy Harris, worked for a local turf accountant and did not have the best of reputations. He had been in court half a dozen times on petty charges, driving a car without a licence, stealing from shops, pestering girls for sex. He said he had watched the couple because if the girl had turned down the man he would have propositioned her himself, which seemed likely enough.

The physical evidence was a sharpened chisel found by a workman among the debris in the area beyond Allgood's house, which had inevitably become a haven for the homeless, among them some drug-takers and meths drinkers who had settled into the ruined houses. Burned into the handle were the initials DA. There was a good deal of blood on the chisel, but according to forensic this was not just from one person but from two or even more, one of whom could have been Lily Devon. Shown the chisel, Allgood agreed that it was his, but said – or rather Mary Silver said for him – that since the bombing and the occupation of the wrecked houses they had been burgled twice, and the chisel was among the things stolen. They had not bothered to report the burglaries to the police because they knew nothing would be done about them. Why did Derek have an offensive weapon? For self-defence. Twice in the past he had been beaten up because of what Mary called his little weakness. She had sharpened the chisel and told him to carry it in case he was in trouble, but he never did carry it. Forensic agreed that it could have been used to slash the girl's body.

So the chisel could mean something, or perhaps not. As for Mary's statement that they had spent the time between nine and eleven on that Friday evening in the Four Feathers, that simply didn't hold up. They had gone to the pub together, but she had left within a few minutes, which she admitted after several people said she had spent most of the evening playing bingo, something they remembered because she had won a prize. And Derek? The landlord and the barman recalled seeing him in the pub, but couldn't say when or whether he left. Friday night was busy, the pub packed, and the characters Derek claimed to have been with were dodgy villains and hangers-on.

Jacko had an uncomfortable twenty minutes with

the Big Man after he expressed a belief that Derek was their man, but said it wasn't easy to find the clincher. The Big Man looked at him hard, and said the clinching evidence was always there if you looked in the right place. Jacko thought of himself as an easygoing type, but he came out of the interview sweating. It was true that the day, like many others in that June, was warm.

It was with little optimism about getting a result that he put Allgood up for an identity parade, and he was genuinely surprised when he got positive identification from both Billy Harris and Moshe. Billy picked him out without hesitation; Moshe seemed unhappy about it but still fingered Allgood. So he was brought in again, and this time four of them took it in turns really to put pressure on − nothing outside the rules, just pressure − and in the end he broke down, fairly cried his eyes out, admitted everything.

With the admission made he kept apologizing both for causing so much trouble and for being so wicked. All sorts of people had tried to help him, he said, but it was no good, he did things he couldn't really remember afterwards, and some of them were very bad. Did he remember this particular bad thing, playing a game with this girl and then getting angry? He agreed it was true that sometimes he did feel angry, and since people had recognized him he must have been there, although he could not imagine why he should have done such terrible things . . . Eventually a weeping Derek made a statement about what he must have done, and insisted on adding how sorry he was to have done it. He wanted Jacko to be there when he made the statement, and afterwards

smiled when Jacko patted him on the shoulder and
said he'd feel better now.

And that, Jacko felt, really just about wound it
up. As he said genially to Stopper, he'd always
thought his Sergeant looked as if he might be the
son of Jack the Ripper and now he knew it. They
had a boozy celebratory evening and on the following morning he saw the Big Man.

'You think you've got a case? The last time we
spoke you weren't sure.'

'He's our man right enough, sir. Admitted everything, pleased to get it off his chest. Whether the
CPS give us the go-ahead isn't for me to say. There's
the two positive identifications and supporting evidence, but a lot depends on his admission.'

The Big Man congratulated Jacko without showing too much enthusiasm. Then he called Johnno
and said he could tell anyone interested that a man
had been charged.

'That's very good. Thank you so much.'

'You might also like to tell this interested person
that what we've got seems to me fairly thin.'

'I see. But, well then – I mean, somebody *has*
been charged.'

'Indeed. Let's hope all will go smoothly. I'm
simply pointing out that the case is by no means
watertight, and I wouldn't want to give any other
impression.'

Johnno passed on the information, and received
a bleak look. 'This was a matter that concerned you,
I believe. You told me you were making inquiries
from your cousin.'

'Yes, sir, but – '

'I'm happy it's cleared up. Thank you for telling

me. And now let me brief you on something else, something I'd like you to do for me. I think you know Charles Nugent.'

Charles Nugent was Belinda's brother, ten years her senior. He was in a merchant bank, and had steered Johnno into what seemed some very good investments, but how did his boss know of their relationship? He contemplated the possibility that his apartment was bugged, a shivery yet delicious thought, for a bugged apartment would mean he was involved in something truly secret.

'You're friendly with him I hope, as with other members of the family?' Johnno, mind still on possible bugging, nodded. 'Nugent's bank handles the Pitcombe financial affairs, did you know that? I'd like you to mention to Nugent that my brother Donald is extremely interested in the preservation of our native wildlife, and looking for a cause to which he might make a sizeable contribution. He's seriously considering the Animal Protection League as a beneficiary, although you know a couple of other worthy causes are under consideration. Can you do that? Casually, mind, don't make lunch and dinner out of it.'

'Yes, I expect – I'm sure I can.'

'You sound surprised.'

'It's just that when you think about – '

'The publications my brother's interested in, you mean? But really his association is indirect, he gives complete freedom to his editors. I shouldn't want a good cause to be left out in the cold because of prejudice against my brother. Nor would you, I'm sure.'

'But you and Allen Pitcombe – the things you've said about him in the House – '

'In the House, yes. I think Pitcombe is a canting hypocrite who smears sincerity over everything he touches like a boy spreading jam on bread.' For a moment the short hair bristled, the deepset eyes gleamed. 'So you'll understand that if I approached Gwenda Pitcombe personally, or even if my brother did, it might not be well received. But still, Donald has this wish to help. Nothing to stop you mentioning it, I hope?'

Johnno said again there was not. He spoke to Charles, who was pleased to have this tit-bit of information to pass on. It was marginally useful to Johnno also, because he was able to make a peace offering to Belinda, to the extent of taking her out to lunch.

'I wish you'd come back.' Belinda, seen across the table in Plato's Cave, a new and fashionable restaurant, looked extremely attractive.

'I don't know. I like this place. Is it your boss over there?'

In the glass behind Belinda Rex Calendar could be seen talking animatedly to the chief political correspondent of the *Express*, or perhaps the *Mail*. 'Do you think he's attractive? Most women seem to.'

'In a way. Rather brutish.'

'He is. Well, not brutish but brutal. But marvellous too.'

'I believe you're in love with him.'

'It's you I love.' They finished eating little fishy things. 'Why don't you come and meet my people next weekend?'

'Oh, your *people*. Do grow up.'

'What does that mean?'

'I'll tell you something. Tell George to move out.'

'I like him.'

'I know. That's the trouble. There's something wrong with him. Unclean.'

'I could tell him to take more baths.'

'You make silly jokes when I'm serious. There's something wrong about him, I tell you. I shouldn't be surprised if he's got a wife and children somewhere.'

'Don't be ridiculous. He was at Magdalen with me.'

'He'll land you in trouble.'

They spent the rest of lunch bickering. When they left, Calendar and the newspaper man were drinking brandy. Belinda didn't come back to the flat. George Kaiser reappeared that evening after being away three days. Johnno asked what he'd been doing. 'Belinda thinks you've got a wife and children tucked away.'

George placed a hand on his heart. His fingers were long, thin, elegant. 'I swear that's not so.'

'So where have you been?'

'This might interest you.' He opened the evening paper to an inside page and pointed to a story about three terrorists on trial for possessing a quantity of Semtex and a store of arms. Evidence had been given by two agents who had penetrated the group. They told their stories behind a screen and were not named.

'Are you saying you were one of them?'

'I'm not saying anything.' A revolver appeared in his hand, blue-black, impressively powerful.

'Is that real?'

'Very much so. You want me to make a bullet pattern on the wall like Sherlock Holmes to prove it?' The revolver vanished, George's long head was shaken. 'I'm in a small group, less than half a dozen of us, what I do is useful, sometimes dangerous but more often boring. I can't say any more.'

Johnno was not sure whether he believed any of this. Discreet inquiries from those with links to SIS brought no acknowledgement of anybody called George Kaiser, but also the information that three or four unofficial groups were, as it was said, roaming around doing odd jobs.

The Pitcombes gave two or three parties during the summer months at their Belgravia home, although *parties* gives an unjustifiable impression of flowing hospitality. There was wine, of course, although orange juice and a drink which blended the pressings from eight vegetables were prominently displayed. And there was finger food, little pieces of cheese, meat and some fishy mixture, wrapped up in fragments of lettuce leaf. There were tiny cakes that tended to crumble in the hand before they could reach the mouth, and small cups of decaffeinated coffee. No spirits were served.

The guests were a mixture of NatLib politicians, supporters of Gwenda's animal causes and Allen's battle to save the countryside, and a spatter of artists, stage, TV and media people who backed NatLib and animal causes. These last were in a minority, people connected with the arts for some reason not warming to the Pitcombes. Bernard Bannock of course was there, talking a little but mostly listening. He had mastered the art of being in one group while hearing what was said in another, alert for phrases that might give a whiff of scandal. And Donald Calendar was there with his wife Norah, who had been a centre-page attraction in Calendar's magazine *Raunchy* a few years back, but since then had gained weight and lost her looks. Allen had been surprised to find their names on the invitation list. Gwenda explained.

'A little bird told me he's ready to make a contribution to animal welfare. Perhaps quite a big one. In fact I heard it from two quite different sources.'

'Absolving his sins. Which include the disgraceful things he's said about the party.'

'That was his editors.'

'You think they don't hear their master's voice?'

'Whatever his papers may say, if he makes a contribution to the League he'll be doing good, and I shall thank him for it.' She greeted Donald warmly. He was a jaunty laughing man who resembled his brother very little in manner and appearance. Their careers also had been different. 'Rex has the brains, I just make money,' was one of Donald's jokes, and it was true that while Rex had got a scholarship and then a first in politics and logic, Donald had saved five hundred pounds out of his job with a secondhand car dealer and used it to start a cartoon magazine called *Stink* which was immediately and immensely successful. Out of *Stink* was born the equally successful sex magazine *Raunchy*, and the profits ensured financial support from banks when Donald bought two dying papers, the daily *Bulletin* and the *Bulletin on Sunday.* They were launched with a typographical facelift and the slogan 'If it's Printable it's in the *Bulletin,*' interpreted by enemies as 'If it's Dirty we Bathe in it.' Since then Donald had acquired weekly and monthly magazines, although recently the circulation curve of the *Bulletin* had moved downwards. Perhaps the public had become sated with pictures of big-breasted girls, barrel-chested men wearing jockey shorts that bulged ominously in the front, and tales of four-in-a-bed frolics. Some said Donald yearned for respectability and was toning down his more outrageous papers, others that he was financially overstretched and wanted to get out of the newspaper business. He was diversifying, still others said. Through Rex's influence (again, so it was said) he had got on to the board of SuperPlus, sunk a lot of money in it, and was determined to extend the range of its activities. There was gossip about SuperPlus backing a new electric car, and also gossip that Donald wanted a knighthood.

In any case here he was, a presence noticed and commented on by the three gossip-column writers present. They observed the friendliness of Gwenda's greeting and the coolness of her husband. Gwenda's warmth was never excessive, for she lavished the small amount of passion in her nature on animals, or rather on the idea of their welfare. She did not greatly care for most of the actual creatures, tending as they did to be both smelly and noisy. But still she was gracious to Donald, and took him off to talk to Mary Morris, the feminist MP who was an unofficial fund-raiser for the League. The tycoon expressed enthusiasm for the APL's work and said the *Bulletin* might run a campaign to support it. Mary Morris, who was renowned for being what she called downright, said it would make a change from all the overdeveloped men and women featured every day.

'They sell papers. That's our business.' Donald gave a little bellow of laughter, then said he was absolutely serious about a campaign.

'And so am I. We welcome help from *any* source.'

'You understand I never interfere with my editors.'

'But sometimes you get rid of them.'

Donald appeared not to have heard. '. . . But suppose the suggestion was made that you should have a centre page opposite the editorial to tell readers what the League's all about, what would you say?'

'I should say wonders will never cease. Also I'd say don't expect me to support the paper's politics.'

Donald fairly roared with laughter at that, and at the look on Mary's face. ('As if it was her first bonk and she wasn't sure if it was all right to say she liked it,' he said to the *Bulletin*'s editor afterwards.) But he was seriousness itself when Gwenda took him off to their study and talked for several minutes about things the APL was doing that weren't covered by the RSPCA or any other group of initials. He said 'Yes' and 'I see' and 'Excellent' at intervals. His merry disposition, expressed by his snub nose and the laughter lines round his eyes, made it difficult for him to strike the right note of solemnity, but he managed it as he said he had felt for some time that he should contribute substantially to charitable causes, and the APL was one for which he felt great sympathy. There were other groups, he added, whose activities had impressed him, but he had been moved by what he had just heard from Gwenda. No exact amount of any possible benefaction was mentioned, but Gwenda was somehow left with the impression that it might be in the region of a quarter of a million. They discussed setting up a trust as the most appropriate way of handling it, and Donald did not demur at the names of possible trustees Gwenda mentioned.

Altogether she felt that this had been time well spent, and was pleasantly impressed by what, talking to Allen afterwards, she called Donald Calendar's robust jollity. Allen was less happy. There had been an incident, while she was closeted with her tycoon, when Norah had slipped, almost fallen, been saved by Bernard Bannock and then accused him of feeling her up ('That was the deplorable phrase she used') and smacked his face.

'She was drunk, of course, had been drinking before she arrived no doubt. She certainly didn't get it here.'

'I could believe anything of Bannock.'

'You have no basis for saying that. I was surprised when Mary Morris took her part. Donald Calendar is no more a friend of good causes than his brother.'

'He offered Mary a page in the *Bulletin* to write about the APL.'

'Did that make it necessary for you to take him off to have a private discussion? It will be all over the press tomorrow.' She told him about the possible donation. 'He wants something, no doubt about it.'

'Really, Allen, you are being ridiculous. What possible benefit could he gain from making a donation to a charity like ours?'

He mused, finger on lip, a pose in which a

photographer had once told him he looked like a philosopher. 'The word is he's looking for a K.'

'A donation to the APL wouldn't be likely to help him much. But if it did, would that matter?'

'Gwenda, the man's little more than a pornographer. You know his money came originally, and I believe still does come, from those appalling magazines.'

'Of course I know, everyone knows it.' She raised her head, stuck her nose in the air. 'People who did worse things have got knighthoods and peerages. If you think of the good a large donation would do, your reaction seems to me really rather – thoughtless.' She had been about to say *unworthy* but refrained.

'Thoughtless or not, I can tell you that if you accept that man's money we shall both regret it.'

The Pitcombes never quarrelled, but certainly they had irritated each other over this.

SIX

The Unwrapping

THE FIRST whisper of trouble, the first cloud crossing the blue sky of Jacko's contentment at being
rid of the Blewbury affair, came from the Sergeant
checking out the jewellery items Moshe said he had
bought from Derek Allgood. The purpose of the
check was to discover which of Lily's clients had
made such handsome gifts to her, and Detective
Sergeant Strong made the rounds of the most likely
London jewellers. One of them identified the emerald necklace as a piece he had sold some months
earlier to a boxing promoter named Dudley Gresham, who had given it to a singer who called herself
Peacocks Fairlight.

Dudley told a fascinated DS Strong that his tem-
pestuous relationship with Peacocks had ended
when, in a manner that would have been approved
by any member of his boxing stable, she had knocked
him unconscious, using an iron saucepan rather than
her fists. Peacocks saw no reason to keep a memento
of a fat greasy bastard, which was how she described
Dudley to an even more enthralled Strong, and sold
it for a couple of centuries to a Portobello Road
dealer, who had no market for something he recognized as too classy for him and took a quick profit

of another hundred by disposing of it to Moshe. The point of all this was that the necklace had been sold to Moshe a week before the Blewbury House crime. Moshe, confronted with this discrepancy, conceded he must have made a mistake about the necklace, but still insisted he had bought a similar item from Allgood, along with the others of lesser value, on the Monday after Lily's murder. And he produced another necklace that, again, fitted the vague description Bobo had given.

Stopper, who talked to Moshe, reported to Jacko that the dealer was probably lying his head off and was equally obviously very nervous, but why? A couple of days after this unsettling news Jacko got word that Pisser Jones was in hospital after being beaten up in an alley outside the Waterloo pub. Jacko went to see him, but was not welcomed. Pisser, face badly cut and with a fractured knee that would need an operation, insisted it was the result of a family row. 'And, you don't mind me saying it, Mr Rose, you paying me this visit, gets around, won't do me no good.'

'I just brought you some grapes, Pisser. Sweet. No pips.'

'Yeah, well. Sooner you didn't.'

'You're not telling me your friends don't know you put it about now and again. Must be a dozen people know you're my snout. What I want to know is, all that stuff about Allgood, someone tell you you should feed me that?' Pisser shook his bandaged head. 'Because if so you'd have me to reckon with, and you'd be feeling sorrier for yourself than you do now.'

'Nah nah, Mr Rose, wouldn't do that. Always straight up with you. Said how I got it – '

'Yes, you told me, through this Maureen. And that's what's landed you here, why not say so? If Jimmy Silver's boys did it I don't mind bringing them in.' When Pisser insisted it was a family argument, he gave up. 'Have it your way. Any time you want to talk you know the number.'

The best guess was, he said to Stopper, that Pisser had somehow got in the middle of a row between Jimmy Silver and Speedy Walters, either over territory since both dealt in drugs and women, or because Jimmy really was needled about losing his girl to Speedy. Even so, the reaction against Pisser seemed excessive. And, Jacko said hopefully, whichever way you read it, there was still some hard evidence against Allgood.

Such optimism made the final blow all the more painful.

It came from inside the force, delivered by Detective Chief Superintendent Hilary Catchpole, Miss Hilly to those who disliked him, Catchers to others more friendly. Jacko called him Catchers, but didn't like him that much. Nor dislike him for that matter, just that he didn't fit Jacko's idea of a police officer. Catchers just didn't have the matiness Jacko was prepared to feel for any fellow plain-clothes detective. He was ready for a couple of drinks, but shied away from a real good boozy evening. He was part of a team all right in the office or when working on a case, but when office hours and cases were done with, he gave the impression he'd done with you too.

Nothing wrong about that perhaps – Jacko was married himself and liked putting his feet up and watching the box with his wife at the end of a hard day – but something about the way Catchers separated himself from his fellows seemed to suggest that his attitudes and interests were not only different from those of his colleagues but superior to them. And then, unlike Jacko and a good many other policemen, especially those in the CID, he wasn't a Mason. That was unusual in the upper echelons of the Yard, where having Masonry behind you was widely thought to be an aid to promotion. Saying no to the Masonic embrace could be called a mark of independence, or of course you could say it was what you'd expect of a toffee-nosed bastard. Catch-pole seemed to Jacko also a bit of a cold fish, although there were those who said he had an eye for women. Altogether – well, Jacko had nothing against Catchers but still didn't fancy him.

So it was particularly galling that Catchers brought the bad news. He came into Jacko's office and said: 'Blewbury House. You've got a man named Derek Allgood banged up for it. I have some relevant information.'

Relevant information – was that the way for one copper to talk to another? Jacko said an interrogative '*Yes?*'

'He put up an alibi about being in a Brixton pub, the Four Feathers?'

'Right.'

'Friday evening, June the third. What were the times he claimed to be there?'

'Nine to eleven. But it didn't stand up. He was there all right part of the evening, but nobody could say it was the whole time. Girlfriend lied about being there with him. Chances are he was there for a while around nine, then again maybe just before eleven. Plenty of time to do the job at Blewbury House.'

'Nine to eleven, yes. I was there the whole evening, sitting near him. He could have gone out for ten minutes or so, no more. I can give him an alibi.'

'*You* were there? The whole evening?' The notes of incredulity and indignation sounded clearly in Jacko's voice, and he was not surprised to see Catchpole's quickly stifled grin. What the hell, Jacko wanted to say, was *Catchers* – Miss Hilly – doing spending the whole evening in a pub when he wasn't a serious drinker? And given that he was so outrageously and improbably there, why did he take particular notice of someone as inconspicuous as Derek Allgood?

The answers were straightforward enough. A haulage firm that did a lot of business in carrying machine tools, car parts and spares had been losing items from the loads somewhere between their depots and the places of delivery, almost all of them within a hundred miles of London. The foreman and the works manager had been with the firm for years, the lorry drivers never made more than one short stop before making delivery, but when the goods were checked at the other end there were often from two to half a dozen items missing, heavy machinery in cases that would have taken some shifting. Catchpole had been in charge of a small team, including a detective named Dick Aylesford who was put inside to work at the depot, his identity known only to the firm's managing director. Aylesford learned that the works manager, Moresby, was carrying on an affair with the wife of the firm's accountant, and spending more than he was able to afford on her. Then a lathe worker told Aylesford that Moresby and a loader were very thick, met every Friday in the Four Feathers, and he'd seen money change hands. Aylesford thought either the loader managed to get the missing goods off the lorry after they'd been checked by the drivers, or one of the drivers was in on the job. He managed to make a couple of quick informal checks of the lorries without finding anything wrong, and suggested confronting Moresby and the loader in the pub, when or if money changed hands.

Aylesford was young and enthusiastic, and Catchpole had agreed although not fully convinced by his theory. Catchpole was unknown to the suspects, so he went in the pub while Aylesford waited nearby. Moresby and the loader came in, both in high feather, drinking Scotch. An envelope passed from the loader to Moresby, Catchpole alerted Aylesford, and then confronted the two men, who were at first astonished, then indignant. The loader claimed he had a winning system on the pools, Moresby and a couple of others had come in on a syndicate, and within a month they had two winning lines worth nearly ten thousand pounds. An unlikely tale? He produced a letter from the pools promoters to prove it.

The detectives did the best they could after this disaster. Moresby threatened to sue the police, but was persuaded after a few drinks that the whole thing was a good joke. The drinks led to a fair amount of chat, in the course of which Moresby voiced suspicions of the accounts clerk who made a final check on loads before handing invoicing details to the drivers. A couple of days later the scam was uncovered, operated by the invoice clerk and a driver who was in trouble with his mortgage. It was simple enough. Twenty cases would be checked by the invoice clerk as loaded, and the driver would certify the number, but one or two never went on the lorry. The tools they contained would have left the depot after it closed on the previous night. The depot's owner said he would never have believed it of the driver, a phrase Catchpole had often heard before. Aylesford was apologetic, Catchpole said it never hurt to buy a man a drink.

None of this much interested Jacko, who chewed the gum furiously during the tale, but what Catchpole had to say about Allgood destroyed any possible case against him. Catchpole recognized him immediately because he had brought Allgood in after one of the cases involving young girls. The detective thought him pathetic but potentially dangerous, 'a tit in a trance who could turn into a loose cannon' as he said to Rose, who was surprised to hear Catchers put it in such colloquial terms. So in the pub Catchpole kept an eye on Allgood in case he started chatting up a teenager, but Allgood just drank quietly, talked to a few very minor villains, joined in sing-songs. 'I spoke to him, but it's as if he isn't there half the time, away in dreamland, I couldn't even be sure he knew who I was,' Catchpole said, and Jacko nodded agreement. He had been maddened by that same apparent absence of attention at times during the interrogations. But Catchpole was certain about Allgood's presence in the pub during the period when Lily Devon was murdered. Why had he confessed? As Catchers said, he was the kind of man who would confess to stealing the crown jewels if you told him often enough you knew he had.

This was a bruising half-hour for Jacko but Catchers was so sympathetic, almost apologetic, that the Inspector felt more warmly towards him at the end of it. If you were given a lead like the one Jacko had by a reliable snout, Catchers agreed, you had to follow it up. He didn't add that a wise man would have been more sceptical than Rose, and done a lot more in the way of checking.

'It was planted on me,' Jacko said. 'That bloody Moshe, I knew there was something wrong, he'd been got at. And Billy Harris, I should have known better than to take the word of scum like that. Someone wanted this out of the way, and that's a fact.'

When he used this phrase to the Big Man, however, he got a frosty reception. A brilliant piece of deduction, the Big Man said, but it was a pity he hadn't made it a little earlier instead of making a fool of himself by arresting Allgood. Jacko had known he would be in for a bad time, and it was as bad as he had feared even though the Big Man never raised his voice. At the end of it he was relieved to know he was off the case. There were, the Big Man said without apparent irony, no doubt a good many other things on his plate.

After a brief period of contemplation the Big Man sent for Catchpole and asked after his family, his manner sympathetic. Catchpole said nothing had changed.

'You're still looking after the boys?' The detective's wife, Alice, had left him a few months earlier, after her brother had committed suicide in prison while on remand. She had blamed her husband for not getting him out on bail. 'And you're managing? On your own?'

'I don't have a live-in lady, if that's what you mean. Alice sees the boys at weekends, says she's sorting herself out. I'm hoping she'll come back.'

'I don't mean to pry. Just like to know how you're coping with the pressure.'

'If I couldn't cope with pressure I wouldn't be in the force.' Catchpole resented the questions, but felt he might have gone too far in showing it. 'Sorry, sir. Just take it I can cope with anything I have to. Trouble is Alice doesn't recognize the limits to what a copper can do and what he can't. She's right in a way and I know it, which makes it hard for us both.'

'I think you're getting round to saying if she comes back it has to be on your terms.'

'You could put it I'm trying to avoid saying that.' Catchpole briefly smiled. Handsome fellow, the Big Man thought, wonder if he has got a piece on the side. He apologized again for prying, said Catchpole had saved them from making a nasty balls-up in this affair of the murdered tom, he'd like the detective to take it on. Catchpole said it might look as if he'd deliberately done Inspector Rose a bad turn to get himself assigned to the case.

'I've already taken Rose off it. If he does have that sort of reaction, which I doubt, it's the kind of petty jealousy a man like you should be able to ignore. Being a good copper can involve ignoring other people's feelings. As you've been suggesting yourself.' He waited for a response, but none came. 'This tom who's been killed, it all looks straightforward but isn't. If the answer is simple, why should a phoney solution be dropped in our lap? Someone's playing silly buggers with us, which is something I don't care for and won't have. I want you to dig into it, find out why Allgood was planted on us and who's behind it. And report to me personally, keep me in touch with what you find out.'

The Big Man's heavy eyelids looked half-closed, but Catchpole was aware of being watched more carefully than usual. 'That's all?'

'What else?'

'Find out who killed the girl. You didn't mention that.'

'But of course, Catchers. With a man like yourself there's no need to state the obvious.'

Catchpole spent the next couple of hours reading the files, then went back to the converted chapel in Clapham that was the family home. Alan had made high tea for himself and Desmond, sardines on toast followed by chocolate biscuits.

'What are you having, Dad?' Desmond asked.

'I'm not very hungry. Probably an omelette. A bit later.'

'That's what you had last night.'

'Wrong. Last night was scrambled eggs.'

Alan said, 'You're not much of a cook.'

'None of us is perfect.'

'It'd be better if Mum were back.'

He looked at their faces, Alan's questioning, Desmond's hopeful but on the verge of tears. 'I want her back too, but it's up to her. In the meantime we can manage. You two go up and make a start on your homework, I'll be with you later.'

Later, a good deal later, after helping with their homework, superintending their baths, doing a bit in the garden, overcooking his omelette and watching an American cop show on TV, he sat down to make notes in his journal about the Big Man's skill in passing the buck and in avoiding saying just what it was he wanted, but found himself falling asleep. Outside the chapel voices were raised in a song about Ireland being sprinkled with stardust to make the shamrock green. Within, he listened for a cry from the children, who sometimes woke with bad dreams, but heard nothing. He thought of Alice, and fell asleep.

SEVEN

What's Right is What's Necessary

WITH CLARISSA fed up, as she nowadays too often and openly said, with dirty London and sordid politics, and at the moment down opening a costume exhibition at Bath or Taunton or somewhere else in the West Country, Bladon often found himself alone and lonely in the evenings. Of course there was work to be done and people he could see, but week by week it seemed more convenient to pass most of the work on to one of his multiplicity of secretaries, and day by day the company of dissatisfied or favour-seeking politicians became less congenial. Quite often in the evenings, therefore, he slipped through the connecting door between ten and eleven Downing Street, nodding to any secretary or official who happened still to be around, and went up the wide staircase, lined with cartoons from 'Spy' to Gerald Scarfe, to have a chat with the Chancellor, Rhoda Carpenter.

The appointment of a woman Chancellor of the Exchequer, the first in British history, was one of the few actions in Bladon's second term as PM approved by both his party and the public. Rhoda's father had been no more than an assistant bank manager. She had won a scholarship to university, where she took an economics degree, preferring a Midlands institution to Oxbridge because she said it was more like real life. She had worked in a merchant bank, then as financial editor of a broadsheet daily. At twenty-five she married a business tycoon, had a son and daughter now both themselves at university, stood for Parliament at a time when she was divorcing her husband for his numerous infidelities, rode the rumours about an affair of her own by admitting it, and to the surprise of most people in the party won first the nomination, then the seat.

Her maiden speech was forceful and funny, and it soon became clear that she was one of the few people in any party who understood the workings of high finance and was also able to explain it in terms the ignorant thought they understood. She had been a conspicuous success as a junior minister, but her appointment as Chancellor in a government able to stay in office only with NatLib support had been a daring stroke. Its success was marked finally by the ease with which she had discomfited the critics who said she had been juggling figures like a stage conjurer with rabbits. The mark of a successful conjurer, she replied, was the ability to pull rabbits out of the hat, and she produced from behind her a fluffy toy rabbit to prove the point. The House of Commons is easily amused, and this was regarded momentarily as a master stroke of wit.

A brandy snifter in front of him, Bladon looked round and sighed. 'You have the gift of making it look lived in. Something Clarissa never managed.'

'That's because it is lived in. It's my home.' It was true that Rhoda owned nothing except an apartment in a Bloomsbury square, which she had let on moving to Downing Street.

'But not for ever.'

'Don't be so gloomy, Patrick. Nothing's for ever, but it's a good idea to behave as though it is. And anyway, there's nothing to be gloomy about.'

'I wish I could agree with you. I admire your spirit.' This was true. Rhoda was small and dark, with curly hair starting to grow grey, features marked by high colour in the cheeks, a strong nose and a long chin. Below them were a squarish figure and rather thick legs, one shorter than the other as the result of a polio attack in childhood. Her marked limp did not stop her moving smoothly round a dance floor, and there were those who found the limp and her slightly crooked smile sexy. She was not in Bladon's eyes physically attractive – he thought it must have been her mind that had impressed the tycoon – but she brimmed with an energy he envied.

There were times, especially in this sitting room, when he felt as if this energy was flowing from her into him, impregnating him with her will towards the control and organization of the party and of society. Had he once been like that, had that sort of confidence flowed in his veins? He mentioned the latest unfavourable poll figures for the sake of hearing her rubbish them, and sure enough she did so. Then she leaned forward, emphasizing what was said with stubby fingers.

'You come to see me to be cheered up, admit it.' He nodded. 'But you don't need it, the cards are in your hands, you just have to play them. The party's with you, just waiting. You're the leader they want, and it's your politics we need.'

'It does me good to listen to you.' He felt the brandy warming him. 'But my policies seem to have been hijacked by other people.'

'Say that's true, claim them back. There's not much wrong with what Rex wants to do, the country's got to be dragged screaming into the twenty-first century, better communications, less labour-intensive work, more leisure, new ways of using it provided. We've got to be part of a political Europe and a trading Europe, and some bits of national sovereignty will have to go. We all know that's true, it's the ham-fisted way Rex goes about trying to put it over that's wrong, that and the fact he sees himself as a national saviour. And of course Allen Pitcombe's got something when he talks about preserving our heritage, though the language he uses may make you and me feel a bit sick. So there's nothing wrong with the ideas, but you're the one who can put them over, make the country accept them. People believe you, Patrick, they know their PM is an honest man. All you have to do is lead.'

When she talked like this, all guns blazing, he thought she was rather fine, even though he was still doubtful. 'What I wonder is how many members in the House, how many people in the country, would agree with what you're saying. But you'd be with me if I did that, set out a range of policies, gave a lead?'

'Right you are. I'm of the PM's party, and you'd be surprised how many others are too. You give the lead, we'll follow. That stuff about politics being the art of the possible, I've always thought it was crap. Politics is the art of convincing people that what we know is right is also necessary.'

He pondered on that. 'Give them Calendar's policies or most of them, but sugar the pill? He'd never go along with it.'

'Then it could go along without him. People only think they're indispensable.' They both laughed, her crooked smile showing one gold tooth. Bladon stayed another half-hour before kissing Rhoda chastely on the cheek, and saying being with her was like having a blood transfusion.

The Big Man's voice was cool. 'I told you the case wasn't watertight. Further evidence has sunk it.'

'That's bad news. It's really very important it should be cleared up quickly.'

'Important to you?' Johnno did not reply. 'You can tell whoever's interested, apart from yourself, that I've put a senior officer on to it. When there's something new I'll tell you.'

The thought of what Rex Calendar might say drove Johnno to words that surprised him even as he heard them uttered. 'That's the kind of thing you say to anybody. It's not good enough.'

'It will have to be. If you're able to tell me a bit more about what's needed and why, that would be helpful.' He put down the telephone.

When Johnno passed on the news to his boss, however, Calendar said it just showed what he'd always suspected, that they needed a good shake-up at the Yard and if he was still Home Secretary in a few months' time they'd get it. 'But you can leave your cousin to his afternoon naps, for the moment anyway.'

'You mean drop it? Don't bother any more?'

'Not exactly, Jonathan. Let sleeping dogs lie, you might say. Or let lying dogs sleep.'

Moshe Davis at first tried to say he'd made a genuine mistake about the necklace. Catchpole moved from friendly understanding through impatient incredulity to threats. It was, as so often, the threats that produced a result.

'Look, Moshe,' he said, 'we both know you're lying, that this book entry is a total fake. Eventually we'll be able to trace the other items you say Allgood brought in and show they couldn't have come from the Blewbury House job, but that would waste time. If you make me waste time I promise we won't let you alone. Every deal you do will be checked to see if it's legit, and I wouldn't be surprised if you were offered stuff we knew was nicked just to see if you were tempted. It could be your legit business will fall off because some of my lads might come in when you're in the middle of a deal and ask if you can help re some stolen goods. I pity you, Moshe, I really do. If you go strictly legit your business might be ruined, and if or when there's so much as a sniff of anything funny you'll be banged up so fast you'll think you're being given a ride by Nigel Mansell.'

After a few minutes of such friendly persuasion Moshe gave way. He said he had been told a man was to be fingered for a robbery, and given a photograph and rough details of what he was supposed to have nicked. From the rough details he had provided from his own stock the stuff he was supposed to have bought, after being assured the genuine pieces wouldn't turn up. What was it all about? He hadn't asked, but was insistent he hadn't known he was getting involved in setting someone up for a murder. 'I never would have gone along with that, never in this world. I'm a man of peace, my record shows it.'

'So why do it, why get involved?'

'I was threatened. They said they'd do my kids if I didn't go along with the story. And they meant it. These young ones today, carving a couple of kids or blinding them, it'd mean nothing to them, be a joke. They're not like you and me, Mr Catchpole, they're not gentlemen, nowadays there's nothing they wouldn't do. It's not the world I grew up in, and that's the truth.'

Catchpole was amused to find himself linked with Moshe as a gentleman. He regarded people in terms of villains, punters, narks, and the respectable citizens he was there to defend, never as gentlemen. Looking at Moshe, however, at the carefully trimmed moustache, blue blazer, tight neat trousers, consciously casual cravat, he saw that for the fence the gentleman mask was necessary not only to impress punters but as a prop for his self-esteem. Perhaps he should feel flattered to be put in Moshe's class. He asked which young ones had approached the jeweller.

They were in the back room, a young assistant outside to deal with customers. Even so Moshe lowered his voice. 'This goes no further, understood? What I mean, I know you'll be using what I say, but keep my name out of it. My kids, the girl's thirteen and her brother's eleven. What they said they'd do to Miriam – they're not human, they're something else.'

'You give me the names, it ends there. I heard the whisper from a snout.'

'Speedy Walters, you know him? These were two of his boys, one I know, called Dodo Canter. First I said I wanted nothing to do with it, handling stones now and then that's my limit. Then Canter said they'd wreck the shop, then about the kids and that settled it. I'm a family man, you'll understand.'

'And sympathize,' Catchpole said, and meant it. But why, he asked his Sergeant, Charlie Wilson, should Walters want to set up Allgood? No doubt Pisser Jones had been primed to tell the tale fed to Jacko Rose, but it all seemed to be the wrong way round. Speedy was living with Jimmy Silver's former girlfriend, so it should be Jimmy trying to plant one on Walters. In any case, why should Walters want to get involved in the question of who knocked off a brass?

Wilson did some asking around, and in a couple of days came up with an answer to the first question. It seemed there had been arguments about territory between Speedy and Jimmy Silver, and Jimmy had sent some of his Tooting Boys to knock over a couple of the clubs Speedy used as drug distribution centres. Hence he had a reason for doing Jimmy a bad turn. Why Walters should have interested himself in the brass remained a mystery.

'What about the girl, Maureen?'

'Don't think she comes into it. Jimmy says Speedy's welcome to the slag. What I hear, though, is one of the Tooting Boys put Pisser into hospital, teach him a lesson. I don't know how it got out Pisser fingered Allgood, daresay one of the Boys knew he was a snout.' Wilson saw with amusement the look of distaste on the governor's face, but he nodded when Catchpole said it was like turning over a piece of earth and watching the worms wriggling. Wilson admired his boss, knew he didn't like the need to be on terms with villains. In Wilson's book it was something you had to do, and the better fist you made of it the more likely you were to get a result.

Now Catchers said: 'Very good, Charlie, but it only takes us so far. Speedy's a thug, Silver raided two of his clubs, so torching four of Silver's betting shops would be more his line, not this complicated business of setting someone up for a killing. Someone told Speedy what to do, maybe he got paid, maybe Speedy owed the man a favour.' He sighed. 'I'd better talk to Speedy. I can see you think you'd do it better than me, Charlie, and you could be right, but I'd still want to be there. You come with me, protect me.' Wilson laughed dutifully. 'Get hold of Walters on the blower, tell him we want to talk about his trouble with Silver, something like that, I don't mind what you say. Be polite.' He got up from his desk, crossed to the window, looked down at girls in summer dresses, men in shirtsleeves. 'Beautiful weather.' He continued in the same neutral tone: 'You know, it really hurts me that we have to be polite to scum like that.'

Speedy lived in a big Victorian house in one of the streets off Streatham High Road. He had installed an electrically operated gate, so that to get in you had to call up the house. Once through the gate you were in a conventional semi-circular suburban drive, with a couple of garages on the right. The front door, however, was not conventional suburban

but iron, with a peephole but no lock. The detectives
were inspected through it, then admitted by a black
who towered over them. They went into a wide
hall, with rooms on either side. There was the sound
of tapping on typewriters or VDUs; a girl came
out of a room carrying files. The black led the way
to a lift. Catchpole asked: 'Speedy put this in? No
staircase?'

'Staircase at the back. Mr Walters say he don't
want it in the front, wants to be modern. Front's a
kind of office, he likes that.'

Catchpole nodded. They got in the lift. Wilson
said: 'Don't I know you? Deptford, couple of years
back, you fought Tiger Murphy, lost in the fifth.
You're Delaware Large, right?'

The negro beamed, chuckled. 'You got a good
memory, only one thing you got wrong. I lay down,
understand me? I coulda beat that Murphy with one
arm in a sling, but you gotta look after the money,
right? Speedy was handlin' it and the way he fixed
it left everyone happy. Shouldn't be saying that to
you gents.'

He showed fine teeth in a laugh. Wilson said:
'We won't tell.' Delaware laughed louder.

Their feet made no sound along a thickly carpeted passage. Gold doorknobs gleamed to left and
right. Delaware opened a door ahead of them, stood
aside to let them in, then announced genially: 'The
filth.'

Speedy Walters bounced across the room on what
seemed dainty feet, and shook their hands with a
powerful grip. He had got his nickname as a quick-
moving middleweight, and looked as if he could still
handle himself in the ring. In the ring or out of it.

His face was unmarked except for a nose slightly askew. Small alert eyes were sunk deeply into flesh. His cockney voice had a very thin overlay of culture when he said, 'What d'you think of my headquarters then, gentlemen? Quite something, isn't it?'

'Quite something,' Catchpole agreed. Walters was evidently keen on gold. The pictures around the wall, sporting prints and photographs of boxers, were all in gold frames. The wall lights were on gold brackets, the wallpaper in black and gold shapes. A glass coffee-table was rimmed with golden metal, there were chairs and sofas covered with gold dralon, the carpet was gold with a black motif matching the wallpaper. Walters let them take it in, then gestured to where one wall had been taken out and replaced by a picture window opening on to a long balcony. 'Couldn't have a penthouse, council wouldn't wear it. This was the next best thing.'

Catchpole nodded. 'Very fine, but not much of a view, just houses. Pity you couldn't arrange to buy them, knock them down, put in an Olympic size swimming-pool. Help you to keep fit.'

The little eyes looked hard at him, then Walters said: 'Good joke, Superintendent, that's the right handle, isn't it? Haven't had the pleasure.' He said to Wilson, 'We know each other,' and the Sergeant nodded. 'Now gents, what are you drinking? Just say the word, Del here will do the honours. Not often we have the pleasure of entertaining the force, is it, Del?' Wilson glanced at his boss, opted for beer. Walters asked for a ball of malt, and Catchpole said he'd take whisky too. The drinks cabinet was concealed behind a section of wall that opened out. Walters watched as they showed appropriate surprise.

'I like something unusual, you'll have gathered. Something with taste. OK, Del, leave us to it, I'm safe enough with these gents.' When Delaware had gone he addressed Catchpole. 'I'm told you're worried about possible trouble starting up here in south London. I think if that's so you've got the wrong end of the stick, come to the wrong shop. Any trouble, I'd know about it.'

Wilson said, 'There's been trouble. The word is two of your clubs were raided by the Tooting Boys, lot of stuff got smashed up, two or three people landed in hospital.'

'I heard about it. Some lads getting high, is what I heard. It happens.'

'This wasn't just any old lads, it was Jimmy Silver's boys. You don't mean to tell me you wouldn't want to smack him back.'

'I just don't know what you're on about. Jimmy's a mate, I got no quarrel with him.'

'Not even though you're laying his tart?'

Walters's face reddened, he muttered something inaudible. Catchpole judged it time to intervene. As he started to speak Walters ignored him and said to Wilson: 'You want not to open your mouth so wide or you could find someone shuts it for you. I dunno what you heard but I've had no trouble, I run a clean operation here. This is my home, office too, I run it as a business – '

'With a guard on the gate and an iron door,' Wilson said.

'Maybe that was needed in the past, but not now. You want to get up to date. This place is clean, and so's my business. You want to look around here, you do that, I don't ask for no warrant, you'll find there's no crack or pills, nothing – '

'Guns?' Catchpole said. 'I noticed Monsterman wore one.'

'Any gun in this house there's a licence for it.' Walters leaned forward in his chair. 'What I'm telling you is what's past is done with, what I'm doing now is a straight business operation. I own a cleaning business, I got contracts for – ' He stopped, shouted 'Yes?' then, 'Come in, pet, say hallo. This is Maureen, these two are a big-shot copper and his boy.'

Maureen was dainty. She blinked wide blue eyes at them, said, 'Hallo', then, 'Lover, it's Garry.'

He glared at her. 'For fuck's sake, I said no calls.'

'I know, but then he tells me it's urgent, can I just have a word with you, say he's on the line. So I have.' She pouted.

Walters got up and crossed the room. He looked as if he wanted to hit her, but instead kissed her cheek. 'What you tell him, pet, you just say I'll call him in ten minutes, got it?' She nodded, looking up at him adoringly. 'And if you come in again when I'm doing business and said no interruptions I'll beat you half to death, understand?' She giggled. 'Run along.' When she had gone he looked hard at Catchpole and repeated: 'All straight, the way I said. I'm a businessman, I've diversified.' He poured himself another whisky. Catchpole shook his head. Wilson gave a dutiful head-shake too.

Catchpole said: 'I'm glad to have met Maureen, because it's her I want to talk about, or something she said.' He told Walters Maureen's story about a cousin of Jimmy Silver being responsible for the killing in Kennington. 'The question is, where did Maureen get the story?'

'Couldn't tell you. Heard about this Allgood from Jimmy maybe, just repeating gossip.' He looked from one to the other of them, the slight twist of his nose giving him an artful expression. 'No use you talking to her, that's what she'd say. Who was it she talked to? Maybe I can guess.'

'I daresay you can. Then there's the question of your boy Dodo Canter saying he'd wreck a jeweller's shop – Moshe Davis, I daresay you know him – and then making threats against his young family?'

'Oh dear me, I'm sorry to hear that. Would this Moshe swear out a complaint, d'you think? Doubtful, I'd say. I'll tell you what it is with Dodo, he's a good boy, good as can be till he gets his mad up. But.' Speedy shook his head. 'He's a user, I'm sorry to say, and users are unreliable, you don't need me to tell you. When he gets his mad up he'll do anything, say anything. But he doesn't mean it.'

'Moshe Davis thinks he came from you. That's not right?'

The artful nose looked askew at him. 'Course not, can't think where he got that idea from.'

To Wilson's surprise Catchpole accepted this. 'OK, I'll take your word on it. I didn't come here to fight, I'm asking for help. Since you and Jimmy can't be the best of friends now you're living with what was Jimmy's girl, and he raided your clubs or that's what I was told, you can see why we'd be interested.'

Walters shook his head. 'I told you, I run a straight business now, wouldn't want no gang war. Jimmy might want to put one on me, but the other way round – you're not thinking straight. I've noticed before you coppers haven't got much on top. No offence meant.'

'Just a pity you can't help me.'

'I'm sorry too.' Speedy wiped his face with a gold-coloured handkerchief. 'You shoulda seen your Sergeant's face when I said, "No offence meant." If looks could kill I'd be a dead duck, lucky they don't. Sure you wouldn't like a conducted tour?'

Catchpole declined. Delaware showed them out.

When they were away Wilson let out a deep breath. 'I don't know how you stuck it, guv, that little bastard enjoying himself. And the sodding awful thing is we can't prove anything, pull in Dodo it'd be no help. Ask me, we've got nowhere.'

'I'm not so sure. Who's Garry?' Wilson looked at him blankly. 'The only time Walters lost his cool was when that girl came in and said Garry wanted to speak to him. And something else. He began to talk about running a cleaning business, said he had contracts, then stopped short. Contracts for what, and who from? I'd like to know, especially if there's any connection with this Garry.'

It seemed important to Catchpole to find out something more about Lily Devon, something Rose had not bothered about. He found it hard to believe the girl had lived the totally isolated life suggested by the file, and in pursuit of this idea talked to Myra Gray, who was now a layout artist in advertising.

She had settled into what seemed happy unmarried life with one of her agency's account executives in a Docklands converted warehouse. She talked to the detective there while the executive, introduced simply as Reg, did some cooking. He said hallo, then returned to what he called the galley. Myra had long dark hair, was decisive in gestures, movement, speech. At times she reminded Catchpole of his wife, Alice. The apartment looked out on the Thames, and she made use of one of her emphatic gestures as they stood beside the window.

'I come from here. My dad had a fish restaurant off Commercial Road. Jewish fried fish, best in the world, non-fattening. I'm East End Jewish and a feminist with it, how about that?'

'It takes all sorts.'

'And still not sorted out my sexuality either, ask Reg. Reg, you hear that?'

Reg waved a spatula. 'I'm not complaining.'

'And us, we're it, you know that? We're what it's all about, we're here and now. You know what I think, we're the rising class, Reg and me, could be a new class, read all the new mags, wear the right clothes, got shelves stuffed full with CDs. But you know what? We have all that stuff and still don't know *anything*. We're not *sure*. What am I doing working in a tosspot ad agency, do I hate it or love it? Search me. And what am I doing here in the East End when I couldn't get away from it fast enough when I was fifteen? What for Jesus' sake is the reason? And I say Jesus, how about that too, why do I say it? You think God exists?'

Catchpole said truthfully that he never thought about it. From the galley at the other end of the long room Reg called out that she talked too much and should shut up. Myra (she had changed the name from Miriam – it seemed to Catchpole that all the women involved had abandoned their given names) said no man understood what she was talking about,

but OK, she'd shut up. The detective sipped the
powerful concoction Reg had made, which was
mainly gin but tasted strongly of limes, and said he
didn't want her to shut up but to tell him about Lily,
her friends, habits, character.

'Friends? She didn't have any. Character? That
was the last thing your colleague, call him that,
wanted to know about. Bloody deadbeat your colleague, if there are many like him no wonder crimes
don't get cleared up. You're different. If I labelled
him deadbeat I'd call you Smartypants, the new man
in the landscape. Married?'

'Yes. As a matter of fact you remind me of my
wife, only she doesn't talk so much and what she
says is more to the point. I want to hear about Lily,
not what you think of the police.'

'Lily, OK. Lily was a hard bitch. I'll tell you what
I think about her but I talk a lot about myself, it's
what interests me most, you'll have to put up with
it. People say to me I got some talent as an artist,
what am I doing in the agency game, some of my
stuff's around on the walls here. Well, I tried it for
five years, sold maybe a dozen pictures and a few
more to friends, then I thought hell I got to make
a living, and here I am. You could say I sold out,
but at least I gave it a try.' Reg called out that she
still painted. 'Do I hell, it's slick stuff, you know it
and I know it. But Lily, this girl from the sticks, this
shy maiden who'd been in an art class with me and
then said she was sick of living at home, working in
an office, being paid peanuts, she asks if she can
come stay with me, and the first thing she says is
she's come to London to make money.'

She took a long pull at her drink. 'Like I said I

can understand the feeling, though I thought she
was a bit young to be putting it that way. What I
didn't understand was how she meant to make a
living. It was a month before I knew what she was
doing. She told me she'd got a part-time job, and I
suppose you could call renting yourself out for sex
doing that. She had her own room – I was living in
Camden Town then, not here, this is Reg's place –
and she was careful, I'll give her that, never took a
client when I was likely to be around. I found out
because I was sick one day, ate a bad mussel the
night before and the effect was drastic, came home
and heard noises, thought it was a boyfriend. Then
I saw him leave and it was an old man, around sixty.'

She shook her head. Reg emerged from the
galley wearing an apron. He said: 'I think it's funny,
French farce up to date.' He was no taller than Myra,
blond, sharp-featured. His rolled-up sleeves revealed
white hairless arms. 'You'll stay to supper? Pasta,
with my own sauce. Good, though I say it.'

Catchpole hesitated. Myra said, 'You'd better stay
if you want to hear the best bit.' And in fact she
talked through the fettucini and its basil sauce, then
through the fruit salad that followed. Reg stayed for
the most part silent, perhaps admiringly. Catchpole
was silent too, aware that he was getting for the first
time an idea of what Lily Devon had been like.

'What I couldn't get over was her nerve. To look
at she was, I don't know what you call it, virginal
maybe, innocent, meek and mild. They're not right,
not the kind of words I use, but maybe they give
you the idea. When I asked who the man was she
said, "A client," then when I was so stupid I still
didn't take it in, she went on, "I told you I'd come

to make money, you must know the old story about sitting on a fortune, I'm not sitting on it, doing something about it." ' Myra paused, a forkful of fettucini half-way to her mouth. 'Don't get me wrong, we all want something better even if we're not sure what it is. Grow up in Commercial Road and you want to be here. Maybe.'

'Want it and got it. And it's good.' Reg looked up at the high ceiling, the picture window. London lights, blue and yellow, winked back at him.

'I don't know about that. But go back to Lily, I couldn't believe it, having men in for money in my apartment. I asked if she couldn't get a job, maybe she was desperate and I could help, but it wasn't that, she asked how much I made and when I told her said she already made three, four times that. How about Aids, I said, how about being attacked by some sex nut? She showed me a knife she had – '

'What sort of knife?'

'Ivory handle, thin blade, sort of stiletto I suppose you'd call it. You never found it?' Catchpole shook his head. 'I'd know it again. Aids, she said if you were careful about clients, which is what she called them, kept an eye out for anyone who might be double-gaited, which again was what she called it, I dunno where she got that from it's so long out of date but could be it's the way they talk in the back of beyond where she came from, in a phrase if you were careful she reckoned you were pretty safe. Then she said my place was convenient, offered to up what she paid to double, couldn't understand when I said I wanted her out.' The gin sling or whatever it was had been succeeded by powerful Italian red wine. Myra drained her glass. 'Looked innocent, in a way she was, but kind of a monster. A machine for making money.'

'That's a phrase. Usable.' Reg wrote it on his paper napkin.

'Did she name any clients, give any hint of what they looked like, age, appearance, what they did?'

'She clammed up when I said I wanted her out inside a week, and no more men in my place. Three days later she was gone.'

'The girl who shared her place in Kennington thinks she got in touch with clients through sex magazines and word of mouth. You don't know about the magazines?' She shook her head. 'And that was the last you saw of her?'

'Not quite. She rang me at the office around a month ago, suggested a drink. I said yes, out of curiosity. Like I said, she was a monster but a one-off.'

'Did you meet? I don't have a note of it.'

'Policeman plod never asked me. We met in a swanky wine bar called Sandy's, sort of place I never go, but d'you know why she wanted to see me?' Myra leaned forward, hair almost in her wine. 'She was really needled I'd turned her out, wanted to tell me how successful she'd been, said she reckoned in two or maybe three years she'd be ready to retire. Then she thought of setting up a straight business, possibly as interior decorator – she had a bit of flair, bit of taste – wanted to know if I'd go in with her, knew I'd tried to be a painter. That was what she said, but what she really wanted was to show me she had it made, earned twenty times the money lying down that I made doing layouts.'

They all laughed. Reg looked about to write that

down but refrained. Catchpole asked if Lily seemed familiar with the wine bar, but Myra said not, then whether she had mentioned or shown any jewellery given by clients.

'Certainly didn't, and she would have done, you bet.'

'Did she say anything that might identify a client, where any of them came from, what they did?'

'Nothing, except she said she was in touch with really top people and I wouldn't believe what they paid just for an hour of her time. I asked if she ever enjoyed it, and she said it didn't arise, it was a business transaction.'

'Love is a business transaction.' Reg savoured it. Catchpole asked if she thought it likely that Lily might have tried to blackmail a client. Myra shook her head emphatically.

'You don't get it, do you? And I thought you were bright. She'd never in the world have done anything like that. She thought she'd found a profit-able business, that's all.'

'She adhered to business ethics,' Reg said, and laughed. Catchpole laughed too. Myra banged a fist on the table. Plates shook.

'God, men are so stupid. It's not a joke, it's about discovering your sexual nature and what you want to do with it. OK, maybe it was part crazy and didn't work out but Lily was logical, knew what she wanted to get through sex. I just wish I did.' She put her head in her hands. 'I wish I knew my sexual identity.'

Catchpole got into his car, aware that he was well over the legal drinking limit. He drove more carefully than usual. Although Alan insisted that he and Desmond were quite able to get their own

supper and put themselves to bed, he had rung the
girl who came in and watched TV when he was
working late. (Alan was infuriated by the use of the
word 'babysitter'.) On getting back to the chapel he
was surprised to see she had been thoughtful enough
to turn on the outside porch light. When he opened
the door and called 'Hallo' the voice that replied
was not the one he expected.

Alice switched off the TV as he came into the
living room, and got up. They embraced. She said:
'I decided I was more miserable without you than
angry with you. And I missed the kids.'

'We all missed you. I'd hoped you weren't still
angry.'

'Let's not go into it. I know you did what you
felt you had to do, leave it at that.'

She put her hand over his mouth. He bit it gently.
'I thought she looked like you, but she doesn't. Not
half as pretty.'

'Who?'

'A girl at dinner. I've had an evening with the
young. In Docklands, which is for the young. They
were very friendly to a middle-aged policeman.'

'You're not middle-aged. But you stink of drink.
Are you drunk?'

'Do you know what's worrying the girl who
doesn't look like you? She's trying to discover her
sexual identity. I think I know mine but let's see if
we can discover yours, shall we?'

On the following day he told Wilson to find out
all he could about the people who used a wine
bar called Sandy's, show the owner or barman a
photograph of Lily and see if he recognized it, and
if she'd been there with a companion. Then he

went down to Worcester to see the parents who had wanted to keep Lily wrapped in cottonwool.

The Devons lived on a small newish estate in a village five miles from Worcester. Lily's father was a fresh-faced pipe-smoking man with muttonchop whiskers. Her mother chirped like a sorrowful bird. Catchpole drank China tea, ate a home-made scone, and listened while they disagreed about their daughter.

'She'd changed,' Mr Devon said. 'And I'll tell you when it was, Mother, when I gave up. I used to be a villain.' He chuckled. 'The man you love to hate. Income tax inspector.'

Mrs Devon looked up from the green and gold something she was knitting. 'Assistant inspector. I don't know why you left, it was only a question of waiting.'

'You make it sound as if I was waiting to step into dead men's shoes and found I couldn't. It wasn't that.' He leaned forward confidingly. 'I tell you what it was. I thought, what am I doing, hunting down people who've done a little bit of fiddling, paid a few hundred pounds less tax than they should, calling them for interviews, going through their accounts with a toothcomb, making their lives a misery? When all the while the people at the top of big firms are voting themselves stock worth a million or more, arranging mergers, getting sacked and coming out laughing with more money than I earned in my lifetime. It's all robbery, I thought, why shouldn't the little robbers get their share?'

'John, don't talk such nonsense. The Superintendent will think you're a radical.'

'It isn't nonsense, Mother. I wasn't envious. It

just seemed to me I'd been wasting my life, doing what? Chasing after figures, checking up on statutes to see if people had got round 'em legally, rubbing my hands if they hadn't and thinking "Got you." Why do that when there were books to read and flowers and plants to learn about? So I said goodbye, took a reduced pension which still leaves us comfortable.' He puffed at the pipe.

'You said Lily changed when you gave up?'

'Yes, well. I told her the reasons, and she seemed to understand I'd done the right thing. But soon after that she began to be dissatisfied with the job I'd found for her with a Worcester firm of solicitors. Boring, she said, and I'd given up, why should she stay in a boring job? I told her I'd been in the job for years, she had to walk before she could run.'

His wife's chirp was still indignant. 'That's not the real story and you know it. She was a clever girl, our Lily, could have gone on to university, that was what she wanted. Why didn't she go?' She spoke to her husband but appealed to Catchpole. 'We're comfortable for money, you say. But if you'd stayed just that while longer we'd have had enough to send her to university and not worry. She always hated that job, you know she did.'

'It had possibilities. I'd arranged with the senior partner to keep an eye on her, and he said she was promising – '

'An invoice clerk, just copying stuff and sending out bills, what sort of work was that?'

'It wouldn't have been for long, she'd have been promoted. Only – ' He hesitated.

'Go on, tell him, blacken your daughter's name. She's gone now, so what does it matter?' She put down the green and gold something, went out. Her husband said apologetically she'd taken it very hard, then told Catchpole that Lily had been discovered copying documents in a complicated case about an estate, and passing them on to a partner in the firm acting for the other side. Was she having an affair with the partner? Mr Devon shied away from the question. She was sacked on the spot and, he said, would have been prosecuted but for the personal appeal he had made to the man who gave her the job. Pulling at his muttonchops, Mr Devon absolved himself from blame.

'Sometime in this life you have to look after yourself, don't you agree? If I realized there's more to life than a monthly pay cheque, hadn't I the right to say enough's enough? Mother says I was responsible, but I don't see it. And I'll tell you something else. In my job I had chances, there was money offered to close my eyes and pass dodgy accounts and there'd be a good fat envelope waiting for me, but that's something I never, never would have done. Lily now, she said yes when she could have said no, the very first time she was tempted.' Soon after that she told them she had got the job in London. Catchpole gathered that her father had not been altogether sorry to see her go.

'And she came back, what, once a month? You thought she was doing well, remained on good terms?'

'We loved her.' Mrs Devon had returned and her chirp, just behind Catchpole's ear, took him by surprise. She had a framed photograph which she now thrust at him. It was a head and shoulders studio portrait in which Lily, eyes wide with an expression of astonishment, lips a little apart, looked both alluring and virginal. The detective matched it in his mind with the photograph of the bloody thing on the bed, and thought fleetingly that retirement from the realities of his world was no less tempting than retirement from adding columns of figures had been for Mr Devon.

'She'd met this important man, didn't say his name.'

'Mother.' Mr Devon put down his pipe.

'She'd been out to dinner with him – we had such high hopes for her.' Had she said anything more about him, mentioned or shown them any jewellery he'd given her? Mrs Devon said no, and continued: 'Just that he was important, perhaps in business, what do they call them, a tycoon. Or it might have been someone in the government – '

Mr Devon stood up. 'It's all nonsense, Mother, you know it as well as I do. A pack of lies. She was a prostitute, it was just stories she made up to tell us.' His wife screamed something, put her hands over her face, ran out of the room. 'You see? She just won't face up to it.' He walked to the end of their drive with Catchpole. 'You a gardener? Roses are wonderful this year, since I retired I've taken a lot of trouble with the garden and it pays for it, but you know something? This has knocked us sideways so that sometimes I wish I was back in the office.'

On the way back to London Catchpole reflected that if Lily really had known important people it might explain the Big Man's interest in her death. Back at the Yard he found that Wilson had discovered a possible link between Walters and a south London local councillor named Garry Johnson. A firm called Speedy Demolition and Construction had done a good deal of work for the local council, and had been given contracts to handle refuse and do building repairs. Johnson was deputy chairman of the council and a member of the committee that handed out the contracts. J. R. Walters was a director of Speedy Demolition and Construction. He was also a director of Speedy Cleaners, a firm founded by Garry Johnson, whose name was still on the notepaper.

Interesting, Wilson said, but why should they think it had any connection with the girl at Kennington? Catchpole agreed. 'I'm just following a nasty smell, Charlie, and hoping it will lead to Blewbury House.'

The nasty smell also led back to Bobo Miranda. From what Catchpole had heard about Lily it seemed to him increasingly unlikely that she would have refrained from showing off valuable gifts, especially to Myra. The only person who claimed to have seen the various jewellery pieces was Bobo. Catchpole sent Wilson down to talk to her, because the Sergeant's approach to girls like Bobo, part friendly but a much bigger part threatening, often produced better results than his own cooler interrogation. Sure enough, Wilson's magical combination of flirtatiousness and sympathy, with warnings about the unpleasantness of prison life for Bobo banged up with a collection of bull dykes all eager to own her, worked perfectly. Bobo confessed to inventing the jewellery.

As she eventually told Charlie Wilson, the drummer in her rock group, who was also her drug supplier, had said the day after Luisa's death that he

could put her in the way of some easy money. She
had met a man in the club where she worked, and
he had told her to say Luisa had shown her some
jewellery. He had given her a piece of paper contain-
ing the vague description of the pieces she had passed
on to Jacko. She did what she was told ('No harm
in it I could see, didn't matter to Luisa, did it?') and
was paid two hundred pounds. The man she met was
young, wore an open-neck shirt, wasn't very tall –
otherwise she was as vague in describing him as she
had been about the jewellery. She no longer had the
piece of paper the man gave her. That was her tale,
which Wilson believed, except that he thought she
was too frightened to give more details about the
man who gave her the money.

'That Rose.' Wilson shook his head incredulously. 'Talk about sloppy, never checked anything.'

'No reason why he should have checked it,
Charlie.'

'I dunno. Girls like Bobo, you never want to
believe what they tell you first time. You got to think
they're lying.'

'You've got a nasty mind. But you see what this
means, it was a fit-up from the start. And an elaborate
one too, with the villain all trussed up and ready for
trial.'

'What next then, guv?'

'It all gives off a nasty smell, Charlie. All I can
do is follow my nose, and I think it's leading me to
our local councillor who hands out the contracts,
Garry Johnson.'

EIGHT

Difficulties of a Prime Minister

On the whole, the *Messenger* was the tabloid Bladon most hated, although he disliked them all, and he read the headline on the front page with distaste. 'The Bull and the Beauty' it said, and the story it told was of the affair between Freddy Bullington, Member of Parliament for a constituency in peaceful Somerset, and an actress named Shirley Donovan. Nothing unusual about an MP having an affair, but apparently both the Bull and the Beauty enjoyed a row, or even something like a pitched battle. Shirley had in the past emptied a plate of soup over a waiter, and Bullington had used language to a producer with whom Shirley was having difficulties, language of a kind that the producer improbably said he had never heard.

The story in the paper told of the damage suffered by their theatre critic, who had said Shirley's performance in the John Osborne play was of 'an ineptness even greater than she has shown in the past', adding that 'she often appeared not to know the meaning of the words she was uttering, something very likely to have been the case'. A couple of weeks later the Bull and the Beauty saw the offender at a party. Bullington knocked him down, breaking his jaw and dislodging some teeth, and Shirley joined in enthusiastically with both feet, cracking a rib. The *Messenger* had pictures of the fray and an interview with Mrs Bullington, who said they had a quiet and peaceful home life in Somerset. Above the caption 'A quiet and peaceful life' was a picture of a snarling Bullington about to hit the terrified critic.

Bullington, who was Bullington? Bladon vaguely remembered a self-important man with a loud voice, who looked and evidently was a bit of a bruiser. In the House he could be relied on not to cause trouble, always voted the way he was told, was what Rex Calendar had been known to call lobby fodder. Bladon talked to his press secretary, Nellie Hill, who had been filched from the media some months ago and was supposed to be very bright, although he had seen few signs of it. He tapped the paper. 'I don't expect to learn about stories like this from the press, Nellie.'

'It only happened yesterday evening. Didn't seem worth bothering you with late at night, I thought it would keep until this morning. It's only the *Messenger*, nobody takes too much notice.' Nellie laughed. Her self-confidence was one of the things Bladon didn't care for. 'I've talked to the editor this morning already, told him it would be appreciated if the story was told straight, nothing to do with politics. I think he'll play ball.'

Bladon told her to keep him in touch with any developments. She seemed about to say something more, but didn't. He saw the Chief Whip later and told him Bullington should be told to behave himself in future and keep his head down. The Chief Whip shook his head and said there could be more to come. Bladon vented his irritation, which was partly discontent with his own feeling of inertia. 'Don't tell me he's beaten up another drama critic.'

'Nothing like that. It's quite funny really. I don't suppose it will do any harm, though any scandal's unwelcome. You remember Bullington was once a junior minister at Defence, pretty inefficient from what I can gather, reward for being a good party man, middle of the road and all that.'

Bladon said of course he remembered, and in fact he did now that he was reminded. 'Well, he's obviously susceptible to passionate ladies. The story is he had an affair six years back with a secretary at the Egyptian embassy, and leaked to her the bit he knew about negotiations going on with Israel about all sorts of possibilities in the Middle East. Some way-out ideas were floated, and it seems the lovely secretary sold them to the highest bidder. The leaks didn't last long, MI5 were soon on to it, the girl was sent back home. Bullington was transferred and then discreetly dropped from office. Morland was PM then, which is probably why you didn't hear much about it.'

'Why am I hearing now? It's all past history.'

'Because we think – we're pretty sure – the *Messenger*'s got the story, along with letters Bullington wrote to the girl which I'm told would make juicy reading. My understanding is the paper bought them a couple of years ago in case they might be useful one day, and they may think the day has come. Another thing is that Bullington was what you might call thoroughly peeved when he was sacked, never did accept he'd done anything wrong, thought we were moralistic spoilsports. If the letters are printed he might want to go public himself about how he'd been treated, suffering for private peccadilloes because his chiefs are a lot of holier than thou moralists.' The Chief Whip, an exuberant Welshman, said all this with annoying cheerfulness. 'Hence, although I'll read the Riot Act to him, I can't be sure how much notice he'll take.'

They were in the Cabinet room which Bladon, like Harold Wilson, used as an office. He enjoyed sitting at the middle of the long table, in the only chair with arms, talking to the various secretaries with whom much of his working day was spent. Just now he found himself wishing he could have a chat with Rhoda, and that this eager Welshman wouldn't bother him with something essentially unimportant. Instead he discussed the possible fall-out from Bullington for five minutes and said he didn't want to see the man in person, he was confident the Chief Whip would bring him into line. There was no suggestion of removal of the whip. Bullington was known to dislike Calendar and have no sympathy with NatLib ideas, and hence might be considered one of the PM's men. It was a pity, Bladon reflected, that a good many of his supporters were of similar calibre.

He looked up. The Chief Whip still hovered, and said now: 'There was nothing else you wanted to see me about, PM?' When Bladon said there was not, he nodded and left. Had there been a meaningful note in his voice? The Chief Whip was a great man for mysterious hints and Bladon decided he couldn't be bothered to find out. He settled down to read reports by two expert advisers on likely developments in the CIS, formerly the Soviet Union. Their views were diametrically opposed. Bladon's special adviser on foreign affairs, a retired diplomat, was in favour of getting the views of a third expert Kremlinologist. The PM's mind strayed from foreign affairs to the problem of countering Calendar, and if possible dishing him altogether. There could be no doubt Rhoda was the most popular member of the Government. She was his ally, and she had protégés, bright grammar-school meritocrats like herself, with theories about the control of money by what they called the B route and the H route, theories about hard and soft policing, theories about everything. If it was possible to replace Calendar with one of Rhoda's protégés, preferably a woman, that would make for a smoother-running government, an easier life. But was it within the limits of political possibility?

Associates of Rex and Donald Calendar knew the two were not joined by brotherly love. Rex made no secret of the fact that he thought Norah Calendar deplorably vulgar, and regarded the magazines that had been the basis of Donald's fortune as disgusting at best and pornographic at worst. Donald, on his side, after a drink or two in congenial company, would say: 'Me now, I'm a man of the people, don't pretend to be anything else. I know what the man in the street likes and doesn't like because I'm one myself, like the same things. I believe British is best, I believe in the family though you've got to allow for a bit of nooky sometimes on the side. I've got nothing against foreigners, don't mind what colour they are, only I know they're not up to a native Britisher, whether he's English, Scots, Welsh or Irish. I believe in the royal family, but if they're having a bit of nooky I want my papers to be the first to get the pix and tell the story. So I'm straightforward, but Rex he just isn't. He believes in himself, that's all. I tell you what it is about him, he's power mad. I believe there's a little clock inside him with a button on it that says *power*, and when you press the button he starts to operate. Me, all I ever wanted was a good life, but Rex would like to control everything. For the public good, mind you, always for the public good.'

This kind of thing Donald would say with laughs in between, so that it was easy not to take him seriously. But still, these two did not love each other. Their rare visits to each other's houses were strained and uncomfortable, for the wives also had no joint interests, and Norah always felt that her production of two sons was for her sister-in-law Mariella only another proof of her innate vulgarity. Yet there are ties that may be more lasting than those of affection, shared memories that cannot be wiped out although they remain unmentioned. Such memories joined Rex and Donald Calendar.

It was also true that each admired in the other, however reluctantly, qualities they knew to be lacking in themselves, and they were jointly aware of what they wanted from life and society. Both regarded their wives as functionaries whose role was to help them achieve and then maintain their position. The wives were of course free agents, theoretically as free as their husbands to plan, scheme, have love affairs, get drunk, work for virtuous causes, give interviews, take jobs. Yet theory was not practice. Mariella Calendar knew she had been married for her money and her beautiful manners. In the early days the money had been useful in promoting Rex's career, and she was used to considering any action of her own in the light of its possible effect on him. And although Norah did not adopt so logical a view of her function as a newspaper tycoon's wife, she knew that occasions like appearing drunk in public at the Pitcombes' was a mark against her, in the sense that it might be considered when there was a possibility of Donald getting his K.

Rex and Donald rarely met. They spoke quite often on the telephone, but the possibilities inherent in the death of Lily Devon were such that a meeting seemed to both advisable. It took place in the penthouse roof garden of Donald's inconspicuous house just off Sloane Street, at the back of Harrods. The roof garden was so filled with plants that it looked like a miniature jungle, and they sat there in the shade on a hot summer afternoon. Norah was away having her hair done. A maid brought in tea, poured two cups, went away. Although there was no chance that they could be overheard the conversation was elliptical, almost as if they did not trust each other.

'Your business with Pitcombe. I put in a word.' That was Rex.

'Many thanks. It seems to be working.'

'I'm opposed to the whole idea, you know that.'

'Can't see why. Goes right along with things you've been saying. If it comes off Pitcombe looks a fool, if not you say he's against progress. Isn't that up your street?'

'This isn't personal. Or not for me. I know what *you* want.' Rex had nothing but contempt for his brother's eagerness to be able to call himself *Sir* Donald Calendar. 'What's the situation?'

'Flexible. The banks will play in the end, have to. Don't worry about it.' A rich chuckle, a decisive scissor movement, crossing of legs.

'I don't. Any money problems are yours, not mine. It's the other thing that's important. Your friends seem to have made a fair cock-up of it.'

'Yes. Well. Couldn't be foreseen. But no damage done.'

'I'm not so sure. If there are no further developments, well and good. But if there are repercussions you leave me to deal with them. You do nothing without talking to me. Is that understood?'

'It depends what you're proposing to do. My boys – '

'Your *boys*, or whoever they talked to, have done nothing but pile up trouble and rouse suspicion. And potentially it's trouble for us.'

The scissors uncrossed. When Donald was frustrated, when his handling of affairs was questioned, he could be pettish although in the end he gave way, did what Rex wanted. 'You always think you know best.'

'That's because I do. I can handle all that side of it, the side your *boys* have made such a muck of. But the most important thing I must leave to you. Nothing like this must happen again.'

'Of course I understand that. Do you think I want another evening like that one? It was the worst of my life.' He got up and moved among the plants, so that he was partly hidden by the purple flowers of an outrageously unlikely orchidaceous tree.

'Donald.' Now he looked out from between flowers, his expression sulky. 'All I'm doing, all either of us is doing, is for the good of this country.'

In Rex's presence Donald always felt inferior. If anybody else had used such words to him he would have told them, in less polite language, to cut the cant. But to Rex he simply said, 'I know that.'

'Remember it.'

From the beginning of his political career Rex Calendar had emphasized to Donald that he wanted no stories obviously favourable to him to appear in either the daily *Bulletin* or its Sunday paper. If they were based on insider knowledge, he said, they would be dismissed as planted, and if they were straight news stories they would still be discounted as based on family sympathy. Donald's papers supported Bladon's coalition government, but were critical of the Prime Minister's failure to put forward any positive programme for modernization. On the brutalization of Britain question, an article one week might stress the urgent need for an extended road network that must be nationally co-ordinated, but a counterbalancing article would be likely to appear a few days later lamenting the destruction of one more piece of our national heritage, the blighting of yet another village. A warning about possible dangers in arming the police would be quickly followed by one stressing that the increase in violent crime must be dealt with urgently. Donald regarded this as preserving a balance, and showing that he had put the past of *Stink* and *Raunchy* behind him.

A couple of days after Rex had paid his visit to

the penthouse roof garden Barry Baker, editor of the *Daily Bulletin*, came to Donald with the story. Donald prided himself on being a hands-off proprietor who allowed his editors complete freedom, but still he expected to be kept in touch with any big story, and this certainly might be one. Donald's first reaction was that it couldn't be true. But there were photocopies of letters, there were the tales as told by the driver and the PA on tapes recorded by Barry and then kept in a safe. Donald looked at the letters, listened to the tapes.

'They're OK, but they need back-up. What d'you reckon, Barry?' Donald was much more at home with his editor than he had been with his brother.

'The driver and the PA have gone on the record, say they'll stand to what they said, in court if necessary. And if we don't buy 'em someone else will.' Barry was lean, with a face that looked as if it was made of leather. 'Both of them have left their jobs now, of course. Driver's with a security firm, PA's temping, her story is she was given the push because she spoke out of turn. Maybe so, maybe not, but they both say they're ready to stand up and be counted. It was she who made photocopies of the letters, could be they planned it together. They're using an agent, of course.' He told Donald what the agent was asking.

'Lot of money.'

'Lot of story.'

'Has it gone the rounds?'

'They say not, but the agent would say that. They say we've got the first refusal, could be true, I've only just heard a whisper here and there.'

'It's political, that complicates things.' Barry knew this meant Rex would have to be told. 'All right, buy it. But I want two prices, one if we use it, the other if we don't.' Barry said that was impossible. 'Well, do what you can, and tell me what you're settling for before you sign anything. And I want a guarantee there's a shut-down on it from now on. Total shut down, no more whispers, the driver and the girl keep their mouths shut.'

'I'll say that, but you can't keep the lid tight on a story like this for long, it's bound to get around. The *Mail* and *Express* will hear it and drop hints, others too.'

'Let them hint. We have the tapes and letters, they'll just be building a bigger story for us.' Barry's inexpressive face nevertheless indicated disagreement. 'There are interests to be considered, you can understand that.'

When Barry left the room Donald called Rex on the scrambler telephone he kept in a drawer.

'I don't see what you've got against it,' Gwenda Pitcombe said. 'It's not land we've any use for, and nothing done with it can possibly affect us. In any case they're agreeable to a clause that forbids any industrial use.'

'Something's wrong, I can smell it.' And Allen sniffed as if he really could smell something unpleasant in their spotless kitchen. They were talking about an offer made by Anglo-European Amenities for a large stretch of land Gwenda owned in Wales. Durbridge Manor in Buckinghamshire was their home, but Gwenda's great-grandfather had made the family fortune as owner of three Welsh mines, and had acquired large areas of mostly agricultural land and a good deal of property that went with it. AEA, as they were called, said they wanted to acquire this land for purposes that would improve the area's amenities. They had mentioned as possibilities the creation of a zoo and the foundation of a training college for farming graduates.

'The directors all seem respectable.' That was Gwenda.

'Two Americans, a Belgian and a German. And half a dozen English or Welsh put in for dressing, businessmen or bank nominees. The company's only existed for eighteen months.'

'But none of the directors is – shady?' Gwenda's slang was that already out of date in her youth.

'As far as I can tell. But why should Belgians and Germans, or Americans either, want to back zoos and training colleges in Wales? Of course they're not committed to them, but if industry is excluded just what will they do with the land? What they're offering doesn't make commercial sense unless there's some industrial use.'

'My dearest, I'm as much opposed to that as you are. But I truly don't think it arises. If it does, we say no.'

'We don't need the money.'

'The APL is always in need of money. It seems to me the land would be sold *in* a good cause, and the money could be used *for* a good cause.'

He made a tugging gesture at his collar, one he always performed when faced with an argument he recognized he was likely to lose. The land belonged to Gwenda, so that in the last resort she

could do what she liked with it. Between the Pitcombes, however, that final resort was rarely reached.
Gwenda recognized the collar-tugging gesture as
surrender.

'You're very keen to make this a question of personalities,' Rex Calendar said. 'I'd like to talk about
policies.'

'It's personalities that sell papers.' Angela Angel,
born Jean Smith, had been labelled by some wit the
crumpet man's thinker, an inversion of the good old
cliché, the thinking man's crumpet. The appearance
of crumpet belied the reality. It had lured many into
indiscretions she exploited in articles where she used
her pen like a razor. When Calendar agreed to be
the subject of a profile for the magazine section
of the *Sunday Times* he was aware of the danger. It
was why they were talking in his room at the
House, rather than over a restaurant luncheon or in
his flat. He found her appearance distinctly attractive.
Tall, leggy, early thirties, no doubt well worn but
still wearing well – what would she be like in
bed? Tough, he told himself, tough as overcooked
meat.

'We can turn this off if you like.' The little
recorder was on a table between them.

'No need. Everything I say is for the record.'

'Very well then. Policies. It's no secret you're
dissatisfied with what the government's doing and
planning. What's wrong with it?'

'Nothing wrong with the policies. I support
them, helped to formulate some of them. They're
being stifled, though, partly by a bureaucracy

opposed to change, partly by those who cling to out-of-date attitudes and beliefs. I want to see an expansive Britain, one that accepts the challenge of the twenty-first century and prepares for it. The Channel Tunnel was a wonderful idea, but look at the way we've failed to exploit it. I want to see every city and large town in Britain linked quickly and directly to each other, and then linked to Europe by road, rail and air. And every road, even those a couple of hundred miles away, should lead quickly to the Channel Tunnel, our most direct link to Europe. But forging new links means cutting old ones – '

'And making omelettes means breaking eggs, etcetera. These are politicians' clichés.' Her smile was sweet. 'It's the brutalization of Britain, that's what those who don't like your vision call it. A lot of them are in your party. Are you going to convert them?'

'All of them, I hope. Some, certainly. Enough to get the policies accepted.' He gave her the Calendar smile back. She seemed unmoved.

'And the rest?'

'Spoiling for a fight, aren't you?' The smile was replaced by a Great Statesman look, sober, unaggressive, but chin out. 'I wish you'd convey to your large public that I simply want what's best for Britain. At present the country is standing still, people are dissatisfied, impatient. There are reserves of energy and ingenuity in the British people that will atrophy if they're not used. I want to see them used.'

'Is the current increase in crime a mark of what you're saying? You're Home Secretary. Is your cure for crime to see all the police carrying this experimental repeating pistol that's never been in practical use, plus sending repeated offenders off to a sort of Devil's Island? Perhaps you'd like to see the police all carrying Kalashnikovs?'

'Irony comes easy, Angela, but it doesn't solve any problems. There isn't any single, simple answer to the problem of crime. If there were, don't you think we'd have found it by now?' He spoke with a sort of controlled passion. 'All I've said is that the Baybee should be given a trial – I've seen it tested and the tests were splendid – and that the Outcast Islands idea should be considered seriously. I'm not fool enough to think they'll do more than put a brake on crime, and getting the country moving is the thing that will help most. If the most vigorous elements in the community, whatever religion they are, whatever the colour of their skin, don't find any scope for their energies, quite a lot of them will turn to crime. That vigour can be employed to the country's profit, which means the profit of you and me and everyone else.'

'I hear you.' Angela's lips tightened, the glance given him was almost lupine. 'But your views aren't shared by all the Cabinet, are they? Will you be able to persuade them that you're right and they're wrong?'

'Not *wrong*, don't say that. I respect Allen Pitcombe's idealism, and I think he'll come round to my ideas as making practical sense.'

'If he doesn't?'

'Then we'd both have to consider our positions and act according to our consciences.'

'Are you suggesting you'd push your plans for

brutalization to the point where one or other of you
might resign?'

'The question's purely hypothetical. And mis-
chievous too.' He leaned forward and spoke with a
passion that, as she said in her article, surprised her.
'I'm not a splitter. I don't deny putting my ideas into
practice is going to be painful for some people. But
ninety per cent will be better off, more money in
their pockets, more satisfaction in their work. *And*
with work to do, which lots of people don't have
today. *And* in a country that's not only prosperous
but beautiful. Don't believe this nonsense about the
destruction of the countryside. It will still be there,
more easily reached by Joe Citizen from his town or
city than he reaches it now. For brutalization read
communication.'

She nodded, but stuck to her point. 'You say you
want a united party, but you don't act that way. Some
of what you're saying goes dead against the Prime
Minister's policies. Surely you accept that can't go
on for long?'

'What policies?' he asked, and cursed the slip as
he saw the wolverine look in her eye. Like an attack-
ing army that has found the weak spot in an enemy's
defences, she peppered him with questions about
any points of difference he had with the PM. He
weathered it, of course, praised the great tradition
the PM represented and said their ends were identical, but it had been a stupid slip, and he was not
surprised when her piece was headed: 'Government
Policies, What Policies? Asks Rex Calendar.' But at
least he survived her last question successfully.

'Your friends and enemies agree on one thing,
you're an ambitious man. Putting it crudely, wouldn't

you like to be Prime Minister? A straight answer, please, no evasions.'

'A straight answer from a politician – all right, I'll give you one. The circumstances don't exist. If they arose – *if* – of course I would.' He paused, laughed. 'And so would half the Cabinet.'

NINE

Garry and Faz

CATCHPOLE SAW Garry Johnson at the Linford Christie Sports Centre, a diamond shining in a grubby south London setting of fast-food cafés, cheap clothing shops, and pavement stalls that sold yams, mangoes and green bananas alongside oversize cauliflowers and withered carrots. The centre had two pools, a sauna, and a boxing-ring. There was also a gym with an exercise room where Johnson crouched low over a stationary bicycle, pedalling fast. He waved a hand at Catchpole, got off the bike, changed into trousers and pullover and joined the detective.

'Sorry to keep you, need the workout, didn't expect you just yet.' He patted a stomach that showed no signs of flab and led the way to a small office with pictures of black athletes round the walls. He was a well-set-up Afro-Caribbean perhaps in his late thirties, handsome, a spring in his step, his manner easy. 'Get you something? Soft drink, no alcohol here. Fine place, eh? Had to knock a few heads together before the council said yes to it. Who'll use it, some of 'em said, but the youngsters, a lot of 'em are in the pool every night, and we've had to put up an advance booking list for the ring. We get a

Golden Gloves winner comin' out of here, that'll shake 'em.' Catchpole asked if this was his office. 'Not really, mine to use if no one else wants it, is all. They made me a vice-chairman or somethin' on account of I helped steer the scheme through. Vice-chairperson I should say.' There was a show of good teeth when he laughed.

'You haven't asked why I'm here.'

The teeth showed again. 'Reckoned you'd tell me.'

'You said you steered the scheme through the council. I'm told you also had some influence in placing contracts for the work here.'

'Who coulda said that, I wonder?'

The answer was nobody. Catchpole was proceeding by guesswork based on information from the files, and what Wilson had gleaned by talking to a couple of council members who did not love Johnson. He asked now if Johnson knew Walters.

'Speedy Walters? Sure, everyone knows him. Runs a building firm, gets on with the job, gets things done. Given the contract for a lot of the work here, did a fine job, ask anyone.'

'His firm got the contract although their estimate wasn't the lowest, correct?'

'Who's been tellin' tales? Not the lowest, but gave the quickest completion time.'

'With a penalty clause that wasn't invoked, though he went over it. And over the original price too, is that right?'

'Someone's been talkin' out of turn. We got some dismal Jimmies on the committee, complain about anything. Just what is it you want, Superintendent,

why you asking these questions?' Catchpole was
pleased to see the smile had gone.

'Did you know Walters has a criminal record,
connected with the sale of drugs, among other
things?'

'Knew he'd been inside. Long time ago, what of
it?'

'Did the rest of your committee know?' Johnson
shrugged. 'If they didn't know you didn't tell them,
right?'

'Right. Man's going straight, trying to forget the
past, not my job to step on his face.'

'Do you think Walters's firm would have got
the work from your committee if the members had
known about his record?'

'How in hell should I know? Maybe they knew,
some of 'em, maybe they didn't. I'm not responsible
for Speedy Walters, don't like these questions. You
give me a reason for what you're askin' or I shut up.'

A police interrogation, Catchpole had sometimes
said at talks or lectures, is like fishing. There may be
hints of a bite, little tugs on the line that seem
meaningful yet prove to have nothing tangible at the
end of them, or nibbles that as the line is slowly
reeled in cease to exert their little pull so that the
angler knows his playing of the fish has gone awry
– or, he would add with a grin as he abandoned the
metaphor, would show you had somehow asked
the wrong bloody questions. And then there were
the moments, of which the delight could hardly be
exaggerated, when you found you had done everything right, the fish was hooked.

One of these good moments came when he said
accusingly, still on the basis of nothing more than

guesswork, 'You know Pisser Jones,' saw Johnson's lids flicker, and heard his voice change from a confident note to one of artificial belligerence.

There was a pause before he said, 'If I do?'

'Did you give him some information about the death of a woman who called herself Luisa Devane at Kennington, earlier this month?'

'I talk to a lotta people, see Pisser sometimes, hear bits of gossip, pass 'em on, just don't remember.'

'I think you do. *Somebody* told Pisser a man named Allgood could have done this Luisa Devane, the brass who got it at Kennington. Then that somebody faked evidence to back the story up, only it didn't stick. Whoever it was, they were trying to plant one on my colleague Jacko Rose, and we don't like that. Tell you something, I hate it myself. Somebody did that, somebody has to pay for it, understand me?'

It was warm in the little room. Johnson's face shone. 'I may have passed on stuff I heard to Pisser, but planting evidence, no sir, not me, can't fix that on me.'

Catchpole spoke gently. 'Not accusing you, Garry, don't mind if I call you Garry? Your arrangements with Speedy Walters over contracts, they're not my business today, if you're helpful maybe never will be. We might come to some arrangement, you're an influential man around here, meet every now and then, give the word about what's going on, how about that? But just now my problem is how this story about Allgood got to Pisser. If it was through you say so, it won't go beyond this room.'

'I told you I coulda passed something on, may have heard this bit of gossip, don't remember.'

'Won't wash, Garry. Pisser *planted* this story on my colleague Inspector Rose and it was *planted* on him, there wasn't a word of truth in it. I want to know if you gave it to him, if you did where it came from, why you had it. That clear?'

The fish knew it was hooked, but made a desperate effort to get off the line. 'You can't talk to me that way. I'm the vice-chairman of this borough council, I don't have to sit here, be insulted. I'm not a police nark. This interview is over.'

He pushed back his chair, got up. Catchpole remained sitting, gave an exaggerated sigh. 'Sit down, Garry. Nobody said anything about being a snout, just thought we might have a friendly chat now and then. But you walk out of that door now and I promise you there'll be an investigation of the work that's gone to Walters, not only this place, how much you've influenced it, how close you are to him. And I don't mean we'll start next year, I mean this week, so if there are papers to be shredded you should start tonight.' Johnson sat down again. 'Better. Now, how was the story planted and who told you to do it?'

'It wasn't the way you say. I never planted no story, nothing to do with faking any evidence, nothing at all to do with that. What it was is, I got a call from Faz, you know him, big lawyer.'

'You mean Fazackerley, Ryton Fazackerley?'

'Only one Faz. Barrel of lard, put him on the exercise bike it'd buckle under him. I owe Faz one, on account of he gave me some help when my brother Slim was in a bit of trouble.' Catchpole nodded. He knew about Slim. 'So Faz helped then, maybe other times too. I help you, you help me,

like the Good Samaritan, way things should be. So
Faz calls and says he's got a problem, can I help,
what can I say except yes?' He held up a hand to
anticipate a question. The nails were manicured, a
large diamond glistened on the pinky. 'I tell you
what he says. This brass picked up some man, made
a bad choice, got done, should be cleared up fast.
Don't ask me why, he didn't tell me, I don't ask.
What Faz says is they need a name. So I had a word
with Speedy, seeing he knows most of the bad boys
in the neighbourhood on account of he was one
himself. Speedy reckons this Allgood is the one. And
then it could be, it's possible I mentioned the name
to Pisser.'

'You had no idea Walters was shacked up with
Jimmy Silver's ex-girlfriend and that Silver's Tooting
Boys had raided two of Walters's clubs, so fingering
Allgood was a way of getting at Silver, since Jimmy's
sister's living with him?' Garry said with the earnest-
ness that had impressed a hundred audiences that he
was shocked to hear all that, knew nothing of it.
'And I thought you knew what went on around
here,' the detective said ironically. Johnson said he
had heard nothing more from Faz, and the detective
saw no reason to disbelieve him.

He got back to the chapel early that evening,
and sat down with Alice and the boys to high tea,
which for Alan and Desmond consisted of indigest-
ible concoctions called cheese dreams, and for all of
them cold ham, followed by a sultana and cherry
cake made by Alice, plus apple crumble. Afterwards,
when he was telling the boys good-night, Alan said:
'Cheese dreams are the best. I think I could do them.
Why don't you make them for us, Dad?'

'Too stupid to think of it.'

'It's good Mum's back, isn't it? Not just for cheese dreams, I mean. Are you pleased?' He said he was. 'Is it all OK now? About Brett, I mean.' Catchpole said he hoped so. 'Was it your fault, the way she said?'

'I don't think so. I'm not sure what she thinks now, but don't ask her.'

'OK. Mum won't go away again?'

'Not if I can help it.' Alan looked up at him uncertainly. 'Don't worry, it'll be all right.'

In the big living room, after they had switched off an American made-for-TV thriller when the death count got to double figures, he said: 'You know that stuff in the papers every summer about how filthy our beaches are, and how you can get everything from diarrhoea to Ménière's disease by going in the sea because it's so full of sewage and stuff? I feel as if I've had a long dip in a very dirty sea today. I've been with a local politician who's an absolute bloody crook, and is cosied up to one of the sharpest villains in south London, a man who used to run protection rackets and deal in drugs, now turned to bribing local politicians to get contracts. Tomorrow I'm going to see a lawyer who acts for crooks who don't get caught, ones who live in Westminster or Docklands instead of Stockwell or Stoke Newington.

'And am I going to be able to put any of them inside which is where they should all be? I doubt it. Instead I have to weave and duck and then catch them with a punch when their guard is down. Build a case against them that looks watertight and their lawyers will find a leak somewhere. There'll be

respectable witnesses who'll swear black's white, and
we know they're lying but can do sod all about it.
So you have to play them at their own game, be as
devious as they are, tell lies and parrot something
about it being in a good cause. But you know that's
eyewash, you're swimming in the same dirty water
and you end up swallowing some of it.' He stopped
because she was laughing.

'If you don't like the dirt don't go in the water.
You've just had a bad day.'

'I'm serious.'

'I know you are. It's what I'm not, why you
didn't like Brett. I think it was one reason why I
married you, not someone more suitable. I suppose
it's a sort of virtue, being serious the way you are,
but it makes life hard at times. For me, I mean.'

'A sort of virtue, yes. I suppose that's what I'm
looking for in coppering. If I didn't think it existed
I'd retire and keep pigs.'

'I don't want to hear any more about coppering
and villains. Let's go to bed.' Some time in the night
he nudged her. 'What's up?'

'I'd like it on my tombstone.'

'What?'

'Name, date, then "He had a sort of virtue." '

'You woke me to tell me that?'

He laughed.

'Bastard.' Then she began to laugh too. 'Come
on.'

'Say "Virtuous man, fuck me." '

'Virtuous man, fuck me.'

'If you insist. Don't forget about the tombstone.'

★

Next day it was down again into the dirty water. Fazackerley, Milton and Close did not waste money in outer show. Their offices, a couple of minutes from the Elephant and Castle, were flanked by a hair salon and a fishmonger, and it seemed to Catchpole that the smell of fish and hair spray pervaded them, blended with a musty reek that might have come from old leather bindings or a mushroom farm. The smell was especially notable in Fazackerley's office, which had a window looking out on to a backyard that seemed filled with car tyres and bits of broken bicycles. He identified the smell. 'Dry rot,' he said. 'You've got dry rot.'

Faz laughed. He had no chin, but the rolls of flesh beneath where it should have been were arranged in folds so that they formed three distinct layers, like steps on a folding ladder. 'Very quick, Mr Catchpole, very quick. Dry rot, it's everywhere. I sometimes think the floor will give way under me, but can we get the landlords to do anything? Not they.'

'If you can't, who can? I wonder you don't move to a smarter neighbourhood. Don't tell me you can't afford to.'

'Our clients wouldn't like it. If we had some-where near Lincoln's Inn, say, they'd be worried they'd be robbed. By us, I mean. It's a matter of psychology.' He chuckled, the sound rich and rub-bery. 'Of course a lot we don't see till you've banged them up and they're crying out for a brief. But you've reminded me, I really must get stroppy about the dry rot, though it goes against my nature. I like to settle things in a friendly way if I can, it must be good to be helpful. So how can I help you, Mr Catchpole?'

Catchpole told him what Garry Johnson had said. Faz listened, head sunk down so that the flesh folds merged and his head became one with his neck. At the end, Catchpole said he wanted the name of Faz's client.

'You must know I can't give you that, Superintendent. And let me be quite clear, I made no suggestion that an attempt should be made to incriminate an innocent person. I'm deeply shocked that such a thing should have happened.'

'I'm sure. Why did you tell Garry Johnson you'd like to see the case cleared up quickly? And why choose Garry?'

'He's a local politician, knows everyone in the area, hears things.'

'And owes you a favour, perhaps more than one. He says you made it clear someone had to be fingered for the killing. The phrase he used was "The police need a name." And he provided one.'

In the great slab of Faz's face the eyes were like little berries. They now sparkled with amusement. 'I sometimes think misunderstandings cause more trouble than anything else in life. Garry just misunderstood me. If I could tell you anything more I would, but you know a client's confidentiality has to be preserved, and I'm sure you won't take that the wrong way.'

The feeling of immersion in dirty water was strong. Catchpole could never be sure, on this or other similar occasions, how much of the anger he expressed was real, how much simulated. He was aware, however, from the comments of awed subordinates, that the effect could be impressive. If one of them had been present when he pushed back his chair and leaned over to address the flesh mountain separated from him by a desk, they would have rated this performance up to scratch.

'I do take it the wrong way. What you're doing, Fazackerley, is obstructing the course of a murder inquiry. You think there's nothing we can do to you, and in a way you're right, you're slick and smart and make sure you've got an escape hatch in case of trouble. But don't be too sure you'll always walk away brushing off the dirt and laughing. We can do a job on you if we have to. You could find your clients staying away because there's a whisper you've shopped a couple to us in a deal, you might even find yourself needing a bodyguard when nasty stories get about. Could be one of your clients has drugs on him that he swears were planted, and we'd let him know you fingered him for us. So as I say, I take this the wrong way, very much the wrong way. You can be sure I'll spread the word around where it'll do you no good.'

'What brought that on, now?' Fat fingers picked up a porcelain egg on the desk, caressed it. Little blue-grey eyes looked speculatively at Catchpole's neat pointed collar, bright silk tie. 'I do a job, you know, someone has to act on behalf of people when you put them in the dock. But I do hope you weren't threatening me, although it sounded that way. If it was one of your colleagues I wouldn't be surprised, but you know what they say about you, they say Miss Hilly always does it by the book. I expect you know they call you that.' He had put the egg down and was writing on a notepad. Catchpole said he knew.

'And of course it wasn't a threat, I was just saying

what might happen. I'd be foolish to threaten you, Faz, when you might have a tape running.'

'That wouldn't be friendly. I said before, Catchers, I like to be friendly – Catchers is what friends call you, I believe. I like to cooperate, but this time it's not possible.' A fat hand went to his ear; he rose. 'Do you know, I think I'm needed in the outer office. Back in a couple of minutes.'

When he had waddled out of the room Catchpole leaned across the desk and tore off the page on which Faz had been writing. It contained the name of Stuart Marley.

'Marley is top crime man on the *Bulletin*,' Catchpole told the Big Man. 'He and Fazackerley are close. Faz feeds him inside stories about villains, and Marley gets wind of raids and prosecutions, tips Faz off. Then Faz passes on bits of what seems like inside information, and villains think the sun shines out of his big backside.'

'You'll talk to Marley?'

'Only if you insist, sir. Myself, I don't think there's any point.' The Big Man raised eyebrows. 'Two reasons. First is of course Faz will have warned Marley, but the important one is this isn't just something Marley's heard, he's been told to do it. It was asking a big favour of Faz to say he wanted someone fingered for a killing. There are limits, and Faz knew he was stepping over the limit with this one. But the client's an important one, so Faz goes to work through this black politician, and Johnson makes a pig's ear of it.'

'Why wouldn't Marley do the fingering himself? From what you say he has the connections.'

'Two reasons. One, it's doubtful he knows the people well enough, or that they'd trust him. Two, he'd want to be sure there was nothing to connect him directly with what was being fixed if anything went wrong. If I talk to Marley he'll just clam up, and of course Faz knows that. He just left the name on the desk to keep me quiet, that's all.'

'You're making a case. Tell me – I'm sure you have an answer, but I'll ask you anyway – I know what a slippery fellow Fazackerley is, so what makes you think the name he gave you is the right one? Why shouldn't he have tipped off Marley to tell you any old cock-and-bull story if you get in touch with him?'

'With someone as devious as Faz that's always a possibility, sir, but I don't think it's likely. He knows I could give him a lot of trouble, and although he may have a friend or two here at the Yard, he's got more enemies. He wouldn't like a real dirty tricks campaign going on against him. So he'll have known it would be dangerous to give me a completely phoney story, but he'll have primed Marley to tell me something that might just be believable but won't be the genuine article.'

It had been a cloudy day, but now sunshine slanted across the room, slicing it in two and leaving most of the Big Man's body in shadow, making him momentarily a disembodied shining head and shoulders as he asked gently: 'So what is the genuine article? What conclusion comes out of your questions?'

'I said the favour Marley asked was a big one. He wouldn't have been asking it for himself, and I

don't believe he'd do a favour that big for a friend
or for his editor. I think he was what you might call
ordered to do it. By his ultimate head, the man who
owns the paper.'

The illuminated head nodded, smiled. At least
Catchpole thought he smiled, but he could not be
sure for at that moment the sunlight disappeared,
and it was hard to see his expression. There was no
doubt about his words, however. 'So you have an
obvious lead. Pursue it. But be careful. Bring the
results to me before you take any action. And my
dear Catchers, I hardly need tell you that for the
present this should be regarded as confidential.'

Forty-eight hours later that obvious lead had taken
him nowhere. On the evening Lily Devon was killed
Donald Calendar had given what, according to his
secretary who answered questions readily enough,
was a working supper party at his house off Sloane
Street. The only guests were the editors of the two
Bulletins, daily and Sunday. They discussed matters
relating to the papers, and the secretary had made
notes. Norah had spent the evening with her sister in
Golders Green and then stayed with her overnight.
A buffet meal had been provided and serviced by
Gourmet Cooking and the editors had left just
before nine thirty, the Gourmet Cooking staff a
quarter of an hour later. It was theoretically possible
for Calendar to have gone out immediately to an
assignment with Lily Devon, but clearly most
improbable that he had done so. Just after ten thirty
a telephone call had been made from his number to
that of his brother Rex, and since there was nobody

else in the apartment it was a fair assumption that Donald had made it.

Catchpole talked to Stuart Marley, but as he expected learned nothing useful. Marley, a tough little red-haired Irishman, said he had heard on the grapevine that someone connected with Jimmy Silver had done the job in Kennington. Which grape on the vine? Marley's grin was sour as a lemon.

'You protect your snouts, I protect my sources. Even when the info's wrong, yes. Why did I pass it on to Faz? He likes to know what's around, tells me things, you could call it a mutual benefit society.'

'The way it looks, there's been a deliberate attempt to plant the killing on someone who had nothing to do with it. Luckily for him, he had an alibi.'

'They tell me the price for a good one is down to a century now.'

'Not this one. I'm his alibi.'

The reporter was only momentarily disconcerted. 'So someone steered me the wrong way. It happens.' Catchpole got the lemon grin again. He did not believe Marley, but there seemed no way of pushing him further.

The Big Man gave an edited version of what he had learned from Catchpole to Jonathan, who told his master. To his surprise Rex Calendar did not seem deeply interested.

'I thought you'd be – I mean, this business of trying to implicate someone completely innocent – '

'Disgraceful. We must be happy our police are vigilant.'

'I know things like that happen, of course,

especially when the affair's somehow top secret. Don't you think it's like that with this one, sir? The whole thing can't just be about a tart being murdered, it must have something to do with our relations to another country.'

'An interesting idea, Jonathan.'

'But if so it should be handled by MI5, only it isn't. So perhaps it *is* something to do with MI5 after all.'

The Home Secretary seemed genuinely puzzled. 'Explain yourself.'

Jonathan was only too willing. 'Suppose someone in MI5 got mixed up with this Luisa Devane, really fell for her, told her things that were top secret, and it was thought she'd been passing them on, or even could have been passing them on. This someone would have had a good reason for shutting her up, and making it look like a sex crime.'

He waited for a comment. Instead he got one of the looks that made him shrivel inside. 'Let's get on with our work, shall we?' Calendar said. A couple of minutes later he added: 'You should keep a hold on that vivid imagination of yours. It could land you in trouble.'

Was that an indirect endorsement of what Jonathan had suggested? He decided to try out the idea on George Kaiser.

TEN

Pitcombe's Dog

'ON TO SOMETHING. Blow Calendar out of the water. Finish him – no doubt of it. You're not listening.' Bannock's face was redder than usual. He looked as if about to have a fit.

'I am listening, Bernard. And of course I'm interested. I'm also very busy. There are other things to occupy me. If you could tell me just what you've found out.'

'Dr Layman's brother – '

'I beg your pardon. Dr Layman is – ?'

Bannock's nostrils widened, he gave an enormous snort. 'Layman's dead. Told you about him – doctor treated the Calendars – all the family – friendly with them. This is Layman's brother, younger brother – several years younger – close to Layman – old man now but still got all his marbles – '

Allen Pitcombe found the irritation unbearable. 'Bernard, I'm happy to know Dr Layman's brother is sane, but what is the point you're making?'

Bannock glared. 'Happened in the sixties – doctor certified a young boy – mentally unstable – put in an institution – Surrey, a place near Guildford. Boy's name was Calendar.'

'What then?'

Bannock said there was something mysterious about it, the doctor's brother knew Dr Layman was worried about what he agreed to, though he did nothing further about it.

Pitcombe controlled himself with difficulty. 'Bernard, I appreciate the trouble you're taking, but I don't see anything useful in what you've told me. Assume the story is true, what have we got? It's the early sixties you're talking about, the other Calendar boys would have been teenagers, they could have had nothing to do with putting someone away. It's the parents who would have been involved, not the boys.'

'Yes. Well.' Bannock on the trail was never defeated. 'Something there. I know it. Do some more digging – dig deep enough, find the bodies.'

'Bernard, be careful. This kind of thing could cause trouble for us rather than for the Calendars.'

Later that day the Pitcombes met two directors of AEA for an informal discussion about the sale of Gwenda's Welsh lands. Hans Kessler was a smiling German, Roger Manston a brisk short-back-and-sides non-executive director of several conglomerates. They met over tea in the Pitcombes' house, with no commitment on either side. As Manston said, the lawyers could be brought in later, after they reached preliminary agreement. Lawyers cost money, and there was no point in wasting money. 'I take it the figures we've been talking about are acceptable.'

'Broadly acceptable. We might want to iron out some details.' That was Allen.

'Leave details to the lawyers. What they exist for.'

'What we should like is something more specific about the use to which you'd put the land. You know, I'm sure, that Gwenda and I are both dedicated to the preservation of our rural heritage.'

'We're committed too. There'd be a clause excluding any major road building in the area, and any industrial use. In fact, industrial use of any serious sort would mean at least one major new road. All covered in the draft.' Manston produced a toothpick and began probing quite savagely into his mouth. Gwenda averted her eyes.

'But then, what would you be using the land for?'

Kessler produced drawings, one the plan for a zoo which could contain only creatures that might be expected to flourish in the environment, so that very few of them would be caged at any time. 'Then here are sketches of the training college for farming graduates. You think this would be too theoretical perhaps?' Smiling, Kessler shook his head. 'Not so, we would of course incorporate a small farm. The practical side would not be neglected. These are sketches, but we have a young architect in Hamburg with some fine imaginative ideas, who is eager to produce something in full detail.'

Gwenda was delighted with the drawings. Allen said: 'You're prepared to commit yourself to the zoo and the farm?'

Kessler was gently reproachful. 'It is a little too soon to speak of total commitment. But the organization I represent in my country are all concerned with what we call the greening of the continent, the continent of Europe. Mrs Pitcombe will be aware of this, I am sure.' Gwenda nodded. Kessler was known for his support of groups concerned with animal rights, the damage being done to the ozone layer by leaded petrol, and the harmful nature of industrial pesticides. Now the German turned his ruminant gaze on Allen Pitcombe. 'I would never be associated with anything I believed damaging to animals or to humans. I hope you accept that.'

Pitcombe said of course he accepted it. They agreed that a draft agreement on the lines of the outline should be drawn up, and that a team of experts would inspect the site preliminary to the preparation of more detailed plans for the zoo. Afterwards Gwenda was exultant, Allen dubious. She became impatient. Kessler had an international reputation, one of the American advisers was a celebrated ecologist, why have doubts?

'Manston is a businessman. He wouldn't be in something of this sort unless he could see a profit. Where's any profit coming from?'

She hardly bothered to reply. She was calculating the amount that would come to the APL from the sale of that dismal bit of Wales, plus the possible donation from Donald Calendar.

Johnno took Belinda to lunch, more successfully this time. At least, he intended to take her to lunch, but the day was so fine that they ate sandwiches in St James's Park instead. They found deckchairs, were pestered by pigeons to whom they gave bits of bread, leaned over the bridge and gave the last of their sandwiches to the ducks. The sun shone. They were both cheerful.

'Do you know, beanbag, this is the nicest day

I've had for – oh, oodles.' She only called him bean-bag when she felt loving. 'It's stupid to quarrel.'

'Of course it is.'

'And you're so sweet. Perhaps I might be put on exhibition to your family after all. Only don't call them your people.'

'Whatever you say.'

'I thought I might come back to the flat if you'd like that.'

'More than anything.'

'Only that awful George is still there. I can't bear him.'

'He's only there half the time, maybe less. And you're out all day at your job, you hardly ever see him.' Belinda worked in a dress shop off Piccadilly.

'Once is too much. But still. I'll come back tonight after work, OK?' He beamed. 'You really are a sweet old beanbag, you know that? You make me feel terrifically domestic.'

Johnno bounced along on air back to the office. Two minutes after his return he was called by the buzzer. As he went in, Calendar's PPS came out of the Home Secretary's office, very red-faced. When Jonathan entered he was met with a glare, and a demand to know where he had been. At lunch he said.

'When I need you I expect you to be here, not *at lunch*. And if you are *at lunch* you should leave a note saying where you can be found. Your job is like mine, it lasts twenty-four hours a day.'

'Actually I couldn't have been reached. I had a picnic in the park.'

'A picnic in the park.' The Home Secretary stared

at him. His bristly hair stood up, each spike a porcupine's quill. 'Have you never heard of bleepers?'

'Of course, sir, but – '

'Never mind. You have a primal innocence that preserves you, Jonathan, but one day you will presume on it too far. Something must be done to stop Bannock.'

'Bannock?'

'Bernard Bannock, the NatLib MP. Pull yourself together, Jonathan. I expect you to know what I'm talking about, at least when parliamentary matters are being discussed.'

Johnno confirmed that he knew of Bernard Bannock, had exchanged words with him occasionally. His master broke in to tell him to get in touch with his cousin at the Yard, and see what progress was being made with the Kennington affair. Then Rex Calendar left to discuss with a gathering of police chiefs some new proposals made for that old chestnut, the establishment of a national police force, and to urge on them the virtue of the Baybee. On his return Johnno told him that the Big Man had said at the moment there was nothing new to report. The Home Secretary grunted, then ground his teeth, which was a habit he had at moments of stress. Johnno asked how he had got on with the police chiefs.

'They're inclined to stall everything, not stick their necks out for fear of getting their heads chopped off. Some of them are coming round to the Baybee, but not many. They're all afraid of the implications, don't see what a blessing it would be to every copper in the country. Argument's pointless, what you have to do is knock their heads together, tell them what they have to do. Like a lot of other people in this country.' He lighted a cigarette, smoke shot from his nostrils.

'Bannock, sir. Would that be to do with Kennington?'

'Possibly. Why?'

'You said the other day, let sleeping dogs lie.'

'And lying dogs sleep. But Bannock's not sleeping, he's nosing about. He's Pitcombe's dog, smelling around my childhood, mine and Donald's, looking for dirt.'

Johnno asked boldly: 'Will he find it?'

'There's dirt in every family if you dig deep enough. Things hidden, things that should remain hidden. That was one of the things the Victorians got right. Meddlers like Bannock should be taught a lesson, shown they mustn't interfere.' The Home Secretary's expression became for a moment so bleak that it would have been easy to imagine him a hanging judge about to don the fatal square of black silk.

'If you think this should be kept out of the public eye, sir – I mentioned MI5 before, but there are other agencies – '

'For God's sake stop this schoolboy prattle. Do you think I want to put myself in the hands of some half-dotty figure with delusions about having power over government politicians?' The glare directed at Johnno was for a moment scorching, then it was replaced by the Calendar smile. 'There are other ways of dealing with irritants like Bannock, more subtle ones. He's only – what was it Churchill called Nye Bevan, a squalid nuisance? Bannock's just a squalid nuisance, but it's true he has to be stopped.'

'It's possible I might be able to help.'

The Home Secretary recovered his customary coarse urbanity. 'Any help you can give, my dear Jonathan, will be much appreciated.' The tone made it clear he did not expect it to be useful in solving whatever problem might be posed by Bannock.

That evening George Kaiser appeared after a four-day absence. He brought a small pot of caviar and a bottle of champagne with him, in celebration he said of a couple of loose ends satisfactorily tied up. Or rather, he added with a laugh, cut off. Belinda had rung to say that she would be back late because a cousin from Sweden had suddenly turned up, and they were going out to dinner. She had a number of relatives dotted around Europe, something envied by Jonathan whose family were mostly lawyers or chartered accountants in the Home Counties.

So the two of them drank the champagne, and then washed down the caviar with some powerful vodka allegedly bottled in Russia. The effect produced was no doubt partly responsible for Johnno telling his friend about the Bannock problem, something he regretted on the following morning. George listened attentively, then asked where the Calendars had been brought up. Johnno recited bits of the well-known history of the brothers, adding that the important thing was not their origins, but where Bannock was nosing about. 'It'd be a job to find that out.'

'Not so.' George shook his lean head. 'You say Bannock's working for Pitcombe – '

'Not sure of that, just informed speculation.' Johnno heard his blurring of the last three words with surprise.

'Get hold of Bannock's secretary, say there's an urgent message from Pitcombe, where can he be found? If that doesn't work, put a tap on Bannock's phone, record all messages, he's bound to be in touch. What did Calendar say? He's got to be stopped, that it?'

'Quite right. Spot on.'

'No need for another word. Least said soonest mended, as my old mum says.'

'Didn't know you had an old mum.' Johnno found himself giggling. 'Thought it was an immaculate contraception.'

'Everyone's got an old mum. Secret, though. Leave it to me.'

'All right.' Johnno stood up with some difficulty. 'I'll leave it to you.'

'That's the ticket. Come on, finish the vodka.'

Johnno remembered nothing more. In the morning he had a hangover. Belinda said he seemed to have had a party last night, and asked where the caviar had come from. She had seen the empty pot.

'George. I helped him to celebrate tying up some loose ends. He's just come back from Russia.'

'He bought the caviar at Fortnum's. You were snoring like a pig. He's gone.'

'Gone?'

'Unless it was you who got up, ate some cornflakes, and left everything on the kitchen table. I wish he'd clear things away.'

'I feel terrible.'

'So you should.'

★

'Gwenda, this is Bernard. Bernard Bannock.'

'Yes. I'm afraid Allen isn't available. He's at a dinner of the pro-European Greens.'

'Been trying to get him – ring in the morning – leave message.'

'Leave . . . very well, what is it?'

'Struck pay dirt.'

'Oh. Pay dirt. Very well. I'll pass on the exact phrase.'

'No time now. Meeting someone – details tomorrow. Ring then, talk to Allen.'

'No doubt he will be pleased to hear from you.'

'He will – end of Calendar – snuffed out in politics – tell him that.'

It seemed to Gwenda that Bannock was ordering her to do things, something she was not prepared to tolerate. But still, she was curious. In her iciest Grand Dame voice she said it would be helpful if she could give Allen some idea of what he might hear in the morning.

'Not possible – not on telephone – tell him to do with murder. Girl killed Kennington not long ago – tell him that.'

And with that he hung up.

The sun shone. In green fields cows meditated. The car turned off the motorway on to the B road that led to Deemings. There was not a house in sight. Bladon seemed to feel – what was it the poet had said, 'Peace comes dropping slow' – peace dropped slowly into his veins. He said to Evans: 'No sign of brutalization here. Do you know, there's hardly been a change along this road since my childhood, not a house put up or a hedge cut down. It used to be a great thing, getting away from London, coming down to Deemings for the weekend.'

'Is that so, sir? Of course you only need to go a few miles and things are a bit livelier.'

Was his chauffeur simply obtuse, could he possibly be indulging in irony, or did he really think the new town just off the motorway, carefully devised in the form of a cross with almost identical shops and supermarkets on each of the four arms, and a cluster of fast food places, building societies and pubs in the centre was preferable to country peace? Very likely he did. Bladon was suddenly aware that although Evans had driven him for nearly two years he did not know where the man lived. It turned out to be a London suburb he knew only by name.

'What do you think about what people are calling the brutalization of Britain? Are you in favour?' The question would come through clearly enough on the radio link connecting the back seats of the Rolls to the front, but why was he asking it, what did he care about the reply? Evans did not turn his head, but an increased stiffness at the back of his neck suggested disapproval.

'Can't say I've thought much about it, sir. Got to modernize, I suppose, keep up to date.'

Modernize, a sacred word. The police car in front halted at the gates. The gates too were modern contraptions, installed when he became PM at the insistence of the Ministry of Defence, who said protection against possible intruders was essential, as if any intruder would come in through the front gate rather than gaining access to the grounds by making a way through the West Wood or climbing the wall into the vegetable garden. But it was good to be back at Deemings, the comfortable eighteenth-century house where he had grown up, good to see Clarissa's Daimler in the garage, back from her costume affair, good to be greeted by the dogs and by Mary Miles, who had been housekeeper at Deemings for a quarter of a century.

Clarissa was in the white drawing room, the doors open on to the terrace and the lawn. She was more than a decade his junior, and he was conscious as always of her fashion model elegance as she moved from the sofa, kissed his cheek . . . although of course he had in mind the fashion models of his youth. The half-naked creatures who paraded about now in Paris and London were not what he thought of as fashion models. He said she was looking wonderful.

'*You* look tired. A bad week?'

'Not particularly. Just continual bickering, Calendar and Pitcombe. I get tired of it. And a man named Bullington's been making a fool of himself.'

'Yes, I saw something about it.'

'You did?' Clarissa rarely looked at the tabloids, often did no more than glance at the broadsheets. 'There may be more to come, I'm told. And then Calendar thinks we should go to the country, but I'm doubtful with the polls as they are. Rhoda's against it.'

'What have you decided?'

'I haven't. I sometimes think I'd like to retire gracefully, settle down here with you, write my memoirs.'

Clarissa's delicate features were rarely animated, but now she showed emotion. 'Don't think of it. You'd be bored within a couple of months. You know you're a political animal, you enjoy all that counting of heads and manoeuvring to make non-entities change their minds.'

'You make it sound like a game for clever children. Perhaps it is. But I'm inclined to think I was a political animal, now I'm a political mammoth. I have to repeat it, you're looking particularly lovely.'

He said this, and meant it, without any flicker of desire. Indeed he had never found her slimness, coolness, calm elegance, sexually attractive. The marriage had been tactical, like much else in his life. He had brought to it a family name and a reputation as a rising politician; Clarissa was the only child of an ailing City banker who wanted his daughter to make a socially good marriage. When the banker died Clarissa inherited money, and when the banker's sorrowing widow also conveniently passed away, she was rich. The money had helped to fuel his career. There had been no children, but what he considered a sufficiency of sex. That, however, was in the past, had been so for nearly five years.

His mind moved away from her to the week ahead. There was a visit to Britain by the Australian PM, who was certain to stir up trouble, a group of worried businessmen from the Far East to be placated, a new slant to the endless discussions about Europe . . . He became aware that Clarissa had said something, and apologized for having been in what he still called a brown study. Although why brown?

'I asked if there'd been any other trouble with the press or TV? Apart from Bullington?'

'There's always trouble with the press about one thing or another. It's what they exist for. But nothing special, no.'

'That's a blessing.'

She seemed to spend the whole evening after dinner on the telephone – she had always been a great telephonist. Bladon read Hobbes, whose realism seemed to him a tonic for any politician:

> Those that are discontented with monarchy, call it tyranny; and those that are displeased with aristocracy, call it oligarchy; So also, they which find themselves grieved under a democracy, call it anarchy.

He marked the passage. That was Friday evening.

ELEVEN

Roselands

THE GARDEN at the chapel was eighty feet long, the width no more than half that. They had agreed that he would look after it when they bought the place, and although Catchpole was not a gardener by skill or temperament, he had found the business of digging, planting, sowing new grass where too vigorous an application of weedkiller had left bare patches, oddly pleasurable. After the immersion in moral mud that was a companion of much police work, it was somehow encouraging to handle actual soil, whether thick or friable, to see worms wriggling out of it like villains, try to trace ground elder to its source.

During Alice's absence, however, the garden had been neglected except that he cut the grass. Now she was back he went to work with an intensity that made her laugh, cleared out the finished wallflowers, sprayed the roses which had developed blackspot and a touch of mildew, planted lilies which had died on him earlier. The boys came out, watched him, fetched water and sprayed it around with the cans, splashing each other. Alan said: 'What's the point?'

'How do you mean?'

'At school we're taught it's good for things to

grow naturally. Some of the stuff you put on, one of our teachers says it's interfering with nature.'

Catchpole showed him the black-spotted roses. 'That's natural too, likewise canker, all sorts of diseases. The stuff I put on stops the diseases – well, helps to. If you're lucky. Fetch me that garden hose, will you.'

Desmond, much smaller than his brother, went to get it, but could hardly carry the rolled hose. Catchpole took it from him and said, 'We'll have to put you on one of those machines that stretch you out, or you'll never be a footballer.' He regretted the words as soon as they were spoken, especially because Alan was big and burly, a forceful striker in the school junior soccer team, while Desmond was undersized for an eight-year-old. Even so, the boy's reaction seemed excessive. He stared at his father, then turned and ran indoors wailing. Alice asked what he had done, then wondered aloud how he could have said anything so foolish.

'It was stupid, but not that stupid.' He went up to Desmond, who shouted that he wanted to be left alone. Later he and Alice talked to Alan, asked if there was any trouble for Desmond at school.

'He's just a cry-baby.'

'But has he said anything to you. About being in trouble?' That was Alice.

'He's always saying things. I don't see him much, you know. I'm not my brother's keeper.' After dumbfounding them with the phrase, he announced that he was going on to the Common for a pick-up game of cricket.

'I wonder where he got "brother's keeper" from,' Alice said, then asked how much Catchpole had left

them alone while she was away, and whether they
had been miserable. He stopped her.

'Forget it. Or at any rate don't talk about it. You
did what you felt you had to do, you're back now,
we're pleased, we all love you. Maybe I was wrong,
maybe you were, forget it. It's over.' He kissed her.

'Oh, Hilly. But what about Des?'

'He'll grow up, get bigger, get over it. Let's all
go and see *Honey, I Shrunk the Kids*. This evening.'

'Telephone.' As he picked it up she said: 'Bear in
mind it's your weekend off.'

He heard the Big Man's voice, asking if he knew
an MP named Bernard Bannock. Catchpole said he
knew the name, but not the man.

'He was found dead in his car last night. Just off
the A3, near Cobham. They think he ran into a
tree, though there may be more to it. Are you with
me, Catchers?'

'So far. But there must be more.'

'There is. I have the misfortune to know the
Pitcombes slightly. A tiresome couple, worried about
whether the world will come to an end sooner than
it should because too many of us drive gas-guzzling
cars. Mrs Pitcombe – Gwenda – called me this
morning. She thinks Bannock's death wasn't an accident. It seems he was doing some amateur detective
work for Allen Pitcombe, trying to find out something he could use to discredit our Home Secretary,
and according to Gwenda Pitcombe he'd found it.
He rang last night wanting to speak to Pitcombe,
who wasn't available, left a message saying he'd struck
pay dirt and that what he'd found out was to do
with a girl murdered in Kennington.'

Catchpole knew what was coming next, and it

came. As he said to Alice, for a copper there was no such thing as a weekend off. She took it well, as she always did, rolled her eyes in mock despair, and said at least it was a body near London, not outside Leeds or Manchester.

Esher, Cobham, Oxshott, Greenley: Catchpole contemplated the self-satisfied houses of this rich commuter land, looking from behind the wheel of his modest five-year-old MG Montego at the BMWs and Mercedes nestling in their kennels like waiting obedient dogs, with the occasional Volvo or Peugeot in a kennel adjoining. British cars? Nary a one to be seen. Was it right that the businessmen who occupied these lush houses and showed their indifference to their own country by using foreign cars should live in an area far beyond the scope of a Detective Chief Superintendent? Did he envy them? Supposing he were investigating one, would it be enjoyable to make him wriggle like a garden worm? He decided he didn't really much mind either way, preferred Alice's chapel to most of these houses.

The accident, if it was one, had taken place on a stretch of open land, a rarity in this built-up area, a mile or so out of Greenley, which possessed a post office, a pub, a general store, a group of Victorian houses placed in a rough semi-circle around a green, and not much else. Bannock's car was still there, although the body of course had been removed. The local Detective Inspector, whose name was Whiteley, was there too. A trilby hat perched lightly on the back of his head, his round youthful face beamed. He was chatty, full of certainties. The front of the car was mashed into unshaped metal where it had hit the tree.

'Tried to make it look like an accident, not much doubt it was deliberate. Just look at the back and side of the car, where it's scraped, reckon he was pushed off the road.' Catchpole dutifully looked, nodded. 'Happened around nine thirty, just getting dark, nobody to see, reckon our client knew the area, picked his place. Drove on a yard or two after giving a nudge to this Ford Orion, then came back, mark up the road where he stopped. Might still have been an accident, you're saying? Afraid not. Victim's badly shaken up, but concussed maybe, bleeding from nasty cut on the head, but still with us. Not for long though. Our client opens the passenger door, says, "Very sorry, went out of control didn't you, not my fault, but let me help," or something similar. Leans over, applies pressure to the right spot, carotid artery, does the trick. That's what our forensic god reckons happened. Client hops back into his car, probably stolen, goes off without saying goodbye.'

Three cars had passed while he was talking. Catchpole said, 'He was taking a chance, surely. It's not what you'd call isolated, just here.'

'Not that much of a chance. If another car stops, what he sees is our client on the scene of an accident, trying to help.' Whiteley beamed, wiped his red face with a perfectly white handkerchief. 'Would have been a bit dodgy though, I agree. Got inquiries out, no response so far, early days. Or hours. Motive wasn't robbery, wallet untouched, how we identified him so quickly. But though I say it wasn't robbery, maybe I tell a lie. Victim was in a local pub last night, landlord remembers he had a briefcase with him, none in the car. Could be that was the object of the exercise. Don't take much interest in politics but I know he was an MP, and it wasn't an ordinary hit, rob and run or you wouldn't be hot-footing it down here. My boss was at Bramshill with you, says you were a high flyer even then. What is it, state secrets? Never mind, don't expect you to tell me. Just do all I can to help.'

'You certainly haven't been wasting your time.' Whiteley beamed. 'I'd like to see the body, and the effects, then talk to the landlord of that pub. As to what I'm doing here, I'm not sure myself.' He corrected that. 'I'm here to find out what the late Bernard Bannock was doing here.'

An hour later he was little wiser. A look at the body told him no more than Whiteley had said and the preliminary forensic view conveyed. Bannock had been hurt in the accident and possibly knocked unconscious, but the cause of death was pressure to the carotid artery. His pockets contained keys and loose change, his wallet money and credit cards. The only thing of possible further interest was a sheet of paper on which some names and notes were written: 'George Layman; home near Guildford; Seafield, Waterfield?; name of patient, check back in records; head Dr Phillips; what links?' Catchpole had spoken on the telephone to Allen Pitcombe, so that this made some kind of sense to him. Pitcombe told him Bannock had been pursuing a story he believed to be discreditable to the Calendar family, a story connected with a member of the family being put into some kind of institution.

The paper seemed to indicate the institution was called Seafield or Waterfield, was near Guildford, and headed by Dr Phillips. Greenley was near enough to

Guildford, no more than five miles away, to make his presence in the area plausible. Unfortunately, however, a quick check on nursing and other residential homes in the area showed none with a name resembling Seafield or Waterfield, or any home of which a Dr Phillips was the head. Possibly the missing briefcase contained more information.

The pub in Greenley's single street was called the Grey Goose. A sign over the bar said: 'Your hosts are Barry and Brenda' but Barry, a thin man with lines carved into his cheeks as if with a knife, was not much of a host. His look of misery was not alleviated by mention of Bannock.

'He was in here throwing his weight about, and I said to him I've got a question for *you*, when's your government going to do something about the bloody brewers and the way they're amalgamating here, closing down there, making so a landlord can't earn a living, telling you what you can do and what you can't which is mostly everything? I'm not the government, he says, my party's not the government. You say that, I told him, you got the nerve to say that when you're one of these bleeding NatLibs, your people are in the Cabinet and you say you're not the government. Gave him something to think about, eh, Brenda?'

Brenda agreed. She was as thin and miserable-looking as her husband. However, she volunteered a piece of information. 'Course he was in before, you know that?'

Whiteley looked suitably abashed. Catchpole asked her to tell him about it.

'Same time as now, more or less, soon after midday. That's when he was asking all the questions about places and people we'd never heard of. Course, we've only been here eighteen months.'

'Eighteen months too long, ask me.' That was mine host.

'And he came back in the evening asking more questions?' He stopped. Brenda was shaking her head.

'No, that was the morning. The evening he was pleased with himself, talking politics and the next election, eh, Barry?'

'Not so pleased he bought me a drink.' There were only half a dozen people in the pub, something Catchpole did not find surprising. Barry went to serve an old man with a beard who looked curiously at the policemen. When he returned he said: 'Evening he had this message. On my phone. Using the place like it was a hotel.'

Catchpole shook his head at the impudence of it. 'Have one with us and tell me about it. If you've got time.'

'We're not that busy,' Barry said with masterly understatement. He poured a pint of bitter, held it to the light. 'Not much to tell. Got no pay phone here, just my private one, back of the bar. So it rings and I answer and someone asks for Mr Bannock, and by this time I know the name of this politician feller I've been arguing with, and I say to this Bannock it's for you, and it's a diabolical liberty using my private phone but I suppose you got to speak now this call's come through, and he came back of the bar and talked. Not for long.'

'Did you happen to hear anything that was said? Of course I realize you were busy.'

'Yes, well. It was a real liberty, using my phone

for his private business, I reckon I had a right. Not that there was much, just that he was meeting someone. At the Road House. I never said anything, not my way, but I thought if it's good enough for him to use my pub for his messages it could be good enough to meet this someone. But no, it has to be the Road House.'

Whiteley explained. 'The Road House is two or three miles up the road, fairly new, combined pub and restaurant, group plays there weekends.'

'*And* I hear they got a sort of annexe with rooms, you want to take a look at what goes on there. Can't compete. Some say we should do meals here, but ask me it's the hanky-panky they go there for. Can't compete and wouldn't want to, that's right, eh, Brenda?'

Brenda agreed. 'What goes on in that Road House, what we hear it's a scandal.'

That was the limit of Barry's helpfulness. He had not recognized the voice at the other end of the line asking for Bannock, could not even be sure it was male, and he remembered no more of the conversation. A couple of minutes after putting down the telephone Bannock had left the pub. There was a public telephone in the village a couple of hundred yards down the road, and the detectives agreed that the likely scenario seemed to be that the caller rang from there, waited in his car until Bannock came out of the Grey Goose, then followed him and forced his car off the road. They were about to leave the pub when the bearded man stopped them with a wave of the hand, and said: 'I heard the name of Dr Phillips. I was one of his patients.'

His voice was thin and high, forced out of his

throat as if a hand clutched his windpipe. He wore an old sports jacket with patched elbows, a rather jazzy food-marked waistcoat and khaki trousers. Long grey gloves concealed his hands.

'You were at Dr Phillips's nursing home, Seafield or Waterfield?'

A curious rattling sound came from the old man's throat, his substitute for a laugh. 'Not so much a nursing home, more a place for shutting up people nobody wants to know about. Sit down, gentlemen, sit down. My name is Satterley, but friends call me Satters. Not that I have any friends.' The rattle again. 'I have psoriasis, do you know what that is? It means my flesh scales away, flakes away, I can pull bits of it off. That's why I wear gloves.' He revealed that the long grey gloves went up his stick-like arms, then pulled up his jacket to show the pink flesh peeling above. 'That isn't all. I have diabetes, my liver hardly exists. Should I be here, what do you think?' He looked from one to the other of them, suddenly gleeful. 'And in my youth I had TB. Yet my father was a county cricketer, enjoyed the most robust health, what do you make of that?'

Catchpole sat down at the table. 'I think we could do with another drink.'

'Mine's whisky. Straight.' Whiteley went up to the counter. Catchpole asked how long ago Satterley had left the home.

'Couldn't say exactly. Few years. Time, can't keep track of it, don't know where it goes, flies away. Bzzz.' A sound perhaps like that of a hornet with laryngitis came from his throat. 'They turned me out, turned poor old Satters out. Into the community, they said, and now I'm with Mrs Robinson.

Good cook, Mrs Robinson, all sorts of puddings and tarts, can't eat any of 'em. What do you make of it, you two gentlemen? Should I be in the community?'

'Dr Phillips turned you out? Was the home called Seafield or Waterfield?'

'Lakeside the name was. Little lake in the grounds, girl tried to drown herself in it once. *What a to-do.*'

'Lakeside, good. Tell me about Dr Phillips. I'd like to talk to him.'

'You would?' Another rattle of laughter. The grey-gloved fingers raised the glass, sipped amber liquid. 'You'd have to go a long way. Skipped off, didn't he, to where the nuts come from as my dad used to say. Did I tell you my dad was a cricketer, played for Sussex? With one of the nurses, tarty piece, fancied her myself.' Flakes of dry skin fell on to the small pub table.

Whiteley spelt it out. 'You're saying Dr Phillips left the country three or four years ago, with a nurse. Did he take the home's money too?'

Satterley's thin head nodded. 'All there was.'

'This must have caused a scandal in the area. I was here then, don't remember it.'

'All hushed up. Private home, no scandal. They closed down Lakeside, bought another place not far away. Dr Armitage said all the patients could stay, but not when my dad died. He was a county crick-eter, fine athlete, not like poor Satters. He used to come and pay a visit every month.'

Catchpole said: 'County cricketers aren't that rich. He paid for you at Lakeside, and then the new place?'

'Paid what he could. Mum died when I was a

boy. Dad paid what he could, seemed to be enough, but when Dad died there was no money. Dr Armitage – ' He paused, then piped on. ' – Not like Dr Phillips. Didn't like Dr Armitage.'

'Why not?'

'Said I was well enough to live in the community, turned me out. That's what it's called, the community. Someone there to help you, like Mrs Robinson, but no good, can't eat her puddings. Didn't want to go, I said that.'

Whiteley said, 'So it's not Dr Phillips now but Dr Armitage, and it isn't Lakeside. What's the name of the new place?'

'Roselands. What do you think of that?' Catchpole shook his head to show he thought little of it, and asked where Roselands was. 'Out there somewhere. Made me leave it, don't care where it is.' He took out a fob watch from the food-stained waistcoat. 'Oh dear, lunchtime, got to go. Mrs Robinson gets cross if I can't eat her puddings. Goodbye.' He was up, out of the chair and out of the pub with surprising speed. A faint memory stirred in Catchpole's mind, what was it? The White Rabbit in *Alice*?

'Half-witted,' said Barry back at the bar. 'Should be put away. Sits half an hour over a drink, keeps business away.' Brenda said he did no harm, she felt sorry for him. She was full of praise for Mrs Robinson, a widow who lived in a big house down the road, and took in two or three former patients, discharged as being able to live in the community.

'And who pays for it?' Barry asked. 'They discharge these loonies should be shut up, say they're harmless, just need a bit of looking after, and we're the ones who foot the bill. You gents, you're all

right, soon's you join up you're working out what
your pension will be, at fifty-five is it – '

'If we don't get shot or knifed first,' Whiteley
said, and laughed heartily.

'And who's more likely to get a knife in the guts
or a glass in the face than a landlord asking drunks
to get out of his pub before they smash up too much
of it? And if they do, if glasses get pinched or chairs
are smashed up when the local soccer club's having
a bit of a consolation drink after they've just lost the
semi-final of the Pisspot Cup, who d'ye think pays
for the new ones? I'll tell you who doesn't, and that's
Johnny Brewer.'

Brenda patted his hand. 'It's a great life if you
don't weaken.'

Ten minutes more spent listening to Barry and
Brenda brought no more useful information. They
had never heard of Roselands or Lakeside, knew
little about the area and were eager to get out of it
and back to London. A local directory, however, gave
a telephone number for somewhere listed simply as
Roselands, Residential Home. A woman's voice said
Dr Armitage was seeing a patient and so was not
available at present, and asked if the caller wished to
discuss a possible admission. Catchpole responded
that it was an official inquiry with which he was
hoping somebody at the home might be able to
help, emphasized that it was urgent, mentioned his
rank, and added with what he hoped was evident
irony: 'I'm sure it would be more convenient for
Dr Armitage if he could spare time to see me this
afternoon, rather than come down to the local
station for interview.'

The voice at the other end said, 'Just a moment.'

More than a moment but less than a minute later the voice said: 'Dr Armitage can make time to see you at two thirty.'

Catchpole, still in the ironic vein, said: 'Thank him for me. Say how grateful I am he can spare the time.'

'She,' the voice said, undoubtedly having the last word.

The two policemen had a pub lunch in Oxshott. Whiteley apologized for the look of the place. 'This used to be a decent pub, now it's all been tarted up, Scottish tartans round the walls, shouldn't be surprised if they have a piper Saturday nights.' Catchpole said anything would be preferable to the Grey Goose.

'Too right. You reckon you'll get anything out of this Dr Armitage, anything to do with our friend Bernard? Nothing to show he went near this Roselands, except for that bit of paper. More likely he was up to some political jiggery-pokery, seems to me, stuck his nose in too far, got it cut off. That your angle on it?' Catchpole said truthfully that he had no angle, except that Bannock's death could have a connection with a murder inquiry. Whiteley shook his head, said he could see Catchpole played his cards close to his chest, and promised to be in touch if local inquiries turned up anything interesting.

Roselands was half a mile up a tree-shaded lane. A discreet sign by a large set of open gates read *The Roselands Home*. Catchpole drove another quarter-mile along a gravel drive lined with flowering bushes. Then the bushes suddenly ended, revealing a large well-kept lawn with stone steps at the end of it

leading up to what Catchpole's untutored eye at first
thought to be a church – his Clapham house, the
chapel, as it were run wild. The formidable main
block that confronted him had mullioned windows
and what seemed a proliferation of roofs and gables
topped by slender chimney stacks. The original
colour had perhaps been yellow limestone with lac-
ings of red brick, but this had aged with the years
into a becoming uniform grey. There were some
obviously incongruous later additions, including one
that looked like a gigantic conservatory, and was
perhaps a solarium.

Half a dozen cars were parked in a space to the
right of the main front, and Catchpole parked his
Montego beside a Vauxhall Cavalier and an Astra, a
Ford Sierra and Escort, a small Peugeot, nothing
ostentatious or grand, no Mercs or BMWs. The
house continued round this side to form an L-shape,
the clerical feeling maintained by steep gables and
long narrow windows so that from this side Roselands looked like a pyramid construction of roofs
and gables belonging to different houses. It came as
no surprise to learn later that this was one of the few
country houses designed by the Victorian church
architect William Butterfield.

Beyond the range of stone and wooden outbuildings on this short side of the L were more glimpses
of green. Catchpole resisted the temptation to
explore, and went round again to the front. As he
turned the corner a uniformed nurse came out of
the arched front entrance and went along to the
conjectural solarium, pausing on the way for a word
with two figures sunning themselves in deckchairs.
On the lawn a painter sat beside an easel, brush in

hand, panama on head as shelter from the sun. The detective felt out of place in his sober suit. He went up the stone steps, through the open door under this main entrance.

And moved from light to darkness, or what seemed like darkness. At first glimpse the hall he entered appeared enormous, although it might have been no more than thirty feet long. The impression of great size came perhaps from the height of the roof, which again echoed church architecture with its arched timbers, slight whiff of dampness, narrow windows. But there were incongruous elements, the evidently modern staircase at one end of the hall, bright rugs, modern sofas and chairs, and a reception desk like that found in a hotel, at which a smiling plump-faced woman sat beside a switchboard. Her 'Superintendent Catchpole?' had a touch of archness. 'Take a seat. I'll tell Dr Armitage you're here.'

Half a minute later a white-coated man appeared, and led the way up the staircase at the end of the hall, then along a wide carpeted corridor lined with dark panelled wood. There were doors on either side. Some were blank, others marked in a stylish script *Music Room, Library, Recreation Room*. The style was that of a small good-class old-fashioned hotel. He asked white-coat if he was a nurse.

'Just general handyman. Do all sorts, though, lend a hand.' He was young, perhaps middle twenties, short but sturdy, hair razor cut at back and sides.

'Including dealing with patients?'

'If asked.' They turned left, no doubt into the shorter piece of the L. Here the dark panelling had been painted white and some of the windows knocked out and enlarged, so that the effect was

lighter. Catchpole asked how many patients Roselands housed and the answer was: 'Don't know.'

'You don't know much, do you?'

White-coat turned, revealing a flat meaningless
face. 'Not my job to answer questions. You want to
know stuff about the home you ask one of the
doctors. Or Mr Larkins.'

'Who's Mr Larkins?'

'Dunno what he's called. You a reporter?'

'Policeman.'

The flat face turned away to show again the
razor-cut back of head. They went up a couple of
stairs, stopped at a door marked *Dr P. H. Armitage.*
Razor-cut opened this door. Dr Armitage got up
from her desk, came round it, shook Catchpole's
hand. He placed her in the late thirties. She was
slim, above average height, with fair hair piled on
top of her head that somehow gave her an expression
both severe and enigmatic, the latter quality accentuated by a pair of large rimless spectacles. An attractive
woman deliberately playing down the sex appeal she
possessed, Catchpole thought. Her voice was light,
frosty.

'I agreed to see you at this very short notice
because I understand you need some information
urgently. I have no idea what it can be, but Moira
– you have met her in the hall – said your tone was
threatening. I don't appreciate that.'

He said he was sorry if that impression had been
conveyed, but Moira had seemed unhelpful, and he
was engaged in a murder inquiry. She raised well-
shaped eyebrows and asked with a touch of incredulity if he was suggesting Roselands could be
concerned.

'Possibly.' He told her of Bannock's death, and the paper in his pocket that mentioned a home in this area and the name of Dr Phillips. Incredulity was replaced by indignation as she listened to him.

'You're seriously suggesting, simply on the basis of a sheet of paper that doesn't even mention Roselands, that we have some connection with this MP's death? I can hardly believe it, Superintendent.'

Catchpole was irritated. 'We'll get on faster, Dr Armitage, if you accept that I wouldn't be wasting your time and mine unless I had reasons for thinking links may exist between Roselands, Bannock's death and a recent murder in south London. The links may have nothing to do with the deaths, that's what I'm trying to find out. What I want to know is first of all whether Bannock paid a visit here and talked to you or anyone else. But I need to know also what sort of home this is, how long it's existed, who owns it and who the inmates are. I'd like to have your cooperation, but if I can't have it I'll find out what I need to know without it. You might not like the upheaval that could cause. Am I getting through to you?'

Behind the rimless glasses her eyes were an odd colour, greenish. Her hands were slender. She wore no wedding ring. Her thin lips tightened to a line. 'Again that sounded like a threat. But very well, ask your questions, but don't be surprised if some don't get answered. I've never seen or heard of Mr Bannock, but of course I can't say whether or not he saw some other member of the staff. And I can only tell you about Roselands. If you want to go further back, talk to Fred Larkins. He was here for a while in Dr Phillips's time.'

'Dr Phillips went off to Brazil with a nurse, and some of the home's funds?'

'That is what I heard. I can't confirm or deny it.'

'And then you were appointed? How did that happen?'

'I answered an advertisement, was interviewed, got the appointment. I was chief medical officer at a home in Devon, but here I was in complete charge. The money was better, much better. And it was made plain to me that I'd be starting out with a clean sheet, that Roselands wouldn't be Lakeside.'

'What was wrong with Lakeside?'

'Again, I only know what I heard. Everything very lax, patients in and out of each other's rooms, Dr Phillips having affairs – but I'm just repeating things at secondhand, and I don't like that. I understood from the trustees that they had decided to close Lakeside because of its undesirable reputation. Roselands, as I've said, was a fresh start.'

Her brows came together when he asked who interviewed her. 'Two men and a woman. I remember thinking it was odd that none of them seemed to have medical experience. One man was named Kennedy, I think he had banking connections. The woman belonged to a society for finding homes for the mentally ill. The Roselands Trust had already been set up, they were looking for someone to run the home. I filled the bill.'

The door opened, a head appeared round it, sandy-haired, sharp-featured. It was about to withdraw when she said, 'Come in, Nigel. Superintendent Catchpole, this is my partner, Nigel Straker. The Superintendent is investigating the death of an MP named Bannock. Did you meet him, by any chance?'

The sandy head was shaken. 'Heard about it on the news, that's all. Smashed up his car, sounded like an accident. What's the connection with Roselands?'

'From what I've heard there isn't one.' Nigel nodded, went out. Dr Armitage continued. 'I deal with the medical side here, with the help of consultants I can call on when necessary. I was trained as an alienist and know quite a lot about mental disorders although I don't specialize in them. Hence the consultants. We don't need them often, perhaps half a dozen times a year. Nigel handles the accounts. He makes a yearly report to the trustees, and they seem happy with it. And going back to Bannock. I've never heard of him, Nigel hasn't seen him, but it's still perfectly possible he called on somebody here, a resident. We try to think of them as residents, not patients.'

'How many residents do you have?'

'At the moment, thirty-one. Forty would be the most we'd be wise to take.'

'And they're all mentally deficient?'

'That's right.' For the first time Dr Armitage seemed genuinely interested. 'Whether by chance or skill you've picked the right word. They are a little deficient, that's all, most of them, just missing one card in the pack, got a single screw a little bit loose, aren't *quite* all there. But they're almost all there, none of them is dangerous, and it would be quite wrong to call them loonies. Do you know that Pirandello play about the man who may be mad, but on the other hand could be saner than all the people round prepared to pretend he's a King? Some of our residents are like that. There may be one or two things they're haywire about, but over others they're more perceptive than you or me.'

Catchpole said that was interesting, although he suspected an attempt was being made to overawe him with superior knowledge. When he said he would like to see a roster of residents along with the length of their stay, Dr Armitage flatly refused.

'Unless you can convince me that one of them has a connection with your investigation, I refuse. So far I haven't heard the faintest suggestion of any link.'

Catchpole sighed. 'Let's try another approach. I assume this is a registered home, subject to the usual regulations and inspection?'

'It is. And rated perfectly satisfactory.'

'But you choose the residents, you don't just take anyone harmless with a screw loose?' She did not reply immediately. 'What I'm asking is how do your residents get here, who puts their names up, is it just you who says OK, or alternatively no, I don't think so? Or do the mysterious trustees have a say, do they interview all the applicants?'

'Come here.' She got up from her desk and beckoned him across to a window from which they had a view of a small lawn to the side of the house, where three or four men and women were helping nurses to put tea things on to garden tables. 'They're residents. They look normal enough, don't they? The one in the suit is Fred Larkins.' The other men were wearing shorts, the women summer dresses.

'Yes, they look normal. You haven't answered my questions.'

'I'll answer them. I just wanted you to see some of the residents, it may help to explain why I resent the tone of the questions. Applications come mostly from relatives, sometimes from lawyers acting on behalf of someone who's been left without a guardian and can't cope on their own. They have to be approved by two doctors, which is the usual form, then they're interviewed by me. Not everybody is suited by a regime like this one, or can pay our fees which are high, though the trustees sometimes waive part of them. The trustees don't see the applicants, they're not qualified to judge their condition so there'd be no point. And the trustees aren't mysterious, they're simply people with an interest in Roselands.'

'But people are sometimes accepted, then turned out. Like Satterley.'

It gave him pleasure to see she was disconcerted. Behind those large round panes of glass the greenish eyes blinked rapidly, as a boxer may when caught by an unexpected punch. But she recovered rapidly.

'Satterley, yes. He was admitted in Dr Phillips's time.'

'But he was accepted at Roselands, then turned out, put into the care of the community. Was that your decision?'

'It was. You've seen Satterley, talked to him? Did he tell you why he had to leave? I thought not. The residents here have a great deal of freedom. They are allowed out during the day, although if they're absent for meals they are expected to tell staff in advance. If they wish to visit friends or relatives and stay away for a night or a weekend they can do so providing they obtain an exeat from Moira, which needs to be approved either by me or Fred Larkins.'

'Rather like the Army. Or school.'

'You sound amused. But yes, the comparison has its point. As I said before, some of our residents are intelligent, most are friendly, but there are exceptions. Roselands isn't suited to those who are occasionally violent, severely physically disabled, or likely to upset other people. We're simply not equipped to deal with such cases. Satterley borrowed from other residents and didn't pay them back. He was suspected of stealing from them. He used to spend evenings out and come back drunk, shouting and upsetting other people. In their interests and perhaps in his own he had to go.'

'How was it Dr Phillips managed to cope with him?'

'Since I never met Dr Phillips I can't tell you. I think it's likely that a good many things went on under his regime that I wouldn't have tolerated. Now, Superintendent, I'm a busy woman. If you're curious about the past, talk to Fred Larkins. He was here for a short time when it was Lakeside, and may be able to help you. I must ask you, though, not to question the residents unless you feel that's absolutely necessary and can tell me why.'

Catchpole said he saw no reason to question them at present.

'But you'd like to talk to Larkins? He doesn't have medical qualifications, but he's been more useful and sensible in dealing with the occasional problems that came up than any young houseman stuffed full of textbook knowledge would have been. I had one of those when I took over, but he didn't last long.' It was plain that at Roselands there was only one boss.

She got up from behind her desk. Catchpole

stood up too. He said: 'Is anyone from the Calendar family connected with Roselands?'

If he had been hoping to disconcert her he failed. 'You mean the Home Secretary, that Calendar? And he has a brother connected with the press, isn't that right? I've never had anything to do with either of them, just know their names. Nobody's mentioned them to me in connection with the home.'

She must have pressed a button on her desk, for the door opened and flatface stood there. 'Take this gentleman down to Mr Larkins.' She held out her hand. Catchpole took it, and had the sensation of holding bones rather than flesh.

Flatface was no more talkative on the return trip through the house than he had been earlier. As they passed the door labelled *Library* Catchpole stopped, turned the door handle, looked in. Tall mahogany bookshelves with metal lattice-work fronts held rows of books in standard bindings. A large table in the middle of the room held magazines displayed in rows. There were ladderback chairs beside a couple of small writing tables and two or three armchairs. The room had an unused look, smelt slightly stuffy. Catchpole nodded, closed the door, smiled at flatface, said, 'Just looking.'

In the big hall down below he stopped before the desk where Moira, who had smiled when she mentioned his rank, now smiled again, and responded to his inquiry about any visitors in the last day or two by saying she was not allowed to give out such information. They passed through the arched door on to the terrace. The painter from the lawn came up the steps from the garden. He carried his easel under one arm, his painting held

carefully in the other hand. He said to Catchpole,
'Hallo, how are you?' Seen close to, he was revealed
as a rather handsome man with long curling grey
hair. It seemed reasonable to respond to the greeting,
but when Catchpole did so the man laughed, showing long yellow teeth. 'Caught you. Never saw you
before in my life. Want to look at my painting?'

'Not particularly.'

'More fool you, it's one of my masterpieces.' He
passed on his way, whistling. When he asked flatface
the man's name the response was shrugged shoulders.

The conservatory was indeed that, a genuine
Victorian relic of ribbed iron and glass that had after
all perhaps been built with the house. It resembled
a comfortable untidy drawing room with a glass roof,
very pleasant on this sunny day although no doubt
draughty in winter. Comfortable, but shabby. Armchairs and sofas looked well worn, the rugs on the
tessellated floor were slightly ragged, several iron
columns of candy twist design badly needed paint.
All this Catchpole took in while flatface led him
across to where a couple, both men, stood talking
beside a bust of a broken-nosed Greek or Roman
that topped a white marble pillar. The shorter of the
men, already seen by Catchpole from Dr Armitage's
window, said, 'Mr Catchpole, hallo, Fred Larkins.
This is one of our residents, Alexander Warner,
always known as Alex.' The thin tall man with Larkins gave the detective a smile of great sweetness,
although he seemed on the edge of tears, and turned
away. There were five other people in the conservatory. A nondescript middle-aged man sat reading
The Times, a completely bald fat man wearing a tight-
fitting short-sleeved shirt and shorts had a writing-

pad on his knee and was scribbling furiously in it, two women who could have been characters in a TV soap sat in a far corner chattering like birds. The fifth person was perhaps in his early twenties, much the youngest of those under the glass roof. He was reading a paperback book, and a bubble of semi-intelligible words came out of his mouth as he read. Suddenly he stood up, the book in his hand, and shouted: 'Filth, all fucking filth. Everything, shit, it's all around us.' The two women continued to talk, the man writing did not lift his eyes from the pad, the *Times* reader lowered his paper, looked at the young man, shook his head, then raised the paper again. Larkins excused himself and went across to the young man, who was now tearing pages from the paperback and throwing them on the floor, talking rapidly as he did so. Larkins put an arm round his shoulders and led him out through a door that led to the inner part of the house. Alex Warner nodded at Catchpole and followed them. It was a couple of minutes before Larkins returned.

'One of those little problems.' Catchpole had sat down, and Larkins dropped into a chair beside him. 'Should have taken his medication at lunchtime. Could be he forgot, but someone should have seen he took it. Either way he's OK now. By the way, I said "Mr" not "Superintendent" because I thought you might not want the official status mentioned. No offence, I hope.'

'Of course not.' Catchpole considered him. Larkins had a small square pugnacious face, ears close to the head as if pinned there, nose not much more than a blob, small deep-set brown eyes. He had a bull neck, thick well-muscled arms, powerful hairy hands. He wore a lightweight pale blue gaberdine suit, and trainers. His intonation was cockney, his manner that of a Cheerful Chappie ready to see the funny side of any situation, but there was something forceful about him. Even the little moustache that covered his upper lip managed to look powerful. Now he said: 'Auntie Armitage said you'd like to ask me some questions about this place as I'm sort of an old hand. Fire away.'

'Tell me about the residents. I'm still not very clear what sort of home this is.'

Larkins put a finger to his head, turned it. 'You've seen a few of 'em. Harmless, but a bit batty. You saw old Locksley there, reading the paper. He pretends he sets the *Times* crosswords, copies out the clues from 'em, then says, "Look, here's another crossword I'm setting for the paper", then we have to say "Hey, Tom, you're so clever." The nurses say his room's stuffed with old copies of the paper.'

'Sounds simply like eccentricity, not a reason for putting someone away.'

'Ah well, ask Auntie, she'll tell you they're not put away, this is a *residential institution*, they're residents. True enough in a way. Look. You've got a batty, or eccentric if you like to call it that, relative who's posing a problem for you one way or another. If you know the right doctors they'll say the relative's a danger to themselves or other people. So then they're signed in here and everyone's happy. Including them, mind you. They're not prisoners, can go where they want as long as they tell the front office and don't make a nuisance of themselves outside. Which of course sometimes they do, one way or another.'

'What then?'

'Then they're candidates for medication. Auntie didn't tell you about that, I guess. Putting it crudely, some of 'em are doped up to keep 'em peaceful. I don't mean they're all that fierce or that much trouble. Maurice now, the boy who threw that tantrum, he's an exception. Only been with us a few weeks, one doctor says he's a non-violent schizo, another that he might self-destruct. Whichever it is, I can cope.' He sat back, stroked his little moustache. 'But I'll tell you for free, Super, if he goes on this way Auntie will get rid of him. It's his family who put him in, can't deal with him at home, don't want to put him in a bin. Fair enough, but Auntie Armitage won't keep him here if he makes too much trouble. You could say the whole purpose of this place is avoiding trouble. For the patients and for those who run it.'

'What about Warner, the one talking to you.'

'Alex, he's a model resident, been here a couple of years now. Never has a tantrum, goes out on his own most days for long walks. Bit of a loner, though you get the feeling sometimes he's looking for sympathy. Struck up a relationship two or three times with residents of the other sex, but that isn't approved of by the powers that be. Wife left him, on his own, no relatives, came here of his own accord, as if it was an ordinary home.' Now Larkins laughed, an easy comfortable sound. 'This isn't what you're here for though, Super, not what you want to know about, is it? You don't want to hear me being disrespectful about my employer or this guff about the residents, just waiting to start the tough questioning, isn't that so? So let's have it, hit me where it hurts, crack me on the chin. Tell me how I can help.'

'You don't feel you should talk to Dr Armitage before answering questions?'

'She's given me the OK, but in any case I'm a free agent. She pays my wages, that's all.' He produced a pack of cigarettes, offered them to Catchpole who shook his head, put a match to one. 'Bad habit. She runs the show, that mousy partner of hers adds up the figures, but I do quite a bit of the hard graft. Learned about it in Dr Phillips's time, the boss when it was Lakeside, said everyone should call him Phil and they did. Everyone liked Phil. Trouble is he had expensive tastes, drove a Merc, and had his hand up all the nurses' skirts. I was only a few months with him at Lakeside, not sure I could have stuck it much longer, the way Phil went on and let the patients go on – we called 'em patients then – drink, sex, Lakeside was a bit of a free for all.' His merry smile expressed pleasure rather than disapproval. 'But then Phil ups sticks and goes off, at first they thought it was to Paraguay but turned out it was Brazil, along with one of the nurses. So Lakeside was closed down and this place was bought, Auntie Armitage was appointed, I was asked to stay on. And here we are.' He stubbed out the cigarette, lighted another. 'Don't get me wrong, Super. About Auntie, I mean. I don't much like her, she's like a schoolmistress who's got a ruler in her desk to rap you over the knuckles, but still she's OK, runs the place the way it should be run, started painting classes and tried to get 'em interested in a reading course, but – ' He shrugged. Catchpole recalled the obviously unused library.

He produced the photograph of Bannock, and Larkins recognized it at once. 'He was round here yesterday asking questions. Got choked off by Moira, the plump one on the front desk. Auntie's given instructions that anyone asking questions should be referred to her, case they're press, but Moira said this man said no, he wouldn't bother the doctor. Moira thought he'd left, but it seems he wandered around snooping. I found him talking to a couple of locals who look after the cars, do a bit of gardening and odd jobs. Then I took charge of him, he asked me questions. I thought he must be press. That what he was?'

'His name's Bernard Bannock, and he's an MP. Or was. He died last night when his car ran off the road and hit a tree just outside Greenley.'

'An MP.' Larkins's mouth rounded in a silent whistle. 'I don't get it. Why would an MP be interested in Roselands? And why would him dying in a car accident bring a Superintendent down here?'

'I didn't say he died in a car accident. There are other possibilities. That's why I'm asking questions.'

'Yes. But I still don't see why you're here.' Catchpole didn't enlighten him. Larkins's face was made for movement, not stillness, and the effect was strange when the merry little eyes and the brows above them, the blob of nose with its occasional slight twitch or wrinkle, the moustache that mostly seemed to bristle of its own volition, were all suddenly and surprisingly stilled, planes and sockets made into a single metallic image. Then he exhaled gently, and metal became plastic again. 'Want to know what we talked about, I s'pose. Maybe the things I was saying about Lakeside weren't so far off the mark after all. That's what you wanted to know

about, I s'pose, him too. He wanted to talk about
the past.'

'What in the past?'

'He said he was writing an article, and I took it
for granted he was a reporter wanted a story. So I
was a bit cagey about Phil's fun and games, but that
didn't interest him. He wanted to know how long
the residents had been here and any who'd been at
Lakeside for a while, which of course I didn't know
much about. And if any were violent, to which I
said what I've told you. Again, though, it was the
past that interested him, things that happened years
back, so he drew a blank. He asked if there was any
check on residents' movements in the evening or at
night and I told him the form, if they wanted to be
out all night we'd check in advance with the place
they were staying – '

'Is that always done?'

'Couldn't tell you, Super. I'm telling you and I
told him what's *supposed* to be done. Then he wanted
to know if there was a record book where those out
at night late would be put down, at which point I
began to think there was something dodgy about
him and his questions, and I clammed up.'

'Did he show you any papers, or was he carrying
any?'

'If he was he didn't show 'em to me. That it?' he
said as the detective put away the notebook in which
he had jotted down points. Catchpole said he had
been very helpful, although he had the impression
that helpfulness had been given within careful
limits. Larkins said he still didn't know what the
whole caboodle was about, and again the detective
didn't enlighten him. He opened the conservatory

door and moved from the artificial warmth under
the glass roof into the dulcet air of a summer day.
The green lawn under foot, not of bowling-green
quality but delicate enough, the pink and white
chestnut trees, the mass of flowering bushes border-
ing the lawn at one side, all checked him and moved
him back to some incident of childhood connected
with the only holiday he could recall ever being
taken on by his father and mother. He tried to
remember the incident as he stood inhaling the scent
of grass curiously mixed with lavender, failed to
bring anything to mind, and walked back to his car.

From the local station he talked to Maggie Steel,
said to be a wizard with the computer. As he knew,
she regarded herself quicker on the uptake than any
male colleague of the same rank, and now she did
not flinch when he asked her to trace back the
records of Roselands and Lakeside, who owned them
and what were the names of the residents.

'I'm not sure how much of this information is
available, on the computer or off it. And you may
have problems since it's the weekend,' he warned.

'I'll manage. Anything else?'

'See if you can pick up any link with the Calendar family. Not just Rex and Donald, their parents
maybe, or a brother named Gene. And if the computer comes up with any violent crime connected
with the homes, I'd like that too.'

'You don't want much, do you? Computers don't
work on lucky dips like policemen, they want something to feed on.'

'Here are some names. Calendar, Fazackerley,
Luisa Devane, Lily Devon, Garry Johnson, any links
any of them have with each other. And a couple

more, just to make sure you're not twiddling your thumbs, Dr Armitage, initials P. H., and Fred Larkins. Anything that links any one of them with any of the others could possibly be interesting. Enough computer food?'

'Enough, but not really the right sort. I'll need to use my imagination.'

'Do that, Sergeant Steel.' He told Alice he wouldn't be back in time to see the film, suggested she might take the boys on her own. She said she'd do that, but it would be nice if sometimes he knew exactly when he'd be free. Before he could say he thought so too, she went on: 'Don't tell me, that's coppering, I've heard it all before. Never mind. See you some time this evening. Look after yourself.'

'Will do. Love.'

'Love you too.'

Driving from Greenley to Sevenoaks, from plush green Surrey to plush green Kent, Catchpole felt himself to be in a circle placed around cities, a circle whose charmed occupants were free from the dirt, the poverty, the corruption of the city, free from all the problems that provided him with a living. They fed off the city, their activities were what made the city function as a machine. Some of them found the city very acceptable for eating and drinking, but when it came to the line they didn't find it a good place for living, or not for their kind of living. Lily Devon murdered in Kennington, drug-dealers ruling the roost in whole areas, blacks and Asians terrorized and doing their share of terrorizing in return, these might be a consequence of their own policies or practices, but such consequences could be evaded or forgotten by moving outside the city, growing tall hedges, being selective about neighbours, keeping undesirable characters out of golf clubs – and leaving Catchpole and Co. to clear up the mess. Such heretical thoughts were in the policeman's mind as he drove past the village greens, along tree-lined avenues dotted with four-square houses that testified to the passion felt by the southern English house-builder and house-owner for red brick. Catchpole never voted in elections. He would have admitted, though, that at some point and in some societies a policeman had to become politicized. The conclusion he drew was that such societies should be avoided, so why should the sight of these businessmen's mock mansions have prompted the heretical thoughts? He could not have answered the question.

New Valley, where the Calendar boys had grown up, was outside the charmed circle, one of the many villages that came into existence just after the Second World War through the foresight of entrepreneurs who realized that if land could be bought in a pleasant area outside a town, and houses built on it quickly and cheaply, townees would buy them under the impression that they would be living a rural life. Instead, within a year or two they found themselves in a suburb of the town where they worked, a suburb quickly spreading so that new estates with their accompaniment of linking roads and sewer guts replaced country views. New Valley had once been a real valley, flanked by hills to one side and wooded country on another. That was when the first houses were put up, two-storey structures regarded by their owners as a vast improvement on the post-war government prefabs. But that was long ago. Now bungalows had crawled all the way up the hills, and most of the woods had been replaced by filling stations, car parks and fast food restaurants.

Catchpole was disconcerted. Newspaper stories had said the Calendar boys were brought up in a village, but New Valley appeared to be a small town. He found a place to park in the High Street, drew a blank in a pub when he asked if they knew which shop had been owned in the fifties and sixties by a Mr Calendar. He had more success at the post office. The counter staff, all in their twenties and thirties, looked understandably bemused by the idea of a general shop existing in New Valley, but agreed that if anybody knew about such a shop it would be Arthur in Parcels. A side door was unlocked, Catchpole was let in, taken down to Parcels and introduced to Arthur, who was housed in a small office where he was making entries in a ledger, standing up to do so like a character out of Dickens. He was even using a pen that he dipped into an ink bottle. Arthur's appearance and dress increased Catchpole's sense of having stepped back in time. Arthur was a red-faced gnome who wore a wig of faded brown hair that had slipped slightly so that it curled round his left ear. He stuck the pen behind his right ear, became aware of the slipped wig and adjusted it, removed paper cuffs from his wrists and gave the detective a hearty handshake.

'Just been checking details of parcel deliveries. Some of the youngsters say it's not important, everything gets delivered in a day or two, but to me that's slackness. All you read about now in the papers is efficiency in business, they say they've got machines can do this and that, dispense with the human element. But will your machine tell you how often and at what time of day an attempt was made to deliver a particular package? As sure as my name is Arthur Timms I can tell you, my dear sir, it won't. Who tells the robots what to do, I ask you? Human beings.' He beamed triumphantly. 'But I'm running on. You wanted to know about Joe Calendar's shop, where it used to be. The answer is, just twenty yards or so down the High Street, other side of the road. Gone years ago, now it's New Valley Cycle Mart, nobody there will remember Calendar's. Changed hands, oh, sixty-two or three when Joe Calendar died. What was your particular interest, sir, if I may make bold enough to ask? The two boys, of course, they became very well known. Anybody's heard of New Valley, it will be because of them.'

Catchpole spent half an hour with Arthur Timms, the niceties of parcel deliveries temporarily abandoned, mugs of tea made and drunk. The results, however, were rather disappointing until his own last, almost casual question. In spite of his Dickensian style Arthur was in fact only in his early sixties. His parents had moved out of Sevenoaks to a house in the recently built New Valley when he was in his teens, and although his memories of Joe Calendar were clear enough, he knew little about the rest of the family except that they were not much liked.

'First two or three years we were here this was a pretty quiet sort of place, just the one shop and it was the post office too, those days. When you just got the one shop you rely on it for things, if they run out of stock it meant going into Sevenoaks on the bus, not many cars about then. Joe Calendar, he often ran out of things, maybe not his own fault,

maybe he didn't bother to restock. And then your
village shop, it's a kind of meeting place, people see
each other, stop and have a bit of a natter. Joe didn't
want that, and he let people know it. He wasn't
liked, I can tell you that. Not that he minded . . .
Rest of the family? Can't remember much about
'em. Mrs Joe, she sometimes served in the shop, but
I don't doubt she had her hands full, three kids to
look after – '

'Three? I only remember hearing about the two
brothers.'

'Ah, there was another. Donald, he was the
eldest, then Rex who wants to have all your lot
carrying guns or such. But there was a younger one
too, what was his name? Gene, that was it. See, I
was too old to have anything to do with the boys,
but some as were at school with 'em say they were
a snobby lot, leastways the older ones, Gene I never
heard much about.' He wiped his hand across his
nose, an action which caused the wig to move sideways again. 'Mind, Joe did well out of the shop,
according to what I heard. Good businessman, and
the boys must be too. Wonderful thing, being able
to make money, never could learn the trick of it
myself. But they was a snobby lot.'

By the end of the fifties Arthur had married and
gone to work for a firm of electrical engineers in
London. Donald would then have been in his mid-
teens and Rex three years younger, so that much of
what he was saying must be secondhand gossip. He
had returned to this curious job in the post office as
a widower, only ten years ago.

Friends of the Calendar family? Arthur knew of
none, didn't believe they existed, and he knew

nothing of any Calendar connection with a nursing or residential home. Catchpole was beginning to think his half hour in Parcels had been a waste of time when he asked if Arthur knew the name of Layman. The gnome smacked his hands together, the gesture resettling his wig.

'That's it, Dr Layman. My mum used to take me to him when I had a sore throat, always getting sore throats till I had me tonsils out, not that they take 'em out now, stick these grommets in kids' ears – '

'What about Dr Layman? Did he have some connection with the Calendars?'

'Course he did, don't know how I could have forgotten. Thick as thieves he was with Joe Calendar, so my mum used to say.' Arthur tapped his nose. 'Those days, late forties, year or two after, things was still rationed. That was for the rest of us, but did the doctor go short? Not on your life. My mum said it was a scandal, doctor's car'd be round the back entrance to the shop and Joe'd come out, put cartons of stuff in the back, piece of good ham maybe, dozen eggs, all sorts of things we never even saw. Wicked.' Catchpole asked why they were so friendly. 'I dunno, think it maya been something to do with the kids being ill, can't remember. But Dr Layman getting ham and eggs from Joe Calendar, that was all round the Valley, everyone knew about it. No use thinking you can talk to the doctor, he's long ago gone upstairs, or more likely down. His brother George still lives here though, up on the Hill. And now, if you'll forgive me, I better be getting back to me figures.' He was adjusting the paper cuffs on his wrists when Catchpole left him, the wig perfectly aligned on his head.

In the outer office they knew George Layman's address. Like Arthur Timms, the young assistant who gave it to him said Layman lived on the Hill, and Catchpole found himself driving up what had once evidently been a green slope of considerable extent, but was now spotted by bungalows, some of them in standard red brick, others with the toytown or Legoland appearance to be found in London's Dock-lands, a few mock-Moorish with arched entrances. There were even one or two designed to look like Palladian villas, with fluted columns flanking the front doors. Little roads ran like ribbons between the bungalows. This was the newer, better, richer part of New Valley, and it was shopless. The shops were down the Hill, in and around the High Street.

Catchpole pressed the bell button at a modest red brick bungalow, and a few moments later was confronting George Layman (Lt-Col, retired) in a small square sitting room full of military memor-abilia. The walls were covered with long rectangular photographs of soldiers lined up in rows like school-boys, along with smaller ones of upright shape show-ing no more than two or three figures. A small glass-covered case contained medals displayed on velvet, and its fellow case in another corner housed toby jugs shaped to the features of Wellington, Roberts, Montgomery and others Catchpole could not ident-ify. The man sitting opposite him, back stiff as a ruler even though he was in an armchair, wore his summer-weight light grey suit as if it were a uniform, double-breasted jacket buttoned, trousers with a knife-edge crease. He was a tallish man with a small face, the features neat and regular, the mouth an uncompromising straight line. When he said, 'You'll take a little whisky, Superintendent', the words were an order rather than a question. A surprisingly deep voice came from the narrow frame, its tone staccato. Catchpole took a fair-sized tot of whisky, sipped, nodded appreciation.

'Superintendence,' the voice said. 'That's what we need.' Catchpole waited for explication. It soon came. 'Order. A pattern to life. You're in the forces, y'know there are lines drawn. Stay inside the lines, no one interferes with you, go about your business. Legitimate business. Step outside – ' He smacked little palms together. 'In trouble. Like a brick wall, hit it and you come off worst. Turn around, try another way, you hit the wall again. Smack it two or three times, you learn your lesson. Stay inside the lines.'

'That brick wall sounds very much like prison.'

'Exactly.' He earned a nod of approval. 'In war the armed forces drew the lines. Now it has to be the police. Wish I could feel they were making a good job of it, though the man Calendar has some ideas that could work. Agree?' Catchpole said he hadn't thought about it and earned another nod, not of approval. 'Loss of nerve everywhere. You're not the first, y'know.'

'Not the first what?'

'Said on the telephone you wanted to talk about brother Ralph. Telling you, you're not the first. A couple of days ago there was a man here asking about brother Ralph. Politician, didn't take to him. Name of Bannock.'

'Bernard Bannock. He died last night after a car accident.'

'Didn't take to him, as I say. No loss, like most

politicians. Mind if I smoke?' The side table on which the whisky decanter stood held also a row of pipes. The Colonel selected one of these, filled it with tobacco, struck a Swan Vesta. Blue smoke curled up. The procedure took almost a minute. Was its purpose to conceal surprise at Bannock's death? On the whole Catchpole thought the retired Colonel simply liked to create an atmosphere of mystery and confusion. He asked what Bannock had wanted to know.

'Must understand about Ralph. He was my younger brother, brilliant, passed out of medical school with all sorts of honours, could have specialized. Went to a decent school like me, wanted to go in for doctoring, never could understand it. Doctoring it was, though. Trouble was, Ralph could never stay inside the lines. Had an affair with a patient, lucky not to be struck off, always short of money, hard drinker. Became a GP.' The Colonel's little nose wrinkled in distaste. 'Hobnobbing with shopkeepers like the Calendars, can't do that sort of thing, lets the side down.' Catchpole asked again what Bannock had wanted to know.

'Coming to that. Got to understand Ralph first, though. This politician feller, wanted to know about the Calendars, knew quite a bit about them already. Famous now, don't mean that. He knew about their past history, the scandal. You understand me?' Sharp eyes looked at him above the pipe smoke. Catchpole said he knew nothing about any scandal, got the approving nod. 'Wasn't any scandal. Would have been except Ralph hushed it up, he and Joe Calendar together. I was on a gunnery course a few miles away at Hythe, saw quite a bit of Ralph then, pleased as Punch with what he'd done. Thought he was wrong then, know that's so now. Stay inside the lines, I say. But he got away with it.'

'What happened?'

'You have to understand Ralph and Joe Calendar were very friendly, Lord knows why—' Catchpole broke in to say he knew about the extras loaded into Ralph Layman's car, and got a glare of disapproval. The Colonel did not care to be interrupted, nor to be reminded of disobliging facts. 'Joe Calendar, whatever you say about him, he knew where he thought his lines should be drawn, made sure the family knew it too. Only the youngest one, Gene, often stepped outside and got punished for it. Could be he was sometimes punished for what the other lads did, but Joe Calendar didn't care about that.

'One of Gene's friends, he didn't have many, was a boy called Billy Hinckley. Always together, these days there'd be talk about sex.' The little face screwed up as if at the taste of bitter peach kernel. 'No stuff and nonsense of that sort then. They were, what, nine or ten years old, always together, Billy a few months older than Gene, and from what Ralph said when he told me the story quite a lot brighter. Billy the leader, Gene the follower, did what he was told, got in a few scrapes because of it. So when Billy Hinckley disappeared, naturally enough Gene was questioned. If it was today your fellers would have half a dozen do-gooders there before they'd start asking a boy that age questions, then they didn't wear kid gloves. Soon realized little Gene was lying his head off. First said he hadn't seen Billy that day, then that they'd been together but Billy'd gone off on his own. Couple of other boys had seen 'em together though, heard 'em quarrelling about a knife, one of those Swiss knives with several little blades, corkscrew and so on, Gene wanted to use it, Billy said no. One of these boys saw 'em fighting, Billy crying out for help. He'd tried to separate 'em, Billy had run away and Gene went after him shouting something about killing him. According to Ralph, Gene wasn't violent except when he got his rag out, then just couldn't stay inside the lines. Know the New Valley Canal?'

Catchpole said no. The Colonel's tobacco was pungent, the room seemed full of it, he coughed. The small head nodded, pipe was removed from what could be briefly glimpsed as brownish-yellow teeth, the hint of a satisfied smile showed. 'Mixture a bit strong for you? Not many able to appreciate it. Never mind.' The pipe's replacement in its rack was in some way a symbolic victory for Colonel Layman.

'Half a mile from here, no more, the canal. Where they found Billy Hinckley's body. Drowned, but had some bruises on head and shoulders. Could have been caused when he fell in the canal. Or earlier. In a fight. No money in his pockets, but his parents said he'd been given pocket money that morning. Only a shilling a week or something like it, father worked on the railway, but it had gone. No money on Gene either, Joe Calendar never gave any to him, said he'd only spend it on sweets. But what he had got was Billy's Swiss knife. Said Billy had lent it to him, but he'd told two or three different stories already.' He looked expectantly at the detective.

'So?'

'Exactly. *So* that was all. Billy drowned, Gene

telling stories any or none of which could have been true. What would you have done?'

'On what you've told me, if that's all, nothing. Anyway, of course Gene was too young to be charged with murder.'

'Just so.' Small hands were rubbed together. 'Spoken like an officer of the law. I'll tell you what I'd have done. I'd have shut the little devil up in a room and fed him bread and water until I was sure he'd told me the truth about what happened that day. Step outside the lines as he did, and you're in trouble. Stay inside, and you have my backing.'

It occurred to Catchpole that Colonel Layman was perhaps short of one or two coppers in the shilling, but it seemed pointless to argue with him. Instead he asked what any of this had to do with Ralph Layman. The Colonel, who had been leaning forward so far that it looked as if some buttons on his suit would burst, now relaxed and smiled foxily. Saying that policemen nowadays were as gutless as they had been more than three decades ago evidently satisfied him. His manner changed to one of positive geniality, although a geniality laced with contempt.

'The connection of Dr Ralph Layman, my brilliant brother, with this affair was that of a master bodger. At the inquest the verdict was accidental death. Nothing to suggest otherwise, the coroner said. The boy who gave evidence about the fight and Gene's threat to kill Billy turned out to be a teller of fancy tales, liked to be in the limelight. But that wasn't the end of it. Billy's family, they were certain there'd been a fight, and that Gene had pushed Billy in the canal. They wanted him put away to await release at Her Majesty's pleasure, talked about bringing a private prosecution. And it wasn't just Billy's family, Ralph told me when he was crowing about what he'd done, lots of the villagers thought so too. Some of 'em started to boycott Calendar's shop, even though it meant going into Sevenoaks. Business fell off, the boys got called names, had stones thrown at 'em. So what does my brother Ralph do? He gets the young villain committed to a home. Not a mental home, wasn't called that, but somewhere he'd be shut up and not seen around New Valley. Joe Calendar reckoned it would be out of sight, out of mind, and he was right. Within a few months Hinckley lost his job and the family moved away, Calendar's wife died and then he keeled over himself, the shop was sold. But what my clever brother did – ' He shook his head. ' – It was against my idea of justice, unforgivable.'

'What happened to Gene, did your brother visit him?' The Colonel shrugged narrow shoulders. 'What was the name of the home?'

'Did Ralph visit him? Probably not. After the affair was over, brother Ralph stayed away from the Calendar family, started drinking hard, got mixed up with some damn woman. Knew he'd strayed outside the lines, done what he shouldn't have.'

'He could have seen Calendar, told him he'd made a mistake, the boy shouldn't have been committed to a home.'

Layman glared at him. 'Why not commit him? He'd killed another boy, very likely. Shouldn't he have been punished, that what you're saying?'

Catchpole gave up the attempt at argument. 'What happened to your brother? And what was the name of the home?'

'Place called Caldington Hall, forty or fifty miles away from here in Sussex. Ralph told me the boy wouldn't have minded, he was fairly simple, best place for him perhaps, though said to be fairly tough. Closed a few years later, no surprise, the way some of these private places are run is scandalous. This one was a sort of school, school with a touch of prison.' The sharp little eyes peered at him, the voice was lowered. 'Something else about the boy, Gene, something Ralph told me. He liked to expose himself, his person. Especially to the other sex.'

'And Ralph?'

'Practice fell off, went on drinking.' The Colonel looked down at his well-polished shoes. 'Came to me for help. Told him he'd gone outside the lines over this business and over his woman patient. Have to take the consequences.'

'Which were?'

'Said I couldn't help.' His voice had dropped almost to a whisper. 'Couple of weeks later he cut his throat.' There was the sound of a door closing. In the same near whisper he said, 'My wife.'

The woman who appeared in the doorway was twice his size, and twenty years his junior. She made waving gestures. 'Smoke, smoke, so thick you could cut it. And you've been drinking. Who are you?'

The last words were directed at Catchpole, who told her who he was. Colonel Layman rose from his chair, went towards her with arms outstretched. They embraced. He was choking with sobs, she made soothing sounds, said to Catchpole: 'Ralph?' He nodded. 'Always upsets him. I think you'd better go.'

★

'I don't feel the least bit sorry for the Colonel,' Alice said when he told her the story the following evening as they sat in the only bit of the garden not overlooked by neighbours, eating Brazil nuts and drinking port. They had already indulged themselves with a chicken risotto with bits of sausage and bacon added, accompanied by a powerful Barolo, and in Catchpole's case preceded by two vodka gimlets. 'But I do for the boy. Poor little sod. Just wanting to get him out of sight I can understand, but practically disowning him, expelling him from the family, that I can't. Real bastards, those Calendars. Do you know what happened to him?'

'Maggie Steel's working on it, but no luck so far. Caldington Hall, which seems to have been a kind of tough school-cum-reformatory, folded in the middle sixties. The husband and wife who ran it, name of Pumphrey, are thought to have emigrated to New Zealand after running out of money. These aren't facts, just rumours and stories from old timers at the local cop shop, but at least the old timers knew nothing serious against Caldington Hall, except that it was supposed to be a fairly tough regime. If there are any records, like a roll of those placed there with reasons given, Maggie hasn't found it yet. From the obsessed way the Colonel talked about his brother's part in getting Gene put there, I'd say the odds are Dr Layman was handsomely paid by Joe Calendar for arranging it. Maybe Bannock somehow traced him from there to Roselands, did some guessing and happened to guess right. Or someone thought he had.'

The air was soft as velvet. Moths flew around the lantern that lighted their garden table, the bottle and

half-full glasses, the bowl of nuts. 'The Mediter-
ranean, who wants it?' Catchpole said.

Alice sipped port, crunched a nut audibly. 'Hilly,
you're not going soft on me, I hope. Don't tell me
that unsentimental hard man's got marshmallow for
a heart.'

They were both laughing when they heard the
sound of breaking glass. Catchpole jumped up and
went to the house. Alice followed him. The stained-
glass window in the doorway of the former Victorian
chapel was broken, and bits of glass were scattered
about the hallway along with the half-brick that had
done the damage. Cars were passing in the road, but
nobody was to be seen on foot. From the Common
fifty yards away came shrieks and shouts and the
sound of a ghetto-blaster. The brick thrower could
be up there, could be hiding in a front garden near
by. Either way there was no point in trying to find
him – or her. Catchpole went into the house. Lights
were on at the top of the stairs. Alan called: 'What's
up?' and Alice told him. 'Is that all?' he said, disappointed, and went back to bed.

With the glass swept up and the front door's gap
replaced by cardboard, they returned to the garden.
'Just kids,' Alice said. 'I know you thought that
stained-glass window was hideous, maybe it wasn't
there when the place was a chapel, just a later
addition, but I liked it. Why do kids now have
to be such bloody little vandals?' She added as an
afterthought: 'Some of them.'

'May not have been kids. Could have been a bad
lad who's crossed my path and didn't like it. Or
someone who knows a copper lives here and has it
in for all coppers. All quiet now on the chapel front,

but you go a few yards up the road to the Common and there the bad lads'll be, rowing in pubs, leaving them half-cut all ready to lay one on the first black or Paki they see who's on his own, and what can we do about it? Talk to the ones who've been on the receiving end, ask if they can make any identifications, five times out of ten they can't and the other five they're too frightened. That's what's just up the road, just round the corner. *This*' − he drained his glass and refilled it, made a gesture embracing trees and bushes glowing dark green in the lamplight − 'is an illusion.'

'Hilly, you're depressing me. What are you going to do about the missing Calendar? Ask the Home Secretary what's happened to him? Don't just shake your head, tell me. And I think you've had enough port.'

'As to what I'll do, I've got a nasty feeling I'm just being used in some way, being told half-truths or quarter-truths or downright lies. So what I'll do is play it straight, tell the Big Man what I've found out or been told, and leave him to do what he wants with it. I think this whole thing might really be all about politics, and a copper should have no politics.'

'So you've told me. More than once.'

'And you should never comment on a copper's drinking habits, didn't you know that? All right, no more port. Somehow it's been a nasty day. Let's go to bed.'

They went to bed.

TWELVE

The End of a Story

'SEVENTY CERTAIN, ninety possible.'

'We might get twenty NatLibs. More would be hoping.'

'Too prissy to commit themselves. See how the cat jumps, maybe I would and maybe I wouldn't, circumstances alter cases, all that shit.'

Four backbench MPs were breakfasting in Bruvvers, a flashy up-to-the-minute version of an eighteenth-century coffee-house, with sporting prints around the walls. All were supporters of the Calendar movement to Make Britain Modern, and they came from the North-east, Midlands and South-east. Ratchet, who had sponsored their unofficial soundings, was a Londoner. He said now to the young waiter: 'My usual, Earl Grey, no milk, wholemeal brown toast.' The waiter tossed his head, nodded, and left them. The others had already ordered.

Ratchet looked like an eager-eyed rat. His little nose constantly twitched and he always smiled even when, as now, the news was not what he wanted to hear. His voice was gentle. 'So the numbers don't add up, they don't love King Rex,' he said.

The three looked uneasy. North-east said, 'It's not love, it's trust. They don't trust him.'

Midlands elaborated. 'They like the idea of
arming the police with those little pistols providing
they test out, lot of support for that. The Devil's
Island idea, they mostly think that's way out, will
never happen. New roads, mostly in favour. It's personal really.'

'Lots of admiration. Splendid Home Secretary.
But PM – ' South-east shook his head.

Ratchet said nothing. Breakfast came. Ratchet
gave a disapproving glance at the plate of bacon, eggs
and sausages ordered by Midland. 'I'm disappointed.'

South-east, the boldest of them, said: 'So am I.'

'Perhaps you didn't ask the right questions. About
King Rex.'

'Straightforward enough. If Bladon dropped dead
tomorrow, would you support the Home Secretary
for PM?'

'Didn't put it quite that way.' Midlands spoke
through a mouthful of egg and bacon. 'I asked
whether they sympathized with Making Britain
Modern, the whole package, and almost all said yes.
But when it came to the point of trusting King Rex
to do it – ' He shook his head.

Ratchet, a delicate drinker, sipped his tea. 'Perhaps I didn't make myself clear. What I wanted to
find out was, if the Prime Minister should unhappily,
perhaps for reasons of health, feel he must step
down, who would they support for PM. I wanted
the inquiry to be impartial, not with a question
attached like, "Would you support X or Y
for PM?" '

'Can't see it makes a blind bit of difference how
you put it,' South-east said.

'The difference is that between a shot directed

from a Purdy and one sprayed from a blunderbuss. To ask NatLib members whether they might join a government headed by King Rex – ' He shook his head sadly. Midlands flinched, looked doubtfully at his plate of food. 'Still, there may be something to be said for stirring the waters.' Rat-eyes flicked from one to another of them. 'The research is useful, thank you for it. And keep alert. Things may happen in the next day or two, week or two. Your expert advice could be needed.' The little nose twitched, left and right. It was a signal for their departure.

When they had gone Ratchet finished his tea and toast, and before he left Bruvvers made an appointment to meet the young waiter for a drink that evening. Unwise, he knew, but he felt he deserved a little fun. Then he went to break the news gently to Rex Calendar that if by any chance the PM gave up, the result of a leadership contest would be far from a foregone conclusion.

'No,' the Chief Whip said. 'Not about Bullington. He's been brought to heel. He'll behave himself in future.'

He spoke with less than his usual exuberant cockiness. Bladon looked out of the study window at Jenkins making a dexterous turn on the motor-mower. Some of the roses were already a little over-blown, summer would soon be gone, why was he not out there walking down to the stream alleged to be full of trout, very few of which he had caught?

'If it's not Bullington, what brings you here at a weekend? What's so important or secret that we can't talk about it on a private line?'

'There are no private lines now, Prime Minister, they can all be tapped. In any case I thought it would be better for me to see you. I suppose you have no idea – ' He was uncharacteristically uncomfortable.

Bladon said sharply: 'You may take it that I have no idea of what you are going to tell me. So don't keep me in suspense.'

'I should stress that it can't be confirmed. I can't offer an absolutely factual basis for it.' He paused. 'The story is that Clarissa's having an affair. One of Donald Calendar's papers is said to have letters. I've seen what purport to be copies of them.'

'Clarissa,' Bladon repeated. His first emotion was incredulity. The idea of his fashion model in bed with another man seemed preposterous. The wife of some other Cabinet minister, yes, but Clarissa – no, that was not possible. 'The letters could be forgeries.'

'Perhaps.'

'Is there any other evidence, photographs?'

'No photographs. But one of Clarissa's assistants, some sort of secretary, and her former chauffeur, have talked to the paper. So it's said.'

'You say former chauffeur, and I suppose former secretary. Clarissa may have sacked them.'

'That's perfectly possible. Even likely. But they've told their stories.'

'Who is—' He stopped himself. 'Who are these letters supposedly written to?'

'The name is Manning Strong. An American. He's some sort of expert on costume, been helping Clarissa to put on exhibitions. I understand they met in the States when she was over there early last year, and for the past few months he's been in this country. It's possible you may have met him.'

And indeed the name did bring to mind a face, broad and open, and a voice with a Southern drawl. A young man, younger than Clarissa and twenty years or more his junior. The name brought back an exhibition called something like 'Costume Through the Centuries', the idea being to contrast American and British dress. He was aware that the Chief Whip had spoken, his voice subdued.

'Prime Minister, we have to take this seriously. It's no use just crying forgery, I'm afraid there's no room for doubting the letters are genuine, or about the nature of the relationship. They were presumably stolen from Strong's London flat. The letters suggest the affair started in the States, partly the reason he came over here. He's oil-rich, doesn't know how much he's worth to a million or two.' He ended lamely: 'I thought you should know about it.'

'Of course.'

'You'll talk to Clarissa.' Bladon said he would. The Chief Whip became confidential, dropped the 'Prime Minister' as he said: 'Patrick, would you like me to stay around so that we can discuss the possibilities after you've spoken to Clarissa? You understand, it's not Edward and Mrs Simpson any longer, you can't keep the lid on anything now. If we tried to, it would be leaked deliberately, especially since it's in the hands of a Calendar paper.'

'I understand that. I have a few wits left, I can see how pressure may be put on.' He said it had been good of the Chief Whip to come down, and he appreciated the offer to stay but felt that after speaking to Clarissa he would like a little time to think about his own course of action before talking about it with anybody at all.

When he was alone Bladon went into the garden and walked down to the trout stream, but he looked on the dartingly visible fish without pleasure, almost unseeingly. Clarissa was up in London shopping – it occurred to him that she spent much less time at Deemings than she had done a few years ago – and he passed the afternoon looking through the material relating to the Australian PM's visit, and trying to understand some financial calculations prepared for him by Rhoda's staff, which seemed to relate to something called the E factor and its detrimental effect on the F balance. What was the F balance, why should the E factor (which was unsurprisingly connected with the extent of national commitment to what was called a fully integrated Europe) affect them so greatly? He started to put queries and exclamation marks against some of the figures, then reflected that he could ask Rhoda to explain them next week in the financial equivalent of single-syllable words, and desisted.

Clarissa returned in the Daimler just after six, then bathed and changed for dinner as she invariably did at Deemings. He spoke to her after Mary Miles brought in the coffee, and he knew they would be undisturbed. She listened carefully to his retailing of the Chief Whip's story, then spoke.

'I was afraid of something like this when I heard the letters had gone. Of course Manning realizes he was careless, they should have been under lock and key.'

'*Careless.*' He stared at her. 'It's all true, then. You're having an affair with this American.'

'Why, yes. Is it so surprising? After all, our relationship – ' She shrugged white shoulders, didn't complete the sentence. 'And he's not just *this Ameri-can*, you've met him two or three times. Of course I'm sorry the letters have got into the hands of Rex Calendar's brother. I know you have to be involved with such people, but really – ' She left that sentence too unfinished, looked away from him. Her profile seemed to him breathtakingly beautiful, with the remoteness, inhumanity, that he associated with per-fect beauty. What right did an ordinary errant human have to criticize anything so physically flawless?

But that emotion was succeeded by indignation that it should be she, the daughter of a businessman who had used her to take a step up the social scale, who should adopt the role of one unwillingly descending into the sordid bargaining of the market-place. Yet as a politician he knew genuine anger, distinct from the synthetic article anybody in public life knew how to produce, to be a self-defeating, useless emotion. He had sometimes thought self-control his greatest political asset, and knew it would be pointless now to upbraid Clarissa for having this affair, or complain that she might have found a lover who would take care of amatory correspondence rather than leaving it to be stolen. Yet when he said, 'You never really loved Deemings, did you?' he did not intend to utter those particular words or voice that thought, and when she replied that she found it pleasant but on the whole rather dull, he felt no anger but only sadness.

'If you could have understood something of what I felt for this place – it has meant more to me than anything else in my life. But that simply wasn't possible. For a long while I hoped it might be, but then I understood that for you it wasn't possible.'

'Any more than it was possible for you to love a woman. Don't look at me like that, Patrick, you know it's true. Only two things have ever really meant anything to you, getting to the top in politics and this place. A wife? Useful for playing hostess, perhaps a plus if political friends found her attractive, extremely handy that she brought some money. In fact you might say that was indispensable. But love? No doubt you've heard of it.'

'Clarissa, I don't want to quarrel.' He found it in him to smile. 'I really admire the way you turn things upside down. It's you who've taken a lover, but it's also you who have a grievance. No politician could do better.'

Her next words surprised him. 'What about you?'

'I don't understand you.'

'I'm told you spend long evenings alone with your Chancellor. Are you discussing finance all the time?'

'Rhoda? That's preposterous. I can assure you – but you can't be serious.' She said nothing. 'Let me repeat, I don't want to quarrel, I just want you to realize this is a serious situation. For you as well as for me. And for your American. I don't suppose he'll want to find himself on the front pages of the tabloids.'

'He may be resigned to publicity. I think I am too, although of course I'd be pleased if it could be avoided. I don't think *you* understand the situation. We want to get married.'

'Get married?' He was astonished.

'Manning's just been divorced from his wife in the States, that was the only thing holding us up. I was planning to tell you in the next few days, then you could have sued for divorce, case uncontested, all done with the minimum of publicity. Afterwards we plan to live in Connecticut with an apartment in New York, so we'd be out of the way, out of any limelight. The whole thing would be forgotten in a couple of months, and you could find another chatelaine for this place. That would be the right word, don't you think? Manning's carelessness about the letters makes a difference, and I'm sorry about it, but if I were you I'd get the lawyers moving straight away.'

He recovered quickly from the shock of what she was telling him, and recognized the strategic advantage in what she was suggesting. If the story appeared in one of Donald Calendar's papers along with paraphrased passages from the letters (the letters were still Clarissa's copyright, so that no direct quotation could be made from them without her permission) it would be an embarrassment, no doubt of that, but with an uncontested divorce action already in train it would be no more than a nine-day, or even a weekend wonder. The Calendar guns would be neatly spiked, and the Downing Street publicity machine might manage to make him a sympathetic victim rather than a comic cuckold. He got up and stood with his back to the fireplace, below the portrait of his great-great-grandfather painted by Sir Thomas Lawrence. The Patrick Bladon of the picture was a young man standing beside his horse, a couple of dogs looking up at him. He smiled confidently like a potential conqueror of the world, although he had in fact become a Tory MP with some minor post under Melbourne or

Peel. The present Patrick resembled him strikingly when young, and was pleased even now when the family resemblance was remarked.

Yet even as he stood there agreeing that yes, it might do, and avoiding Clarissa's amused or ironic look, he was conscious of a sinking spirit, a doubt about whether he was really braced for all the snide comments and jokey asides, the pestering of journalists, the personal pieces about the breakdown of their marriage and about Bladon the lonely man, the linking of him with any woman to whom he paid the slightest attention, perhaps even echoing that preposterous suggestion about Rhoda. Could he face all that? He responded brusquely to Clarissa when she said they must both be prepared, and so must Manning (she never forgot Manning), for a ride on the media roundabout in the next weeks, but she was pleased he agreed her suggestion to be by far the best solution. The brusqueness came in part from a feeling that she had created the problem, he was the wronged person, and it was not for her to suggest solutions. He said he had not made up his mind what to do. Then, with uncharacteristic impoliteness, he left her at the dining-table.

Back in his bedroom – for years now they had parted company at night – he felt a lassitude so overwhelming that he was barely able to summon up energy to brush his teeth, remove clothes, put on pyjamas. Was he ill? Sir Grately Lamp, who came down to Deemings once a month, and supervised some hospital tests every quarter, occasionally said he should take a little more exercise or suggested a more fibrous diet, but his general summary was always that the PM was in what he called fine fettle.

The opinion, repeated many times, had brought Sir Grately his knighthood, but was it right? As he lay in bed he wondered exactly what branch of medicine it was that Sir Grately specialized in, and whether it was one that took into account overwhelming lassitude as a significant symptom. Thinking about possible ailments, not at all about Clarissa and her American lover, he fell asleep.

Faz folded his hands across his stomach. 'I said to you before, Mr Catchpole, that a client's confidentiality has to be preserved, and that's so whether the client is one of the most important in the land or one of the humblest. The names of the directors of the residential home you're interested in have been properly registered as they should be, and if you want to know more about Roselands I suggest you approach them.'

'I've done so already. There's a City type who's concerned simply to keep an eye on Roselands' accounts, and a woman who helps to run a society for the mentally handicapped, and is full of gush about the home. And the third director, Mobey, turns out to be one of your clerks. Why should Mobey be a director of a residential home?'

'Because the owners want an eye kept to see the place is running along the right rails. There were some problems in the past, I expect you know that. Mobey's a little terrier I can tell you, pokes his nose into everything.' A fat hand waved up at the ceiling, which was marked with cracks like roads on a map. It bulged ominously in a couple of places where main roads met. 'Mobey's upstairs. I'll call him down, have a word with him if you like.'

'Would it do me any good?'

'I doubt it. The principle of confidentiality – '

'Fuck the principle of confidentiality. You're concealing information that could be of importance in a murder inquiry. I'm not threatening you, just think you don't realize the trouble you may be landing yourself in.'

'I'll tell you what I realize.' When Faz leaned forward part of his stomach bulged over the top of the desk. 'If I gave you names, even if I knew them, which I'm not admitting for a moment, I'd be breaking faith with my clients. And that's something I'd never do, Catchers, not even for you.'

Catchpole gestured at the bulging ceiling. 'Don't blame me if this whole building collapses and buries you under the rubble. I'll tell you something else. What goes on here stinks, and it isn't just the dry rot.'

Laughter bubbled out of Fazackerley, all of his three chins shook. 'That's not polite, Catchers, you've lost your temper.'

'Which is more or less correct,' Catchpole said to the Big Man. 'I was trying to provoke him into telling me something, but had no luck.'

The Big Man nodded. 'So we don't know who's putting up the money for this place Roselands. Does it matter? Run through it for me, tell me why it's so important.'

'We're looking for the killer of Lily Devon. That's what the case is about, or what it *was* about in the first place. We're provided with a patsy, someone who's been set up for the killing, only I happen to be able to give him an alibi. The set-up's been arranged through Faz, who's done it or so he says because he was asked to by the crime man on the *Bulletin*. Faz wouldn't stick his neck out like that for a crime reporter, but he might for Donald Calendar, who owns the *Bulletin*. Next, Bannock's murder – and there's no doubt it *was* murder. Bannock had been digging away at the background of the Calendar family, hoping to find something the NatLibs could use to discredit Rex Calendar. He'd rung the Pitcombes not long before his death to say he'd discovered something that would drive Rex Calendar out of politics.'

'No hint as to what it might be?'

'No hint. But he's been asking questions at this residential home, Roselands, one of those places where the well-to-do send relatives who're troublesome because they're either just a bit gaga or somewhere further round the bend. I talked to the woman doctor who runs the place, and to a man called Larkins who's a sort of general factotum and seemed pretty efficient. Nothing wrong with Roselands that I could see, except maybe families should look after their own as they did in the past.' The Big Man raised a tolerant eyebrow at this eccentricity. 'But the point is that this is another link to the Calendars. I expect you know the story about their father running a general store in a village built post-war near Sevenoaks – '

'Humble origins, one of life's success stories, yes.'

'I went to the village, only it's not that any more, talked to the brother of the local doctor. The doctor's long dead, killed himself. It turns out there was a third Calendar boy named Gene, youngest of the brothers, not very bright, quiet most of the time but occasionally went a bit wild, seems to have been badly treated by the family. It's possible that when Gene was ten he killed another boy, fought with him, then pushed him in a canal.'

'It came to court?'

'No. The local doctor, friend of the Calendars, got him put into a sort of tough reformatory school. Used another name, and sounds as though the father and mother washed their hands of Gene. The school went out of existence long ago, we haven't yet been able to trace any records and don't know what happened to Gene.'

'And you're suggesting he may be at this place, Roselands? That seems to be making a quite unjustified jump. What's the connection?'

'The connection is the Calendars, sir. OK, I know we've got no positive proof they're linked with the home, it's all been handled by Faz, but just make the assumption Gene's at Roselands under some other name and had something to do with Lily Devon's death that his brothers wouldn't want made public, and it explains everything. Bannock must have been on to it, from what he said to Pitcombe's wife. There are three or four men at Roselands about the age Gene will be now, in his forties, and we have to find out if any of them is a likely candidate. Maggie Steel's working on it.'

'But it's perfectly possible that Gene Calendar, or whatever he calls himself, left this country long ago and is settled in Australia or New Zealand or elsewhere. Or that he's dead.'

'Then why are the brothers so concerned to cover up what's happened? What's their interest in Roselands, why are they using a villain like Fazackerley?'

'I take the point. But you haven't told me why Gene would go on that murderous escapade with Lily Devon.'

'I should have mentioned that Gene liked to expose himself to both sexes when he was a young boy. And he'd have had no problem in leaving Roselands, inmates are encouraged to go out on their own providing they don't cause any trouble. If he got to Sevenoaks, the nearest railway, a train gets you to central London in half an hour.'

'That's a long way from showing he's a murderer. And what would his reason be for killing Bannock?'

'I'm guessing. But Bannock must have found out something that marked Gene conclusively as Lily Devon's killer.'

The Big Man looked troubled. He got up, presented his broad back to the detective as he looked down on Broadway. He stared down at the scurrying people for perhaps half a minute, and when he turned round he was smiling. He came over, patted Catchpole on the shoulder, returned again behind his desk.

'Full marks for ingenuity, but you must know yourself it's like a magic cloak woven out of air. If someone gave a puff it would blow away. No, don't interrupt me and say inquiries are still going on, I know that perfectly well. The point is, you're full of theories that sound as enticing as a tub of Häagen-Dazs on a hot day, but you're uncommonly short on fact. You *think* the Calendar brothers are mixed up in this but there's not a shred of proof, you think Gene Calendar was responsible for two murders but you haven't convinced me he even exists.'

'I understand that, sir.' (He did not add, *as well as you do.*) 'You wanted a report on how far the investigation has progressed, and I've given it you.' He looked directly at the Big Man. 'I wanted you to be clear about the way in which inquiries are moving, in which my ideas are moving. And to consider the possible consequences. I know these are still only possibilities, sir, but I thought you would like to know about them. Whether this line of inquiry is pursued is a matter for you.'

The Big Man beamed. 'Catchers, my dear fellow, don't misunderstand me. It's a fault of mine to go off half cock and say more than I mean.' Nothing, Catchpole knew from experience, could be further from the truth. Everything the Big Man said was calculated in advance. 'Of course you must pursue this line of inquiry, as you call it, no matter where it leads. You're a man of tact and sensibility, you know this is an area in which you should tread delicately. But if it comes down to the line, if there's proof of the involvement of any individual in these killings, no matter who it is, justice plays no favourites. For the present, though, we're still in the land of theory and we keep all this to ourselves. And remember that to you I'm available at any time.' Another beam. 'I was delighted to hear any domestic problems you had have been solved. I know Alice very little, but enough to be aware that she has a mind of her own.'

Catchpole agreed that this was certainly true, and departed. When he had gone the Big Man wondered how what he had been told might be useful to him. Was the Home Secretary aware that the AC Crime really was an old woman, not up to the job, and should be replaced? Would it be a good idea to make clear that an ideal replacement was sitting in this chair, already doing the most important part of the AC's work? Might it be possible, even, to go for the big one, Commissioner of the Metropolitan Police? The Commissioner's health was not good, there had been rumours about his possible early retirement, and while it was usual for the new Commissioner to come from outside the Met there was no law that this should be so . . . At this point he rebuked himself for day-dreaming.

Johnno heard the news on the radio, first with disbelief, then horror. When Belinda got back from her dress shop she found him slumped on a sofa, on what he admitted was his third gin. She had read about Bannock's death in the paper, but it had made no impression on her. Now she said: 'So what?'

'George did it. Or had it done.'

'Nonsense.'

'He must have done, it can't be a coincidence, it's absurd to think so. And I'm responsible, that's what's so awful. I've tried to get in touch with RC, can't locate him. And of course George has vanished. What shall I do, Bel, what do you think I should do?'

'Start thinking straight to begin with. I'm sure it's moonshine, anyway, about George – no, don't ask me how I explain it, I can't, just don't believe anything he says. And what's the point of talking to your boss, what d'you think he's going to say? Well done my boy, just what the doctor ordered? Just stay shtum, calm down.'

'I had to tell somebody. I even thought of going to the police.'

'Think again, they'll laugh at you. You had to tell somebody, OK, you've told me. And I could do with some of that gin. It's been a hard day, and I didn't expect to come back to hear you confessing incitement to murder. I suppose that would be the charge, don't you? For God's sake don't look like that, I'm joking.' A couple of drinks later she said: 'You really are a stupid old beanbag, aren't you? Shouldn't be let out on your own.'

The telephone rang. Johnno looked at it, whispered, 'George. To say the job's done.'

Belinda picked it up, made a face, said ironically, 'RC.'

The confident, hectoring voice said: 'Jonathan. You've seen the news. About Bannock.'

'Yes.'

'It calls for some biblical text, don't you think? Something about the Lord smiting one's enemies. You'll think I'm blaspheming, and so I am. I believe you said you might be able to help about Bannock, but of course that won't be necessary. I called chiefly to say I'd like to see you early on Monday morning, nine o'clock. Right? Enjoy your evening.'

Johnno put down the instrument. 'I think he was fishing, trying to find out exactly what I'd done.' Belinda replied that it would be nice if sometimes he believed what people said instead of looking for secret messages.

When he began to say how foolish he had been to tell George Kaiser that Bannock was a problem, she said: 'You're beginning to bore me, I can't listen to this stuff all weekend. Why don't you put me on show?'

'On show?'

'To your family, your *people*. Or would they be too horrified?'

'Bel, what a marvellous idea. I'll call them now, invite ourselves for Sunday lunch. They'll love to see you.'

So it proved. Johnno fenced off his father's questions about the prospect of political changes, and his mother's about his intentions in relation to Belinda. She charmed the Major-General, who said she was a spirited young filly and he wished Johnno the best of luck. Johnno's mother was not quite so approving of the spirit, said there could be only one master in the home and he would have to make sure she understood that. Belinda, both of whose parents had remarried after divorce, said they were sweeties. She was uncharacteristically silent on the return journey, then said: 'Expect you'd say you had a happy childhood. Loving parents and all that.'

'I suppose so, yes.'

'Trouble is, life's not like that. Sometimes I think life's just awful. What about you, beanbag?'

He had the sliding roof of his little Fiat open, and he pointed upwards. 'The sky's blue.'

'I s'pose so.' She sighed. 'I think I love you, beanbag. Thing is, do I want to live with someone I'll have to look after?'

'I'm not a bloody invalid.'

She sighed again, said nothing more. At the apartment there was no sign of George Kaiser.

★

The Bannock affair prompted one of the Pitcombes' rare disagreements. Allen said it was obvious he had picked up a hitchhiker, probably with sex in mind. The man had attacked him, then stolen his briefcase, what could be plainer? Gwenda replied with the unquestionable fact that he had not heard those last words of Bannock's on the telephone. It was absurd to believe that after saying he had found out something discreditable about Rex Calendar he had been murdered by pure coincidence . . . the argument simmered and occasionally bubbled over the weekend. On Monday Gwenda telephoned Scotland Yard again. Catchpole was out, but a subordinate told her inquiries were continuing, a response that led her to complain to Allen of police slowness and inefficiency. He paid little attention, more concerned with rumours floated in a Sunday paper that the Prime Minister was thinking of resigning on health grounds, and speculating on a battle for Number Ten in which he and Rex Calendar would be likely candidates. Like Calendar he had his men out making estimates of possible voting patterns, and the results were not particularly cheerful. But an unexpected blow fell on Tuesday, when he was discussing the nuts and bolts details relating to Gwenda's Welsh land with his solicitor, Geoffrey Langrish.

'Of course, you realize that the clause excluding industrial use means exactly what it says. I mean, there are other uses to which the land could be put that you and Gwenda might not like.' Allen asked what he had in mind. 'Nothing in particular. I'm simply pointing out the possibility.'

'But any project of any size would involve a new main road. The expense would be enormous, and the whole thing might be rejected by the local council.'

'Just so. I only mention it. The price seems handsome.' Allen said with some satisfaction that Gwenda drove a hard bargain, and Langrish acknowledged this with a nod and a smile. He said there was nothing unusual in the draft agreement, and that the other side had been almost surprisingly accommodating in relation to one or two minor points he had raised. 'They gave you no idea of what they intended doing with the land?'

'Why, yes. Hans Kessler is an international celebrity, famous for his belief that animals should be encouraged to live in an environment natural to them. So part of the plan is for a very open zoo. He's also concerned to encourage organic farming. He showed us plans for a zoo and a training college that would leave us very happy.'

'They'd be unlikely to offer a quick return on the capital expenditure involved. Or even a slow one.' Allen said that was not their concern, nor was it likely to be Kessler's. 'But it is Roger Manston's. He hasn't made a fortune by philanthropy. Since he's involved, and apparently the banks are ready to back him, he's got something in mind that could be a quick earner. That doesn't worry you?'

'I don't see why it should. As long as there's no industrial use.'

'I've been asking around here and there about Manston's recent activities – he's the kind of man who's always got something new cooking. One of his schemes, which came to nothing because of problems with the local administration, was for a theme park somewhere near Boulogne.' He paused.

'Another point. His chief partner in that theme park scheme is said to have been Donald Calendar.'

Pitcombe's narrow head reared up. The solicitor went on, choosing his words carefully. 'It's my under-standing from what Gwenda has said to me that Calendar is thinking of making a substantial contri-bution to her Animal Protection League. If he's associated with Manston in buying this land – '

'No need to spell it out,' Allen Pitcombe said. 'But this is all conjecture.'

'Just so, Allen. But conjecture based on one firm fact. Roger Manston is involved in this deal, and he's not in it because of a concern for animal welfare, nor does he have a passion for organic farming. The zoo and the training college are the icing, and you're not meant to look at what may be in the cake.'

'What do you suggest? Extending the clause about industrial development to exclude the possi-bility of anything like a theme park?'

'Obviously you could do that.'

'But then the sale might fall through. Gwenda would be upset. Otherwise I suppose it wouldn't be that important.'

'Perhaps not. Although I think you should bear in mind the possible involvement of Donald Calendar.'

Allen thought for a moment, then said he saw what the lawyer meant. That evening he talked it over with Gwenda. She listened disapprovingly, dip-ping her head occasionally like a long-necked, stately bird. At first she said Geoffrey Langrish was imagin-ing things, making a fuss about nothing.

'I don't think so. Let's assume that we go ahead, and Manston gets permission for his theme park and Calendar gives a hundred thousand or more to your

Animal Protection League. The media are going to say we've sold out, taken a bribe from Calendar, and for all our talk about preserving the countryside we've sold our land for a theme park.'

She said reluctantly that she could refuse Calendar's money and condemn the theme park, saying they'd been tricked.

'Then we shall look like fools.'

Gwenda looked down her long nose, an effect not lacking dignity, as he continued remorselessly. 'They have us over a barrel. Go ahead and the media will say we've forgotten our principles, sold out. Do the other thing, insist on a clause which will stop any kind of commercial development and tell Calendar we don't want his money. The deal falls through, and the media will say we're killjoys who want to stop people having harmless fun, and the money's been turned down out of pique.'

'That would be only in Calendar's papers, surely?' But still she knew *the media* to be a terrible threat, a dragon that delighted above all to crunch up politicians. They were the dragon's favourite food, with pop musicians and artists of all sorts agreeable as *hors d'oeuvre* or pudding, but as a main course not up to politicians. So she was not surprised when Allen said the Gadarene swine would all be at it, and then with a shift of animal metaphor that once the jackals had smelt blood they closed on the wounded lion. In his slightly piping voice he said they had fallen into a trap set by those villainous Calendars, and bewailed the loss of Bernard, that gallant helper with a nose for genuine scandal.

At that, with the memory of Bernard's last message and her curt dismissal of him when she might have persuaded him to tell her some details of what he had found – and having in mind also that the munificent donation almost as she felt promised by Donald Calendar to the APL was probably mere moonshine – she gave a long wail and cast herself into her husband's arms. He stroked her hair, which had a curious sweet smell about it from the shampoo she used, and said that in the morning they would light a fire under those slowcoaches at Scotland Yard. It would be easy enough to delay signing the agreement by raising some unimportant points in the draft, and in the meantime perhaps the piece of infamy mentioned by Bernard that spelt disaster for Rex Calendar would come to light. He was aware that this was a pious hope, but Allen Pitcombe was a pious man. He believed virtue must triumph in the end, and knew himself to be virtuous.

'Jonathan, what are you talking about?'

When Johnno was worried he sweated, and he could feel himself doing so now. Was a drop forming at the end of his nose? He gave it a quick wipe, and went on trying to explain about George Kaiser. 'I did say I might be able to help.' Why did the words sound like a plea rather than an assertion?

He certainly had his master's full attention. Rex Calendar, short hair bristling, stared at him with an intensity as great as if he were a creature of an unknown species. 'You told this friend of yours, this friend who calls himself *Kaiser* – '

'That's his name. He was up at Magdalen with me.'

'You told this friend Bannock was causing me

problems, and asked him to do something about it?'

'Not exactly. It wasn't like that. You said yourself he was a squalid nuisance, you'd appreciate any help.'

'You gossiped to your *friend from Magdalen* about things I'd mentioned to you in the privacy of this office.'

Johnno protested again that it hadn't been like that. He could feel the drops of sweat gathering on his nose.

'I knew Oxford was a factory for producing know-nothing wiseacres, but I didn't know they cultivated gibbering idiots as well.' Without raising his voice, but pausing between the words so that Johnno felt as if they were darts, each one piercing his skin, Calendar said: 'Get out of my sight.'

Johnno stared at him unbelievingly, not moving from his chair.

'Jonathan, I'll decide what is to be done with you later. At present I want you out of this office. So go away. Don't come back today. If you see your friend Kaiser, try to keep your mouth shut.'

Rex Calendar had forgotten Jonathan two minutes after he had left the room, but the incident moved him to a decision. He called his brother on the scrambler telephone and said the time had arrived to go ahead. His temper was not improved when Donald expressed doubts. There was a policeman from the Yard nosing around, he'd been talking to Marley, and although of course the journalist had stonewalled, that was uncomfortable. 'And this officer, his name's Catchpole, has been talking to Faz. Asking questions, some about Roselands.' First Jonathan's idiocies, then his brother expressing doubts – it was really too much. But he contained himself, merely said there was no need to worry about Scotland Yard, he could close down any inquiry if necessary.

'Then there's Bannock. He's dead, Rex. There'll be a fuss about it.'

'An inquiry, yes. I'm the Home Secretary, Donald. I'll look after it.'

'I'm worried about Gene.'

Rex stopped him saying anything more. Even scramblers were not completely safe nowadays. He pointed out that the Clarissa story would have purely political effects, was not in any way connected with the past. But Donald, typically, still had doubts. It was, he said, the wrong time to make a political move.

'I think using the story is going to get Bladon a lot of sympathy. And once MPs sense that's happening, they'll think they're better off with nurse.'

'Are you telling me you won't use the story?'

'No, I'm saying let's see how things shake down, Bannock and the rest of it. The Clarissa story won't lose anything by being kept for a day or two, give Barry time to prepare a really big splash with it. But I think we should take care, wait and see which way the cat jumps.'

'I can tell you the way the cat jumps if you wait too long. It jumps on you.'

Bladon woke feeling wonderfully well and energetic. He had his usual breakfast, half a grapefruit followed by dry toast and marmalade. He discussed making a new rose garden and an arbour for next year with Jenkins, who still liked to be called the head gardener although his assistants were now only a couple of part-time youths. Clarissa did not appear, nothing unusual about that. After the chat with Jenkins he spoke to the Chief Whip, and said he had decided to call Donald Calendar's bluff. Publish and be damned would be his attitude. There was silence at the other end. It occurred to Bladon that in a leadership election where he was not a candidate, the Chief Whip's vote would certainly go to Rex Calendar. And if they were rivals, which way would he vote then?

'You've talked to Clarissa?'

'Of course. The story's true enough. Apparently the affair has been going on for some time.'

'So it's not a bluff.'

'Yes, I think it is, politically speaking. What will it be, a nine days' wonder if that. Just think of what goes on in other countries, politicians siphoning money out of every business deal in Italy, the tales about Clinton and his girlfriends, Mitterrand's liking for the ladies – '

'There is a difference, Prime Minister. Clinton and Mitterrand are supposed to like the ladies. In this case it's your lady liking a man.'

'Yes, that's true.' It's also true, Bladon thought, that you may have broken the news to me yesterday at Calendar's suggestion, and that our conversation may go straight back to him. 'Even so, I don't think the fact that the Prime Minister's wife has taken a lover is an event of government-shaking importance. Do you?'

The Chief Whip became uncharacteristically flustered, emphasizing that he had thought it his duty . . . possibly distressing nature of any revelations . . . no question of pre-judging the

issue . . . With every fresh phrase Bladon became
more certain that he was in Calendar's pocket. He
said of course, much appreciate your sympathy my
dear fellow, but convey to anyone interested that the
PM has every intention of riding this and any other
storm that may be in the offing.

Extraordinary, he thought as he put down the
telephone on a Chief Whip he had decided to
replace at the first convenient moment, how a crisis
can clear the mind and act as a stimulus to decisive
action. He went in search of Clarissa, whom he
found writing letters at her davenport in what she
called the morning room. Absurdly pretentious, he
thought, to use such an out-of-date term, especially
in a modest house like Deemings. This thought
lingered in his mind even as he said that he realized
some of his inadequacies as a husband, would put
no obstacle in the way of a divorce, and hoped she
and her American would have a very happy life
in New York – and, he added as an afterthought,
Connecticut. He wondered whether their house in
Connecticut would have a morning room, and said
aloud: 'I should have realized life at Deemings was
too quiet for you.'

It was not in Clarissa to show emotion, but she
said that was generous of him, and that she was sorry
to have caused him trouble of such a disagreeable
kind. When he replied that politicians should always
be prepared for trouble she exclaimed wonderingly:
'I almost think you're enjoying this.'

'We're two people who have discovered rather
late in the day that they have very little in common,
aren't suited to each other. That's surely nothing to
cry about.'

She asked what steps he was taking to stop publication of scurrilous material in the tabloid press, and was visibly shaken when he said none. 'I should have thought – ' she began, then shook her head.

'You'd have thought an old-fashioned man like me would do anything to avoid publicity, the interviewers, the photographers, the raking over of all the details of our private lives in search of a bit of scandal, a school friendship that can be the basis for a story about homosexuality, your sessions with a psychotherapist a few years ago which can be called an attempt to stop the breakdown of our marriage. Calendar's papers may start the hunt, but half a dozen other papers will be scraping the barrel for dirt.'

'It wasn't that.'

'What wasn't?'

'When I saw the psychotherapist. It was about adopting a child. He thought it would be no help, but I knew you'd never agree. When I mentioned it to you, you simply dismissed the idea, never even asked why I went to see the psychotherapist. I thought I was marrying a human being, but really I was just a hostess for a politician.'

He was only momentarily disconcerted. 'It was a politician you married, yes. I don't think you ever accepted that. If we were going to quarrel about all this we should have done so long ago. But we never quarrelled, and you might say this is the result.'

'What will you do?'

'What any politician with guts would do, ride the storm. It may never break, we shall see. I think what really should concern you, my dear, is what *you* will do. My advice to you and your American

friend would be to make yourselves scarce for the
next month or two. I'd suggest going to the States,
perhaps to that delightful house in Connecticut. But
cover your tracks, there may already be one or two
camera clickers and paragraph writers who've got a
whiff of the story. On the other hand, they may
follow me.'

'Where are you going?'

'To Downing Street.' She gave a brief involuntary
shudder. 'It's the Prime Minister's power house, and
that's where I should be.'

Before he left he had to endure a litany of complaint from Allen Pitcombe about some sort of skul-
duggery in relation to the sale of Gwenda's land in
Wales. One or perhaps both of the Calendar brothers
were trying to play a disgusting trick on Allen and
Gwenda. He was not precise about details, and
Bladon did not listen very closely, but he was moved
to attention when Pitcombe said he might have to
withdraw NatLib support from the government.
Bladon suggested that might be unwise, since the
cause was so personal.

'I hope you don't think I should let personal feelings influence me. The fact is, Prime Minister, that
Rex Calendar wants to harm me, and since his
political campaign against me has failed he's chosen
this underhand way of doing it. Really, it's des-
picable.' A pause. 'Patrick, we've had our differences,
but you know I respect you and regard you as a
friend. I hope for your support over this.' Another
pause. 'If nothing is done to check Calendar or his
wretched brother I shall have to consider my position
carefully. Did you know Bernard had uncovered

some information he said would drive Rex Calendar out of politics?'

'Bernard? Ah yes, Bannock. I was sorry to hear that news, he was devoted both to your party and to the House. Allen, I'd be grateful if you could leave coming to any decision for the next couple of days.' Then a few clichés about taking on board all that had been said, understood the problem, agreed some action was necessary – and he put down the receiver, reflecting that politicians were the first to be soothed by political guff. He spoke to Rhoda, learned that she was spending the weekend at Number Eleven and would be happy to see him. Then he called his press secretary and his personal private secretary Naomi, who looked after his appointments, and told them both that he wanted to see them at nine the following morning. Both were surprised – a weekend at Deemings usually meant he was not in Downing Street much before midday on Monday – and Naomi was curious, asked if there was something particular she should know about or prepare. Bladon said no, just be ready for a busy week ahead. She said afterwards that she hadn't heard the PM sound so chipper and confident for months.

Evans, who stayed at Deemings when the Prime Minister was in residence, was cheerful on the drive back to London, no doubt pleased to get back to his wife and what Bladon, with a consciousness of neglect in that he had never discovered their existence before, ascertained were three children. 'Girl, boy, girl,' Evans said. 'That's the right order. Ronnie's a real little troublemaker, but the girls sort him out, Eileen our eldest slaps him down when he gets out of

line, Mary cheers him up when he's miserable or
hurts himself. Good girls they are, look after him.
What girls are for, looking after us, shoulder to cry
on I always say.'

'You'd better not let their politically correct
teachers hear you say that.' Bladon immediately
regretted the facetiousness, knowing it would be
taken seriously. Sure enough Evans said, 'I don't hold
with any of that,' and added that in his view it had
got out of hand. 'When you come right down to it,
sir, it's the women who produce the kids, only
natural they should look after them seems to me.'
The Prime Minister, uncomfortably reminded of
what Clarissa had said about adoption, busied himself
with his papers, and Evans relapsed into his usual
silence.

On this late Sunday afternoon Downing Street
was empty, and so was Number Ten. The door-
keeper was there, of course, and a couple of policemen, but there was no clamour of secretarial voices
from the Green Room, and none of the seventeen
expert advisers on foreign affairs, the economy or
the new maximum efficiency unit was there. It was
as he wished. He climbed the staircase alone,
giving as often before an appreciative nod to the
portraits of all those other PMs who had succeeded
or failed – or thought they had succeeded but were
deemed by the opponents who replaced them to
have failed – in making Britain a prosperous and
contented country. All this was as he would have
wished, and he felt positive exhilaration as he looked
at his own image in the bathroom of the private
apartments made by Neville Chamberlain and his
wife, much changed by the Wilsons, Thatchers and

others, and detested by Clarissa who pronounced the apartments as a whole dismal, beyond redemption, unimprovable. The image confronting Patrick Bladon in the glass was of a handsome silver-haired man, elderly no doubt, but alert and bright-eyed and with not an ounce of superfluous flesh on him, trim-waisted as he had been thirty years ago. He felt exultant, almost youthful. 'You'll do, my lad,' he told the figure in the glass, 'you'll do.' His heart positively beat faster as he spoke to Rhoda and opened the door that went through to Number Eleven, though this was not a lover's exultant heartbeat but that of a thoroughbred too long away from competition, eager to race again.

As always he awarded Rhoda a kiss on both cheeks, then sank into an armchair with the brandy she had placed beside him, and began to talk. He admired the lucidity with which he set out the situation, Clarissa's unfaithfulness, the fact that her letters were in Calendar hands and might be used at any time, Pitcombe's complaints and his half-hearted threat to desert the government and provoke an election. Rhoda listened and did not interrupt, her thick brows drawn together once or twice in a frown. When he had finished she said: 'You don't sound like a man who's just had some hard knocks, more like one who's won a big pot at poker.' She reconsidered. 'No, like someone who believes he's got the cards to win that big pot.'

He laughed appreciatively. 'Very good, Rhoda.'

'So what are the cards?'

'Did you know about Clarissa?'

'I'd heard rumours, that's all. What are the cards?

I can't see you've got a strong hand. If I were up
against you I'd say you were bluffing.'

'He's the one who's bluffing, Rex Calendar. He
wants to use these letters to force me to retire, that's
the only way they're any use to him, agreed?' She
nodded. 'I don't know if he realizes this himself,
but revelations like these are only damaging if the
publicity would very much upset the people
involved. Clarissa won't like being plastered over the
scandal sheets, but I've advised her to go to the States
with her American tycoon or whatever he is, and
stay there till the fuss dies down. And as for me, I
may be an old fogey but I'm not a delicate plant.
I shall admit to all those newshounds that it was a
shock – as it was – say I've always been faithful
myself, which is more or less true, and that we have
to accept the realities of the situation, which is also
true. I think I may come out of it rather well. After
all, Macmillan was cuckolded for years, everyone
knew about it, and it did him no harm at all politically, even earned him some sympathy.' He laughed.
'I'm being eloquent, Rhoda.'

'You certainly are.'

'The strength of my hand is that the Calendars
can publish and be damned, and *I don't care*. I am
not going to resign. On the contrary, I shall call an
election.'

For the first time she showed surprise, and the
colour in her high cheeks deepened as she repeated
his last words.

'It's what Calendar, damn him, has been urging
on me for weeks, and I've said no in the cause of
unity and balance in the party. Now he's determined
to wreck any prospect of unity by the way he's

behaving to me and to Pitcombe. You understand Pitcombe's threat to take his NatLibs out of the government – '

'He's such a pain in the neck I'd call it a promise really.' She said it without smiling.

'Whatever you call it, we'd be left without a majority, so we'd have to go to the country. Call it a promise or a threat, it provides an ideal opportunity. And do you know, Rhoda, the prospect of it has really galvanized me. I haven't felt so, what shall I call it, *party political*, for a long time. It's taken a schemer like Rex to wake the sleeping giant.' She said nothing. 'I shall want you by my side in the campaign, and afterwards of course you'll remain Chancellor. You know how much I value your judgement, not only about economics, where I'm a babe in arms.'

'What about Rex?'

'Oh, I'd find a place for him somewhere, though not at the Home Office. Don't you see, by taking the initiative I'll have removed his threat of challenging for the leadership? Anything I offered would be a demotion, and if he didn't accept it, never mind.'

'He's popular, or those anti-crime measures he wants to enforce are.'

'If that's true – I'm not sure it is – someone else can enforce them.'

'The polls are wavering about; they certainly don't look encouraging. You might let the others in. That would be awful.'

He agreed about the awfulness, but said with the kind of campaign he felt capable of waging that wouldn't happen. Then he stopped, conscious that something was not as it should be. Rhoda's hand, stubby and competent, a workman's hand, was tapping the arm of her chair, her frowning gaze examining him as if he were an unexpected object suddenly found on a plate. Then she said: 'It's too late in the day.'

'What do you mean? The last time we talked you said the party was behind me, all they wanted me to do was lead.'

'I think maybe I was talking about the past, not the present. I know Rex has been taking soundings, and the word on the grapevine is that in a leadership contest he wouldn't have enough support to get a majority, nothing like it. Pitcombe doesn't come into it, the kind of support he gave us did more harm than good, whining about the countryside even when they voted with us. And the rest of the party, maybe two-thirds of our MPs, certainly more than half – they don't want you to lead us into the next election, whenever it's called.'

'You told me there was a Prime Minister's party. You said if I led, they'd follow.'

'I wasn't talking about going into an election, only giving a lead to the party today, or rather yesterday. It could be I was wrong even then. Now you don't have winning cards, you don't even have good ones. If you call Rex's bluff, as you put it, you won't get sympathy, you'll be laughed at. It's no use talking about Macmillan, he wouldn't get an easy ride today, with all the papers being discreet. That was then, this is now. And the party's decided you belong to then, belong to the past.'

'This is your doing if it's true. Something you've organized.'

She got out of her chair and stood looking down

at him. He was unwillingly impressed by the way every inch of her seemed to radiate toughness, inflexibility, the will to succeed. And that head with its dark, almost black hair, thick brows, strong features, how was it possible not to admire it? What was that line of Swinburne? 'The implacable beautiful tyrant, rose-crowned, holding death in his hand.' To remember something like that, he thought, was the mark of an aesthete rather than a serious politician. But a few years ago wouldn't he have said one shouldn't be completely serious about anything? He had missed something Rhoda was saying, something about consultations, discussions she'd been having with senior figures in the party, the group known as the Inners although they might also have been called the Elders. She had been talking to the chairman of the Inners, the sage, immensely influential Radley Jevons. Radley had always been a Bladon man, but the term he used now, Rhoda said, was 'burnt out'. It was Radley's belief that a way should be found of persuading the Prime Minister to retire gracefully before the next election certainly, perhaps sooner.

Now Rhoda looked at him – quizzically, happily, sadly, which was it? – and said: 'It's what they want, Patrick, not what I want. They're keen to stop Calendar and they don't think you can do it, not nowadays. The Inners would have been telling you this very soon, but since you're here – well, you know I don't flinch from saying difficult things.'

From the haze of her words, and others he did not bother to listen to, he took the message that they wanted him to go, to take this opportunity of leaving the scene with honour so that Calendar could derive no conceivable benefit from publicizing his marital problems. Now Rhoda was saying she had argued for him, told them he was the cohesive that held the party together, but it had been no use, the Inners had decided. He took it all in, but commented on it as it were from a distance, from a point beyond or above the battle.

'There was something in my kind of politics, you know. I've never had a passionate belief in any system or theory, simply tried to run the country in the way most people would like. All those claims that we should be better or happier if we worried about the ozone layer or gave up our cars or tried to provide work for everybody, or made soft and even hard drugs legal, or shut up persistently violent criminals for good and all, I never believed in them. Some people will always be defeated, unhappy, find their way to the bottom of the pile, and there'll always be some like the Calendars who rise to the top, getting some dirt attached to them on the way. My father used to say what rose to the top was scum, but there's scum at the bottom too. To recognize all that, to know some of the winners are villains and some of the losers are good unlucky people who'd never be winners, and then after that to forget them and try to guide the country in a way that will make Middle England happy, guide it rather than dictate a particular course – that's what I tried for, and I can't think it was wrong.'

He had been talking to himself rather than to Rhoda. Now, still looking down on him, she said: 'You'd better have another brandy.'

'No, thank you.' He stood up, a head above her.

'You're telling me to resign before they get rid of me, that's the message.'

'There isn't any *message*. You came to see me and I felt bound to tell you, that's all.' She put out her hands to him, but he turned away. 'And I'll tell you what will happen if you try to face it out. A deputation from the Inners will tell you that the party has lost confidence in your leadership, an election for the leadership is necessary and the Inners can't support your candidature. If you persist in standing you'll be humiliated. I should hate that to happen.'

'And their chosen candidate?' She said nothing. 'That's you, isn't it?'

'My hat will be in the ring, yes, and some of them say they'll support me, chiefly I think because they're afraid of Calendar.' Now she positively took his hand. In the reflected light cast by a standard lamp there seemed to be tears in her eyes, but he could not be sure of that. 'We've been allies, I think we've been friends, I hope we can be friends still.'

'Why not? You want my job, that's all.' He disengaged his hand, left her standing in the middle of the room, went down the stairs and through the connecting door, nodded to the duty policeman and climbed his own staircase, past the State rooms and the prints and photographs of predecessors, up to the private flat. His earlier energy had been replaced by the kind of numbness he felt after a dental injection. He prepared mechanically for bed, was surprised to find himself wearing nightclothes, then unable to remember whether he had brushed his teeth, and so perhaps brushed them again. It occurred to him that he might telephone Clarissa and tell her what had happened, but the icy ennui with which she was likely to receive the news deterred him. Rhoda's sympathy had been hard enough to bear. If Clarissa showed indifference (after all, his retirement would not affect their separation), that might move him to an outburst he would regret. For that matter he regretted any outburst, no matter what its cause.

Not until he was in bed did he contemplate the possibility of rejecting Rhoda's advice. For a moment, no more, he felt indignation as he lingered on her betrayal, then reflected that she had perhaps been telling no more or less than the truth. But still, why not face it out, put it to the test of a leadership election? Another quotation moved into his mind, something about fearing your fate too much if you failed to put things to the touch. But the exact words escaped him, and he fell asleep before making up his mind.

He woke to daylight dazzling as arc lamps, the usually sunless bedroom and breakfast room transformed. He had an earlier springiness about him, crunched breakfast toast decisively, felt the capacity to outface any opposition. What had he been thinking of to accept Rhoda's dismal arguments? He would talk to the Inners, convince them that he was still the man they wanted, the man to slap down Rex Calendar, and when he'd convinced them Rhoda would come to heel. He told his press secretary, Nellie Hill, that he would be making a statement of his intentions in the next hour, told her also to get Donald Calendar on the line, and quickly. His principal private secretary appeared, and was told to call an urgent meeting of the full Cabinet. Would it be better to talk to Rex Calendar first, have things out once and for all? He decided it would, cancelled the Cabinet meeting, told his PPS to find Calendar, say they must talk. And why in hell wasn't the other Calendar, Donald, on the line? He rang for Nellie Hill, but when the door opened it was Clarissa who appeared, arm in arm with a tall dark man. 'I thought you'd like to meet Manning again,' she said. The stranger put out a large hand, one that seemed to grow bigger every moment, but he ignored it, asked what they were doing there, was suddenly aware of his own extreme danger at the exact moment when the arc lamp lighting failed and plunged them into darkness . . .

He woke to darkness, and a pain moving around inside his chest. When he turned on the bedside light the pain changed direction, shot up his left arm as if he had touched a live wire, then attacked again intensely inside his chest. That fool Grately, he thought, Grately with his fibrous diet, why didn't he tell me I had heart trouble? And now the pain grew overwhelming, seemed to occupy the whole of his chest so that he called out, 'Oh, oh.' He tried to reach the telephone on its bedside table, clutched but then dropped it as the pain struck again, and fell to the floor as he made a desperate attempt to get out of bed. On the floor, at some time said by the pathologist to have been between three and four o'clock in the morning, died Patrick Rooth Bladon, Prime Minister of Britain, from what his personal physician, Sir Grately Lamp, certified had been a massive heart attack. Sir Grately attributed the attack to the immense load of responsibility the PM bore, together with worrying problems in his personal life.

It had been as much a shock to him, Sir Grately handsomely admitted, as to all the PM's other friends. 'I gave him a thorough check-up six weeks ago,' he said, 'and he was in fine fettle.'

THIRTEEN

Reactions: People

THE RADIO CLOCK said six thirty when the telephone rang. Rex Calendar picked it up, said, 'Yes?'

'Donald. The PM's dead. They say a heart attack. Some time in the night.'

'Yes.'

'We can run the story about the affair and the letters in the *Bulletin* tomorrow. And we'll get Fertie Maclane to write one of her pieces on did the PM know, was the knowledge connected with the heart attack. There's a heart specialist who'll do his stuff about stress and post-this or pre-that, pretty well say learning about the affair could have killed him. Plenty of pix of Clarissa and her American.'

'No.'

'Rex, if the heart man worries you he's no quack, he's a specialist at St—'

'I mean no to the whole story. Don't run it. Just a solemn serious straightforward piece and a handsome obit.' Donald's voice became a complaining shriek. 'Listen, just listen. Bladon was lazy, hated making decisions, let things go, but nobody disliked him. Now he's dead, for the next few weeks he'll be a sort of martyr, died at his post, part of a vanishing Britain, all that guff. You print the Clarissa story, you'll do me no good or yourself either. I'll guarantee within a week there'll be a backlash where you'll feel it, in the circulation.'

'But it's a great news story. I know we talked about holding it over for a day or two, but it's different now he's dead.'

'The story died with him.' They argued for another five minutes and Donald gave way, as he always gave way in the end to Rex. What Rex wanted in the paper was profiles of any possible candidates who might stand in a leadership election within the party, with any available dirt dished out about them. Donald agreed to this, as something that could be helpful to Rex. It seemed to him sometimes that too much of his life had been spent in doing things that might be helpful to his brother.

Rex spent the next two hours talking to supporters, to media men and women, to his appointments secretary, his adviser on police matters, his economics adviser, the road transport specialist through whom he filtered his ideas about the new road systems network. When he finally washed and shaved he was confident he had set in motion the preliminary moves for a leadership challenge in an election by the party's MPs. He had instructed that Jonathan's secondment to his office should be ended so that he would return to his Civil Service job, something he momentarily regretted until he reflected that Jonathan was too big a fool to be tolerated, even though he liked him personally. Rex believed in facing trouble only when it became unavoidable, and put any possible problems about Bernard Bannock's death out of his mind. Later in the morning he expressed his sympathy to Clarissa, who received it coolly.

As indeed she had received all the pleasures and assaults of life, including the dubious joys of marriage and the undoubted boredom of listening to politicians. Boredom rather than enthusiasm had driven her to become an expert on costume, and it was enthusiasm for Manning Strong's knowledge of eighteenth-century clothing rather than physical attraction that had prompted their affair on her side. All the physical urgency had been on his. She had been at first amused by something so different from Patrick's characteristic behaviour, and in the end responded to it. When Manning suggested they should get married, she had no objection.

Now she did everything necessary. She told the staff, made arrangements for the funeral to be here at Deemings as Patrick would have wished, spoke to the lawyers and learned that apart from small bequests to staff and friends she was the sole beneficiary of the not very considerable estate. And of course she told Manning, who equally of course expressed his regret. They agreed that the sad event, and the likely publication of scurrilous articles about their relationship, need not affect their plans for marriage.

'An interesting situation, Gwenda,' Allen Pitcombe said. 'There's no Deputy Prime Minister to take over. Really no provision for something like this.'

'A general election?'

'That's what Calendar would like, he's very good on the stump, likes hearing himself talk. So they'll try to avoid it, the older heads I mean.'

'So there'll be an election simply for the leadership, with all the party MPs voting, is that what will happen?'

'It's what the rules lay down, but they'll try to avoid that too. The last time was such a scandal.' He referred to the time when Bladon had taken over as party leader after the resignation on health grounds of the existing incumbent, John Major. A sudden unexpected shifting of votes on the second ballot had given him the majority he needed over the favourite, Kenneth Clarke. After a general election which Bladon won handsomely, several of those who had changed allegiance were rewarded with government jobs. They included Rex Calendar and his then small group of supporters. Their switch had been dramatic, since a few days earlier Calendar had called Bladon a 'milk and water neo-Socialist'. Calendar had been appointed Secretary of State for Defence then promoted as Home Secretary in Bladon's second administration. The scandal of the vote-shifting had died down but not been forgotten, and the party would certainly not wish to see it repeated.

So Allen said now: 'I think they'll try to return to the old way of doing it, reading the tea-leaves you might say, finding the new party leader by consultation. I wonder – '

'Yes?'

'Calendar as PM would split the party, some of the Cabinet might not serve under him. So they'll be looking for a compromise candidate.'

'Rhoda Carpenter?'

'Another woman, after Thatcher? One was enough. Besides, she's just a jumped-up financial journalist. I think it might be worth having a word with Radley Jevons. A lot of them will do what he says.'

'But Allen, we're NatLibs.'

'Yes. What then?'

'We have our principles, our policy. They're not the same as the Tories', you've made that plain a dozen times. And our members won't even be able to vote if there is a vote, they won't have any say in the choice of a new leader.'

'My dear Gwenda, I'm perfectly aware of that. Of course we are a separate party. I'm just suggesting that a little flexibility may be possible. On both sides, of course.'

So Allen Pitcombe had a word, a good many words, with Radley Jevons. He praised the lost leader, deplored his demise, stressed his own wish to compromise but emphasized that the NatLibs could never be part of a government headed by Rex Calendar, and yet made clear his own willingness, even eagerness, to serve in a government of national unity in any capacity that the wisest heads in the government and the party should think fit. He also emphasized that, as he saw it, there was no outstanding candidate in the party except for Calendar. Radley listened, said an occasional yes and no, then in his soft voice thanked Allen for being so frank, and said of course he would make Allen's views known to the Inners when they met, as they urgently must, to decide on a course of action.

Radley Jevons was not a great laugher, but when the conversation ended he allowed himself a chuckle.

Just as Ted Heath had underestimated Margaret
Thatcher, Allen Pitcombe had failed to take account
of Rhoda Carpenter's political intelligence.

That instrument clutched and then dropped by
Patrick Bladon had alerted the exchange to the fact
that something was wrong at 10 Downing Street.
The police had been told, and the Prime Minister's
death had been discovered just after four thirty in
the morning. The Chancellor of the Exchequer,
housed next door, was among the first people to be
told, and quickly though Rex Calendar acted to
establish his position, Rhoda was quicker still. At
five a.m., hours before Allen Pitcombe made his call,
she wakened Radley Jevons with the news. Radley,
chairman of the Inners, expressed incredulity, dismay,
distress at having lost a dear personal friend. Rhoda
heard this a little impatiently, and at length interrupted him.

'Patrick came to see me last night. Donald Calendar's papers have got hold of some letters Clarissa
wrote to her American lover – you've heard the
story, no doubt, there's been a lot of Westminster
gossip – and Patrick thought there'd be a threat to
print them. He was intending to face it out, said
he'd be calling Rex Calendar's bluff.'

'Dear, dear.' Radley was in his early seventies.
His voice and manner were misleadingly gentle, his
diction often old-fashioned and even pompous. Now
he said: 'So unnecessary. I sometimes think it would
be a good thing if the popular press did not exist.'

'So I felt I had to tell him what we'd discussed.
I said he no longer had the support of the Inners.'

'You did? That was very bold.'

'It was what I understood. From your committee.'

'What one is told as an expression of personal opinion at a private meeting is not necessarily to be passed on as a definitive statement. An expression of opinion is not an official decision.'

Rhoda glared at the instrument in her hand. 'You must see I was in a difficult position. I couldn't let Patrick go away thinking he had full party support.'

'I understand that. If I may ask – ' He paused, then went on. 'Did he appear to be shocked and upset by what you told him?'

'Hard to say. He rambled on a bit about there being something in his kind of politics, the middle way, accepting that there'd always be rich and poor. Clichés really. But when he left me I think he'd accepted resignation was inevitable.'

'You don't think he was so upset that he may – ah – ' Radley's voice dropped almost to a whisper, 'have taken an overdose of pills or some medicine?'

This idea, later floated in some sections of the press and then summarily dismissed by Sir Grately and the pathologist, had not occurred to Rhoda. She denied the possibility of it brusquely, and Radley said he sincerely hoped she was right. The conversation was not going as she expected. She had thought Radley would immediately raise the question of the succession, and was determined to force the issue.

'Patrick's death is a tragedy, but we have to think about what follows. Nobody wants a general election at this moment, with the polls the way they are. It might be playing into the hands of the Labour Party, or it could mean Calendar's candidates romping home on the basis of his promising everything people want to hear and the rest of us struggling to keep our seats, which would be almost worse. Are you with me so far?'

'You put it clearly, as always.'

'Then the rules say a ballot should be held, with the voters the party's MPs. There might be several candidates, and we know what happened last time over the switched votes. We don't want that to happen again.'

'Indeed.'

'Or a new leader could be arrived at by general consensus. That was what I thought had been agreed when I met your committee last week. There was general dissatisfaction with Patrick's lack of leadership, and his resignation, perhaps on grounds of health, would be suggested. I understood I was being asked if I would take on the burden of leadership, at least until the time for a general election two years ahead.'

She ended with a snap, like the click of a handbag closing.

'How clearly and cogently you put it, Rhoda. I do congratulate you on your clarity.' A little cough then, one of the Radley coughs that often preceded a disclaimer. 'I think, though, the feeling of the meeting was much more tentative than you're suggesting. These were all possibilities that we discussed, nothing more. Suppose, for example, Patrick had declined to consider a suggestion that he might resign, we certainly hadn't made up our collective minds about the possible courses of action. It was not at all cut and dried. I sensed a great deal of opposition to any idea of forcing Patrick out.' His voice became positively dulcet. 'We all loved and admired him. It was just that in the last months he seemed to have lost his way.'

Did any thought cross her mind of the way she had pushed the necessity of resignation a few hours ago? If so, it was not apparent when she said: 'What are you telling me?'

Again his reply was calm, even soothing, the words carefully chosen. 'You should be patient. There are decisions to be made, negotiations under-taken perhaps. In Parliament we can't do without the support of the NatLibs, and they know it.' She made an impatient sound. 'Then there is the ques-tion of what Rex Calendar might be offered. If you vacate the Chancellorship he might demand it.'

'He's not an economist, knows nothing about finance.'

'He would have expert advisers. You don't like the idea? Very well, but we must still negotiate, give a little here, make a little ground there. In a week, or perhaps two or three, I hope these things will have arranged themselves through consultation. I shall do my best to see that they do, I can assure you of that.'

And with that she had to be satisfied. It con-firmed her view that Radley Jevons was the most adroit and devious strategist in Parliament. Was he on her side? She could not be sure of that.

The news was too late for the early papers. The Big Man heard it on his car radio, on the way up to the Yard. By the time he reached his office he had decided it was possible to apply a little pressure. His

call to the Home Office passed through the barricade
of secretaries, then he was told that his nephew was
not in the office and was put through to Rex Calendar himself. The Home Secretary's 'Yes?' was not
welcoming. The Big Man mentioned his relationship
to Jonathan, to be told that his nephew's secondment to the Home Office had been terminated, and
given a growled reminder that this was an extremely
busy morning. Silence succeeded the growl when
the Big Man suggested that a meeting might be
useful. Then, sharply: 'With what purpose?'

The Big Man said some further information had
come to light relating to the death in Kennington
in which he understood the Home Secretary had an
interest. He added, 'It may also have some connection with the recent death of the MP Bernard Bannock,' and it may have been the last sentence that
produced the result of an appointment that afternoon. The Big Man put down the telephone satisfied
that whatever might be involved was important to
the Home Secretary. But just what *was* involved?
About that he remained unsure, but felt certain it
could be turned to his benefit.

Johnno would not have thought anything could
make him feel more miserable than the news that
his secondment to the Home Office was finished
and he was being returned to the Civil Service, but
the news of the PM's death had that effect. He was
not solaced by Belinda's view that being back in his
old cosy job would really suit him much better.
Didn't she understand that this could have been his
big chance? Very likely Calendar would take over,

and Johnno would have been the confidant of the Prime Minister. 'He liked me, I know he did.'

'But you didn't like him.'

'I admired him.' He poured them drinks but barely sipped his own, looking at it gloomily. 'You don't have to *like* your boss.'

'Oh beanbag, you are a creep. You really need someone to look after you, tell you what to do. You make me feel quite motherly.'

'You're not – '

'No, no, I just feel motherly, not going to be a mother, don't want to be anyway. But I liked your father a lot, he's a real antique, and I reckon your mother could get used to me. Time I settled down too. Perhaps we should give it a try.'

'Get hitched?'

They embraced. He nuzzled her neck, but cheerfulness did not last long. He raised his head from her neck to say: 'Where's George? Do you realize if he's arrested I shall be too?'

Catchpole took little interest in politics. Alice had voted NatLib at the last general election in support of their resistance to Calendar's roads and building programme, but was outraged when the NatLibs became a junior partner in the government. Neither of them felt Patrick Bladon's death was likely to change anything, either in their personal lives or in national politics.

In any case Alice had something else on her mind. On Tuesday morning after breakfast, just as Catchpole was about to leave for the Yard, she said: 'Something you should know. Alan's headmaster wants to see us.' He did not take it in fully, said he'd be busy all day, might be late home, she was much better at all that school stuff than he was, liked discussing the boys' progress or lack of it.

'Hilly, you're not listening. The head wants to see *us*. Both. I can't make out exactly what's happened, the boys have clammed up and I didn't want to bother you.'

'You mean you don't know what it's about?'

'Oh yes, I know that. It's about bullying.'

'Bloody hell, that can be serious.' He had been involved in a case twelve months earlier when a twelve-year-old Indian girl had hanged herself after persistent taunting by white schoolmates about her colour, religion, and alleged stupidity. 'I suppose some of them have been getting at Desmond?'

'You don't understand. It's Alan. He's been accused of bullying.'

FOURTEEN

What the Media Said

EXTRACT FROM *The Times* leader, 19 July:

... Patrick Bladon will not go down in history as one of Britain's great Prime Ministers, but in his first administration the diplomatic skill with which he urged this country's claims to play a leading part in Europe while avoiding commitment to the idea of political union won him praise even from those most opposed to his stance. He seemed similarly able to conciliate the factions within his own party while exercising the lightest possible control over them. At the last general election seats were lost to Labour and the NatLibs, but confidence in the Prime Minister enabled him to form a government, even though one kept in office with the support of Mr Pitcombe's party. Minority governments are always difficult to handle, and in his second administration Bladon seemed to have lost his touch, so that the outspoken modernizing views of the Home Secretary, Rex Calendar, and the total opposition to them of the NatLibs seemed more important than anything the

Prime Minister did or said. The second
Bladon government was one in which the
helmsman had lost control, and no longer
seemed to care in which direction the ship
was heading. Now the question arises, not
only of who should replace him, but what
the procedure should be by which the new
leader is chosen . . .

Extract from the *Bulletin* leader, 19 July:

. . . The new Prime Minister has not yet been
named. It is said wise heads are consulting and
deliberating, but we see no reason for delay.
Those so-called wise heads are slowcoaches.
Our industries ask for action, so does the
City. One man has been calling insistently for
the modernizing decision to be made that
will cut the red tape at present strangling
our manufacturers and our exporters. Rex
Calendar is the only possible choice to get
action now, and there is no reason at all to
delay his appointment as Prime Minister . . .

Extract from the *Independent* leader, 20 July:

. . . In the situation created by Patrick Bladon's tragic death there is a good deal to be
said for the early appointment of a new party
leader, whether at an election in which the
party's MPs vote or, as is said may be the case,
by consultation. There always is a good deal
to be said for immediate action. There is
also a good deal to be said for a period of

contemplation. Again, there always is. In a few days the House will rise for the summer recess, a breathing space to be treated this year less as a holiday than as a period of reflection for the factions that make up the government. The country will be best served by the appointment of an interim Prime Minister to handle all current affairs, appointed on the understanding that the party will go to the country in a general election during the next few months, certainly no later than next spring. A general election would come like a breath of fresh air after the devious manoeuvrings now going on in the corridors of power. Let the party's MPs appoint a new leader, but then *Let the People Vote* should be the cry. The result of a general election may surprise the pundits – and the present government . . .

Extract from interview with Rhoda Carpenter by Isabel Denton on BBC TV, 21 July:

DENTON: . . . You were the last person to talk to the Prime Minister, just a few hours before his death.

CARPENTER: Yes. I was his nearest neighbour, you might say, and he often dropped in for a chat – you know, I'm sure, that 10 and 11 Downing Street have a communicating door. I think and hope we were friends. Patrick was gregarious, yet still in some ways a lonely man, and I think he appreciated being able to put his feet up and chat. The feet up is metaphorical, of course. (*Slight laugh*) In fact, he used the armchair you're sitting in.

DENTON: There were rumours – still are, as I'm sure you know – that a scandal was about to break involving his marriage. Did he mention this on that last evening?

CARPENTER: Patrick was a very private man. It wasn't the sort of thing he talked about.

DENTON: So he didn't mention any personal problems?

CARPENTER: I would never have raised such things –

DENTON: He didn't mention them?

CARPENTER: And with Patrick only just dead I don't propose to discuss them now.

DENTON: Very well, but what about problems inside the Cabinet? It's well known Rex Calendar and Allen Pitcombe don't see eye to eye, and that Calendar wanted action about which the Prime Minister was reluctant to commit himself, like arming the police with this little revolver called the Baybee after it's passed its tests. Did you get any idea of his thinking about those particular things?

CARPENTER: You're right in saying he was reluctant to commit himself. He wanted to make sure we carried the country with us over any measure we advocated. Patrick believed in government by the consent of the people. So do I.

DENTON: Did you talk about those things on that last evening?

CARPENTER: We did.

DENTON: Had he decided on a course to follow?

CARPENTER: In the sense I think you mean, no. He thought the mass of our people hadn't made up their minds about most of the forceful measures being talked up at the moment – *our people*, not just our party. Patrick was never just a party man.

DENTON: You mean Rex Calendar is? Is totally a party man?

CARPENTER: (*Laughs*) Come along now, I never said or implied that.

DENTON: Would you agree Rex Calendar is much more a party man than the Prime Minister ever was? So that, for example, there'd be no place for Allen Pitcombe in a Calendar government, and perhaps no place for any NatLib in the Cabinet?

CARPENTER: You want to see everything in terms of personalities, but these are issues of principle. Certainly Patrick thought the public wasn't prepared to see all the police armed with Baybees.

DENTON: Even though violent crime increased by eight per cent last year, seven per cent the year before that?

CARPENTER: Killing or injuring more thugs won't stop thuggery. It will simply mean the thugs get better, more lethal weapons.

DENTON: That's your opinion?

CARPENTER: And it was Patrick's. He believed in government by consensus, not confrontation. That's what our people want.

DENTON: But who could head such a government? Isn't your party split, quite decisively? Not down the middle, but cracked all over?

CARPENTER: Picturesque but untrue. There are factions, but the *party* isn't split.

DENTON: Seems to me it has at least two opinions about any subject. Like arming the police.

CARPENTER: We encourage free speech. And we're prepared to change our minds if circumstances change. Unlike the Labour Party.

DENTON: Will you change your mind about arming the police with Baybees?

CARPENTER: Me personally? No.

DENTON: Would you serve in a government prepared to arm the police with them?

CARPENTER: I don't answer hypothetical questions . . .

Extract from interview with Rex Calendar by Lucinda Summers in the *Daily Mail*, 22 July:

... He said the Prime Minister's death had left him with a sense of deep personal loss. 'Patrick was a great gentleman, a great Englishman. I admired him immensely, almost revered him.' But what about his policies? 'I'll be candid, and say in my opinion, in these last months he'd lost touch with some of the country's needs.' Would his own policies be more in touch? Including the arming of the police with machine-guns, and what the opposition is calling a plea for unemployed men to be put to work on road building? Isn't that forced labour?

He threw back his head and laughed. 'Two questions, two mistakes. The Baybee, which is now undergoing its final tests, is nothing like a machine-gun, it's a very small revolver with an automatic reloading device. And yes, I believe in putting the able-bodied unemployed to work, but it would be voluntary, no forced labour.'

If he were Prime Minister, would he be able to work with colleagues like Rhoda Carpenter and Allen Pitcombe? More laughter.

'I'm an immense admirer of the way Rhoda juggles with figures and makes them come out right. Of course she'd have an important place in any government of mine. As for Allen, I always value his views. He'd have to make up his own mind whether he could work with me.'

Would it have been a good idea to appoint a Deputy Prime Minister, so that the present power vacuum wouldn't have occurred? 'I

think so, yes, but no use crying about that
now.'

If there was an election for leader inside
the party, would he be a candidate? 'If you
haven't understood that by now, you're not
the bright girl I think you are.'

There's no doubt that if you're affected by
personal charisma Rex Calendar has got it . . .

FIFTEEN

Logical Solutions

MAGGIE STEEL was short, kept her hair cropped, had a freckled face and a wide friendly smile, and was a lesbian ready and eager to announce changes in her partners, something that seemed to happen every year. She was also one of the most skilful analysts and interpreters of the department's computer. She said now: 'I've come up with a name. Wanna know how I got it?'

'Not particularly, because I shan't understand when you tell me, but all right. Not too long.'

'The tiny tots class. OK, first all the old records have gone. Lost, destroyed, whatever, records of Lakeside don't exist. I put in a call to the boss lady at Roselands, spoke to her, and you know what? I was at school with her. Thought the name sounded familiar.' Catchpole asked what she had been like. 'What you might expect. Head girl type who never got to be head girl, cool, ambitious, calculating, only she never worked out the calculations quite right. Loved exercising power, only she never had much. Know what her Christian name is? Poppy, we all thought that was a scream. Mind you, she was attractive.'

'Did you?'

Maggie shook her head. 'She had no time for short freckled girls who lacked class, but she took some of the others to bed. There was a row about one of them, a girl called Gabriella something or other, her parents took her away. Still, Poppy seemed quite pleased to hear from me, we chatted away about those good old days, and she gave me a list of residents who've left Roselands since it's been going, which isn't that long, along with another list of people she thought might have been at Lakeside. So I checked out the names she gave me, not very many of them actually, and drew blanks. Mostly dead, and dead or alive couldn't find any link with the Calendar family.

'So we're down to the existing residents, right? There were only seven long-term ones and I checked 'em all carefully, ran them through the computer. Nothing.'

'Did you check both sexes? There were semen traces on Lily Devon, but there could have been two people involved in her death, just possibly a man and a woman.'

'You think that wouldn't occur to me, me with my inclinations?' She grinned, showing slightly crooked teeth. 'The answer's yes, and that was a blank too. It also occurred to me that Poppy could have left a name or two off the list deliberately. I don't know why she'd do that, but it's a possibility. But then I had my brainwave. How about the staff?

'I thought very likely there was nothing to it, but I went down and had another chat with my friend Poppy and she was sweet as pie, said she remembered I was a persistent little bitch at St Wini-fred's only she didn't put it quite like that. Anyway,

she put me in touch with a staff member named
Larkins, said you'd talked to him. And he's helpful
too, everyone cooperating with the fuzz, goes against
nature seems to me. But before I saw Larkins I'd
already eliminated the helpers and nurses, most of
'em don't go back more than a year or so anyway.
Then I had a look at the odds and sods, and came
up with this name. Ted Copeland. Listed as a porter,
but he does any old thing, sweeping up around the
place, cleaning cars, even washing down the loos.
And Larkins is friendly with Ted, tells me about
him. There's some story about Ted once having been
a resident, but I drew a blank with Poppy about that,
she said she wasn't sure. As I told you, there are no
old records, so no one's sure how long Ted's been
there. He's simple, it's said, simple but harmless. He's
like an institution, everyone I spoke to seemed to like
him, but does he go back thirty years or so, which
he'd have to do if he's Gene Calendar. So it seemed
a long shot.'

'There's more?'

'Apart from the coincidence of initials, which
you were no doubt waiting for me to point out. EC
for Edward Copeland, EC for Eugene Calendar.' She
grinned at him again.

'Congratulations. But it's all hearsay. I'm waiting
for the computer to come up with something.'

'Which it has done. Give it the right food and it
cooks a perfect meal. It recognized one Edward
Copeland who likes to show people his willy, women
especially. He's been up four times, for indecent
exposure twice, indecent assault twice – tried to pull
down a teenager's pants to see her vagina, and
wanted to play sex games with a couple of girls aged

ten and thirteen. First offence was twenty years ago, address given as Lakeside Residential Home, most recent one a couple of years back at Roselands. Got probation twice, then suspended sentence. Magistrate last time said he needed looking after, and was told they paid particular attention to just that at Roselands. General view is he's not quite all there and getting less so every year.'

'Four offences in twenty years, none violent. Doesn't sound like a sex killer.'

'Plus maybe others that weren't reported. Still, I agree.' Maggie hesitated. 'I did have the feeling with a couple of people – one of the male helpers and Larkins – that maybe they weren't telling the whole story. They all like Ted, don't want to say things against him.' She chewed a fingernail. 'One thing I forgot. He likes dressing up as a woman, so Larkins told me. They have a Christmas party and he dresses up, pretends to be Lady Muck, doesn't have to say more than a few words and look haughty, loves it. May mean something or nothing. Lot of my friends like cross-dressing.' She grinned amiably, and Catchpole grinned back.

Afterwards he looked through the papers Maggie had left with him, and was stopped by the name of the solicitor employed by the defence on the most recent charge: R. J. Fazackerley. Then he sat back, considered what he had got, and decided it still didn't amount to anything solid. Another session with Fazackerley? But that master of evasion wouldn't give away any secrets, and even if Ted Copeland was Gene Calendar, what then? If the links were made, the Calendar family could be praised for looking after their younger brother, although of course a less generous interpretation was possible. What had Copeland's movements been on the night Lily Devon died? If there was positive confirmation that he had been at Roselands between nine and eleven o'clock that night he was ruled out for the Kennington murder. As for the death of Bannock, the use of force seemed out of keeping with his character. He decided all this was too sketchy to be passed on to the Big Man.

Another plunge into deepest Surrey was indicated. He took Maggie with him, because she thought there might be more to be learned from the staff, in particular from Moira. He left her chatting amiably with Moira, and went to see Dr Armitage. It was one of the hottest days of a dry summer and her long-sleeved dress made no concessions to the weather, yet she looked wonderfully or intolerably cool. Catchpole opened on that note of false indignation every successful interrogator has mastered, a note all the more impressive, as here, when the false indignation has a genuine basis.

'The last time we talked I asked you about Ted Copeland, one of the staff here. You didn't tell me he'd been in court four times for sexual offences. Sergeant Steel found his name on the computer.' A blink behind the rimless glasses was her only reaction. 'Why did you conceal it?'

'The private affairs of – ' There was a moment's gap before she continued ' – those who live here concern themselves only. Ted's problems seemed to me to have no connection with your inquiry.'

'You were going to say "the private affairs of residents", weren't you? Ted Copeland is a resident, right? Why conceal that?'

He was pleased to see her thoroughly disconcerted. 'I – you must understand – '

'No, Dr Armitage, *you* should understand that
hampering a police investigation by concealing matters of possible importance is a serious matter. If Ted
Copeland is a resident someone pays for him, and
you must know who that someone is.'

She shook her head. 'All I know is that he's paid
for by the Trust, and the money comes through a
lawyer.'

'Whose name is Fazackerley.'

'Yes. Does the name matter?'

'Perhaps. So Ted Copeland is a resident. Is that
his real name?'

Her reaction when she said she had never heard
he had another name seemed genuine enough. 'As
for being a resident, yes, in the sense that he's paid
for. He's been here and at Lakeside for quite a time,
but it's no use asking me how long because we have
no records of the Lakeside period. But he *isn't* a
resident, in the sense that here at Roselands, and
probably before then, he's been employed to do odd
jobs. He enjoys that, feels he's being useful, likes
being paid a weekly wage. He's a sex offender it's
true, but not a very serious one, and he's been out
of trouble now for two years, which is good. A year
or so back he took to sleeping in an outhouse, part
of an old barn which he renovated with Fred Larkins's help. He lives there now and he likes that too,
gives him a feeling he's independent and also helps
in running the place.'

All this was, for Dr Armitage, wonderfully forth-
coming, and she continued in the same vein. 'By
all means talk to Ted, though you won't find him

tremendously coherent. He has patches of being comprehensible and chatty, then shuts up. Try not to upset him, we're all rather fond of him.' The idea that she could be fond of anybody was as surprising to Catchpole as if a teardrop had fallen from her steely eye. She was similarly gracious when Catchpole said Maggie was talking to members of her staff, and might like to have a few words with her partner, Nigel Straker, and the mood was maintained when Larkins was summoned via the switchboard and told that the Superintendent wanted to talk to Ted Copeland.

'What's Ted been up to? No trouble, I hope.' Larkins's little square face, inappropriately small for his powerful body, showed concern. Catchpole said he just wanted a chat.

'He's down in the workshop mending some furniture.' Larkins hesitated. 'If you don't mind my saying so, the best way of approaching him is to show an interest in what he's doing. Ted's very friendly, loves to talk about his work, but tends to clam up if he thinks he's being criticized. Clams up or gets flustered, can't get his words out. So take it as easy as you can. Anything I might be able to help with?'

'I'd like to know if he was here all night on the third of June. And where he was when that MP died.'

'You don't suspect – that's ridiculous.' Dr Armitage seemed genuinely shocked. 'If those were both acts of violence you can rule out Ted Copeland. He's been in therapy with me, and I'd stake my professional reputation that he would never do anything violent to another person.' She appealed to

Larkins, who agreed, but as it seemed to the detective with less conviction. He said so when they had left the doctor and were walking through the house. Larkins ran a hand through his curly hair.

'He's a sweet-tempered lad, Ted. I think of him as a lad, though of course he must be older than me. But there are times when he gets in a paddy, and then it's as if he doesn't know what he's doing. It happens when something he wants is taken away, that sort of thing. Might happen say twice a year, rest of the time he's good as gold. One other thing. You'll find he sometimes talks about himself as if he was someone else – in the third person I think it's called, though Doctor A and the other specialists who're on call have probably got some long name for it. Here we are.'

They had been walking round the side of the house, past garages and a vegetable garden, to a small group of outbuildings that had originally perhaps been a large barn, and were still under one long pantiled roof. The first section of the barn was open, and contained a big motor-mower, rakes, forks, and other bits of garden equipment. Some hung on nails, others were arranged neatly on shelves. Larkins called 'Ted,' a reply came from the barn's interior, and a figure appeared in the doorway of a section cut off by a wooden partition.

Catchpole blinked, momentarily almost blinded by the change from the strong outside sunlight to the darkness within the barn, so that the figure he saw seemed a giant filling the door space, a monster with an enormous misshapen head in which it was impossible to distinguish any human feature. Then the monster advanced a couple of steps and was revealed as a man of no more than normal size, the featureless effect caused by a goggled helmet which he now removed, saying he'd just been using the lathe. Catchpole had met Rex Calendar twice, at an official party and when he had come to give a talk to the Police Federation, and was struck immediately by this man's resemblance to the Home Secretary. The same square head, small ears clamped back close to it, the same low forehead and formidable torso. But in Gene (if this was Gene) all the characteristics that made Rex look as if a rock would come off worse in any conflict with him seemed to have melted, become amorphous and unthreatening. He had the trusting look that marks many adolescents as his gaze moved inquiringly from one to the other of them. Larkins asked why he had been using the lathe.

'That chair, you know the one going in Ted's room, needed a new leg.' He smiled, again with an effect of youth and shyness quite unlike the Rex Calendar smile. 'Shouldn't be smoking, not in here. Not anywhere. Bad for you.'

Larkins stubbed out his cigarette. 'You don't miss much. This is Mr Catchpole from London, wants to ask you a few questions.'

The smile was transferred to Catchpole, succeeded by a pout, regret that there was nowhere to sit, and a suggestion that they should go into Ted's rooms. Larkins winked at Catchpole as they were led through the neat workshop into another part of the barn that had been made into a self-contained flat, sitting room, kitchen, small bedroom, bathroom and lavatory. It had all been done by him, Ted Copeland said proudly, he had made the windows, done the electrics, decorated it, only thing he couldn't manage was the plumbing. Then he checked himself and said with boyish shyness: 'Fred helped.'

It proved difficult to ask questions that elicited useful replies. Ted Copeland said he had been at the home a long time but he had no idea how long. He remembered nothing of where he had lived or what he had done before being there, and appeared to make no distinction between Roselands and Lakeside. He answered in the third person only when he found the question awkward, and then tended to refer to Larkins in the hope that he might provide an answer. He never wanted to know why the questions were being asked, but was eager to talk about his achievements as a handyman and home-maker, and Catchpole tried to open up obliquely the question of Lily Devon by this route. Wouldn't it be good to have a partner to share the work in his home? Ted said he managed very well.

'But it would be good to have a girl around, surely? I mean, you like girls, don't you?' Ted muttered something, then brightened. 'You want to see something? Something big?' He fumbled at his belt.

Larkins said: 'No, Mr Catchpole doesn't want to see your willy. Try to answer the questions.'

'You do like girls, don't you? Like to play with them?'

Copeland's voice suddenly became thin and high, as if he were reciting a ritual. 'Ted likes to play with girls, but sometimes girls won't play.'

'And then you get cross? Try and make them play?'

'No. Ted never gets cross.'

'Then perhaps sometimes you go up to London, try to find a girl who'll play with you.'

A long pause. Then: 'Perhaps. But only games.'

'Of course only games, that's all you want. But then if she won't play sometimes it makes you angry. Do you remember a time like that?'

'No. No. Ted doesn't do bad things. Ted's going to make tea.' He got out of his chair, shaking slightly, went to the galley. Larkins's shrug suggested nothing further would be got out of Ted Copeland, and that proved to be the case. They drank their tea, but Copeland said he didn't want any more questions, they were nasty. The look directed at the detective suggested he thought Catchpole was nasty too.

Afterwards Larkins was apologetic. 'Hope you didn't think I was a stumbling block. Tell you the truth, I think he'd have clammed up sooner than he did if you'd been on your own.' Catchpole said he was sure that was right. 'So what now?'

'Now we go through the process of checking whether Ted Copeland went to London on the evening of June third, by rail or bus. As far as Bannock's concerned, anyone could have been waiting for him by appointment and done the job in the car – anyone at all, no need to connect it with Roselands, except that Bannock had been rooting about here. But it's the Kennington case I'm concentrating on, and Copeland has to remain a candidate for that. You didn't happen to see Ted Copeland that evening, I suppose?'

'Afraid not. After the evening meal, I usually go around making sure everyone's happily settled – no need to do it really, Auntie Armitage always makes her rounds too, but no harm in double-checking.

Then I settle down in my room to watch the box. Didn't see Ted.'

'Pity. If you'd been with him part of the evening – '

'But I wasn't. Wish you luck.' He sketched a mock salute and was gone.

Afterwards Catchpole met up with Maggie, who gave him an account of her afternoon. She had talked to Nigel Straker, whom she called Poppy's Plaything, and to several members of the staff, of whom Moira to Catchpole's surprise had been the most forth-coming.

'Next time she's in central London she's coming to have a drink at a club I belong to. I think we recognized each other.'

'Glad you've found a friend.'

'Yes, Moira's OK. But back to Poppy's Plaything. He knows Ted Copeland's fees at the home are paid for by the Trust, but says he hasn't got any details, and I believe him. He also said nobody else is paid for in the same way, almost all by their families or distant relatives. Said Poppy and he make a decent living out of the home, no more, but she loves running the place so he's happy too.' Maggie shook her head in disbelief at the complaisance of Poppy's Plaything. 'Most of those I talked to seemed con-tented enough, get good money, one or two com-plained about the dictatorial ways of la Armitage. Moira was the only one who told me anything interesting – well, it might be interesting. She's in charge of the book which staff and residents have to sign if they're going to be out for a lunchtime or evening meal, but she said nobody bothered a lot about it, and there was no signing out for the evening

of the third of June. So you might call that drawing
a useful blank. I had a bit more luck with another
of your queries, about whether any washing or dry
cleaning had been sent out for servicing that week.
Moira also dealt with that, and it so happened the
home's own washing machine had broken down, so
that almost everything was sent out locally. Moira
thought she'd be able to get a list of who sent what,
although I don't know what good it'll do you.'

'Probably none. Just that *if* someone here was
involved in the Kennington business they'll have got
blood on their clothes. Quite a bit of it.'

'Wouldn't they wash the clothes themselves? Or
burn them?'

'Perhaps. But either might be risky, especially
burning. So there just might be a shirt, socks, a
sweater, something with a lot of blood marks sent
for cleaning. And it could have been noticed.' He
sighed. 'A long shot, I know.'

'Fifty to one outsider, you ask me,' Maggie said
cheerfully.

The Big Man emerged from the Home Office port-
als humming a little song of which he could not
remember the words, in an excellent temper. He
strolled back to the Yard through the park, a trilby
hat placed a little askew on his head. Another warm
day, the sky egg-blue, the grass showing a faint tinge
of brown because of the drought. He looked with
a benevolent eye upon everything, the couples in
deckchairs and those lying sun-dazed on the grass
with torsos burning gently, the mothers pushing
prams, even the inevitable layabouts investigating the

contents of litter-bins, sitting on benches reading yesterday's papers, upon occasion doing a bit of begging. The Big Man disapproved of beggars, thought they should be arrested if they caused trouble, should be forcibly removed from shop doorways at night and sent firmly back to the Sally Army or if necessary to cardboard boxes. But today was a good day, today the actual sun shone on him in the park and a metaphorical sun had beamed on him at the Home Office. When a reasonably dressed young man, bearded and a bit shabby, came close and asked if he could spare the price of a cuppa, guv, he did not tell the beggar to clear off but chuckled, felt in his pocket for a coin, and then in a burst of good feeling took a fiver out of his wallet and handed it to the fellow.

The bearded man looked at the bit of paper, put it in his pocket, spat and said: 'Stupid rich fucker.' The Big Man chuckled again and went on his way, happy that this was the way the world went round.

Catchpole had the gift of being able to relegate a case he was working on to the back of his mind, and bring forward something immediately urgent. The habit served him well that evening when they went round for their interview with Alan's headmaster. A fatherly talk with Alan, on which Alice had insisted, produced no result. Alan, usually chatty, was uncooperative. Yes, Wilkins, the boy whose parents had complained, was younger than him, and smaller. Yes, Alan had hit him, knocked him down.

'He said you kicked him when he was on the ground. Did you?'

'Might have done. To make him get up.'

'And that you waited for him outside the school, took off his cap and threw it into someone's garden, emptied everything out of his satchel. It was raining and the things got wet. Is that right?'

'I never took any stuff out of his satchel, it dropped out. He's lying if he says so. He's a dirty little liar.'

'What about the cap?'

'Might have done that. Can't remember. My cap's been pulled off, got thrown in a pond once. Who cares?'

'We would, if we had to buy you a new one.' Alan shrugged. It was uncomfortably like an interrogation at the station, and the boy's apparent indifference was exasperating. 'It may come down to them asking us to take you away. Is that what you want? I thought you liked it there.'

'It's OK.'

'Why pick on Wilkins?'

'Don't like him. He smells, doesn't wash.'

'Where d'you think you'd go if it wasn't South Clapham Modern? This is a good school. We want you to stay there, and you want it too. Don't you?'

'Don't mind. Plenty of other schools where I know some people. They get bullied too, everyone does. Don't go crying to their mum and dad, though.'

'But you weren't being bullied, were you? Tell me if you were, I wouldn't make any complaint about it, just like to know.' Alan shook his head. 'Right, so you were doing the bullying. Why?'

Looking at his son's handsome sullen face, turned away from him, Catchpole felt a twinge as if his heart had missed a beat. Brief questioning of

Desmond proved no more profitable. Where Alan had retreated into silence, Desmond went in for tears and shouting.

'I *don't know* nothing about it,' he shouted. Did he know Wilkins? 'Yes, and I *don't like him*. He makes stinks, everyone says.' Did he know any reason why Alan should fight with Wilkins and torment him? When Alan was bigger and in a different class? At that Desmond wept, ran away to his room, barricaded the door, and Catchpole called the questioning off.

'It's not like Alan, is it, Hilly?' Alice said pleadingly in bed that night. If he had replied truthfully he would have said experience had taught him almost anybody might do almost anything, but he knew the answer she wanted and gave it. No doubt, he added, it would be cleared up when they saw the headmaster.

Catchpole's heart sank, however, at the sight of Mr. J. E. Hook, LL B, BA. He wore a tight-fitting short-sleeved shirt open at the neck, jeans and trainers, and had a gold circlet in one ear. Catchpole had seen dozens dressed like him at demos, eager to be arrested and then complain about police brutality, sometimes with justice. Mr Hook made it plain at once that he was not overawed or even impressed by Catchpole's rank as a police detective. The school had conducted its own investigation, he said, Alan had admitted bullying Fred Wilkins, and they now had to decide what should be done about it. Alice asked how long the bullying had gone on, and what exactly it consisted of. Mr Hook beamed at her.

'Very natural question. Teachers here at South Clapham Modern look out for bullying, some of it's just horseplay, not to be taken seriously. There's also a bit of sexual jealousy or rivalry, they grow up young nowadays, and we take account of that.' Another beam. 'But in this case – twice your son was seen fighting Wilkins, a very unequal fight because Alan's taller and bigger. According to Wilkins, Alan has more than once followed him home, tormenting and threatening him. And demanding money, which Wilkins gave him under threat of being beaten up.'

Alice gasped. Catchpole said incredulously: 'Demanded money. Alan gets – how much is it, two pounds a week?' She nodded. 'He doesn't spend it all, saving up for a computer.'

'With experience, a teacher learns that often the money isn't really the important thing. It's imposing your will on someone else – boys, and girls too, can be very primitive.' Mr Hook spoke almost with relish.

'I'd like to know more about Fred Wilkins. What's his background, do other pupils like him, has he been in any trouble before?'

Mr Hook's smile disappeared. 'As I said, the school has conducted its own investigation, and I'm perfectly satisfied with the result. Your son has admitted the acts I'm talking about, threatening Wilkins and demanding money from him – '

'How much money? Did Wilkins say?'

'Mr Catchpole, I know you're a police superintendent, but this isn't a police interrogation. You must accept that I know how to run my own school.'

'Of course. I'm not a police officer here but a concerned parent, but I won't be fobbed off by being told everything's settled.'

Alice said warningly: 'Hilly.'

'It's all right, I'll keep my temper. I just want Mr Hook to understand everything isn't settled. I want to know whether there are other boys or girls Alan is supposed to have bullied, and I want to ask Fred Wilkins some questions. That's reasonable.' He glared at the headmaster. 'Don't you agree?'

Mr Hook gave a watered-down version of the smile. He told them Wilkins was more than a year younger than Alan and much smaller, a little more than a year older than Desmond. He was the son of a postal worker made redundant two years ago and since then unemployed, and there were two younger children, boy and girl, both in junior school.

'As to his academic abilities, I don't teach him myself, but he's certainly not one of our show per-formers. Nobody holds that against him. We bear in mind he may have troubles at home. We make allowances, we always make allowances.'

'What sort of troubles, what sort of allowances?'

Alice said 'Hilly' again before subsiding under his glare, and Catchpole repeated the question. Mr Hook looked a little uneasy before saying: 'The trouble was to do with other children, I believe mostly girls. I couldn't say he's popular.' He essayed a smile that vanished when the question about allow-ances was repeated. 'I believe the parents aren't get-ting on well. The father drinks since he lost his job, and sometimes takes it out on the children.'

'Sorry to hear it. But you said you make allow-ances. What are the allowances *for?*'

At that, as he said afterwards to Alice, Mr Hook was definitely hooked, the barb in his throat. 'Wilkins has been in trouble – with both sexes – he's not a big boy, but I suppose it could be called bullying. Or threatening perhaps, but I don't think he ever actually hit anybody whereas Alan, you see – '

'I know what Alan did. What sort of threats? Did he ask them to do things, humiliate them?'

'Nothing like that.' A small gasp, then: 'He asked for money. You understand, I didn't deal with this myself, it was in the very capable hands of his form teacher, Miss Barmby. She discovered Fred's pocket money had been stopped, no doubt as a result of his father's redundancy. And, well, Fred Wilkins had been asking for money and I believe saying he had a gang who would do something or other if he didn't get it. I'm sure there was no gang. That is, Miss Barmby was sure.'

'Is this still going on?'

'I don't know that anything went on, Mr Catchpole, as you call it. There were two complaints, Wilkins didn't admit anything, and one of the complaints was withdrawn. Miss Barmby talked to the lad, and told him quite severely that if anything of this kind had been going on it must stop.'

'Doesn't it strike you as odd that Wilkins had been demanding money, and our son is now accused of demanding it from him?'

A faint smirk touched Hook's features. 'There is a difference. Fred Wilkins never admitted it. Alan did.' He went on smoothly. 'Believe me, I hate punishing the boys and girls, but I feel this is something that can't be overlooked. At the same time Alan's work has always been good, he is one of our high-flyers, and I should be sorry to lose him. I'd like us to make a decision together, for you to go away and think about it and let me know your own feelings. Then we can decide.' He beamed at them both, gave them a warm, deep handshake.

Back in the car Catchpole said: 'He's a creep.'

'I knew you wouldn't like the jeans and shirt, but I thought he was reasonable.'

He thumped the steering-wheel. 'It's all wrong, don't you see? Wilkins demands money with menaces, probably gets it, then Alan does the same to him. The two have to be connected, but how?'

'I don't see it helps if they are. I'm so miserable, Hilly, Alan doing that. It must be something we've done wrong.'

'That's just liberal crap.' He put a hand over hers. 'Sorry. But don't start blaming yourself.' They drove in silence until they were within half a mile of the chapel, then he said: 'Of course. That's it.' With the front door open, he ran up the stairs. Alan was bent over an exercise book, doing a French translation for homework. He looked up at his father, who waved at him then went on to Desmond's room. Desmond was on his bed listening to a cassette-player, headphones over ears. Catchpole removed them, sat on the bed, and said: 'Now, Des, tell me about you and Fred Wilkins.'

Desmond turned his head away, his eyes filled with tears. He shook his head. 'All right then, I'll tell you. Wilkins asked you for money, maybe said his pocket money had been stopped, just enough to buy a KitKat bar or a choc-ice, and you gave it to him. Then he said he wanted all your pocket money and had a gang that would beat you up if you didn't give it, very likely told you some others were giving him money already. And you gave it to him. More or less right so far?'

Desmond wiped his nose with his sleeve. 'He did have a sort of gang, three or four of them. At first it was just to get some sweets, then they got me on the ground and took what was in my pockets. So after that I just gave it to them, there were too many of them.'

'And then you told Alan?'

'He found out, because I hadn't got any money, asked what I'd done with it, and I told him. And now Alan – oh Dad, I'm sorry, but he said I mustn't tell you, he could handle it.'

'So that was it,' Catchpole said later to Alice. 'Simple enough really. Anyone except that creep Hook and his half-witted Miss Barmby would have seen there was something wrong at once when a straightforward boy like Alan with a reasonable amount of pocket money has been beating up a smaller boy to get more.' He said meditatively: 'What really impresses me is the nerve Wilkins showed in complaining. I suppose he thought it was the most likely way he could get away with it. I shouldn't be surprised if Fred Wilkins has a bright criminal future.'

'So what happens now?'

'In the morning I ring up the creep, tell him just what happened and why, and suggest that someone a bit tougher than Miss Barmby talks to villainous Fred. Alan's given me the names of three other victims of Wilkins, and they'll all be willing to tell their stories now what Fred and his lads were doing is out in the open. After that – well, I've talked to Alan, he'd like to stay at South Clapham Modern, says a lot of the teaching's very good. Des, I don't know. Not sure he likes it much, but if we took him away and left Alan there, he might feel he'd failed some sort of test. I'd think leave him another term or two, see how it goes. How about you?'

'Me, I go along with it all. I'm full of admiration. You're a cunning old bugger, Hilly, figuring that out so fast. Sometimes you give me the shivers. Just one thing. When you call Hook in the morning, don't crow.'

'Another touch of cunning – it'd be better if *you* ring in the morning. And play down my part in it, say *we* talked to the boys, or you did if you like. Mr Hook will always love you more than he does me.'

So it was settled. In the morning Mr Hook was first astonished, then when he was convinced horrified, by what had been going on at South Clapham Modern. The other victims spoke up. Fred Wilkins made piteous pleas about his ill-treatment at home, and said he had been led astray by his friends. In accordance with Mr Hook's policy of avoiding scandal he was allowed to leave at the end of term, no more than a couple of weeks ahead.

'We could do with air-conditioning,' the Big Man said. Behind him a bluebottle buzzed vainly against a window. The only possible exit was a louvre at the top, and it seemed unlikely the fly would be bright enough to reach it. The Big Man went to the window and partly lowered a venetian blind, with the effect that his face was in shadow while Catchpole remained blinking at the sun. The bluebottle buzzed against the blind. Catchpole said: 'Do you mind, sir?' and shifted his chair out of the direct sunlight. Then he brought his superior up to date about what he had learned at Roselands. The Big Man listened carefully, then said: 'Your conclusions?'

'I don't think I've come to anything so conclusive as conclusions.' A nod and a smile acknowledged the verbal joke. 'It seems to me an overwhelming probability that Ted Copeland is Gene Calendar, and that the family have paid over the years to keep him in homes. He could be an embarrassment to them with his habit of exposing himself and interfering with young girls, and if it's true as Larkins says that he goes berserk at times, then he must be a candidate for killing Lily Devon. As to Bannock, anybody could have arranged to meet him near that pub where he was telephoned and murdered him. It doesn't seem to fit what we know about Copeland, but if Bannock had threatened him I suppose he could have had a violent reaction. Or Bannock may have made an assignation with a sexual end in mind.'

'And the next steps, as you see them?'

'Get Maggie Steel to go on checking the background. Try to find out whether the Calendars own Roselands through the directors. Check every possible means by which Copeland might have got to Blewbury House that night, and check over again the evidence of any witnesses of people going in or standing outside it at the relevant times. Run another check on Bannock's movements the day he was killed – the local Inspector's bright-eyed and eager, he'll do that. And make a thorough search of Copeland's apartment at Roselands looking for any connection with Lily Devon.'

'Clear and concise, Catchers – I'd expect nothing

less from you. But it's still shadow-boxing. Copeland may be a Calendar brother as you say, but what then? As for Bannock, as you say, he may have picked someone up hoping for sex, and got more than he bargained for.'

'But I did say too, sir, that that would be a pretty tall order in the way of coincidences.'

'In life coincidences happen.' The bluebottle stopped buzzing – in appreciation of this wisdom or because it had escaped? 'What you've told me is interesting but a long way from making a case. And really I value your work too highly to see so much of your time being wasted as one might say on the desert air, or on the problem of who murdered a common prostitute.' Catchpole realized that these compliments were somehow ominous, but he heard what followed at first with incredulity, then simply with shock, as the Big Man said he thought the Lily Devon case should be passed over to Detective-Superintendent Lowry, which in view of Lowry's known laziness and desire for a peaceful few months before his retirement was like closing the file. And Bannock? Certain political nuances existed there, the Big Man said, not only those connected with Bannock's sexual preferences. It was important not to offend Pitcombe and the NatLibs, all the more so because Pitcombe was on bad terms with the Home Secretary. So Bannock's death could perhaps best be handled by the man on the spot, who knew all about the area and its gays who might perhaps also be criminals. When he had finished the Big Man said: 'You don't like it?'

'No, sir.'

'You're a reader, Catchers. Have you ever come

across a book by Kropotkin – he was a Prince and an anarchist, unusual combination – called *Mutual Aid*?' Catchpole said no. 'I read it when I was young, and it impressed me. The general idea was, you might say, I help you, you help me. A natural idea, Kropotkin thought. So if you help me I owe you one, do I make myself clear? And I'd regard it as helpful if this Lily Devon affair was passed on to Bill Lowry without it being discussed in the corridors or the canteen, or mulled over in the local hostelry after the third Johnny Walker's. I'm sure I can rely on you.'

'Of course, sir. But do I have a choice – about it being passed on or staying with me?'

An exhalation that could hardly be called a sigh came from across the desk. 'No, you don't have a choice, since you compel me to put it like that. Lily Devon will be Lowry's pigeon from now on. But I shall bear in mind your good work, on this case and in the past. I shan't be keeping this seat warm for ever. Administration can be more rewarding, in its own way, than field work.' The Big Man rose, extended a hand. 'Have a look at *Mutual Aid* sometime. And if you can't find the book remember the principle.'

As Catchpole left the room the bluebottle started buzzing again.

Back in the chapel that night he raged at Alice. 'He's been got at, warned off or more likely bought off. Put a damper on this and you won't have to wait long for promotion, something like that. Could have been money, but I don't think he'd be tempted. Promotion, yes, he's ambitious, longs to be top dog.'

'Don't you?'

'Not that way. There was a hint promotion for me might come my way if I behave myself, stay mum. It makes me sick.'

'You want to be careful, carrying around a ton weight like that conscience of yours or it'll sink you, just a few bubbles coming up on the surface. It helped to kill my brother, don't let it lose you your job.' He glared at her. 'I'm sorry, Hilly, but there are times it seems to me you forget you've got a wife and kids.'

'Look,' he said. 'I've told you before, in my book there are things a copper does and things he doesn't. I'll pay snouts, make a deal with a petty crook to get a real villain, go along with a crime if that'll help to expose a bigger one. I'll lie and cheat and threaten if I think it'll help to get at some truth or other. But there are things I won't do, like taking bribes and faking evidence. Packing in a case because someone upstairs is putting on the pressure, that makes me sick, and the fact that I've got no choice about packing it in doesn't make it any better.'

'So what will you do?'

He shook his head and put it in his hands. She had always admired his thick glossy black hair. Now a few strands of grey showed among the black, and the sight so overwhelmed her with love, and shame at her lack of sympathy, that she embraced him, pulled frantically at his trousers, and they made love on the carpet, something they had not done for years. She waited for him to say afterwards that making love didn't solve any problems, but instead he said he had always loved her and that he wouldn't do anything foolish.

In the morning they were both more cheerful,

but it was true that no problems had been solved. When she asked him what he would do when he got to the Yard he grinned. 'Play it by ear. Just hope I'm not out of tune.'

SIXTEEN

Wrapping It All Up Tidily

THE FAG-END of July. The heatwave still unbroken, the atmosphere humid, the sky thick with thunder that didn't clap, rain that didn't fall. Regent Street and Oxford Street full of bare male torsos, black and brown skins shining beautifully, many white ones like uncooked meat. A sudden fashion for painting faces and bits of bodies with battle scenes and land-scapes, claims made by some art critics that this was a new movement, Impermanent Body Art. Parliament in recess, no new Prime Minister, no word of one: 'An atmosphere thick with rumoured plots, betrayals, stories of unlikely alliances, murmurings that if the delay goes on much longer the Queen will send for the Leader of the Opposition,' said *The Times*.

To Rex Calendar came Ratchet, bearing what he said was good news. 'People are sick of it,' Ratchet said. 'They want action. That means they want you. There's been a shift of feeling in the country, people want *attack*.' His mobile nose twitched.

Ratchet was always strong on the feeling in the country. But surely, Calendar said, his policies on law and order, road building, all his policies implied attack? Ratchet shook his head. 'With the deepest possible respect, they don't go far enough. People now want a clear statement of aims, a programme for national recovery. No offence to the rest of Europe, but a programme that says Britain first, second and third as well.' Tremendous nose twitches there. 'And strengthen ties with the States by all means, but don't knuckle down to 'em, we talk as partners as we did in Maggie's time. In foreign policy Britain first, at home get the wheels moving, give the City confidence, slap down the shirkers, support the bosses of our industries so that they know we're on their side, not sitting carping on the sidelines.' Ratchet subsided, overcome by his own eloquence.

'You're telling me what I already know,' Calendar said, then added as consolation: 'But you may have something. Stress half a dozen simple points, so that even the morons understand. But what you call feeling in the country's one thing, party votes are another. If it comes to an election in the party for leader – '

'With the greatest possible respect, it wouldn't. A statement of aims, clearly put out and phrased in the way you'd put it, would sweep the country. Call it the National Recovery Programme, excellent title. Clear the decks for action, that's the thing.' Ratchet's eyebrows, mobile as his nose, shot up and down.

'Ratchet, you're not listening to me. What I want to know is, in a party election just how will the votes go? What about the Inners? Have you talked to Radley Jevons?'

'Lot of has-beens. Go which way the wind blows.'

'I said, have you talked to Jevons? Or anyone

close to him?' Ratchet said he had tried to but they were cagey, wouldn't commit themselves. His information was that half or more of them were sitting on the fence but all ready to move off it if they were given a little push. Was Ratchet taking his wishes for horses? It was impossible to be sure, but it did seem time to make a move.

With Ratchet gone, Calendar called in his press secretary and the replacement for Jonathan, a greasy-looking young man who impressed him as a potential back-stabber where Jonathan would hardly have known one end of the dagger from the other. He gave them the outline of what was needed, and they went away to flesh out the details of Recovery Programme, which was the briefer title he had decided on. Calendar strengthened the draft with some of his own pungent phrases and the press release went out quickly. It made the lead story not only in the *Bulletin*, but in the other broadsheets and most of the tabloids. Only the *Guardian* had the wit to put a question mark after the heading. As the *Independent* pointed out, the Recovery Programme was not much more than Make Britain Modern rejigged and given a note of urgency. But that note of urgency, Rex Calendar believed, might be just what was wanted at the moment.

He talked to his brother, who was enthusiastic about what the *Bulletin* called the Six Points, but worried by other matters. The Home Secretary reassured him. 'The heat is off.'

'My information is that the police are still poking around.'

'Donald, I said the heat is off. I've made arrangements. The Kennington inquiry is closed. Forget it.'

In conversations with his brother Donald's voice often took on a pleading, even whining tone. It did so now when he mentioned Gene. Rex stopped him. 'Donald, this is an open line.' His brother said something about sitting on a time-bomb, and Rex became impatient. 'If there was a bomb it's been defused. The trouble caused by the elephantine antics of your subordinates has been put right. The matter's settled. I hope I'm making myself clear.'

'Clear, yes. I just hope you're right.' He then told Rex that the Pitcombes had backed out of the Welsh land deal, and reluctantly agreed that this was not the time to alienate the NatLibs completely by printing the story, with its conclusion that the leader of the party concerned so much with the people's welfare was puritanically opposed to the fun and games of a theme park. At the same time, Donald was not pleased. 'This is another exclusive we're sitting on.'

Rex said they were playing for bigger stakes than printing good stories. '*You* are,' Donald responded. 'I can't see what *I* get out of it.' But, as always, he did what Rex wanted.

Rex put down the telephone without saying goodbye. He spent a couple of hours that afternoon discussing publicity matters with Rosie Raymond.

Johnno and Belinda were drinking sherry while trying to decide which of the local restaurants they would dine at, when the bell rang. The tall woman standing outside said: 'Have you seen him?'

Johnno gaped at her.

'My son. George.'

'Come in. Please come in.' She followed him into the living room.

'Belinda, this is George's mother, Mrs Kaiser.'

'I don't know where you get that Kaiser from, the name's Kavin. Was Kavinsky but Moshe, my husband that was, said Kavin was more English. That's my name. And George's. It's George I'm looking for. He lives here, is that right?'

'Not exactly, he's just here sometimes. But how can that be his name? I was at Oxford with him, and his name was Kaiser. He as good as told me his father had been a member of the German royal family, the Hohenzollerns.'

'Did he say that? George was always a liar, from a little boy. Clever, but a liar. Got his scholarship to Oxford, but never wanted his father or me to come up and see him, too Jewish, too low-class. The authorities there, they must have known his real name, but there's no law to say you can't call yourself what you like, though it could be they'll soon pass one.'

Mrs Kavin looked more like a man than a woman, an impression enhanced by her height, by shoulders as wide as those of a front-row forward, and by her clothes. She wore stretch trousers striped in red, white and blue, and a cherry red jacket. Her shoes were also red, of a darker shade than the jacket. She brushed aside the offer of a drink and said: 'Where is he?'

Johnno found himself tongue-tied, and it was Belinda who replied. 'He only stays here occasionally, Mrs Kavin. There must be other places he lives most of the time.'

'Of course there is. He's got a flat in Redbridge, near the works.' Her searchlight gaze shifted from

Johnno to Belinda, then back. 'That's where I found your name and address. Reed, Jonathan Reed, that's you?'

Johnno acknowledged it. 'But I don't quite understand why you're looking for him.'

'Because he's disappeared, why else?'

'Then perhaps I can explain, or be of some help. I expect you know George is in government employ, involved with one of the secret services. A few days ago I gave him some private information – I work, or I did then, for the Home Office – about a problem that had come up. George said he would deal with it, and I'm afraid he did. I can't reveal details, but somebody's been killed. I'm sure George was involved, and that's why he's gone under cover.'

He wriggled unhappily under the glare, waiting for an explosion. After a moment or two it came, a roar not of indignation but of laughter. 'George told you that stuff? And you believe it? Let me tell you what George Kavin does. When Moshe died – there he was one minute, my Moshe, on the blower shouting at one of our clients if he didn't pay in seven days we'd take him to court. Next minute he's dropped down dead. He liked a shouting match, my Moshe, we'd yell at each other all day long. You got to shout to make yourself heard in this world, though George would sneak out of the room away from it. Trouble with George, he's got no guts. Can't face up to things. Can't shout. A dreamer.'

Belinda nodded emphatic agreement. 'That's what I've always said. So what—'

'I think I could use that drink, after all.' She downed what Johnno poured in a gulp, said with disgust, 'Sherry,' then, 'You won't help?'

'Mrs Kavin, we have no idea – ' Johnno started again. 'George has always been a bit of a mystery man, never mentioned his parents or told us what he did. Except recently he's dropped hints about being in government employ. He was very convincing.' There was a sound of dissent from Belinda. 'Well, he convinced me. Especially when he promised to take care of someone causing trouble and the man died, could have been murdered.'

Mrs Kavin shook her head disbelievingly, poured herself more sherry, and downed it with a shudder. 'I'll tell you what George does, and what he did. He was a salesman for KTP and a good one, he's a real spieler is George. Then when my Moshe died, he'd always looked after the accounts Moshe, chased 'em like a tiger if they didn't pay up on time, I made George the finance director. The biggest mistake of my life.' Belinda asked what the initials stood for, and received a glare. 'Kavin Toilet Preparations, everything for the bathroom. Started with toilet rolls in ten colours – that was Moshe's idea, why stick to white or pink, we put out light grey, green, blue light and dark, rainbow – very successful, rainbow – then expanded. *Everything* for the bathroom from KTP, six different sorts of loofah including one in the shape of a gentleman's doodah, four different scents to make the air sweet, rambler rose the most popular. Everything.'

Johnno asked what had happened, although by now he had a good idea of the answer. 'George was fiddling the books. Cheating KTP. Defrauding his mother. Three years he's been at it, then it came to a crisis with this year's audit, and he's done a bunk. And you know where the money went?'

Belinda said: 'Not on women.'

'Right you are, my dear. George never showed interest in that aspect. Gambling. Not even a gentleman's sport like horse-racing. The dogs. I've been over his flat since he skedaddled, and he's in hock to three bookies, thousands he owes to each one of 'em. And he's borrowed from a loan shark. He used to go off for days at a time, supposed to be following up slow payers and looking for new business. In his filofax, after your name, he'd written "hideaway". So I came here.'

When she had gone Belinda said: 'At least you don't have to worry any more about being responsible for a murder.'

'No.'

'She was wonderful, wasn't she? Those clothes. Those shoulders. I'd back her to survive after a shipwreck, or in a prison camp.'

'I suppose so, yes.'

'I loved the way she swigged the sherry, even though she didn't like it.'

'Yes.'

'You don't seem very cheerful.'

'It's just that I liked – like – George. Most of us live such dull lives, and he seemed to give a glimpse of an exciting one. Only of course it wasn't.'

'Oh, I don't know. Fiddling the books and spending the money on some crackpot greyhound racing system sounds quite exciting to me.' Silence. 'Don't you see, beanbag, it's all terribly funny? Just think of George going around selling all that loo paper, rainbow the most popular. And I can't wait to get my hands on one of those loofahs.'

'I think it's pathetic. I don't like to think of George as pathetic.'

'Come on then, misery, let's go out and eat. I want to go to the Greek place, eat some vine leaves and a pilaff, and drink lots of filthy retsina. Does it taste like leather, or more like one of those sticks of black liquorice we used to eat when we were kids? Tonight I'm going to make up my mind.'

They went out. He cheered up.

Catchpole spent the next days in a state similar to his experiences after being concussed when hit on the head by a man in a pub during the course of a drugs raid. He went about his work perfectly competently, so Charlie Wilson and the typing-pool girls said afterwards, but couldn't remember a thing about it. Since the work consisted mostly of reading and approving memos about what travel expenses could permissibly be charged, and an elaborate new system for speeding up interdepartmental communications, his blankness of mind was not important.

He did not pass the bulky Lily Devon file on to Lowry, although this was not out of conscious rebelliousness but simply because he did not think about it. He looked at the newspaper headlines that said things like: 'Calendar's Great Recovery Plan . . . Calendar, the Way Forward . . . Home Secretary's Play for Leadership . . .' and read the stories without really taking them in. It was almost a relief when he was sent on a course, his name put forward no doubt at the Big Man's instigation, on 'The Use of Information Technology in Ensuring the Cooperation of International Police Forces'. The course lasted almost a week, was held at a hotel in Suffolk where drink flowed freely all day and night, and the food was approved by the attendant cast of senior police officers from six European countries, all of them speaking good or excellent English. Catchpole was one of the most junior officers on the course. He took part in lengthy discussions on the problems involved in using the new technology, but at the end of each day could hardly remember a word he had said.

An agreeable interlude, provided chiefly for the other Europeans, was a testing of the Baybee, which none of them had seen although all knew of its existence. When tested it performed well up to a range of about ten feet, after that became inaccurate and much less penetrative. The general view, expressed particularly by officers from countries where there was most violent crime, was that the Baybee was an ingenious but not very effective toy. It was stressed by the small-arms expert who supervised the testing, and had played a large part in developing the Baybee, that improvements were still being made and this was not the final model. In the meantime all of them, Catchpole included, were presented with Baybees, loaded and ready for use, in their neat chamois leather containers that fitted unnoticeably around the hip.

The Baybee was an entertainment, an agreeable debating subject, but for the most part Catchpole felt wrapped in a cocoon of unbeing, his only contact with reality the conversations held every evening with Alice and the boys. This sensation was not lessened when he returned to the Yard and found on his desk a thick wodge of papers, the top one headed: 'Suggested Techniques for Fulfilment of the Multiple Protection Plan'. What was the Multiple Protection Plan? Something to do with a scheme floated by the Home Secretary for closer links between police forces in large towns and cities. He pushed it aside. His telephone rang, and at the same moment a red light on his intercom glowed. He picked up the telephone. The switchboard girl said, 'Dr Armitage from Roselands wants to speak to you. Rang twenty minutes ago. Said it was urgent.'

He pressed the intercom buzzer. Maggie Steel said: 'That long shot of yours, looks as if there might be something in it. Nothing exciting about the washing, but two jackets were sent for dry-cleaning. Moira remembers it because they came back with one of those notes cleaners sometimes put in, saying they've done their best but can't get the stains or marks out completely. Jackets and trousers, actually, but the trousers didn't have a note attached. And who do you think they belonged to?' She told him, then went on: 'The computer turned up something about our Poppy and her partner. She's got a couple of speeding fines, lost her licence for twelve months. More interesting, she was involved in a case when she was heading a psychiatric clinic. She was responsible for letting a wife killer out into the community on the ground that he was now harmless, and within a week he'd searched out his daughter and stabbed her to death. No prosecution or anything like that, but she had to leave the clinic, seems to have taken odd jobs for a year or two before she came to Roselands. And partner Nigel was up on a drugs charge six years ago. Not just using, handling and maybe dealing. He got away with it, admitted using, said

he'd been under stress. The other charges were dropped, he got probation.'

He sensed something held back. 'There's more?'

'Well, yes.' For once in her life Maggie sounded
embarrassed. 'You know what they say, everyone
says, about computers, ask the right questions and
you get accurate answers. I fed a lot of names in.
And in one the operator pressed a wrong button.
Generally doesn't matter much, if you press an "o"
or an "e" for the second "a" in Armitage, the computer will still come up with a lot of names near to
what you've asked for, Armitage included. But this
time the operator pressed the wrong initial letter, so
what she got was a lot of names that were no use at
all. Kind of thing should never happen, but once in
a thousand times it does. And I should have spotted
it, but didn't. It could be important.' She told him
why.

Dr Armitage's voice was cool as ever when she
said: 'We've had a tragedy here at Roselands, Superintendent. Last night Ted Copeland hanged himself.'
The coolness turned icy as she continued. 'You were
talking to him, and I understand that afterwards he
was upset. I don't know whether your interview had
any connection with his death, but I thought you
should be informed.'

Catchpole said he would be down at Roselands
in an hour, and asked that nothing should be
touched.

'A little late for that, I'm afraid. I'm sure you'll
understand that he had to be cut down. But there's
no doubt he hanged himself. I can testify to that in
person.'

Again, Catchpole's reaction was automatic. The

instruction to let the Lily Devon case alone was simply not in his mind as he drove himself down to Roselands. And it was not by conscious decision that he took neither Charlie Wilson nor a driver. His mind was blank of everything except an image of the hanged man.

Publication of the Recovery Programme, the attention it received in the media, and the instant requests by TV and radio pundits for Rex Calendar to explain his plans in detail – requests to which he willingly acceded – had effects he did not foresee. He realized it would upset the NatLibs, but the NatLibs as a party and Allen Pitcombe as their leader would as he thought be neutralized by the wave of enthusiasm with which the press greeted what *The Times* called a bold, brave and above all decisive programme, and by his own immediate rise in the polls as potential leader of the party. It seemed to him that Pitcombe was only important while the party was uncertain of its objectives as it had been under Patrick Bladon. With the Recovery Programme accepted there would be enough NatLib waverers to make Pitcombe's objections unimportant. 'Do you know what gives me most pleasure out of the whole shebang?' he said to his press secretary. 'The fact that I'll be able to ignore that canting po-faced bore.' The press secretary laughed dutifully, but his master detected a certain counting-your-eggs-before-they're-hatched scepticism behind the laughter. There was nothing of the wide-eyed wonder Jonathan would have shown. It came to him with a shock that he missed the idiocies and innocence of Jonathan.

The press secretary was right to be sceptical. Rex
Calendar had forgotten the devious skills of Radley
Jevons.

Or perhaps he had given too much credit to
Ratchet, when he said Jevons was a has-been and
the Inners would go with any prevailing wind.
Radley was lazy, anxious always to preserve the status
quo, had always refused any important post in
government. He was reluctant to take positive action
– indeed, political inaction seemed to him almost
always preferable to actually doing anything – but
the stridency, assertiveness and dogmatism of the
Recovery Programme appalled him. He had discour-
aged Rhoda because of her eagerness, but this was
far worse.

Radley had reckoned on spending the recess
partly looking after his Leicestershire constituency,
and partly doing what he called a spot of fishing in
one of Scotland's loveliest salmon rivers. But that
was all given up, for Radley recognized a crisis, and
fairly put himself about. Scotland was postponed, his
attendance at local shows and dinners reduced to a
minimum. He disliked the telephone, but now used
the awful instrument to talk to several Inners, even
pursuing some of them to holiday fastnesses where
they had thought themselves free from any parliamentary voice. He had himself driven in his vintage
Daimler to see a dozen possible waverers in Wales,
the Midlands and the NatLib South-west, and then
made the final sacrifice of returning to London,
which even in the recess was the country's political
nerve centre.

It was still disgustingly hot, and in London
Radley abandoned the lightweight tweeds that were

his usual summer wear, in favour of blue and dark grey linen suits made especially for tropical use. His red face, fluffy sideboards and quiff of fine white hair were seen in clubs, at dinners in private houses, even in a restaurant or two. His host or companion or guest was always a Member of Parliament who might be persuaded that a Recovery Programme led by Rex Calendar was not in the national interest and, as Radley said with hand upon heart, would have horrified his old and dear friend and colleague Patrick Bladon.

Some word of this activity filtered through to Calendar, but he took little notice of it. Radley shunned rather than courted publicity, and his rare appearances on the box suggested that he was a bumbling old fellow.

The end of Radley's to-ing and fro-ing, probing and persuading, was Downing Street. Not Number Ten, still awaiting an occupant, but the house next door, where Rhoda was busy, indeed busier than usual. The City had reacted calmly to the lack of a Prime Minister, feeling perhaps that Bladon's hand on the tiller had been very slack in his last months, and the markets had been cautiously friendly to the idea of the Recovery Programme.

Rhoda received Radley with courtesy rather than enthusiasm, remembering their telephone conversation. She asked what he would drink.

'Lime juice, my dear, lime juice and soda. Alcohol in this weather – ' He shook his head. 'But you look wonderfully cool. Cool, calm and in control.' He beamed at her. His tropical dark grey suit shone silkily, the face above it was very red.

She poured his lime juice, gave herself a small

whisky and water. 'Why aren't you catching salmon in Scotland?'

'I wish I were. I felt the situation called for my presence down here.'

Rhoda raised her thick brows.

'Rhoda, my dear, when we last talked I said I thought there should be a delay in appointing the new PM. I was wrong. I hadn't anticipated Calendar's forcing the pace in the way he has done, or the fuss the wretched media would make about his so-called programme. So I was wrong, and I'm very sorry. I've been trying to put things right, and hope I may have succeeded.' At that she merely nodded, and Radley Jevons thought in admiration: 'My word, she's a tough one. She could take Calendar on, take anybody on.'

He continued: 'I've been talking to the Inners. Not to every one of them, but to the most important, talking enough for me to know their opinions. Their feeling, with not a single dissentient voice among them, is that you should have their blessing. They would like you to form and head a government. By a general consensus rather than an election within the party which might be divisive. That's the gut feeling, to use a coarse phrase, of the party.'

'So I have their blessing. And the Inners have a gut feeling, good for them. But blessings and gut feelings aren't enough. Have you been counting heads?' The white quiff nodded. 'Then you'll know they aren't enough. The Inners are the soul of the party if you like, and perhaps the majority of the party will go along with them, but that still isn't enough. There are forty members, fifty, maybe as many as seventy, who really do think the sun shines

out of Rex Calendar's backside. Or if that offends
you, they've been hanging on to his coat-tails so
long they'd be in free fall if they let go.' At the
mention of *backside* Radley had indeed averted his
face. 'And even if we persuaded a few of them to
hang on to a skirt instead of a jacket, we'd still need
some of the NatLibs.' She leaned forwards, jabbing
at him with a finger. 'I thought this might have been
done, we could have got agreement in the immediate
aftermath of Patrick's death. But what did you say
then? *People must be consulted, decisions have to be made,
be patient.* I appreciate your efforts now, but they
come a bit late. All I can see ahead is a leadership
ballot with two or three or more candidates, a no-
holds-barred fight, and at the end of it a badly
damaged party.'

'Could I have a little more of this very refreshing
lime juice?' After taking a couple of sips Radley said:
'You do me an injustice, Rhoda, if you think I'm
not aware of the potential pitfalls. But they're possibilities, not certainties, and I've been exercising my
poor old brain and any powers of persuasion I pos-
sess, in trying to circumvent them. We have two
ends in view – first, to convince our friend Rex that
his public assault can't succeed because too many
people in the party will never accept him as PM.
And second, to persuade Rex and his colleagues, and
our allies the NatLibs, that you're Patrick's natural
successor. This is a matter of strategy. I'll tell you
what I propose.'

When he had finished she said wonderingly:
'You've got a villain's mind, Radley. Nobody would
think it to look at you.'

'I shall take that as a compliment. All I've done

is to prepare the ground. The difficult part has to be done by you.'

'Just one thing. At the end of it, if it comes off, what do you want yourself? A Cabinet post? You could pretty well name it. A knighthood? Of course.'

'You misjudge me, Rhoda. I want nothing for myself, simply the knowledge that the government is being carried on by the right people in the right way, Patrick's way when he was in his prime. If I thought Rex could do it I'd support him. But I don't.'

What you want, Rhoda thought after he had gone, is to play kingmaker. But then, should she complain? That night she looked at herself in the mirror and said: 'Rhoda Carpenter, you may be Prime Minister.'

The news from Roselands diverted Rex Calendar temporarily from the publicity campaign. He talked to Donald, who was almost beside himself with distress and fear. 'You weren't there on that terrible night – it was such a *shock* to me. If what we'd done, what we agreed to, came out – '

'It won't.'

Rex rang the Big Man, who was for a few moments lost for words as he listened to the flow of invective. Then he said: 'But as I told you, all inquiries have been stopped. The case has been put on the back burner.'

'After the damage had been done. Your man – what's his name?'

'Catchpole.'

'I shall remember it. Your man subjected

Copeland to what I don't doubt was a savage inter-rogation, one that left him so fearful he hanged himself.' The Big Man protested that they had only talked about stopping inquiries into the Lily Devon affair. He was brutally interrupted.

'If you didn't understand that that included stop-ping any poking about at Roselands, you must be a bigger fool than you seemed.'

'They were to be left in the hands of the local police. Catchpole had already spoken to the man Copeland before we talked. And he's the most dis-creet of officers, I'm sure his questioning will have been probing perhaps, but not savage.'

Calendar ignored this. 'I want you to understand, any provisional arrangement we may have made is cancelled, am I making myself clear? That conver-sation never took place. Neither did this one.'

The Big Man endured another few seconds of vituperation before the telephone was slammed down at the other end. Then he composed himself, assessed the damage. The AC, inefficient beer-swilling golf-mad figure that he was, would see out his term as boss of the Met. His replacement by the Big Man would not be made in the near future, perhaps not ever. But that was all. There was no threat to his present position, and it was unlikely one would be made. It was also possible, of course, that Calendar would come a cropper and a new Home Secretary with different views could be appointed . . .

It was typical of the Big Man that during this period of contemplation no thought of Catchpole or of the hanged man crossed his mind.

★

'So you knew he was Gene Calendar all the time.'
Catchpole shook his head, sighed.

'You have to understand. I was bound by my
agreement to say nothing, and so far as I could see
it was a family matter, no concern of yours. His
tragic death changes things.'

'He might not be dead now if you'd told me his
identity the last time we talked.'

'I can't accept that for a moment. As I've said,
we were bound by a solemn agreement.'

'Rubbish. What bound you was your own past
history. I'll tell you the way I see it. When Dr Phillips
skedaddled with his lady and the money, the other
Calendar brothers were put on the spot about Gene.
They suspected he'd killed another boy when he was
ten, and he was subject to fits of rage when he could
be violent. He should really have been in a secure
mental home, but let's say they loved their brother,
or at least loved him enough not to put him away
in a mental home. But they wanted also to keep
control over the place he went to, so they got Fazackerley, who should be inside though we've never
been able to put him there, to look around for
someone to run the new place they were prepared
to set up, who was basically respectable but had
something dodgy about them. And Faz found you.
You'd been in trouble, your husband was an addict.'
She began to protest. 'Save your breath. Maybe partner Nigel's cured, maybe you acted from the best of
motives and were unlucky. Doesn't matter.'

'Nigel *is* cured.' She glared at him through the
rimless glasses. 'And Ted – we always called him
that, Ted was cured too. The idea of curing him, that
was part of the reason for appointing an alienist

who'd look after him. Fazackerley told me that, one
of the only two or three times I saw him – I never
spoke to either of the Calendar brothers, but Fazackerley told me Ted's real name, and said it wasn't to
be revealed if any snooper came round asking questions. And Ted was cured, I'll swear it. He suffered
from a fairly rare form of schizophrenia, and I'm
convinced the tendency to violence had been what
we call phased out. He still liked what he called
playing games with girls, he was interested in sex,
but violence – not now. Fred Larkins would tell you
the same thing, I'm sure.'

'But he hanged himself.'

'I don't understand it. He seems just to have fixed
the rope around a hook in the ceiling and stepped
off a chair. Fred found him when he went in around
nine o'clock this morning – Ted was always up by
eight – and called me. I examined him, then waited
for Dr Roper, the nearest doctor we have on call,
then he was cut down. We both think he did it
around midnight last night. There was no farewell
note, nothing. I'm afraid we failed him, I don't know
how.' She looked down at her desk, then up again.
'Is Maggie Steel with you?'

'Not today. I'm on my own.'

'She's a bright girl.'

'She turned you and your partner up on our
computer.' Dr Armitage flinched slightly. 'I'd like to
see the body. And talk to Fred Larkins.'

'Of course. You'll find him somewhere around.
He was closer to Ted than anyone, though everyone
liked him. You'll find the residents rather subdued,
news of this sort affects everyone. We've laid Ted
out in his own bedroom. Of course there'll have

to be an inquest, but there's no doubt about what happened. Or what made him do it.'

'Dr Armitage.' Catchpole put his arms on the desk that separated them. 'Nothing I said when I talked to him could have made Ted Copeland hang himself. I think you know that.' She looked at him for a moment, then away, and said nothing.

Subdued was the right word for the atmosphere of Roselands. On his way back to the entrance hall Catchpole passed Poppy Armitage's partner, Nigel, who hesitated at the sight of him, then bolted into the nearest room, the library. In the entrance hall he stopped to speak to a red-eyed Moira. Like Dr Armitage she asked if Maggie was with him, and was disappointed when he said no. At mention of Ted she shook her head.

'I can hardly believe it now, he was always so cheerful. And so much better, though he still had his little ways, know what I mean. Once you got to know him you took no notice of them.'

'But he wasn't violent?'

'Not that I ever saw, I can't imagine it really.' She lowered her voice. 'Those lists I gave Maggie, were they any use?'

'They were a help, yes. What you gave her was a photocopy, have you still got the actual lists?' She nodded, opened a filing cabinet, took out a folder.

'I kept them in case there should be any queries, we don't usually send things out. And they'll be needed when Mr Straker makes up the monthly accounts. This was the laundry for that week, and then here are the accounts for the jackets and trousers that were dry-cleaned.'

Catchpole put them in his pocket, thanked her,

and made his way around the back of the house to the barn that had been Ted Copeland's home. The day was sultry, the sky dark with thunder. He opened the barn door and went through the workshop into the living quarters. The body lay in the narrow bedroom, a purplish circle round the neck where the noose had been cut away, the face mottled, the trousers smelling of urine. The cut noose and the rest of the rope lay on the bed beside the body. The room held little furniture other than a chest of drawers and a cupboard that looked as if Gene might have made them himself. The chest of drawers contained vests, pants, shirts, pullovers, all neatly folded. Beneath the shirts were half a dozen old black and white photographs in an envelope. One showed the shop in New Valley, with a man, presumably Joe Calendar, standing outside it hands on hips, his stance aggressive. The others showed three boys whose identity he would not have recognized but for the wording on the back that said 'Rex' and 'Donald', and one that showed them all together, labelled 'Rex, Donald, me.' Me was smaller than the others, his hand holding Donald's, his expression blank where theirs was cockily assertive in their father's style. Catchpole thought of his own Desmond, and shook his head. The clothes in the cupboard were similarly neatly hung. Catchpole looked at them closely, then took out a greeny-grey jacket and a pair of grey trousers, both obviously recently cleaned.

He went into the living room, saw the hook in the ceiling from which Copeland's body had hung, and stood on a chair to examine it. He was about to get down when he noticed, two or three feet along from the hook, a couple of newly made marks in the beam as if something had been screwed into it. But what? He marked the position of the holes on a piece of paper, then went into the workshop and looked around for something that might fit them. A ceiling fixture for a light fitting matched the holes perfectly, but there seemed no conceivable purpose in putting a light fitting on the beam. Then, lying loose in a tool box full of odds and ends, he saw a small pulley wheel with holes for screw fixing. When he stood on a chair and fitted the pulley to the screw holes they matched. Catchpole pursed his lips in a silent whistle, went into the bedroom, partly uncoiled the rope and ran it through the groove of the pulley, where it went smoothly and easily. He was back in the living room, the pulley in his pocket, when Fred Larkins appeared in the doorway and said: 'You've seen him?'

'Yes. You were the one who found him this morning. Did you see him last night?'

'Sure. Saw Ted pretty well every evening. He liked to chat, drink a glass of beer. Last night same as usual. I left him around nine o'clock, he liked to turn in early.'

'Did he give any hint of what he was going to do, was he depressed?'

Larkins hesitated. His small square face was a mask of indecision, the Cheerful Chappie was worried. 'Not sure how much I should say, what you know.'

'I know Ted Copeland's name was Gene Calendar, and who his brothers are. My guess is you had a brief from them to keep an eye on him.'

'Good guess. Auntie Armitage didn't know about it. I only saw Mr Calendar, the politician I mean,

just the once. I suppose he'd been told I got along
with Ted, and he asked if I'd look after him, keep
him out of any mischief. He and his brother didn't
want any publicity about what Ted thought of as his
little games, showing his willy and all that. Suppose
they were afraid some people'd cotton on to who
he was, and make trouble for them. I got an envelope
every month from some solicitor, the money was
handy. And I did my best, managed OK the last
couple of years. Till now.'

'What about last night?'

Larkins took out a cigarette from a packet, then
pushed it back. 'What you're after is who did that
tart in Kennington a few weeks ago, right? It was
Ted. I knew it at the time, but didn't want to admit
it even to myself. What happened that night was I
took him up to London in my old banger. He loved
going up to town as he called it, could spend a
couple of hours playing pinball machines and games,
once he was in an arcade it was hard to get him
away. I had a mate I'd arranged to meet down Kennington, pub near the Oval, so we went in there.
Idea was we'd have a pint or two, then take in a
movie – Ted loved Westerns – have a meal, come
back. Just an outing, nothing exciting. There's a
couple of pin-tables in the pub, Ted goes over to
play 'em, then when I look round he's not there,
skedaddled.

'I wasn't much worried at first, reckoned he'd
gone in an arcade near by he knew about, but he
wasn't there. Knew there were only two things
would interest Ted, pin-table games and girls. After
a bit I went back to the Queen of Hearts, that was
the pub's name, reckoned Ted'd have to come back

there. My mate got fed up with waiting around, cleared off. Then after maybe half an hour or a bit longer Ted comes in, calls me, I go out in the street with him, he's in a terrible state. Blood on his clothes and he's shivering and shaking, won't tell me what happened except he was with a girl and there was an accident. I asked him where it was and first he says he doesn't know, but then he takes me to it, block of flats, can't remember the name.'

'Blewbury House.'

'Blewbury House, right.'

'Did he say how he got in the girl's flat?'

'No. Maybe she was out on the street, or could be he saw one of those cards tarts put in newsagents' windows. Anyway I was set to ring the bell, find out what had happened, but Ted wouldn't have it. He was half crying, half screaming, saying I shoulda looked after him, which is true in a way, and he wanted Rex or Donald, they'd know what to do. Seemed to me that wasn't a bad idea, and we went to brother Donald's flat. He'd been having a party or something, though he was on his own. Can't say he was pleased to see us, but he certainly went into action. We got Ted cleaned up, then he rang his brother. After talking to him, he said we should go home and forget anything ever happened. Mind you, Ted couldn't remember anyway, so he said, and I believe him. He had these blackouts when he was violent, not more than once or twice a year.'

'And last night?'

'Last night he'd remembered, and it upset him. He said, "Ted did something very bad last time we went up to town, didn't he. There was a girl, Ted wanted her to play, and she wouldn't. Then he began to cry. And *then* – ' Larkins's little brown eyes seemed about to pop out of his head. 'Then I said to him if he really believed he'd done something very bad he should go to the police, tell them, then give himself up. I'll never forgive myself for saying it.'

'Don't try.'

'How d'you mean?' Larkins's hands, dark hair over their backs, were posed on the table like two small animals, but all they did was fidget with the cigarette packet.

'You should be telling fairy stories on radio for the kids. Lily Devon never walked the streets, and she didn't use notices in shop windows, she had too much class for that.'

'Maybe not. I don't know how Ted found her.'

'He didn't. It was you who found her, through one of the sex magazines was it, or through another girl on the game? You took Ted along, told him he could watch, maybe take part. You're on the computer, Larkins, though it wasn't spotted because the programmer made a slip, printed P for L, and came up with Parkins. Tying girls up and then giving them half an hour of torture, that's how you get your kicks. I don't know what the judge was thinking about, giving you only three years. Not as if it was the first time.'

'That was a long time ago. Not been in trouble for years now, your computer must have told you that.'

'So you've been lucky. Don't tell me you haven't been at it. And looking after Ted Copeland was a plus, you had some fun with him, I'll bet. Playing games, eh?'

The little animals took the cigarette packet,

looked for a moment as if they would twist it in pieces, they extracted a cigarette, lighted it. Catchpole went on.

'Let me tell you what happened that night. You'd got in touch with Lily Devon, I'd guess by dropping the word through another girl that you were connected with high-ups in the government, that would have impressed her. She'd have thought there'd be rich pickings if you'd dropped a hint you'd be bringing along the brother of a government minister. Maybe she agreed to a spot of bondage before she saw the colour of your money, then objected when she saw the brother was only going to watch, and you were the active one. What did you offer her, fifty? From what I hear the tariff would have been four times that. So then you went wild and did what you did. Maybe Ted gave a helping hand at some point, more likely he put his hands over his eyes. Whatever way, there was a lot of blood, some got on your clothes even though you may have thrown a lot of them off, and some got on Ted's. Then you had the idea of telling the Calendars it was Ted who'd done the girl, not you, or if you didn't tell them that you implied it. It could be you threatened him, he worshipped you and was frightened of you at the same time, or maybe you didn't have to say anything, he depended on you so much. Whether the Calendars believed you or not you knew they'd protect Ted, certainly didn't want publicity about a brother who'd been mixed up in a murder. It was quick thinking, going to see Donald Calendar.' He paused. 'Any comment?'

'No need. It never happened, just talk.'

'And more coming,' Catchpole said cheerfully. 'There's the pulley.'

'What pulley?'

'This one.' Catchpole produced it from his pocket. 'Fits perfectly with those screw marks in the beam. Shall I tell you what it was used for? Games.'

'I don't know what you're talking about. You keep saying games. What games?'

'Sex games, you bastard.' Catchpole's voice was level, but the tone was bitter. 'That's what the poor sod liked, isn't it, sex games that made what he called his willy stand up. And you went along with him, taught him ways of jerking off, exciting himself. Could be you even found it fun to watch.'

'I've no need to sit here, listen to this.'

'You'll listen till I've finished. There's a game you can play on your jack, where you half choke yourself by hanging, get a hard on, then relax the rope at the moment of ejaculation. Hard to know if it's the danger or the physical act of near-strangulation gives the pleasure, so it's said. It's a game of solitaire, only Ted played it with his friend, and I don't think this was the first time. So Ted and Fred played the game as they had before, with Fred hauling on the rope that ran through the pulley, only this time he didn't let go. Then when the job was done you took him down, unscrewed the pulley and hooked him on to the place where he was supposed to have done the job himself, kicking away the chair he was supposed to have stood on. Nice work.'

The little brown eyes looked from side to side, never at Catchpole. 'Said before it's all talk, rubbish talk. Trying to fit me up.'

'We can get prints off the rope. And the pulley.'

'Course they'll be on the pulley, Mr Cleverdick. I've used it often enough in the workshop.'

'Then there's DNA, genetic fingerprinting, you'll have heard of it.'

For the first time the little furry animals were withdrawn from the table. 'What's DNA got to do with any of this?'

'On the seventh of June two pairs of trousers and two jackets were sent to the dry-cleaner, one lot yours, the other Ted Copeland's.'

'Right. They were dirty, so they went.'

'Moira remembers they had marks on as if something had been spilt. Natural enough to send the things to be dry-cleaned, not try to wash out the stains yourself. But a mistake, definitely a mistake. Burning would have been better. Dry cleaning – ' He shook his head. 'It may have got out the surface stains, but there'll be enough left for a DNA sample, using a microscope and probably ultra-violet illumination. I've got Ted's jacket and trousers, and if you'll let me have yours – '

Larkins was on his feet. He said nothing, but moved backwards towards the workshop.

'I'll also be taking you in, to help us with our inquiries, and to get your story on tape.'

Larkins shouted: 'No.' He had reached the workshop door, and disappeared beyond it. Catchpole moved after him, and was in the doorway when he saw the scythe coming at him, ducked and moved aside. The scythe stuck in the door frame for a moment, then fell to the ground with a clatter. Larkins plucked a pitchfork from the wall behind him. The bright tines looked viciously sharp.

Catchpole said: 'This is stupid. You're an intelligent man, you know now we've got your record you'll have to talk to us.'

Larkins shouted *no* again. His little brown eyes were fixed on the detective, the merry face was grim. Words came out of his mouth in bursts, not quite coherently. 'Not taking me in – fitted up, fitted up, they always fit you up – little bitches all of them pretending they don't like it – I'll stick you, you come any nearer, I swear I will.' They shuffled round the room in a kind of slow motion comic ballet, Catchpole edging towards the outside door, Larkins making thrusts with the pitchfork to keep him away. It occurred to the detective, late in the day, that it would have been wise to bring along Charlie Wilson. He hadn't done so because the visit was wholly unauthorized and he might have landed his Sergeant in trouble. While he thought of this, a vicious jab caught the sleeve of his jacket. He swayed slightly, felt the Baybee hard against his hip, took it out, said to Larkins: 'Put that thing down.'

A laugh was the first response, another pitchfork jab aimed at his chest the next. Catchpole was suddenly very angry. He said, 'If you don't put it down I shall shoot.'

Larkins laughed again. 'Bloody little peashooter, poncey policeman.' Then he suddenly sank to the floor still holding the pitchfork, a look of surprise on his face. The sound made by the Baybee had indeed been no more than the *pop-pop* of a motorized bicycle, and Catchpole barely realized he had pulled the trigger. He had aimed at the lower part of Larkins's body. Sure enough a stain was spreading in the region of his groin, and now the hand holding the pitchfork abandoned it and moved to the lower abdomen. Catchpole shook his head, looked at the Baybee, and put it back in its little pocket.

The difficult part, as Radley Jevons had called it, proved difficult indeed. Tentative approaches made at second hand to Allen Pitcombe met with the response that he would not be prepared to bring the NatLibs into a government in which he continued in his present post. What did he want, what might he accept? About this he was vague, apart from complaining bitterly to Rhoda's emissary about the attempt made by Donald Calendar to trick his wife into selling some land in Wales which a company involving Calendar intended to turn into a theme park. The purpose was to blacken the Pitcombes' reputation as defenders of rural delights, and Pitcombe implied that the whole thing was a plot concocted by the villainous brothers Calendar.

Rex Calendar's response to a Deputy Chief Whip was more direct. He roared with laughter, said he'd sooner talk to the boss than to one of the foremen, walked the short distance between Whitehall and Downing Street, and confronted Rhoda.

'It won't do,' he said. 'You're a clever woman, Rhoda, but it won't do. Radley can fiddle about all he pleases, but there's a solid block of the party behind my Recovery Programme. They think I'm the one to do it, and they won't settle for anything else.'

'You mean you won't.'

'Put it how you like,' he said, and gave her the Rex Calendar smile. 'But there'll have to be an election in the party. And quickly.'

'You couldn't be tempted?' Radley's idea had
been that if Calendar and Pitcombe were offered
jobs more important than those they occupied, they
would both be pleased, and ready to serve under
Rhoda. Calendar's reaction, though, made it look as
if Radley's bright idea was not so bright after all.
The interview with Rex Calendar did seem to rule
out any possible negotiation.

Until the file of papers arrived.

It came in the post, the postmark London, with
a brief typed note: 'To the Acting Prime Minister.
This is a matter that should be brought to your
attention.' Ministers often receive communications
saying something similar and they are usually the
work of cranks, but the secretary who looked
through the file saw that this was something different. She brought the papers to Rhoda, who glanced
at them with distaste and asked what they were
about. The secretary said they seemed to be photocopies of part of a Scotland Yard file about the
investigation into the murder of a prostitute named
Lily Devon, and she thought Rhoda ought to look
at it.

Rhoda had never heard of Lily Devon, and was
by no means convinced the secretary was not wasting
her time. She glanced at a page or two, then turned
to Catchpole's final report. After that she turned back
and read the file page by page.

Who sent the file, and with what purpose, was
never discovered, nor indeed was any attempt made
to do so. It was felt that any information turned up
by an investigation would be profitable to nobody –
or at least, to nobody connected with the government. It had clearly been the sender's intention to

damage Rex Calendar's political future and harm the reputations of both Rex and his brother Donald. That was not quite how it worked out.

When Rhoda asked Rex Calendar to come and see her again, she pushed the file across to him. He looked at the first sheets, which described the finding of Lily's body and Rose's investigations, then pushed the file aside. 'How did you get this?'

'It was sent through the post. Anonymously. I presume you know about it.'

'Of course I remember the case. Indeed, the climax of it came only this week when the Scotland Yard man had to use his Baybee in making an arrest. It proved remarkably effective.'

'I'm not sure I should put it like that. The suspect died.'

'Yes, he turned out to have a heart condition. That was unfortunate. But he was more than a suspect, you know. There's no doubt he did for the girl, and for Bannock too. All this won't be news to you, if as I presume you've read the whole thing. I can't say I have.' He permitted himself a modified version of the smile. Rhoda admired his nerve, but was determined to break him.

'Rex, I think you must have forgotten what else is in the file. It says you had a brother named Gene, a sexual exhibitionist who lived in a home financially backed by you and your brother. It says the bloodstains show Gene was present when Lily Devon was murdered, whether or not he took part in the killing, and that then you and your brother staged an elaborate attempt to plant the crime on a completely innocent man. It names the people who were involved and the connections you used, working through a

solicitor named Fazackerley, who acts for some of
the biggest crooks still out of prison – '

'One thing I admired about Patrick, Rhoda, was
that he never preached. When he was really on form
he could turn you down flat, suggest you'd made an
almighty balls-up of something or other and weren't
up to your job – I've seen him do it, and he was so
gentle the poor sod he was talking to didn't understand he was being told to resign – but he never
preached. So don't bloody preach at me, all right?
Yes, Gene was our brother, had some bad trouble
when he was a kid and we looked after him, Donald
and I, as best we could, which wasn't always perfectly.
And we used old Faz. He's clever, keeps his mouth
shut, and it's not only crooks who employ him. And
the rest of it, well, someone at the Yard put a fellow
named Catchpole on the case, and he's too smart for
his own good.'

'About not preaching, I'll try to remember.' She
leaned forward almost confidingly. 'But Rex, you're
the Home Secretary, the man in charge. You can
imagine what would happen if this got out.'

The bristles on Calendar's head seemed to rise,
his voice wavered slightly. 'What are you saying to
me?'

'Just that if this got out you'd have no future in
politics.'

'That would be bad for the party.'

'But curtains for you.'

The wavering of his voice had been only
momentary, he was a match for her in toughness.
'All right, you can call the shots, I accept it. What
do you want? My resignation, health problems,
spend more time with my wife?'

'I didn't say that, that's not what I want at all. Shall I tell you the vision I have? It's of a party united as it hasn't been for years, all of us working together towards the great idea of a revived industrial Britain, carrying out your Recovery Programme or most of it, but doing it gradually. Urbanization, yes, get rid of our clutter of outdated legalisms and government-arranged quangos, but again do it gradually. Upset as few people as possible, not declare war on everyone who differs from us. That was dear Patrick's idea until he lost his grip in the last few months. The inevitability of gradualness, it's a Fabian phrase but I don't hold that against it. But I should need your cooperation to carry it through.'

'It sounds like my programme watered down, but if that's how you want to play the game – '

'Play it any other way and you split the party and the country, perhaps let in Labour.'

'So what do you want from me?'

'You remember when we talked the other day I asked whether you could be tempted. I hope you may have changed your mind.'

She got the smile at full power. 'You could say you've changed it for me.'

'I don't think you can stay as Home Secretary, you're too closely identified with giving the police these semi-automatic toys that kill people rather too easily.' He made an irritated gesture. 'I know he suffered from a heart condition, but his heart wouldn't have failed if he hadn't been shot. Besides, there's an idea being touted in the media that all the Baybees will do is increase the number of killed and wounded.' Another irritated gesture. With no hint of sarcasm she said: 'You know all about the power

of the media. My secretaries tell me the number of
interviews you've given about the Recovery Programme is well into double figures.' She waited for
comment or question, but none came. 'So it seems
to me Home Secretary is out. Chancellor? I don't
think you'd claim to have any background of financial expertise, and anyway I have Angus McLaverty
in mind for the job. He's a Scot, has hankerings after
a Scottish Parliament, and is altogether the kind of
man you want inside the tent pissing out rather than
outside pissing in, as Lyndon Johnson put it.'

'And his views about cutting loan credits and
national expenditure happen to coincide with yours.
No problem about the PM and Chancellor saying
different things.'

She ignored the remark. 'That's two of the three
most important government positions covered, leaving the Premiership aside. The fourth, some people
would say next in importance to the PM, is the
Foreign Secretary. I'd like Rex Calendar to be my
Foreign Secretary.'

He was silent. There was no doubt he was taken
aback. She laughed, heartily, easily. 'We both know
what's going to be said. You've been concerned with
conditions inside the country, cutting crime, improving communications, no experience of foreign diplo-
mats and negotiating with them, too blunt to get on
with them, etcetera. I say to hell with that, experience doesn't matter at this moment in time, what I
want is someone who'll stand up for British interests
not just against the French and Germans, but everyone else too. That old has-been Alfred Hooper that
Patrick put in quite obviously can't cope, spends half
his time in a gin daze from what I hear. Anyway

he's quite ready to take his peerage and sleep after-
noons away in the Lords. And you won't have me
breathing down your neck, as you might if you were
concerned with home affairs. I'd like you to feel it's
a challenge, but if I say anything like that you'll tell
me I'm preaching. Think about it. I'd like an answer
in twenty-four hours.'

There were still twenty-two hours left when he
called back to say yes. He added that there was a
little unfinished business at the Home Office, and
she said of course he should attend to it.

If Rex Calendar had been surprised, Allen Pitcombe
was astonished to be offered the post of Home Secretary, with the understanding of course that he
would be able to bring the other NatLibs along with
him. He took longer than Calendar to make up his
mind, because he had to persuade both his colleagues
and Gwenda. The colleagues, eager for any crumb
in the way of minor posts that might fall from the
government table, were more easily convinced than
Gwenda, whose distaste for any association with the
name of Calendar had become profound. But in
the end the thought of undoing all the things Rex
Calendar had set in train, relaxing prison conditions,
abandoning the idea of distributing Baybees to the
police, and undoing most of what had been planned
in the way of urbanization (another NatLib was to
be given the number two post at the Environment
Ministry) converted Gwenda. Allen Pitcombe too
said yes.

Radley Jevons was full of admiration, said he
couldn't understand how she had managed it at all,

let alone so quickly. A little tact, Rhoda said, a little persuasion, one or two juicy carrots and a few gentle taps with the stick . . .

'But we've been plugging the Recovery Programme, playing up a new view of it every day. There are features arranged about the way it'll affect different areas, interviews with out-of-works who say the Programme has given them hope for the future for the first time in years. The *Bulletin* can't just go into reverse on all that. We have a reputation for telling the truth.'

They were in Donald's green and white office at the top of the *Bulletin* building in Dockland. The walls were a bright glossy white, the carpet was white, everything else was green and most of it seemed to be made of glass. Even the chairs crackled at the least movement, as if glass were being trodden underfoot. Donald moved now uneasily, and there was a respondent crackle. His brother, by contrast, was splendidly at ease.

'I thought the art of journalism was to make readers believe today the opposite of what they were told yesterday.' Donald did not smile at this quip. 'Anyway, there's no need to go into reverse, just use the brake pedal gently. Rhoda's filling up some of the minor jobs now before making an official announcement, that'll come in a day or two, when she's got the rest of the Cabinet settled. And the Recovery Programme won't be sabotaged, just slowed down a bit. You haven't congratulated the Foreign Secretary on his appointment yet.'

'We've been plugging you every day as the next party leader and PM.'

'I've told you why that isn't possible.'

'We're in that lame woman's hands, I know that. But I don't see there's much cause for congratulation. You may have got something out of it, I've got nothing. What about those letters of Clarissa's, and the stories of the chauffeur and the secretary? We paid good money for them.'

'They're of no interest now Patrick's gone. His widow had an affair, who cares?'

'And you say hold up on the Pitcombes' story, backing out of a deal for a scheme that would have given pleasure to hundreds of thousands.' He moved a green glass elephant on the desk. 'Millions.'

'He'll be my colleague in a new government. You must see it's not the time to stick the knife in. It could come in useful later on, that story.' Rex favoured his brother with his grin, a demonic affair quite unlike his smile.

'And in the meantime, for me the whole business is a dead loss. Money down the drain, and I can tell you what will happen when we hit the brake pedal, as you call it, on the campaign we've been running for you as PM. Circulation of the papers will drop. Our readers aren't the fools you take them to be.'

Rex thrust his bullet head forward. He looked dangerous, a mastiff straining at the leash. 'Brother mine, you've forgotten something. If that bastard Larkins had survived, both of us would have been in a very dicey position indeed. We'd have had to stop him talking, you tell me how. As it is, that meddling policeman did us a service, though if he'd done as he was told and dropped the case there'd

have been no trouble at all. He's saved trouble, but
it's trouble he caused in the first place. I don't like
people who cause trouble.'

'We ran a feature, did you see it?' Rex shook his
head. 'First use of the Baybee, it stopped a killer.
Some pix of the copper, name's Catchpole.'

'I know his name.'

Catchpole was in no doubt that there was trouble
ahead. He had been suspended from duty while a
committee decided his fate. He had refused to be
interviewed either by tabloids, broadsheets or TV
pundits, and they had to be content with shots of
him waving the boys off to school. Alice felt he was
being too pessimistic. After all, what had he done?
Used the Baybee when he was attacked by someone
he was about to arrest for murder. All the papers
had been praising his courage and coolness. Larkins
wouldn't have died from the bullet wounds, although
the slightly misdirected one that hit him in the abdomen had caused internal bleeding. It was just bad
luck that he had a dodgy heart.

They were in the kitchen having a sandwich
lunch. Catchpole temporarily abandoned his BLT.
'Why am I in trouble? I did everything wrong. First
of all I shouldn't have gone down to Roselands, I
was off the case. Next, if I *was* going and thought
trouble was likely, as I did, I should have taken
Charlie Wilson with me. I didn't because I knew I
was stepping out of line and didn't want to land
Charlie in the shit. But that's no excuse. There isn't
any excuse.'

'Except that you caught a murderer.'

'Even that's not certain. The DNA samples off both men were Lily Devon's but getting them off clothes that have been dry-cleaned is a chancy business and only doubtfully accepted by a jury, unless it's backed by other evidence. Officially the case is closed. Larkins killed the girl after some sex play that went wrong, with Ted Copeland either watching or taking part. Larkins killed Bannock because the MP had somehow got on to his past, though the meeting could have been arranged as a possible homosexual tryst. And Ted Copeland hanged himself because of guilt feelings. That's the official version. Case closed.'

'But most of that's what you think too, except about Ted Copeland.'

He bit into his sandwich, swallowed the rest of his half-pint of beer. 'What I think, but I doubt if it would have stood up in court. And there's something else. I wanted to pin the murders to Larkins, but I wanted to show the lying and chicanery by which those two brothers tried to plant false leads, finger an innocent man for Lily's murder, and do it all through third or fourth parties. I've known real villains I liked more than those two.'

She said, half admiringly but with a touch of sarcasm too: 'The knight in shining armour is unhorsed.' Then she was sorry as she saw the words had stung him. He rarely raised his voice when talking to her, but he did so now.

'No bloody knight in armour, just a policeman trying to do his job. I've told you before, in my book there are things a copper can do and some he can't. One of the things he can't is to break the rules just to help someone, and I mean anyone, which is why I couldn't help Brett. And a policeman doesn't like it when politicians and media men are giving him false leads and making a murder investigation into a sort of obstacle race.' He said to his empty glass: 'After what Maggie told me, what came up on the computer, there was no way in the world I could let Lowry squash the case by sitting on it with his big bum.'

'Don't squash me too, I'm on your side. What do you think'll happen? To you, I mean.'

'At best it's on my record, goodbye promotion this year or the ones after. At worst, resignation. I shouldn't think they'd go that far.'

'I thought the Big Man liked you, was always friendly.'

'Just I was useful at times. Could be he'll need some friends himself.'

In that Catchpole was right. When the Big Man heard Rex Calendar's voice on the telephone, brisk but equable, he expected the worst and was not mistaken.

'I'm sure you'll be interested to know I'll be moving very soon, doing another job. Rhoda Carpenter will be the new PM and I'm taking the FO, the papers will have it tomorrow. I've made one or two recommendations. I think the Met needs stirring up, the AC's a bit of an old woman as I'm sure you'll agree – '

A pause. Was the news good, after all? He began to say it was not for him to comment, when Calendar spoke again.

'I've recommended he takes early retirement.

Replacement will be Dick Reynolds from Wales. Seems a live wire, no nonsense about him, give some of the lazy and disobedient sods at the Met a kick up the arse. He's asked for another provincial as his sidekick, a lad from Lancashire I've had my eye on for some time. I thought you'd like to consider your own position. Oh, one other thing. Next time you plant a bomb, make sure it doesn't blow up in your face.'

No comment was expected on that. The Big Man spent five minutes regretting the impulsive move to get revenge on the Home Secretary, who, he felt, had betrayed the promise made in their verbal arrangement. Revenge without an ulterior motive was, he reflected, almost always a mistake. But then he found his anger moving to the source of all his troubles, Detective Chief Superintendent Hilary Catchpole, and the spirit of revenge moved him again. He wrote a minute to the committee deliberating on Catchpole's fate, describing the way he had ignored instructions, his determination to go his own way and certainty that he knew best, and his reckless use of the Baybee, which had caused an unnecessary death. He felt there was no alternative but to recommend Catchpole's resignation, or if necessary dismissal.

That done he put out feelers, and soon got a response. Within a couple of weeks he had signed a contract to take charge of all security matters at the international giant MultiCorpus, at a salary more than double what he was paid at the Yard. He had regrets, of course he had, but money was money.

★

The Big Man's memo was felt to be over the top, obviously motivated by personal feeling. At the same time it was recognized that Catchpole had stepped intolerably far out of line. He was informed of the committee's decision by telephone. When he put down the instrument he was laughing.

Alice stared at him. 'What is it? What have they said?'

'I clear up a case where there are two murders, maybe three, and does anybody say thank you? They do not.'

'But you never expected them to, you told me – '

'I know, I know, but they're still bastards.'

'So what is it? Resignation?'

He began to laugh again. 'But can you believe it, here I am one of the Met's most senior detectives, and a successful one – '

'Hilly, pull yourself together. What did they say?'

He took out a handkerchief, wiped his eyes. 'I'm being transferred to the Traffic Police. The *Traffic Police*, can you imagine?'

She knew it would be foolish to say well, that wasn't as bad as they'd feared. Instead she kissed him, and to her surprise discovered he had an erection. Afterwards, lying on the bed upstairs momentarily exhausted, he said: 'Ah well, it could be worse. About the job.'

'I thought you meant the sex.'

'Now that *would* have been serious.' They both started laughing.

The postcard came a couple of days before Johnno and Belinda got married. The picture was of the

Plaza Mayor in Salamanca; the message said: 'Sorry left urgently, job done, touch and go Mossad. Moving safe house Saudi Arabia, writing.' It was unsigned, but Johnno recognized George's writing. 'Do you suppose he's really had trouble with Mossad and is going to Saudi Arabia?'

'No,' Belinda said. 'And neither do you.'

'I suppose not.' He sighed.

They were married at St George's, Hanover Square. The reception was at the Savoy. Belinda turned out to have a great many relatives, close and distant. Her father had been married three times, her mother twice, and former husbands and wives abounded, European and American. They all screamed delightedly at Belinda and congratulated Johnno, one or two ex-wives or perhaps ex-mistresses telling her he was a handsome young man, she must be careful. The Major-General, his wife and the few relatives on the male side (Johnno had invited the Big Man, but he pleaded an urgent meeting) collected in a little cluster, sipping champagne and talking in lowered voices. Belinda said she had hoped Uncle Potto would be there, but it looked as if he'd been unable to make it. Johnno asked if he was on her father's or mother's side.

'Oh, he's not a real uncle, I just call him that. He's fabulously rich.' She suddenly screamed: 'There he is.' The throng parted to reveal a tall figure in headdress and burnous. For a wild moment Johnno thought it might be George Kaiser, then he was in the hawk-faced man's embrace, caught a whiff of some fragrant spices, and received what he hoped was a blessing in Arabic. A minute or two later Belinda told them Uncle Potto was giving them as

a present a honeymoon in Dubai – they could cancel
the projected one in Cornwall.

He was surprised again, by the arrival of Rex
Calendar. Johnno had not dared to invite him, but
Belinda had made an approach and received a positive response. Now he put an arm round each of
them, asked if Jonathan would like to work for him
again, and at the eager stammered affirmative said
he would arrange it. An arm still round Belinda, he
said Jonathan should thank his charming wife.

They went to watch TV in an adjoining room
where Rhoda, standing in Downing Street, was
extolling the qualities of her Cabinet. She reached
the peroration of her brief speech.

'In the past, let me admit it, there has been
division in the party. But now we are marching in
step together, our sole concern the making of a
Greater Britain. That means men and women with
work to do, and happy in doing it, in factory, office
or home. It means a nation of independent indi-
viduals who are yet cared for by the state when they
are in need.' She opened her arms wide. 'This will
be a government of the people, and for the people.
And above all it will be a government devoted to
raising national standards, a government of integrity.
This is a good day, the day a new world opens.
Everybody should be happy today.'

Belinda turned from Johnno to Rex Calendar,
kissed them both, and repeated ardently: 'A government of integrity, the day a new world opens. Isn't
that fine? Yes, we should all be happy today.'